*Text Book Of*

# FINANCIAL MANAGEMENT

## For M.B.A. : Semester - II

### As Per New Syllabus of Anna University : Chennai

## Dr. Nachiket M. Vechalekar

Associate Dean – Post Graduate Programmes
IndSearch
Pune 411 004

## Dr. Mahesh Kulkarni

M.Com., M.Phil., L.L.B., D.T.L., Ph.D. (Management)
Associate Professor and Research Guide,
BYK College Research Institute, Nashik – 422001.

## Dr. Suhas Mahajan

B.A., M.Com., Ph.D. (Finance)
Associate Professor and Research Guide,
Ness Wadia College, Research Institute, Pune – 411001.

NIRALI PRAKASHAN
ADVANCEMENT OF KNOWLEDGE

N3787

**Financial Management  (MBA - Sem. II) (AUC)**                    ISBN 978-93-5164-995-3

First Edition     :     February 2016

©               :     Authors

**Published By :**

**NIRALI PRAKASHAN**

Abhyudaya Pragati, 1312, Shivaji Nagar,
Off J.M. Road, PUNE – 411005
Tel - (020) 25512336/37/39, Fax - (020) 25511379
Email : niralipune@pragationline.com

☞     **DISTRIBUTION CENTRES**

**PUNE**

Nirali Prakashan     :     119, Budhwar Peth, Jogeshwari Mandir Lane, Pune 411002, Maharashtra
Tel : (020) 2445 2044, 66022708, Fax : (020) 2445 1538
Email : bookorder@pragationline.com, niralilocal@pragationline.com

Nirali Prakashan     :     S. No. 28/27, Dhyari, Near Pari Company, Pune 411041
Tel : (020) 24690204 Fax : (020) 24690316
Email :  dhyari@pragationline.com, bookorder@pragationline.com

**MUMBAI**

Nirali Prakashan     :     385, S.V.P. Road, Rasdhara Co-op. Hsg. Society Ltd.,
Girgaum, Mumbai 400004, Maharashtra
Tel : (022) 2385 6339 / 2386 9976, Fax : (022) 2386 9976
Email : niralimumbai@pragationline.com

☞     **DISTRIBUTION BRANCHES**

**JALGAON**

Nirali Prakashan     :     34, V. V. Golani Market, Navi Peth, Jalgaon 425001,
Maharashtra, Tel : (0257) 222 0395, Mob : 94234 91860

**KOLHAPUR**

Nirali Prakashan     :     New Mahadvar Road, Kedar Plaza, 1$^{st}$ Floor Opp. IDBI Bank
Kolhapur 416 012, Maharashtra. Mob : 9850046155

**NAGPUR**

Pratibha Book Distributors     :     Above Maratha Mandir, Shop No. 3, First Floor,
Rani Jhanshi Square, Sitabuldi, Nagpur 440012, Maharashtra
Tel : (0712) 254 7129

**DELHI**

Nirali Prakashan     :     4593/21, Basement, Aggarwal Lane 15, Ansari Road, Daryaganj
Near Times of India Building, New Delhi  110002
Mob :  08505972553

**BENGALURU**

Pragati Book House     :     House No. 1, Sanjeevappa Lane, Avenue Road Cross,
Opp. Rice Church, Bengaluru – 560002.
Tel : (080) 64513344, 64513355,Mob : 9880582331, 9845021552
Email:bharatsavla@yahoo.com

**CHENNAI**

Pragati Books     :     9/1, Montieth Road, Behind Taas Mahal, Egmore,
Chennai 600008 Tamil Nadu, Tel : (044) 6518 3535,
Mob : 94440 01782 / 98450 21552 / 98805 82331,
Email : bharatsavla@yahoo.com

niralipune@pragationline.com  |  www.pragationline.com

Also find us on  [f] www.facebook.com/niralibooks

# Preface ...

Financial Management is one of the most critical and important activities for the professional business managers. It is a fact that consequences of all important management decisions, financial and otherwise, are immediately and/or eventually will be reflected in the financial performance of the business organisation. It therefore is a great pleasure to present the book on 'Financial Management'.

This book is written as per the new and revised syllabus prescribed for MBA students, by the Anna University, Chennai, effective from 2013. The authors have tried their level best to ensure that all the points have been covered as per the prescribed syllabus. The authors also hope that this book will definitely help in meeting the growing requirements of the students of Financial Management.

All the topics included in the syllabus are explained in simple but lucid and apt language.

We are very grateful to Mr. Dineshbhai Furia and Mr. Jigneshbhai Furia and the entire staff of Nirali Prakashan, Pune especially Mr. Amol Mahabal, Mr. Akbar Shaikh and Prasad Chintakindi for their earnest help in bringing out this book with vigour and accuracy. We have taken maximum efforts to make the text error free. Nevertheless, we do not rule out the possibility of certain shortcomings or misprints still remaining, we will be obliged to the readers if such errors are pointed out from time to time.

Any constructive comments for improving the contents will be warmly appreciated.

We have given our best inputs for this book. Any suggestions towards the improvement of this book and sincere comments are most welcome on niralipune@pragationline.com.

**Authors**

■■■

# Syllabus ...

### Unit I: Foundations of Finance                    [09 Lectures]

Financial Management - An Overview - Time Value of Money - Introduction to the Concept of Risk and Return of a Single Asset and of a Portfolio - Valuation of Bonds and shares - Option Valuation.

### Unit II: Investment Decisions                    [09 Lectures]

Capital Budgeting: Principles and techniques - Nature of Capital Budgeting - Identifying Relevant Cash Flows - Evaluation Techniques: Payback, Accounting Rate of Return, Net Present Value, Internal Rate of Return, Profitability Index - Comparison of DCF Techniques - Project Selection under Capital Rationing - Inflation and Capital Budgeting - Concept and Measurement of Cost of Capital - Specific Cost and Overall Cost of Capital.

### Unit III: Financing and Dividend Decision         [09 Lectures]

Financial and Operating Leverage - Capital Structure - Cost of Capital and Valuation - Designing Capital Structure.

Dividend Policy - Aspects of Dividend Policy - Practical Consideration - Forms of Dividend Policy - Forms of Dividends - Share Splits.

### Unit IV: Working Capital Management               [09 Lectures]

Principles of Working Capital: Concepts, Needs, Determinants, Issues and Estimation of Working Capital - Accounts Receivables Management and Factoring - Inventory Management - Cash Management - Working Capital Finance: Trade Credit, Bank Finance and Commercial Paper.

### Unit V: Long Term Sources of Finance              [09 Lectures]

Indian Capital and Stock Market, New Issues Market Long Term Finance: Shares, Debentures and Term Loans, Lease, Hire Purchase, Venture Capital Financing, Private Equity.

■■■

# Contents ...

■■■

# CHAPTER 1

# Foundations of Finance

## Contents ...

## 1.1 Financial Management - An Overview

### (A) Definition of Financial Management

The term *'financial management'* can be defined as *the management of flow of funds and it deals with financial decision-making*. It is basically concerned with raising of funds and the utilisation of funds in the most optimum manner so as to maximise the return for the owner.

Since raising of the funds and the best possible utilisation of the same is a very crucial part of the success of an organisation, financial management as a functional area has got a place of prime relevance in every firm. All business decisions have financial implications and therefore financial management is inevitably related to almost every aspect of business operations.

### (B) Modern Approaches to Financial Management

In order to understand the concepts of financial management in a better manner, it is necessary to understand the difference between the traditional and modern concept of financial management.

Though financial management is a relatively new discipline, finance as a function has been known to business organisations even in ancient times. The traditional concept of financial management can be summarised as mentioned below:

(a) Finance function was mainly concerned with raising funds for various requirements like diversification, expansion and so on. It was not considered to be a regular part of managerial functions.

(b) Attention was given to the long-term funds only. The concept and day-to-day management of working capital was not considered.

(c) Sources used for raising funds were mainly equity shares, debentures and preference shares. The knowledge of legal framework necessary for raising funds through these sources was considered essential.

**Modern Concept of Financial Management**

Due to increasing competition and growth in business as well as occurrence of trade cycles, the scope of the finance function expanded. It was no longer a fund raising activity only. The finance function became more analytical and decision oriented. Apart from fund raising, utilisation of funds became of paramount importance. A Finance Manager became a professional manager and he had to seek the answers to the following questions.

(a) What is the projection of the requirements of funds for the organisation? How should this amount be raised?

(b) How to utilise the funds in an optimum manner in order to maximise the returns of the shareholders?

## (C) Goals of Financial Management

Financial management is concerned with the following activities:

1. Raising of funds

2. Investment of funds

3. Other decisions like dividend decisions.

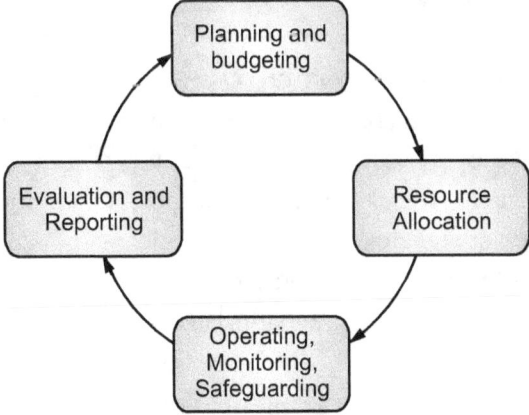

**Fig 1.1: Financial Management Cycle**

1. **Raising of Funds:** A finance manager has to take a crucial decision regarding the selection of source for raising of funds. Funds can be raised from owned sources as well as from borrowed sources, with the right balance between the owned funds and borrowed funds.

These sources have their own peculiar features and characteristics. While owned funds do not have any obligation such as repayment at maturity and interest payments, borrowed funds have both these obligations. However, borrowed funds are comparatively cheaper, however will have a risk element always. This risk is known as financial risk, i.e. risk of insolvency due to landing in a debt trap. Equity shares, preference shares and retained earnings are owned sources of raising funds while debentures and term loans are borrowed sources of raising of funds. There is a need for striking a right balance between the owned funds and borrowed funds. These sources have their own peculiar features and characteristics. The main difference between them is that in case of borrowed funds, there is a commitment of fixed amount in the form of interest payments as well as repayment of principal amount. In case of ownership funds, these commitments are not there and hence they are considered to be risk free sources.

A business organisation normally has a combination of both the types of funds. There should be a balance between the two types of funds so that there will be a balance between the risk and profitability. While planning the debt-equity mix, various factors should be considered. These are cash flow analysis.

- EBIT-EPS analysis
- Debt-equity ratio
- Financial and operating leverage
- Capital market situation
- Capital structure models
- Cost of funds
- Management perception of control.

A finance manager must tap new financial instruments for raising finance and therefore should be aware of financial engineering.

To summarise, three crucial aspects should be taken into consideration before financing decisions are taken.

(a) Requirement of funds during long-term and short-term.

(b) Deciding about optimum combination of owned funds and borrowed funds for raising the funds.

(c) Determination of the financing pattern for long-term and short-term requirements of the funds.

2. **Investment of Funds:** Another important decision that is to be taken by the finance manager is about the investment of the funds. Resources at the command of the firm are always scarce and there are several demands on the same. It is therefore necessary for the finance manager to provide a framework for taking appropriate decisions.

   Investing decisions are normally related to the following areas.

   (a) **Fixed Assets:** Investment in fixed assets is made with a long-term perspective and the main objective behind this decision is to enhance the earning capacity of the organisation. Investments in fixed assets also called capital. Budgeting decisions, are normally irreversible and involve heavy amounts. Therefore capital budgeting decisions are to be taken with utmost care and only after ensuring that the projected benefits will be more than the projected costs.

   (b) **Working Capital:** Working capital is required for the day-to-day requirements of a business organisation. It is defined as the excess of current assets over current liabilities. Current assets are basically created with an intention to convert them into cash or other current assets within a period of one year, while current liabilities are the liabilities which are expected to mature within a period of one year and paid either from existing current assets or by creating new current liabilities. A Finance Manager has to take decisions regarding the amount of funds to be invested in the working capital. He has to ensure that there is neither excess working capital nor shortage of the same. For this, he has to take several decisions like how much inventory is to be kept, how much credit is to be allowed to customers etc. He also has to prepare the estimate of working capital and arrange for the same through various sources.

3. **Dividend Decisions:** Another major area of decision making by a finance manager is known as the dividend decisions. Dividends are paid out of divisible profits of a company. These profits can either be retained as reserves or distributed as dividends to the shareholders.

   A Finance manager has to comply with the legal provisions and consider the financial aspects also. Though there is no legal restriction on the rate of dividends, there are several considerations which are to be complied with before dividend decisions are taken. These include:

   • cash flow positions
   • capital structure planning
   • shareholders' expectations

There should be a balance between a liberal and conservative dividend policy. Reactions of the shareholders are also to be considered. Similarly, the likely impact on the prices of the shares is also to be taken into consideration.

A finance manager must also decide about the declaration of bonus as a policy of the company. Since the dividend decisions have long-term implications, utmost care must be taken. Several considerations like cash flow positions, capital structure planning, shareholders' expectations etc. are to be taken into consideration before finalising the dividend policy.

Keeping in mind various areas of importance of financial management, the financial manager has to take numerous decisions as seen above. It is therefore necessary to understand what the goal of financial decision making is. These goals can be listed as given below:

1. **Maximisation of Profits:** Any commercial organisation is established for profits. Therefore maximisation of profits is considered to be the primary goal of financial management. This goal advocates that when there is any issue of decision making, the objective which will maximise the profits should be selected. The profit is measured according to accepted accounting principles. The argument in favour of this objective is that the profit is a parameter for measuring the performance of a business organisation and hence profit maximisation is the most appropriate objective of financial decision making. It is argued that if every firm tries to maximise profits, there will be maximising of the social welfare of the society. If all the firms keep this target, the resources of the economy will be used for the most productive uses, resulting in efficient utilisation of the same.

   However, it has been observed that there are flaws in the profit maximisation concept. It is said that profit maximisation cannot be the goal of financial decision making as the interests of various stakeholders should also be taken into consideration. Profit maximisation ignores the interests of other stakeholders except the shareholders.

   The arguments against profit maximisation can be summarised as given below:

   (a) The profit maximisation objective aims at maximisation of profits only and ignores other aspects. For example, it ignores the financing aspects this means that in order to earn maximum profits, it may ignore financing options and a firm may be tempted to borrow beyond its capacity to finance an investment proposal.

   (b) Risk factors are also ignored if the profit maximisation objective is to be pursued. Even risky investment proposals may be undertaken to earn higher profits and it can bring the firm in trouble.

(c) Profit maximisation does not take into consideration the time value of money.

(d) The profit maximisation concept is considered to be vague. Exactly which profits a firm wants to maximise? Whether accounting profits or cash profits? Pre-tax profits or post tax profits? Long term profits or short-term profits? These questions remain unanswered and hence the concept is considered to be quite vague.

(e) This objective aims at maximisation of profits but it remains vague as to whether shareholders' interests are to be protected or not. It remains to be seen whether this profit will be distributed among the shareholders so that their wealth will also be maximised. This question remains unanswered. It is also said that this goal is shortsighted and in an anxiety to maximise profits, the long-term impacts may be ignored. Ethical and moral considerations may also be overlooked in order to maximise the profits as the firm may try to achieve the objective by hook or by crook.

This is the reason why wealth maximisation objective of financial management is gaining more importance. The rationale of this goal is discussed in the following paragraphs.

2. **Wealth Maximisation:** The wealth maximisation may be described as the prime objective of financial management. Shareholders are the main stakeholders in a firm and are the owners of the firm as per relevant laws. It is natural for a firm to strive for the maximisation of the wealth of the shareholders. All decisions should be taken by keeping this objective in mind.

It is necessary to understand the concept of the wealth of shareholders. The wealth of shareholders is measured in terms of the value of shares of a firm. In case, the shares of a firm are not quoted on stock exchange and hence no market value is available, the wealth can be measured in terms of earnings per share and the intrinsic value of the share.

Wealth in financial management is measured in terms of economic value which is the present value of future cash flows which result from a particular decision regarding capital investment.

When a firm takes a decision regarding any capital investment, it is based on the *net present value* generated from that decision. The net present value is calculated by discounting the future cash flows at an appropriate rate of discount and deducting them from the initial investment made in the project. Decision regarding capital investment is taken if the net present value comes positive. Therefore the concept of wealth is based on cash flows rather than the accounting profits.

When the net present value is positive, it is reflected in the overall performance of the firm and the shareholders get the benefits in the form of increased dividends and appreciation in the market value of their shares. Thus economic value of the shareholders' wealth is finally the market value of the shares of the company.

The objective of maximisation of wealth of shareholders implies that all the financial decisions should be taken by keeping the shareholders' interest in mind. The decisions should result in higher dividends and increased market price of shares that will benefit the shareholders. Thus, it will be necessary for the management to allocate the scarce resources for the most efficient use and thereby maximise the returns to the shareholders.

Few points that need to be considered in this regard are discussed below. This objective of financial management is quite acceptable as it is realistic and recognises the importance of the stakeholders. It is but natural that as the shareholders supply the capital and in fact they are the owners of the firm, their interests should get priority and get protected. However, some questions arise regarding the measurement of wealth of shareholders. The first one is concerned with the measurement of wealth, if the shares of the firm are not quoted on a stock exchange, how does one measure the wealth of the shareholders? In such cases the earning per share as well as the intrinsic value of the share should be taken into consideration. If the earnings per share are constantly increasing and the intrinsic value is also constantly higher than the face value, it can be concluded that the wealth of shareholders is growing.

Another consideration is that the share prices are dependent on several factors. Performance of a firm is one of the factors and not the only factor. Market price of a share is influenced by the overall economic and political scenario in the country and by speculative transactions. Hence it is very difficult to decide whether the market price has appreciated due to the good financial performance of a firm or whether due to other factors.

One more consideration that goes against this objective is that shareholders are not only the stakeholders in a firm. There are also others like creditors, suppliers, employees as well as the members of the general public. At times there might be a conflict of interests between the interests of shareholders and interests of the other stakeholders.

Despite the above limitations, it can be concluded that as compared to the profit maximisation objective, the objective of wealth maximisation can be considered to be superior as it takes into account the present value of the future expected cash flows arising out of an investment decision and hence it is more realistic and objective.

## 1.2 Time Value of Money

## (A) Introduction to Time Value of Money

Money has time value. Because of the following reasons a rupee today is more valuable than a rupee a year hence.

(i) Individuals, in general, prefer current consumption to future consumption.

(ii) Capital can be employed productively to generate positive returns. An investment of one rupee today would grow to $(1 + r)$ a year hence (r is the rate of return earned on the investment).

(iii) In an inflationary period a rupee today represents a greater real purchasing power than a rupee a year hence.

Many financial problems involve cash flows occurring at different points of time. For evaluating such cash flows an explicit consideration of **time value of money** is required.

The recognition of the **time value of money** is extremely important in financial decision-making. Most of the financial decisions affect firm's cash flow in different time periods. Purchase of a fixed asset results in immediate outflow of cash and will also generate future cash inflows during the life of the fixed asset. Similarly, borrowing funds from banks or financial institutions results in inflow of cash, but, creates an obligation on the part of the firm to pay interest and return the principal sum in an agreed future period.

If the firm raises funds by issuing equity shares, there will be an inflow of cash at the time of issuing shares for cash, but, as the firm pays dividends in future, the firm will have to meet the outflow of cash. Sound capital budgeting decision-making requires logical comparison of the present cash outflows with the future cash inflows. Absolute cash flows which differ in magnitude and timing, do not render themselves comparable. The comparison becomes meaningful only when it recognises the **time value of money** and makes appropriate adjustment for time.

**"Time Preference for Money":**

An individual's preference for possession of a given amount of cash at the present time, rather than the same amount at some future time is called **"time preference for money"**. An individual's **time preference for money** could be traced to the following reasons:

(i) Since future is uncertain, an individual prefers receiving cash now.

(ii) Most people have subjective preference for present consumption over future consumption of goods and services.

(iii) Most individuals prefer present cash to future cash because they like to employ present funds to tap the available existing investment opportunities.

The justification for corporate time preference for money lies only in the availability of investment opportunities. In financial decision-making, a firm has to compare cash inflows of one investment opportunity with that of the other.

**"Time Preference Rate":**

**Time Preference Rate** is also known as discount rate. It is generally expressed by an interest rate. If an individual's time preference is 18%, it means that he is prepared to forego the opportunity of receiving ₹ 100 now if he is offered ₹ 118 after one year. Thus, the individual is indifferent between the choice of ₹ 100 now and ₹ 118 after one year as he considers these two amounts equivalent in value. Discount rate enables a firm to translate different amounts received at different times to amounts of equivalent value to the firm in the present at common point reference.

**Discounting:**

**Discounting** is a popular technique used in evaluation of capital projects which meets the financial goal of maximisation of present wealth of the firm. Selection of projects under discounting method basically, involves the use of a discount rate calculating the present value of future cash inflows allows us to isolate differences in the timing of these cash inflows.

In any economy, in which capital has value, a rupee today is worth more than a rupee to be received 1 year, 2 years or 3 years from now. Therefore, we need a means for standardising differences in timing of cash flows so that the time value of money is properly recognised. The following example will clarify the concept very well.

**Example:** A firm has an opportunity to receive with complete certainty ₹ 1,000 at the end of each of the next 2 years. If the firm's opportunity cost of funds is 10% per annum, what is this proposal worth to the firm today?

**Answer:** In this case, we have the terminal value i.e. future value as well as the required interest rate, we must solve for the appropriate beginning value.

Consequently, we divide the future value by the required rate of interest and this operation is called "**Discounting**".

Present value of ₹ 1,000 to be received at the end of 1st year is,

$$PV = \frac{₹\,1,000}{(1.1)}$$

$$= ₹\,909.09$$

Present value of ₹ 1,000 to be received at the end of 2nd year is,

$$PV = \frac{₹\,1,000}{(1.1)^2}$$

$$= ₹\,826.45$$

Thus, ₹ 1,000 received 2 years from now, has a lower present value than ₹ 1,000 received 1st year from now. Therefore, the opportunity is worth ₹ 909.09 + ₹ 826.45 = ₹ 1,735.54 to the firm today.

In solving present value problems, it is useful to express the interest factor apart from the amount to be received in the future:

Present value of ₹ 1,000 to be received at the end of 1st year is,

$$PV = ₹\,1,000 \left[ \frac{1}{(1.1)} \right] = ₹\,909.09$$

Present value of ₹ 1,000 to be received at the end of 2nd year is,

$$PV = ₹\,1,000 \left[ \frac{1}{(1.1)^2} \right] = ₹\,826.45$$

In this way, we are able to isolate the interest factor, and this isolation facilitates present value calculation. In such calculations, the interest rate is known as the discount rate.

The general formula for finding the present value of $X_n$ to be received at the end of year n (where, K is the discount rate) is,

$$PV = X_n \left[ \frac{1}{(1 + K)^n} \right]$$

**Note:** Using present value tables we can calculate the present value of various future streams of cash flows. The present value of an amount of money to be received in the future decreases at a decreasing rate, as the discount rate increases.

Present value, when interest is compounded more than once a year.

When interest is compounded more than once a year, the formula for calculating present values will be:

$$PV = \left( \frac{X_n}{\left( 1 + \dfrac{k}{m} \right)^{mn}} \right)$$

Where,

(i)    $X_n$ is the cash flow at the end of year n.

(ii)   m is the number of times in a year interest is compounded.

(iii) k is the discount rate.

**Annuities:**

An **annuity** may be defined as a series of uniform receipts occurring over a specified number of years, which results from an initial deposit.

Present value of an annuity is given by the following formula:

$$PV = \frac{A}{i} \left[ 1 - \frac{1}{(1 + i)^n} \right]$$

Where, A represents an annuity.

$$i = \frac{r}{100}$$

where,                      r = Rate of interest

                               n = Number of years

**Example:** An equipment requires an initial investment of ₹ 6,000. Annual cash inflow is estimated at ₹ 2,000 for 5 years. Cost of capital is 20%.

(i) Calculate present value of cash inflows.

(ii) What is Net Present Value of the project?

**Answer:**

$$PV = \frac{A}{i}\left[1 - \frac{1}{(1+i)^n}\right]$$

$$= ₹\frac{2,000}{\frac{20}{100}}\left[1 - \frac{1}{\left(1 + \frac{20}{100}\right)^5}\right]$$

$$= \frac{₹\,2,000}{0.2}\left[1 - \frac{1}{(1.2)^5}\right]$$

$$= ₹\,10,000\left[1 - \frac{1}{2.48832}\right]$$

$$= ₹\,10,000\,[1 - 0.4018775]$$

$$= ₹\,10,000 \times 0.5981225$$

$$= ₹\,5,981.23$$

$$\text{Net Present Value} = \text{PV of cash inflow} - \text{PV of cash outflows}$$

(i.e., initial investment)

$$= ₹\,5,981.23 - ₹\,6,000$$

$$= ₹\,-18.77.$$

The period for which an annuity is payable is called "**Status**". The persons who receives the annuity is called "Annuitant."

When an annuity is payable for a fixed number of years, it is called **"Annuity Certain"**. Annuity which is payable till the happening of a certain event is called **"Annuity Contingent"**.

An annuity is a **"Perpetual Annuity"** when payments are to continue forever.

When payments are made at the end of each period, it is known as **Immediate Annuity or Ordinary Annuity**.

When payments are made at the beginning of each period, it is known as **"Annuity Due"**.

**Unless specifically stated, it is taken as Immediate Annuity.**

An annuity that is to take effect after a certain number of years is known as **Deferred Annuity**. An Immediate Annuity deferred for n years implies that its first payment is due at the end of (n + 1) years.

**Present value of an annuity** is present **worth of various payments**.

A freehold estate is one that yields a perpetuity **known as rent**.

**Future Value of Annuities:**

Amount of any annuity is the total sum of unpaid instalments together with the stipulated compound interest at the end of the given number of years.

*Symbols used:*

$$A = \text{Annuity}$$

$$M = \text{Amount of Annuity A left unpaid for n years or period}$$

$$PV = \text{Present value of an annuity A for n years or periods}$$

$$C = \text{Interest on unit sum for 1 year (unit sum means one rupee)}$$

Amount of n Immediate Annuity certain.

$$M = \frac{A}{i}\left[(1 + i)^n - 1\right]$$

Amount of an Annuity Due:

$$M = (1 + i)\left(\frac{A}{i}\right)\left[(1 + i)^n - 1\right]$$

Present Value of an Immediately Annuity:

$$PV = \frac{A}{i}\left[1 - \frac{1}{(1 + i)^n}\right]$$

Present Value of an Annuity Due:

$$PV = (1 + i)\left(\frac{A}{i}\right)\left[1 - \frac{1}{(1 + n)^n}\right]$$

# (B) Concept of "Time Value of Money"

The concept of **time value of money** deals with the fact that an amount of money received in future is not as valuable as the same amount of money received in the present. This is because:

(i)    The future is uncertain;

(ii)   Individuals prefer current to future consumption;

(iii)  The opportunity exists to invest the amount received in the present at a specific rate of interest;

(iv)  Inflationary trends are a common feature reducing the value of money in the future.

All this means that future benefits should include some compensation for waiting. In other words, the future benefits should be equal to the sum of the present benefits and an amount equivalent to the compensation for waiting.

Suppose a person gets 10% per annum as interest on a savings bank deposit. He would be indifferent between the two options of getting ₹ 100 today and receiving ₹ 110 after a year. Here the sum:

(i)    ₹ 100 is the present value of the receipt.

(ii)   ₹ 10 is the compensation for waiting.

(iii)  ₹ 110 is the future value of the receipt.

It can also be said that the future value is the sum of the present value compounded at a given rate of interest. The present value is therefore calculated by reverse compounding. It is the formula used to compute compound interest, and not the one used to compute simple Interest, that is involved in computing the future value of a receipt. The reason for this is that it is not only the original amount that earns interest but also the earned interest that earns further interest.

## (C) Need of "Time Value of Money"

The concept of the maximisation of corporate wealth necessarily involves the study of the time value of money. This is because the benefits that a firm expects to receive from an investment are usually spread out over a period of time. Such benefits need to be translated into their present value so as to facilitate their comparison with the initial investment and thereby to ascertain whether the investment has really added something to corporate wealth.

The concept of time value of money is also relevant to the shareholders, who make present sacrifices in the form of dividend foregone for investment in the expectation of future benefits. They would thus like to know the present value of future benefits so as to find out whether these future benefits exceed their present sacrifice.

## (D) Importance of "Time Value of Money"

Time Value of Money recognises that cash benefits emerging from a project in different years are not identical in value. This is why annual cash benefits of a project are discounted at a discount rate to calculate total value of these cash benefits. At the same time, it also gives due weightage to risk factor by making necessary adjustments in the discount rate. Thus, cash benefits of a project with higher risk exposure is discounted at a higher discount rate (cost of capital), while lower discount rate is applied to discount expected cash benefits of a less risky project. In this way, discount rate used to determine present value of future streams of cash earnings reflects both the time and risk.

It is equally useful for stockholders too who do not directly participate in management of the enterprise but are supposed to see that the management is working in their best interest. This can be ensured if they have gained the knowledge of "time value of money".

Fig. 1.2 indicates the **methods used for computation of Time Value of Money** as shown below:

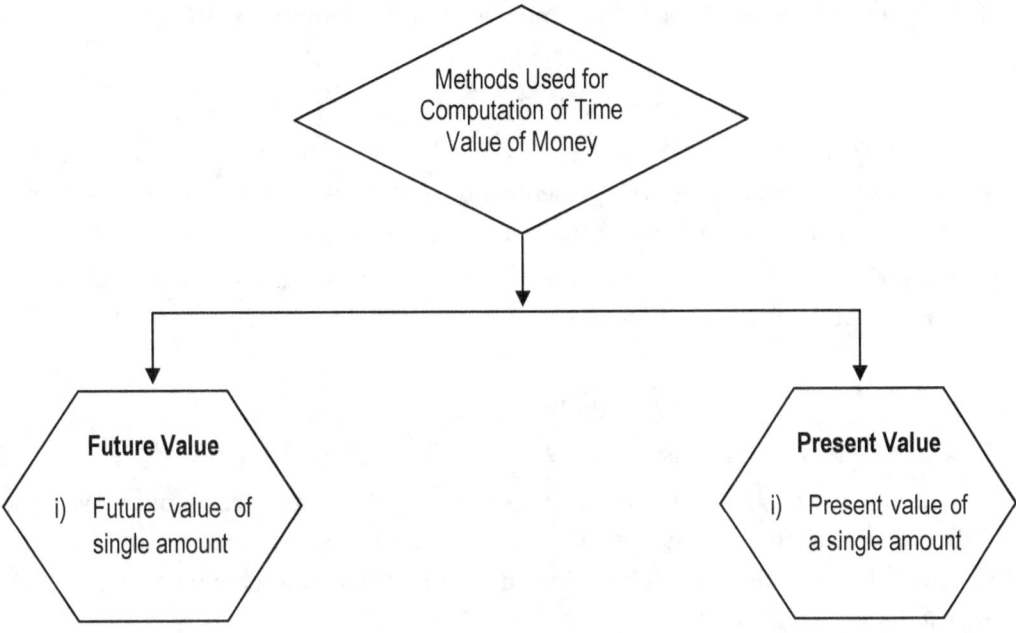

**Fig. 1.2: Methods used for Computation of Time Value of Money**

## (E) Future Value

### (i) Future Value of a Single Amount:

The future value of an amount at the end of a Period 1 (A1) will be equal to the product of the original value (P) and the rate of interest plus 1. This can be expressed in the form of an equation as follows.

$$A1 = P(1 + r) \qquad \qquad \text{... (1.1)}$$

Here, the subscript denotes the end of the specific period. For example,

If P is ₹ 100 and r is 10%, A after a 1 year period will be,

$$= ₹ 100 \times 1.10$$

$$= ₹ 110.$$

Similarly, the future value of the amount P at specific rate of interest r at the end of Period 2 will be,

$$A2 = \{P(1 + r)\}(1 + r) \qquad \qquad \text{... (1.2)}$$

Continuing on the basis of the above example, A after a 2 year period will be,

$$= ₹ 100 \times 1.102$$

$$= ₹ 110.2$$

Again, the future value of an amount of money at the end of period n will be,

$$An = P(1 + r)n \qquad \ldots (1.3)$$

The future value of ₹ 5,000, 10 years from now at 8% rate of interest will be,

$$A10 = ₹ 5,000 (1.08)10$$

$$= ₹ 10,749.50$$

Normally, it is difficult to raise $(1 + r)$ to the nth power. In order to overcome this difficulty, one uses numerical tables. The present value is multiplied by the compound factor (CF) given in the table in order to arrive at the future value $(P \times CFr, n)$.

As per the table, the CF for 8% rate of interest for 10 years is ₹ 2.1589. On multiplying it by ₹ 5,000, one gets the future value as follows:

$$= ₹ 5,000 \times 2.1589$$

$$= ₹ 10,749.50$$

Future Value of a Series of Payments:

When a single amount is not involved, rather a series of receipts occurs over a specific period of time, the total future value of these receipts can be found out by adding up the individual future values at the same future time. If P1, P2, P3 and so on are the receipts, their future value at Period n will be,

$$A_n = P_1 (1 + r)^{n-1} + P_2 (1 + r)^{n-2} + P_3 (1 + r)^{n-3} + \ldots + P_{n-1} (1 + r) + P_n \ldots \qquad \ldots (1.4)$$

The future value of a series of three annual receipts of ₹ 1,000, ₹ 500 and ₹ 800 respectively at the end of the third year at 5% rate of interest will be,

$$A3 = ₹ 1,000 (1.05)2 + ₹ 500 (1.05) + ₹ 800$$

$$= ₹ 2,427.50$$

## (ii) Future Value of an Annuity:

In the preceding sub-section, the size of receipts in different years was not uniform. But there are cases when the size of receipts over time is equal or uniform. Uniformity of cash flows represents a case of annuity. Annuity may be of two types:

(a)  Regular annuity where the cash flows, equal in size, occur at the end of each time period;

(b)  Annuity due where the uniform cash flows occur at the beginning of each period.

Irrespective of whether the cash flow occurs at the beginning or at the end of each period, P in equation (1.4) is equal and so it becomes a common factor. Equation (1.4) can be re-written in cases of regular annuity as follows:

$$A_n = P \{(1 + r)^{n-1} + (1 + r)^{n-2} + \ldots + (1 + r) + 1\}$$

or $\qquad\qquad A_n = P [\{1 + r)^n - 1\}/r] \qquad \ldots (1.5)$

Here too, the difficulty of raising $(1 + r)$ to the $n^{th}$ power does arise if the value of n is large. In such cases, the amount of annuity is multiplied by the annuity compound factor (ACF). This can be expressed in the form of an equation as follows:

$$A_n = P \, (ACF_{r,n} - 1) \qquad\qquad\qquad ...\, (1.6)$$

The future value of an equal annual investment of ₹ 1,000 at the end of a 10 year period at 10% rate of interest will be,

$$= ₹ 1,000 \, [\{(1.10)^{10} - 1\}/0.10]$$

$$= ₹ 15,937.40$$

Alternatively, P multiplied by $ACF_{r,n} - 1$ and then divided by r will be

$$= ₹ 1,000 \times 1,59,374/0.10$$

$$= ₹ 15,937.40$$

In case of an annuity due where cash flows occur at the beginning of a particular period, the amount is invested for the year. As a result, in this case, equation (1.5) can be re-written as follows:

$$A_n = P \, [\{(1 + r)^n - 1\}/r] \times (1 + r) \qquad\qquad ...\, (1.7)$$

The future value of equal annual investment of ₹ 1,000 made at the beginning of each year for 10 years at 10% rate of interest will be,

$$= ₹ 1,000 \, [\{(1.10)^{10} - 1\}/0.10] \times 1.10$$

$$= ₹ 17,531.14$$

### Frequency of Compounding:

Normally, the interest rate is given in per annum terms and compound is also done on an annual basis. But there are cases when compounding is done on a half-yearly or quarterly basis. In specific cases, it is even done monthly. If the frequency of compounding increases, which means that it is done more than once a year, the future value of the receipt will be greater. This is because the Annual Percentage Yield (APY) is greater than the Annual Percentage Rate (APR). The greater the frequency of compound, greater is the APR and the larger the future value of the receipt.

APY is the effective annual rate of interest. It is computed by compounding the period of rate for the compounding frequency. This can be expressed in form of an equation as follows:

$$APY = \{1 + (APR/m)\}^m - 1 \qquad\qquad\qquad ...\, (1.8)$$

where,                                        m = The number of compounding periods per year

If the annual interest rate is 12% and compounding is done on a monthly basis, the APY will be,

$$= \{1 + (0.12/12)\}^{12} - 1$$

$$= 12.68\%$$

**(I)  Formula for the Future Value of Single Amount:**

The general formula for the future value of a single amount is,

$$FV_n = PV (1 + k)^n$$

where,                                    $FV_n$ = Future value n years hence

$PV$ = Cash today (present value)

$k$ = Interest rate per year

$n$ = Number of years for which compounding is done

The above equation is a basic equation in compounding analysis. The factor $(1 + k)^n$ is referred to as the compounding factor or the future value interest factor ($FVIF_{k, n}$). It is very tedious to calculate $(1 + k)^n$ unless you have a calculator. To reduce this tedium, published tables are available showing the value of $(1 + k)^n$ for various combinations of k and n.

Table 1.1 shows some illustrative values of $(1 + k)^n$.

**Table 1.1: Value of $FVIF_{k, n}$ for various combinations of k and n**

| n/k | 6% | 8% | 10% | 12% | 14% |
|-----|-----|-----|-----|-----|-----|
| 2 | 1.124 | 1.166 | 1.210 | 1.254 | 1.300 |
| 4 | 1.262 | 1.360 | 1.464 | 1.574 | 1.689 |
| 6 | 1.419 | 1.587 | 1.772 | 1.974 | 2.195 |
| 8 | 1.594 | 1.851 | 2.144 | 2.476 | 1.853 |
| 10 | 1.791 | 2.159 | 2.594 | 3.106 | 3.707 |
| 12 | 2.012 | 2.518 | 3.138 | 3.896 | 4.817 |

**Example:** If you deposit ₹ 1,000 today in a bank which pays 10% interest compounded annually, how much will the deposit grow to after 8 years and 12 years?

**Answer:** The future value 8 years hence will be,

$$= ₹ 1,000 (1.10)^8$$

$$= ₹ 1,000 (2.144)$$

$$= ₹ 2,144$$

The future value, 12 years hence, will be,

$$= ₹ 1,000 (1.10)^{12}$$

$$= ₹ 1,000 (3.138)$$

$$= ₹ 3,138$$

**(II) Formula for the future value of a single amount when compounding is done more frequently.**

The general formula for the future value of a single cash amount when compounding is done more frequently than annually is,

$$FV_n = PV\left(1 + \frac{k}{m}\right)^{m \times n}$$

where,                                    $FV_n$ = Future value after n years

PV = Cash today (present value)

k = Nominal annual rate of interest

m = Number of times compounding is done during a year

n = Number of years for which compounding is done.

**Example:** How much does a deposit of ₹ 5,000 grow to at the end of 6 years, if the nominal rate of interest is 12% and the frequency of compounding is 4 times a year?

**Answer:** The amount after 6 years will be,

$$= ₹\,5,000\left(1 + \frac{0.12}{4}\right)^{4 \times 6}$$

$$= ₹\,5,000\,(1.03)^{24}$$

$$= ₹\,5,000 \times 2.0328$$

$$= ₹\,10,164$$

**(III) Formula for Future Value of an Annuity:**

In general terms the future value of an annuity is given by the following formula:

$$FVA_n = A\,(1+k)^{n-1} + A\,(1+k)^{n-2} + \ldots + A$$

$$= A\left[\frac{(1+k)^n - 1}{k}\right]$$

where,                                    $FVA_n$ = Future value of an annuity which has a duration of n periods

A = Constant periodic flow

k = Interest rate per period

n = Duration of the annuity

The term $\dfrac{(1+k)^n - 1}{k}$ is referred to as the future value interest factor for an annuity ($FVIFA_{k,\,n}$). The value of this factor for several combinations of k and n is given in Table 1.2.

**Table 1.2: Value of FVIFA$_{k,n}$ for Various Combinations of k and n**

| n/k | 6% | 8% | 10% | 12% | 14% |
|-----|------|------|------|------|------|
| 2 | 2.060 | 2.080 | 2.100 | 2.120 | 2.140 |
| 4 | 4.375 | 4.507 | 4.641 | 4.779 | 4.921 |
| 6 | 6.975 | 7.336 | 7.716 | 8.115 | 8.536 |
| 8 | 9.897 | 10.636 | 11.436 | 12.299 | 13.232 |
| 10 | 13.181 | 14.487 | 15.937 | 17.548 | 19.337 |
| 12 | 16.869 | 18.977 | 21.384 | 24.133 | 27.270 |

**Example:** Four equal annual payments of ₹ 2,000 are made into a deposit account that pays 8% interest per year. What is the future value of this annuity at the end of 4 years?

**Answer:** The future value of this annuity is,

$$= ₹ 2,000 \ (FVIFA_{8\%, 4})$$
$$= ₹ 2,000 \ (4.507)$$
$$= ₹ 9,014.$$

# (F) Present Value

**Computation of Present Value of Cash Flows:**

The present value shows today's value of a future sum of money. If today's investment of ₹ 100 at 10% rate of interest brings in ₹ 110 after a year, the latter is the future value and ₹ 100 the present value. It means that if future value is found out through compounding the present value can be calculated through the reverse of compounding.

**(i) Present value of a Single Amount:**

**Example:** 'X' promises to give you ₹ 1,000 three years hence. What is the present value of this amount if the interest rate is 10%?

**Answer:** The present value can be calculated by discounting ₹ 1,000, to the present point of time, as follows:

Value three years hence = ₹ 1,000

Value two years hence = ₹ 1,000 $\left(\dfrac{1}{1.10}\right)$

Value one year hence = ₹ 1,000 $\left(\dfrac{1}{1.10}\right)\left(\dfrac{1}{1.10}\right)$

Value now (present value) = ₹ 1,000 $\left(\dfrac{1}{1.10}\right)\left(\dfrac{1}{1.10}\right)\left(\dfrac{1}{1.10}\right)$

**Formula:** The process of discounting, used for calculating the present value, is simply the inverse of compounding. The present value formula can be readily obtained by manipulating the compounding formula:

$$FV_n = PV \ (1 + k)^n \qquad\qquad\qquad … (1.9)$$

Dividing both the sides of equation (1.9) by $(1 + k)^n$, we get,

$$PV = FV_n \left[\frac{1}{1+k}\right]^n \qquad \qquad \text{... (1.10)}$$

The factor $\left[\dfrac{1}{1+k}\right]^n$ in equation (1.10) is called the discounting factor or the present value interest factor ($PVIF_{k,n}$). Table 1.3 gives the value of $PVIF_{k,n}$ for several combinations of k and n.

**Example:** Find the present value of ₹ 1,000 receivable 6 years hence if the rate of discount is 10%.

**Answer:** The present value is,

$$= ₹\, 1,000 \times PVIF_{10\%,\, 6}$$
$$= ₹\, 1,000\, (0.5645)$$
$$= ₹\, 564.5$$

**Table 1.3: Value of $PVIF_{k,\, n}$ for various combinations of k and n**

| n/k | 6% | 8% | 10% | 12% | 14% |
|-----|-----|-----|-----|-----|-----|
| 2 | 0.890 | 0.857 | 0.826 | 0.797 | 0.770 |
| 4 | 0.792 | 0.735 | 0.683 | 0.636 | 0.592 |
| 6 | 0.705 | 0.630 | 0.565 | 0.507 | 0.456 |
| 8 | 0.626 | 0.540 | 0.467 | 0.404 | 0.351 |
| 10 | 0.558 | 0.463 | 0.386 | 0.322 | 0.270 |
| 12 | 0.497 | 0.397 | 0.319 | 0.257 | 0.208 |

**Present Value of an Uneven Series:**

In financial analysis we often come across uneven cash flow streams. For example, the cash flow stream associated with a capital investment project is typically uneven. Likewise, the dividend stream associated with an equity share is usually uneven and perhaps growing.

The present value of a cash flow stream – uneven or even – may be calculated with the help of the following formula:

$$PV_n = \frac{A_1}{(1+k)} + \frac{A_2}{(1+k)^2} + \dots + \frac{A_n}{(1+k)^n} = \sum_{t=1}^{n} \frac{A_t}{(1+k)^t}$$

where,                                     $PV_n$ = Present value of a cash flow stream

$A_t$ = Cash flow occurring at the end of year t

$k$ = Discount rate

$n$ = Duration of the cash flow stream

Table 1.4 shows the calculation of the present value of an uneven cash flow stream, using a discount rate of 12%.

### Table 1.4: Present Value of an Uneven Cash Flow Stream

| Year | Cash Flow ₹ | $PVIF_{12\%, n}$ | Present Value of the Individual Cash Flow |
|------|-------------|------------------|-------------------------------------------|
| 1 | 1,000 | 0.893 | 893 |
| 2 | 2,000 | 0.797 | 1,594 |
| 3 | 2,000 | 0.712 | 1,424 |
| 4 | 3,000 | 0.636 | 1,908 |
| 5 | 3,000 | 0.567 | 1,701 |
| 6 | 4,000 | 0.507 | 2,028 |
| 7 | 4,000 | 0.452 | 1,808 |
| 8 | 5,000 | 0.404 | 2,020 |
| ∴ Present Value of the Cash Flow Stream | | | 13,376 |

### (ii) Present Value of an Annuity:

**Example:** Suppose you expect to receive ₹ 1,000 annually for 3 years, each receipt occurring at the end of the year. What is the present value of this stream of benefits if the discount rate is 10%?

**Answer:** The present value of this annuity is simply the sum of the present value of all the inflows of this annuity.

$$₹\,1,000 \left(\frac{1}{1.10}\right) + ₹\,1,000 \left(\frac{1}{1.10}\right)^2 + ₹\,1,000 \left(\frac{1}{1.10}\right)^2$$

$$= ₹\,1,000 \times 0.9091 + ₹\,1,000 \times 0.8264 + ₹\,1,000 \times 0.7513$$

$$= ₹\,2,486.80$$

**Formula:** In general terms, the present value of an annuity may be expressed as follows:

$$PV_n = \frac{A}{(1+k)} + \frac{A}{(1+k)^2} + \cdots + \frac{A}{(1+k)^{n-1}} + \frac{A}{(1+k)^n}$$

where,

$PVA_n$ = Present value of an annuity which has a duration of n periods

A = Constant periodic flow

k = Discount rate

$\left[\dfrac{(1+k)^n - 1}{k(1+k)^n}\right]$ is referred to as the present value interest factor for an annuity ($PVIFA_{k, n}$).

It is, as can be seen clearly, simply equal to the product of the future interest factor for an annuity ($FVIFA_{k, n}$) and the present value interest factor ($PVIF_{k, n}$). Table 1.5 shows the value of $PVIFA_{k, n}$ for several combinations of k and n.

Table 1.5: Value of PVIFA$_{k,n}$ for different combinations of k and n

| n/k | 6% | 8% | 10% | 12% | 14% |
|-----|------|------|------|------|------|
| 2 | 1.833 | 1.783 | 1.737 | 1.690 | 1.647 |
| 4 | 3.465 | 3.312 | 3.170 | 3.037 | 2.914 |
| 6 | 4.917 | 4.623 | 4.355 | 4.111 | 3.889 |
| 8 | 6.210 | 5.747 | 5.335 | 4.968 | 4.639 |
| 10 | 7.360 | 6.710 | 6.145 | 5.650 | 6.216 |
| 12 | 8.384 | 7.536 | 6.814 | 6.194 | 5.660 |

**Example:** What is the present value of a 4-year annuity of ₹ 10,000 discounted at 10%?

**Answer:** The PVIFA$_{10\%,4}$ is 3.170.

Hence,                    PVA$_n$ = ₹ 10,000 (3.170)

                                = ₹ 31,700.

## 1.3 Introduction to the Concept of Risk and Return of a Single Asset

### (A) Introduction

Financial Management provides answers to three important questions. These questions are what is the amount of funds required for the business? How the funds will be raised? How the funds will be invested? In taking appropriate decisions in relation to these questions, a finance professional has to take into consideration two important aspects i.e. risk and return. A manager has to find out how much risk he is taking and how much return he is expecting from a particular decision. In raising funds from various sources, risk and return has to take into consideration while even in investing funds, risk and return are involved.

Decisions which will balance risk and return will create value for the shareholders of a firm. Therefore the concepts of risk and return have assumed significant importance in the modern finance theory. In fact it can be said that they are the pillars of the modern finance theory. A detailed study of these concepts has thus became of paramount importance for any finance professional. The aim of this chapter is to discuss various aspects of risk and return and also discuss various theories associated with these concepts.

### (B) Concept of Return

The important question is what is return? How it is measured? Let us try to find out answers to these questions. Suppose, an investor has purchased 10 equity shares of a company at a price of ₹ 1000 each. This means that the investment made by him is ₹ 10000. If the company declares a dividend of 10%, the investor will earn ₹ 100 per share, which means he will get total ₹ 1000 as dividend. The rate of return will be therefore

₹ 1000/₹10000 × 100 = 10%. It should be remembered that the dividend is always paid on the par value i.e. face value. In this example, ₹ 1000 is the face value and hence the return received by him is 10%. However if suppose the shares are listed on the stock exchange and the market value of each share is ₹ 1050, the total market value of the investments will be ₹ 1050 × ₹ 10 = ₹ 10500 and the rate of return will be ₹ 1000/₹10500 × 100 = 9.52%. This means that the rate of return has fallen due to rise in the market price. On the other hand, if the market price of shares falls, the rate of return will increase. The amount of dividend is always paid on the face value and hence the return fluctuates as per the market price. Now suppose, the investor sells these shares after one year for ₹ 15000, he will gain ₹ 5000 which is the difference between the purchase price and the selling price. This gain is called as capital gain. Thus the investor will get dividend as well as capital gain. Hence his total income will be dividend of ₹ 1000 + ₹ 5000 = ₹ 6000. If this gain is computed in percentage, the gain will be ₹ 6000/10000 = 60%. However if the market price goes down as compared to the face value, there will be a loss which means the return from capital gain will be negative.

## (C) Risk

Risk is present everywhere. Risk is there in everyday life. When a finance manager selects an investment avenue or a marketing manager finalises an advertising campaign or a production manager selects a plant and machinery, there is always an uncertainty about the expected cash flows resulting from these activities. When a common man selects a particular avenue for investing his funds, there is a risk involved in it as the return can vary. If a person invests in equity shares, he takes a risk of uncertain dividend and also capital gain. On the other hand, if he decides not to take risk at all, he will have to be satisfied with a comparatively lesser rate of return. For example, if he decides that he will invest only in nationalized bank fixed deposits or post office deposits, there will not be any risk but at the same time the returns will be quite less as compared to other avenues like investment in shares and so on.

Risk is divided into diversifiable and non diversifiable risk. Risk can be reduced by diversifying the portfolio in more than one type of securities. For example, rather than investing in only one company's shares, an investor can choose more than one companies from various sectors and thus reduce the risk considerably. Thus instead of investing into only one company, diversification will reduce the risk. This will ensure that if there is a loss from one sector, there will be profit from other sectors and thus overall risk can be reduced. There cannot be losses from all the sectors at one time. However it should be remembered that even though diversification will reduce the risk, it will not eliminate the risk. After a certain limit, the diversification will not reduce the risk. This is due to the reason that certain types of risks are non diversifiable. For example, even if an investor spreads his investments in several companies, if the economy of the country is not doing well, all sectors will suffer and hence this risk always remains. Thus it should be remembered that risk can be reduced but cannot be eliminated.

## (D) Measurement of Risk

The risks arising out of investments in financial assets are measured in terms of the riskiness of the cash flows. Thus variability of cash flows is the major criteria for measuring the risk arising from a financial asset. The risk measurement and its relation to the return is done in the following manner.

## (E) Risk and Return of a Single Asset

If an Investor invests in equity shares of a company, he will get certain returns. These returns may fluctuate from year to year. The risk is measured after taking into consideration these variations. This means that risk is measured by measuring the deviations in the returns from the average rate of return. In other words, standard deviation or variance are used as measures for such dispersion. Standard deviation is the square root of the variance. The calculation of standard deviation is illustrated in the following example.

**Illustration:**

Mr. A has invested ₹ 10,000 in the equity shares of company X. His rate of return during the last five years were respectively, .10, .15, .05, .12 and .07. The standard deviation and variance will be calculated as follows:

| Sr. No. | Rate of return | Deviation from average | Square of the deviations |
|---------|----------------|------------------------|--------------------------|
| 1 | 0.10 | 0.002 | 0.000004 |
| 2 | 0.15 | 0.052 | 0.002704 |
| 3 | 0.05 | − 0.048 | 0.002304 |
| 4 | 0.12 | 0.022 | 0.000484 |
| 5 | 0.07 | − 0.028 | 0.000784 |
| Average | 49/5 = 0.098 | | 0.00628 |

The standard deviation will be $= \sqrt{0.00628}$

$$= 0.00792$$

The variance will be 0.00628.

The standard deviation of this security will be compared with the standard deviation of returns from another security to find out the comparative risk of the two securities.

The standard deviation can be calculated from the historical data as well as from the expected returns, i.e. from the forecast of the returns in the future period.

## (F) Capital Asset Pricing Model

The capital asset pricing model [CAPM] is a model that provides a framework to determine the required rate of return on an asset and indicates the relationship between the return and risk of the asset. [Sharpe]This model indicates the relationship between risk and the expected rate of return on a risky security. According to this model, risk and return are related in a linear function and is indicated by the following equation.

$$E(R_j) = R_j + \beta_j [E(R_m) - R_f]$$

Where,

$E(R_j)$ = Expected return on security j

$R_f$ = Risk free return

$\beta_j$ = Beta of security j

$E(R_m)$ = Expected return on the market portfolio

**The assumptions of this model are as follows:**

1.  Individuals are not keen on taking risk, i.e. they are risk averse.
2.  Individual investors want to maximise their expected return on their portfolio over a single period planning horizon.
3.  Expectations of the investors are similar to each other as regards to the risk, variations and returns.
4.  The capital market is efficient which means that the share price reflect all available information. As happens in perfect competition, individual investors are not able to influence the share prices.
5.  The interest rate is risk free which means that all investors can either borrow or lend at an interest rate which is risk free.

## 1.4 Risk and Return of a Portfolio

A portfolio is the total collection of all investments held by an individual or institution, including stocks, bonds, real estate, options, futures and alternative investments, such as gold or limited partnerships. Most portfolios are diversified to protect against the risk of single securities or class of securities. Hence portfolio analysis consists of analysing the portfolio as a whole rather than relying exclusively on security analysis, which is the analysis of specific types of securities. The risk-return profile of a portfolio depends not only on the component securities, but also on their mixture or allocation, and on their degree of correlation.

### (A) Portfolio Returns

The return of a portfolio commensurates with the return of its individual assets. The return of a portfolio is the weighted average of the return of its component assets.

**Formula:**    $\text{Portfolio Return} = \sum_{k=1}^{n} \dfrac{\text{Amount of Asset}}{\text{Amount of Portfolio}} \times \text{Return of Assets}$

n = Number of assets

### (B) Portfolio Risks

Portfolio risks can be calculated by taking the standard deviation of the variance of the actual returns of the portfolio overtime. This variability of returns commensurates with the portfolio's risk, and the risk can be quantified by calculating the standard deviation of this variability.

**Standard Deviation Formula for Portfolio Returns:**

$$S = \sqrt{\frac{\sum_{k}^{n} = 1 \, (\gamma_k - \gamma_{expected})^2}{n-1}}$$

where,        $S$ = Standard deviation,

$\gamma_k$ = Specific Return,

$\gamma_{expected}$ = Expected Return,

$n$ = Number of Returns (Sample size),

$n-1$ = Number of degrees of freedom, which in statistics is used for small sample sizes

## (C) Portfolio Variance and Standard Deviation

The variance/standard deviation of a portfolio reflects not only the variance/standard deviation of the stock that make up the portfolio but also how the returns on the stocks which comprises the portfolio vary together. Two measures of how the returns on a pair of stocks vary together are the covariance and correlation coefficient.

## 1.5 Valuation of Shares

## (A) Meaning of the Concept

There are different motives for which the shares are valued, viz.; speculation motive, investment motive, and control motive. Some persons are interested in purchasing shares for speculative purpose, they want to dispose-off shares when the price rises in the market. They are influenced by price fluctuations. Some persons want to purchase shares purely from investment motive. They are influenced by security cover offered by the assets of the company. While some others are interested in purchasing the shares to acquire the control of some others while some are interested in purchasing the shares to acquire general prospect and other factors. Expected yield is the main factor which affects almost all the cases.

- In most cases, shares are quoted on the stock exchange and generally, the price prevailing on the stock exchange may be taken as the proper value. But all the shares are not quoted on the stock exchange.

- Valuation of shares is required for transfer of shares in private companies and of other unquoted shares. It is not only the shares of private companies and the unquoted shares of public companies that need valuation. Sometimes, as in the case of proposed merger or for acquisition of large blocks of shares, it becomes necessary to value even the quoted shares of public companies.

- The stock exchange price of shares may not represent the correct financial position of the company because stock exchange prices are affected by external factors such as demand and supply, the bank rate, taxation policy and political conditions which are beyond the control of the company.

**Need for Valuation of Shares:** Shares of a company are valued on some special occasions like:

(a) At the time of purchase and sale of unquoted shares.

(b) For estate duty and wealth tax computation purposes.

(c) For acquiring control on block of shares.

(d) For schemes of amalgamation or absorption of companies.

(e) When a company is reconstructed under Section 94 of the Companies Act and there are dissentent shareholders.

(f) Conversion of shares of one class into another.

(g) Acquisition of shares of dissentent shareholders under Section 395.

(h) Valuation of assets of a finance or an investment trust company.

(i) Government acquisition.

## (B) Special Factors affecting Valuation of Shares

(a) The nature of the business and its history.

(b) The economic outlook in general.

(c) The position and outlook for the specific sector.

(d) Role of management, vision, and strategy.

(e) The book value of assets and liabilities.

(f) Financial condition of the business.

(g) The earning capacity.

(h) Dividend paying capacity.

(i) Intangible assets, and goodwill.

(j) The size of the block to be valued.

(k) The marketability of shares in private companies.

(l) Rights attaching to shares, minority interests.

(m) Market share and strategic positioning.

(n) Risk/reward aspects.

(o) Level of gearing.

(p) Accounting adjustments

## (C) Methods of Valuation: (a) Net Assets Method, (b) Yield Basis Method, (c) Fair Value Method

(a) **Net Assets Method:** The method aims to find out asset backing per share. An investor though interested mainly to the possible return always cares to see that his investment is well secured by valuable assets.

Under this method:

(i) Take present or market value of each tangible asset including Goodwill. Non trading investment will also be taken. If current realisable values are not given, then the Balance Sheet figures will be taken as Realisable Values. Fictitious items like Preliminary Expenses, or Discount on issue of shares, or Debentures will be eliminated.

(ii) From the total assets third party or external liabilities (revised values) including any contingent liabilities will be deducted. This will give us the Net Assets,

(iii) Net Assets = Realisable Assets – Outside Liabilities.

(iv) If there are preference shares, then from the net assets, preference share capital will be deducted being preferential as to return of capital, and the remaining balance will form the asset backing for equity shares.

(v) The balance of net assets available for equity shares is to be divided by the number of equity shares subscribed (of the same paid-up value) and the result will be the intrinsic value of shares.

$$\text{Intrinsic value} = \frac{\text{Net Assets for Equity Shareholders}}{\text{Number of Equity Shares}}$$

(vi) Where there are equity shares of different paid-up values, the total asset backing for Equity shares or Equity Fund being dividend by the total amount of paid-up Equity capital (not number of shares) gives the value per Rupee of paid-up equity capital. This will be multiplied by the actual paid-up value of each class of shares useful for formulating amalgamation schemes for acquiring controlling shares. In case of liquidation, intrinsic value will be the price that will be paid. Sometimes, the asset backing is calculated by excluding the value of Goodwill.

**(b) Yield Basis Method:** An investor is primarily interested in the yield and so the price he will prepare to pay will depend upon the return that he expects from his investment. This means that the price which he is prepared to pay directly varies with the expected yield.

Under this method, the annual profit available for distribution to equity shareholders is estimated on the basis of company's past performances. Out of the future maintainable profits:

(i) Transfers to reserves.

(ii) Transfers to Debentures Redemption Fund.

(iii) Taxation.

(iv) The Preference dividend will be deducted.

This is done with a view to know the possible amount of profit available to equity shareholders.

The next step is to find out expected rate of return or dividend on Equity Capital by:

$$\frac{\text{Adjusted average profit available for Equity Shareholders}}{\text{Paid-up Equity Share Capital}} \times 100$$

The expected rate of return or dividend will be compared with the normal rate of return in similar business to get the market value of each share.

$$\text{Market Value} = \frac{\text{Expected rate of Return or Dividend} \times \text{Paid-up Value Per Share}}{\text{Normal Rate}}$$

- Alternatively, the annual profit available for distribution to shareholders as calculated above, are capitalised at a normal rate. This captialised value thus arrived is to be divided by the number of equity shares subscribed. The result is the market value of each equity share value based on earning of the company.

- Generally, the dividend declared by the company is much lesser than the rate of its earning. As retained profits are likely to be distributed in the form of bonus shares, the market value is to be based on the earning of the company rather than dividends earnings (i.e. profit before appropriation to reserves, debenture redemption fund, preference dividend etc. but after tax called distributable  profit) rather than dividend (i.e. profit left after transfer to reserves, debenture redemption fund, preference dividend etc. called distributed profit) are often considered as a better measure of share value since this relates the value to the real efficiency as measured by the profitability of the company.

$$\text{Rate of Earning} = \frac{\text{Profit earned}}{\text{Capital employed}}$$

Where profit earned is before debenture interest, preference dividend transfer to reserve but after tax and capital employed is the total capital including long-term borrowings.

$$\text{Value of Share} = \frac{\text{Rate of earnings as calculated} \times \text{paid up value per share}}{\text{Normal rate of earning}}$$

(c) **Fair Value Method:** Fair value is taken as the arithmetic means of Intrinsic value and market value of the share.

$$\textbf{Fair Value of the Share} = \frac{\text{Intrinsic value of the share} + \text{Market value of the share}}{2}$$

## 1.6 Valuation of Bonds

Bond valuation is the determination of the fair price of a bond.

Bonds are long-term debt securities that are issued by corporations and government entities. Purchasers of bonds receive periodic interest payments, called coupon payments, until maturity at which time they receive the face value of the bond and last coupon payment. Most bonds pay interest semi-annually.

**Important Terms used in Bond Valuation:**

(a) **Par or Face Value:** The par or face value of a bond is the amount of money that is paid to the bondholders at maturity. It also represents the amount of money borrowed by the bond issuer.

(b) **Coupon Rate:** It is generally fixed. It determines the periodic coupon or interest payments. It is expressed as a percentage of the bond's face value. It also represents the interest cost of the bond issue to the issuer.

(c) **Coupon Payments:** The coupon payments represents the periodic interest payments from the bond issuer to the bondholder.

(d) **Maturity Date:** The maturity date represents the date on which the bond matures, i.e., the date on which the face value is repaid.
   The last coupon payment is also paid on the maturity date.

(e) **Call Price:** The amount of money the issuer has to pay to call a callable bond. When a bond first becomes callable, i.e., on the call date, the call price is often set to equal the face value plus one year's interest.

(f) **Required Return:** The rate of return that investors currently require on a bond.

(g) **Yield to Maturity:** It is the rate of return that an investor would earn if he bought the bond at its current market price and held it until maturity.

**Basic Bond Valuation Formula:**

A bond's value is the present value of the payments the issuer is contractually obliged to make - from the present until maturity. The discount rate depends on the prevailing interest rate for debt obligations with similar risks and maturities.

Using the basic DCF method, a bond's value is:

$$B_0 = \text{Sum} [1 + n] I / [1 + i]^n + M / [1 + i]^n$$

$B_0$ = Bond's value at time zero,

$I$ = Annual interest payments,

$i$ = Discount rate,

$n$ = Number of years to maturity,

$M$ = Par value (payment at maturity)

Bond valuation is an application of present value. The value of the bonds is the present value of all the cash flows the investor receives as a result of holding the bond.

**Example of Bond Valuation:** Suppose 'Goodwill Inc.' issues ten-year bonds (par $ 1000), with an annual coupon at 8.6%. Similar ten-year bonds are paying 8.0% interests. What is the value of one of Goodwill's new bonds.

$$B_0 = C + (1 + i)^n + M/(1 + i)$$
$$= \$ 86 \times (\text{PV of ten year } \$ 1 \text{ annuity at } 8.0\%) + \$ 1000 \times (\text{PV of } \$ 1 \text{ to be paid in 10 years at } 8.0\%)$$
$$= (\$ 86 \times 6.710) + (\$ 1000 \times 0.4632)$$
$$= \$ 577.06 + \$ 463.20$$
$$= \$ 1{,}040.26$$

**Relationship between Coupon Rate and Yield to Maturity (Y) or Current Interest Rates:**

(a)  When $Y = $ Coupon rate, $P_b = P_n$.

(b)  When $Y < $ Coupon rate, $P_b > P_n$

 (Bond sells at a premium).

(c)  When $Y > $ Coupon rate, $P_b < P_n$

 (Bond sells at a discount).

## 1.7 Option Valuation

An option contract or option is defined as a promise which meets the requirements for the formation of a contract and limits the promisor's power to revoke an offer.

Options contract are often used in securities, commodities and real estate transactions.

## (A) Forms of Options Contract

**(a)  Call option:** It gives the beneficiary the right to require the grantor to sell or convey the property to them at an agreed price on exercise.

**(b)  Put option:** It gives the beneficiary the right to require the grantor to buy or receive the property at an agree price on exercise.

## (B) Valuation of Options

**(a)  Protective Put:**

(i)  Buy the underlying asset and a put option to protect against a decline in the value of the underlying asset.

(ii)  Pay the put premium to limit the downside risk.

(iii)  Trade-off between the amount of protection and the price that you pay for the option.

**(b)  Put-Call Parity:**

(i)  If the two positions are worth the same at the end, they must cost the same at the beginning.

(ii)  This leads to the put-call parity condition,

$$S + P = C + PV[E]$$

(iii)  If this condition does not hold, there is an arbitrage opportunity, i.e. Buy the "low" side and sell the "high" side.

**Example:** Finding the Call Price

$$\text{Current stock price} = \$50$$
$$\text{Put price} = \$1.15$$
$$\text{Exercise price} = \$45$$
$$\text{Risk - Free rate} = 5\%$$

Expiration in 1 year

$$\therefore \qquad \text{Call price} = 50 + 1.15 = \frac{C + 45}{(1.05)}$$

$$\therefore \qquad C = 8.29$$

**(c)  Put value:**

(i)  The value of a put can be found by finding the value of the call and then using put-call parity.

**(d)  Equity as a Call Option:**

(i)  Equity can be viewed as a call option on the firm's assets whenever the firm carries debt.

(ii)  The strike price is the cost of making the debt payment.

(iii)  The underlying asset price is the market value of the firm's assets.

(iv)  If the intrinsic value is positive, the firm can exercise the option by paying off the debt.

(v)  If the intrinsic value is negative, the firm can let the option expire and turn the firm over to the bondholders.

**(e)  Valuation at Expiration:**

**For a Put Option:**

(i)  Assume: the strike price = $100.

(ii)  For a put, if the stock price is greater than $100, the option is worthless at expiration.

(iii)  The downward sloping line represents the intrinsic value of the option.

**For a Put Option:**

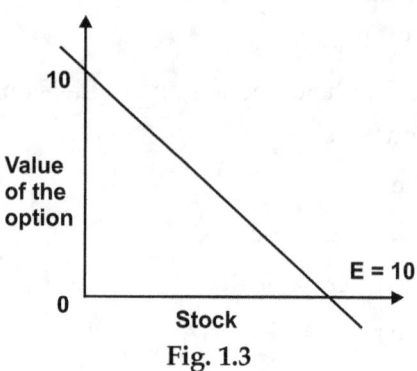

Fig. 1.3

**For a Call Option:**

(i) Assume: the strike price = $ 100.

(ii) For a call, if the stock price is less than $ 100, the option is worthless at expiration.

# (C) Determinants of Option Value

(i) **Variables Relating to Underlying Asset:**

    1. **Value of Underlying Asset:** As this value increases, the right to buy at a fixed price (calls) will become more valuable and the right to sell at a fixed price (puts) will become less valuable.

    2. **Variance in that value:** As the variance increases, both calls and puts will become more valuable because all options have limited downside and depend upon price volatility for upside.

(ii) **Variables Relating to Options:**

    1. **Strike Price of Options:** The right to buy (sell) at fixed price becomes more (less) valuable at a lower price.

    2. **Life of the options:** Both call and puts benefit from a longer life.

    3. **Level of interest rates:** As the rate increases, the right to buy (sell) at a fixed price in the future becomes more (less) valuable.

**A Summary of the Determinants of Option Value:**

| Factor | Call Value | Put Value |
|---|---|---|
| (i)   Increase in Stock Price | Increases | Decreases |
| (ii)  Increase in Strike Price | Decreases | Increases |
| (iii) Increase in Variance of Underlying Asset | Increases | Increases |
| (iv)  Increase in Time to Expiration | Increases | Increases |
| (v)   Increase in Interest Rates | Decreases | Increases |
| (vi)  Increase in Dividends Paid | Increases | Decreases |

## Practical Problems

**Problem 1:** The following is the Summarized Balance Sheet of ABC. Ltd. as on 31.12.2015.

| Liabilities | ₹ | Assets | ₹ |
|---|---|---|---|
| **Share Capital:** | | Fixed Assets | 38,00,000 |
| 10,000 5 % Preference | | Investment | 10,25,000 |
| shares of ₹ 100 each, | | **Current Assets:** | |
| Fully paid | 10,00,000 | Stock in trade | 5,72,000 |
| 2,00,000 Equity shares of | | Sundry debtors | |
| ₹ 10 each, Fully paid | 20,00,000 | (Less: provision) | 12,78,000 |
| **Reserves and Surplus:** | 15,00,000 | Cash and Bank | |
| General Reserve | | Balances | 2,25,000 |
| Profit and Loss A/c (Cr.) | 12,00,000 | | |
| **Secured loan:** | | | |
| 6 % Debentures | 8,00,000 | | |
| **Current liabilities:** | | | |
| Sundry Creditors | 2,75,000 | | |
| Liabilities for expenses | 1,25,000 | | |
| | 69,00,000 | | 69,00,000 |

For the purpose of valuation of shares, Fixed Assets are to be depreciated by 10 %. Investments are to be taken at ₹ 10,80,000, and Sundry debtors are to be further reduced by 5 %. Interest on Debentures is due for 9 months and Preference Dividend for 2015 is also due; neither of these has been provided for in the Balance Sheet.

Calculate the value of each Equity share.

**Solution:**

| Particulars | ₹ | ₹ |
|---|---|---|
| **Net Assets:** | | |
| Fixed Assets (₹ 38,00,000 – 3,80,000) | 34,20,000 | |
| Investments | 10,80,000 | |
| Stock | 5,72,000 | |
| Debtors (₹ 12,78,000 – ₹ 63,900) | 12,14,100 | |
| Cash at Bank | 2,25,000 | 65,11,100 |
| **Less: Current Liabilities** | | |
| Sundry Creditors | 2,75,000 | |
| Liabilities for Expenses | 1,25,000 | |
| | 4,00,000 | |

*contd ...*

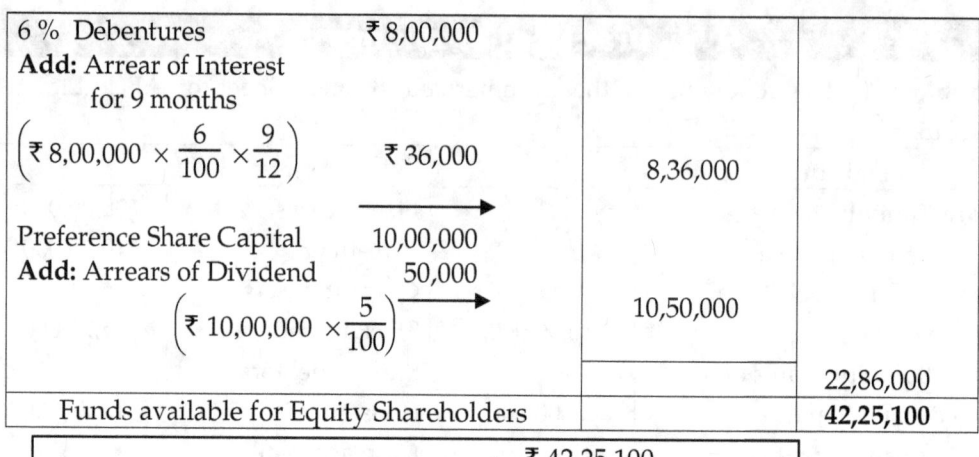

| 6 % Debentures | ₹ 8,00,000 | | |
|---|---|---|---|
| **Add:** Arrear of Interest for 9 months $\left(₹\,8,00,000 \times \dfrac{6}{100} \times \dfrac{9}{12}\right)$ | ₹ 36,000 | 8,36,000 | |
| Preference Share Capital | 10,00,000 | | |
| **Add:** Arrears of Dividend $\left(₹\,10,00,000 \times \dfrac{5}{100}\right)$ | 50,000 | 10,50,000 | |
| | | | 22,86,000 |
| **Funds available for Equity Shareholders** | | | **42,25,100** |

$$\therefore \quad \text{Intrinsic value of each Equity Share} \;=\; \frac{₹\,42,25,100}{2,00,000 \text{ Shares}} = ₹\,21.13$$

**Problem 2:** The following is the Summarised Balance Sheet of X Co. Ltd. as on 31.12.2014.

| Liabilities | ₹ | Assets | ₹ |
|---|---|---|---|
| **Authorised, Issued,** | | Goodwill | 5,000 |
| **Subscribed Capital:** | | Land and Building | 1,05,000 |
| 1,000 Equity Share of | | Machineries | 55,000 |
| ₹ 100 each, fully paid | 1,00,000 | Stock (at cost) | 45,000 |
| 1,000 Redeemable Preference | | Sundry Debtors | 20,000 |
| Shares of ₹ 100 each fully paid | 1,00,000 | Cash in Hand | 5,000 |
| General Reserve | 15,000 | Cash at Bank | 1,15,000 |
| Dividend Equalisation Reserve | 5,000 | | |
| Employee's Compensation | | | |
| Fund | 5,000 | Investment in National | |
| (Represented by Investment in | | Plan Certificates | 5,000 |
| securities ) | | | |
| Reserve for taxation | 5,000 | Preliminary Expenses | 5,000 |
| Employees Saving A/c | 10,000 | | |
| Sundry Creditors | 20,000 | | |
| Profit and Loss Account | 1,00,000 | | |
| | **3,60,000** | | **3,60,000** |

On 1.1.2015, all the Preference shares were redeemed at a premium of ₹ 10 per share out of profits otherwise available for dividends. You are asked to ascertain the intrinsic value of each of the Equity Shares by Assets Backing Method, on the basis of the Balance sheet immediately after redemption of Preference shares.

Take into accounts the following information:

(a) Goodwill to be taken at ₹ 50,000.

(b) 10 % of Sundry Debtors are bad.

(c) A claim for compensation to an employee has been admitted on 2014, the amount involved being ₹ 1,000.

(d) All the other assets are taken at their book values as shown in the above Balance Sheet.

**Solution:**

| Particulars | ₹ | ₹ |
|---|---|---|
| **Net Assets:** | | |
| Goodwill | 50,000 | |
| Land and Building | 1,05,000 | |
| Machineries | 55,000 | |
| Stock | 45,000 | |
| Sundry Debtors | 18,000 | |
| (₹ 20,000 – ₹ 2,000) | | |
| Investment | 5,000 | |
| Cash in hand | 5,000 | |
| Cash at bank | 5,000 | |
| (₹1,15,000 – 1,10,000) for payment to Pref. | | |
| shareholders with premium | | 2,88,000 |
| **Less: Current Liabilities:** | | |
| Employees Saving Account | 10,000 | |
| Sundry Creditors | 20,000 | (–) |
| Employees Compensation Claim | 1,000 | |
| Reserve for Taxation | 5,000 | 36,000 |
| Funds available for Equity Shareholders | | **2,52,000** |

$\therefore$ **Intrinsic value of each Equity Share** $= \dfrac{₹\,2,52,000}{1,000} = ₹\,252.$

(Assume current liability i.e. like provision for taxation.)

**Problem 3:** The capital of a company consists of 20,000 Equity shares of ₹ 10 each fully paid. The annual profits of the company is ₹ 20,000 which is expected to be maintained in future. The normal rate of return on the paid-up value of shares for the similar business is 8%. Compute the value of each Equity share.

**Solution:**

$$\text{Capitalised Value of Profit} = \frac{\text{Profit}}{\text{Normal rate of return}} \times 100$$

$$= \frac{20,000}{8} \times 100 = ₹\,2,50,000$$

$$\text{Value of each Equity share} = \frac{\text{Capitalised value of profits}}{\text{Number of Equity shares}}$$

$$= \frac{2,50,000}{20,000} = ₹\ 12.50$$

**Problem 4:** Two companies A Ltd. and B Ltd. are found to be exactly similar as to their assets, reserves and liabilities except that their Share Capital Structures are different.

The Share capital of A. Ltd. is ₹ 11,00,000 divided into 10,000 6 % Preference shares of ₹ 100 each, and 10,000 Equity shares of ₹ 10 each.

The Share capital of B. Ltd. is also ₹ 11,00,000 divided into 1,000 6 %. Preference shares of ₹ 100 each, and 1,00,000 Equity shares of ₹ 10 each.

The fair yield in respect of the Equity shares of this type of companies is ascertained at 8 %.

The profits of the two companies for 2013 and 2014 are found to be ₹ 1,10,000 and ₹ 1,50,000 respectively. Calculate the value of the Equity shares of each of these two companies on 31.12.2014 on the basis of this information only. Ignore taxation.

**Solution:**

| A. Ltd. | | B. Ltd. | ₹ |
|---|---|---|---|
| $\dfrac{₹\ 1,10,000 + ₹\ 1,50,000}{2}$  = ₹  1,30,000 | | Average profit<br>**Less:** Pref. Dividend | 1,30,000 |
| **Less:** Preference Dividend 6 % on | | | |
| ₹ 10,00,000 | ₹  60,000 | Maintainable Profit | 6,000 |
| Maintainable Profit | 70,000 | (6 % on ₹ 1,00,000)<br>Capitalised Value of Profit<br>$\dfrac{1,24,000}{8} \times 100$ = ₹ 15,50,000 | 1,24,000 |

$$\text{Capitalised value of Profit} = \frac{70,000}{8} \times 100$$

$$= ₹\ 8,75,000$$

∴       Value of Each Equity Share       Value of Each Equity Share.

$$= \frac{₹\ 8,75,000}{10,000} = \frac{15,50,000}{1,00,000}$$

$$= 87.50 = ₹\ 15.50$$

**Problem 5:** The issued share capital of a company was ₹ 5,00,000 consisting of 50,000 Equity shares of ₹ 10 each . The net profit for the last 5 years were ₹ 40,000; ₹ 50,000, ₹ 60,000 ₹ 80,000; and ₹ 70,000 of which 20 % was placed to Reserve. This proportion being considered reasonable in the industry in which the company is engaged and where a fair investment return may be taken at 10 %. Compute the value of the companies share by the yield basis method.

**Solution: Calculation of Average Expected Future Profits:**

$$\text{Average Profit} = \frac{₹\,40,000 + ₹\,50,000 + ₹\,60,000 + ₹\,80,000 + ₹\,70,000}{5} = ₹\,60,000$$

**Less:** Transfer to Reserve @ 20 %

$(60,000 \times 20/100)$                                          $= ₹\,12,000$

**Maintainable Profits**                                          $₹\,48,000$

$$= \frac{₹\,48,000}{10} \times 100$$

$$= ₹\,4,80,000$$

∴ **Value of each Equity Share**

$$= \frac{₹\,4,80,000}{50,000} = ₹\,9.60$$

---

**Problem 6:** Sri Das holds 5,000 Equity shares in Hindustan Ltd. The nominal and paid-up capital consists of:

(i)  ₹ 20,000 Equity shares of ₹ 1 each.

(ii) ₹ 10,000 5 % Preference shares of ₹ 1 each (Note: The Preference shares do not participate further in the profits)

It is ascertained:

(a) The normal Annual Net Profit of such company is ₹ 5,000, and

(b) The rate of normal return by way of dividend on the paid-up value of Equity share capital for the type of business carried out by the company is 8 % .

Sri Das requests you to value his share holding based upon above figures.

**Solution:**

| Particulars | ₹ |
|---|---|
| Annual Net Profit | 5,000 |
| **Less:** Preference Dividend @ | 500 |
| 5 % on ₹ 10,000 | |
| **Maintainable Profits** | **4,500** |

$$\textbf{Value of Each Equity share} = \frac{\text{Profit}}{\text{Normal Rate of Return} \times \text{Number of Equity Shares}} \times 100$$

$$= \frac{4,500}{8 \times 20,000} \times 100$$

$$= ₹\ \textbf{2.8125}$$

Alternatively, $\text{Rate of Dividend} = \dfrac{\text{Profit}}{\text{Equity capital(paid-up)}} \times 100$

$$= \frac{₹\,4,500}{₹\,20,000} \times 100 = \textbf{22.5 \%}$$

$$\frac{\text{Value of each}}{\text{Equity share}} = \frac{\text{Rate of Dividend}}{\text{Normal rate of return} \times \text{Paid up value of each Equity share}}$$

$$= \frac{22.5}{8} \times ₹\,1 = ₹\,\textbf{2.8125}$$

∴ Value of 5,000 Equity shares will be

$$5,000 \times ₹\,2.8125 = ₹\,\textbf{14062.50}$$

**Problem 7:** The following is the Balance Sheet of Mithu Ltd. as on 31.12.2014.

| Liabilities | ₹ | Assets | ₹ |
|---|---|---|---|
| **Share Capital:** | | Land and Building | 55,000 |
| 10,000 Shares of | 1,00,000 | Trademark | 10,000 |
| ₹ 10 each | | | |
| General Reserve | 20,000 | Stock | 24,000 |
| Taxation Reserve | 30,000 | Debtors | 44,000 |
| Workman Saving A/c | 15,000 | Cash at bank | 26,000 |
| Profit and Loss A/c. | 16,000 | Preliminary Expenses | 6,000 |
| Sundry Creditors | 49,000 | Plant at cost less Dep. | 65,000 |
| | 2,30,000 | | 2,30,000 |

The plant is worth ₹ 60,000, and Land and Building have been valued at ₹ 1,20,000. Debtors include ₹ 4,000 as bad. The profit of the company have been for 2011 ₹ 40,000, for 2012 ₹ 45,000, and for 2013 ₹ 53,000. It is the Company's practice to transfer 25 % of Profit to Reserve.

Similar companies give a yield of 10 % on the market value of shares.

Value of Goodwill is 80,000. Ignore Income Tax. Find out the fair value at the equity share.

**Solution: (a) Under Asset Backing Method:**

| Particulars | ₹ | ₹ |
|---|---|---|
| Goodwill | | 80,000 |
| Land and Building | | 1,20,000 |
| Plant and Machineries | | 60,000 |
| Trade Marks | | 10,000 |
| Stock | | 24,000 |
| Debtors | 44,000 | |
| **Less:** Bad Debt | 4,000 | 40,000 |
| Cash at Bank | | 26,000 |
| **Less:** Workman Saving A/C | 15,000 | 3,60,000 |
| Secondary Creditors | 49,000 | 64,000 |
| **Funds available for Equity Shareholders** | | 2,96,000 |

∴  **Intrinsic Value of each Equity Share:**

$$= \frac{₹\ 2,96,000}{10,000} = ₹\ \textbf{29.60}$$

**Note:** It is assumed that Taxation Reserve represents a Contingency Reserve which may be created out of appropriation of profit, and not like provision for Taxation.

**(b) Under Yield Basis Method:** Since the trend of profit is rising, weighted average method is so be used to find out the average maintainable profit.

| Years | Profits (₹) | Weights | Products (₹) |
|-------|-------------|---------|--------------|
| 2011 | 40,000 | 1 | 40,000 |
| 2012 | 45,000 | 2 | 90,000 |
| 2013 | 49,000 (₹53,000 – ₹ 4,000) | 3 | 1,47,000 |
| | | 6 | 2,77,000 |

Hence, **Average Maintainable Profit** $= \dfrac{2,77,000}{6}$

$= ₹ 46,167$

**Less:** Dep. say 5 % on increased value of
Land and Building ₹ 65,000
$(₹ 1,20,000 - 55,000) = \quad 3,250$

$\overline{₹ 42,917}$

**Less:** Transfer to Reserve 25 %

$\left(₹ 42,917 \times \dfrac{25}{100}\right) = ₹ 10,729$

Actual Maintainable Profit $= \overline{₹32,188}$

∴ Capitalised Value of Profit $= ₹ \dfrac{32,188}{10} \times 100 = ₹ 3,21,880$

∴ **Value of Each Equity Share** $= ₹ \dfrac{3,21,880}{10,000} = ₹ 32.188$ (approx)

∴ **Fair Value** $= \dfrac{\text{Intrinsic value} + \text{Yield basis}}{2}$

$= \dfrac{₹ 29.60 + 32.188}{2} = ₹ 30.894$

## Questions for Discussion

1. What is Financial Management? Explain the various goals of Financial Management.
2. Explain the concept of Time Value of Money.
3. Explain: Valuation of Bonds.
4. Explain: Option Valuation.
5. Write short notes on:
    (a) Risk and Return of a Single Asset.
    (b) Risk and Return of Portfolio.
    (c) Valuation of Shares.
    (d) Future Value.

■■■

CHAPTER 2

# Investment Decisions

*Contents ...*

## 2.1 Capital Budgeting - Principles and Techniques - Nature of Capital Budgeting - Identifying Relevant Cash Flows

### (A) Capital Investment Decisions

Any business organisation has to incur various expenses in order to run the business effectively. These expenses are required for improving the earning capacity of the business as well as for running the business effectively on day-to-day basis. Expenditure incurred by a business organisation can be broadly divided into:

(a)  Capital expenditure

(b)  Revenue expenditure and

(c)  Deferred revenue expenditure.

While capital expenditure is incurred basically for a long term objective, this expenditure also results into acquisition or creation of fixed assets. On the other hand, revenue expenditure is incurred for short term purpose and mainly for running the business on day-to-day business. The examples of capital expenditure are acquisition of land, construction or acquisition of building, modernisation of plant and machinery, creating additional production capacity etc. Examples of revenue expenditure are salaries paid, wages paid, repairs and maintenance, rent etc. The deferred revenue expenditure show the characteristics of both, capital expenditure and revenue expenditure. For example, heavy amount spent on advertising will be beneficial for next 3-5 years and hence it is treated as deferred capital expenditure. Decision regarding incurring capital expenditure on a particular aspect is a major decision for any business organisation. A business organisation has to quite often face the problem of capital investment decisions. Capital investment refers to the investment in projects whose results would be available only after a year. The amounts invested in these projects are quite heavy and even if the investments are made currently, the return will be available only after a period of time. These investment decisions, popularly known as capital budgeting decisions, require comparison of cost against benefits over a long period. Such investments may affect revenues for the time period ranging from 2 to 20 years or more.

In other words, the system of capital budgeting is employed to evaluate expenditure decisions, which involve current outlays but are likely to produce benefits over a period of time longer than one year. These benefits may be either in the form of increased revenues or reduction in costs. The following basic features of capital budgeting may be derived from the above discussion.

(i)     Capital investments involves comparatively a large amount.

(ii)    The benefits from these decisions are spread over a large time horizon.

(iii)   There is a greater degree of risk involved in these decisions.

(iv)    Capital investment decisions are either not reversible or reversible at a heavy loss.

## (B) Reasons for Capital Investments

**(a) Projects which are means to maintain or improve profitability:**

(i)     Certain projects may result in cost reduction, e.g., Replacement of manual operations by labour saving device.

(ii)    Certain projects may lead to increased output and, therefore, increased earnings.

(iii)   It may become necessary to invest in certain projects in order to protect the company's earning potential, in view of growing competition. It may be either a protective investment or even an investment, meant to ward off competition.

(iv)    Many Capital Investments become necessary because of technological changes and innovations. If a machine with a better design comes into the market, the existing machines (in the same line) become obsolete. If a new manufacturing process is developed (which results in greater economy and/or more output), the existing process has to be discarded.

(v)   Certain investments may be made because of strategic reasons. If a company wants to acquire or maintain leadership in the industry, it spends vast sums of money on Research and Development which may in some cases appear to be output of proportion to its existing level of activities.

The primary motive in making the above types of investment is profitability in contract to the five types of investments classified under (b) below. What we are going to discuss in this chapter is relevant to the investments which are made for reasons of profit.

**(b) Projects for which profitability is not the criterion:**

There are certain projects, in which every company has to invest funds, though such projects do not have any direct impact on increased profitability either in the short–run or in the long–run.

**Examples:**

(i)    Projects, which are statutorily required, e.g., Effluent clearing plant in a fertilizer factory, dust collection in a cement factory, special equipment to treat noxious gases, released by a chemical factory.

(ii)   Service Department Projects, e.g., Building and Furniture for administrative, finance, legal departments, and so on.

(iii)  Welfare Projects such as Health Clinic Recreation Club for employees.

(iv)   Educational Projects such as Schools for employee's children.

(v)    Safety Projects, e.g., Fencing equipment, special protective cages, and so on.

However, it does not mean that some of these projects do not result in increased productivity and profitability in the long–run, they may. But what is necessary to remember is that in making these investments, profitability is not the Chief Criterion.

## (C) Meaning and Nature of Capital Budgeting

Capital Budgeting is the exchange of present expenditure for future benefits which is the distinctive feature of capital expenditure situation.

Capital Budgeting includes both raising of long-term funds as well as their utilisation.

Capital Budgeting is the long-term planning for proposed capital outlays and their financing.

Capital Budgeting decisions require an assessment of future events which are uncertain.

The effect of capital budgeting decisions inevitably affect the cost structure of a company.

## (D) Aspects of Capital Budgeting Process

The most important part of the capital budgeting process is decision making in some very crucial areas. These areas can be broadly identified as given below.

(i)      The total amount that the firm has to invest in capital budgeting proposals.

(ii)     The projects in which the amount is to be invested have to be identified and accordingly the ranking of projects according to their relative importance in the overall strategy of the firm.

(iii)    The sources from which the required amount is to be raised should also be decided. The cost of funds depends on the sources from which the funds are raised.

(iv)    The techniques which are to be used for the evaluation of the capital budgeting proposals should also be decided in advance so that fair evaluation will be possible.

## (E) Types of Capital Budgeting Decisions

Capital budgeting decisions are normally of the following types.

(i)      **Replacements:** Existing fixed assets will need replacements either due to the end of their useful life or due to advancement in technology, otherwise their productivity will come down. For replacing such assets, capital budgeting decisions become essential.

(ii)     **Expansion:** Enhancement of existing capacity becomes necessary due to increased demand for the products. For this enhancement, additional funds will be required.

(iii)    **Diversification:** A firm may be interested in diversification with the objective of reducing the risk. Diversification may be in the form of introducing additional product lines or entering into several markets rather than operating in a single market. In such cases, capital investment decisions become inevitable.

(iv)    **Other projects:** A firm may have to invest money in such projects which are not directly resulting into profits but are mandatory. For example: installation of pollution control equipment, undertaking welfare projects for workers etc.

Capital Expenditure Proposals may also be classified into the following types.

(a) **Mutually Exclusive Proposals:** These types of proposals are alternatives to each other and the decision making is to be done for selecting any one of these proposals. For example, if a firm wants to replace its Plant and Machinery and two alternatives are available, any one will be selected by applying the decision criteria for the same. Similarly there can be options like buying v/s leasing, which means that either an asset can be purchased or the same can be taken on lease. Comparative costs and benefits of both the options will be worked out and appropriate choice will have to be done.

(b) **Independent Proposals:** These are independent proposals and do not have any alternatives as such. For example, a company may be considering to expand its production capacity or it may be considering of introduction of a new product. These proposals do not have any alternative and the acceptance depends on the comparison of costs and benefits.

(c) **Dependent Proposals:** Sometimes, it so happens that certain proposals are dependent on a particular proposal. For example, if a manufacturing company decides to open an additional production facility in the rural area, along with the plant and machinery, they will have to invest in other infrastructure facilities like housing for workers, roads, hospitals, schools and colleges and so on.

## (F) Steps in Capital Budgeting Process

Capital budgeting decisions have long term implications and hence careful planning and effective implementation of the same becomes extremely important. The following steps are normally involved in the capital budgeting process.

(a) **Finding out investment avenues:** Before formulating any proposal of capital budgeting, it is essential to find out the profitable investment avenues for capital investment. Identification of proposals is dependent on generation of ideas and the ideas are generated at various levels. It has been observed that several proposals of cost reduction or modernisation or even of product improvement may be generated by workers at the lower or middle level while the expansion or diversification proposals may come from the top Management. The various ideas generated at different levels will have to scrutinize carefully before accepting any one of them.

(b) **Screening and Evaluation of Ideas:** A very careful evaluation of the proposals generated at various levels is of utmost importance in the capital budgeting process. Evaluation of these proposals is done on the basis of the projected cash inflows and the proposed cash outflows. For this development of cash inflows is important. In real life situations, this is quite difficult as the future is uncertain and lots of risks are involved in various proposals, which may make the prediction rather difficult. Estimation of cash flows requires collection and analysis of all qualitative and quantitative data, both financial and non financial in nature. Large companies would generally have a Management Information System providing such data. While estimating the cash flows, the time horizon over which the estimate is to be made is also to be decided in advance. The time horizon depends on the estimated life of the proposal which may vary from proposal to proposal. However, a time horizon of over 10 years is highly risky as lot of uncertainty creeps in. After the estimation of cash flows, appropriate technique is used for evaluation of the proposal for the sake of decision making.

(c) **Authorisation of the proposal:** It has been the practice in several organisations that before the commencement of a proposal, there is an authorisation of the proposal in a formal manner. Proposals are presented in a formal manner by submitting a detailed description of the proposal which includes the initial investment required, the description of the proposal, detailed projections of cash flows with appropriate justification of the same. Additionally, the expected annual accounting rate of return along with the pay back period may also be given in the detailed description. Due to the importance of the capital budgeting decisions, it is but natural that the proposal is submitted to the Top Management which may have a committee to look into this matter. However, considering the pressure of time on the Top Management, companies may fix up ceiling limits on the amounts of the proposals and may prescribe that proposals above a particular amount only should be submitted to the Top Management and proposals of lower amounts may be sanctioned at the Department level itself. The authorisation of the proposal signals the start of the proposal.

(d) **Implementation:** After a careful evaluation of the proposal, if it is found viable, the implementation of the same commences. Care is taken to ensure that there is no time and cost overrun and the project is completed in time. For effective implementation, network analysis proves to be extremely useful. Techniques used in the network analysis, i.e. Project Evaluation and Rating Technique [PERT] and Critical Path Method [CPM] help companies to implement the proposals effectively to ensure that the proposal is completed within given time and there is no cost overrun.

(e) **Post Completion Audit of the cash flows:** It is of paramount importance that there should be constant review of the capital expenditure proposals after their commencement. In this review the actual results are compared with the estimated results that were included in the investment proposal. There should be some method of evaluation similar to the method used for the evaluation of the proposal itself. Post completion audit will compare the actual performance with the standard one, but the difficulty here is that no pre determined standard will exist for any capital expenditure proposal. Comparison of actual and estimated cash flows will be very difficult to evaluate basically because even if there is a deviation between the actual and the projected, ascertaining the reasons for such deviation will be difficult. There may not be any method to find out as to how much of the deviation is due to incorrect forecast and how much is due to other factors. In such situations, what can be done is that the investment proposals should be scrutinized very carefully in the screening stage itself and incorporate the estimated results of individual projects into departmental operating budgets. Although the results of individual projects cannot be isolated, their combined effect can be examined as part of the conventional periodic performance review.

Another important factor to be considered is that capital investment decisions are long term decisions. Naturally, a forecast of future cash inflows is to be made and if the actual cash inflows do not match with the projections, the project may be a failure. Future is always uncertain and hence even if technique like sensitivity analysis and probability analysis are used, one negative event may severely affect the outcome of the project. Hence it will not be appropriate to blame any one particular department or person for failure of capital investment proposals. Actually, it is not the intention of the post completion audit also as otherwise it will kill the initiative and promote a policy of over cautious approach. There is a danger that only safe proposals will be undertaken and it may hamper the profitability in the long run.

However, in any case, post completion audit of capital expenditure proposals should be undertaken. A record of the performance and the mistakes committed can be a guidance for the future for avoiding such mistakes in the future. Similarly, this audit will also inculcate a tendency among the manager to screen every proposal very carefully and thus have a realistic appraisal of the proposals.

## (G) Importance of Capital Budgeting

Capital budgeting decisions are quite crucial and critical business decisions. The reasons for this can be summarised as given below.:

(a) The capital budgeting decisions relate to fixed assets and the fixed assets represent the true earning assets of the firm. They enable the firm to generate finished goods that can be ultimately be sold at profit. Thus, it can be said that capital budgeting decisions determine the future destiny of the company. While an opportune investment decisions can yield spectacular returns, a few wrong decisions may force a firm into bankruptcy.

(b) The effect of capital budgeting decisions will be felt by the firm over a long time, and inevitably affect the cost structure of a company. For example, if a particular plant has been purchased by a company to start a new product, the company commits itself to a sizable amount of fixed costs, in terms of labour, supervisor's salary, insurance etc. If the project is unsuccessful, the entire burden of fixed costs will fall on the firm, thus, affecting its profitability.

(c) In most cases, capital budgeting decisions are irreversible. The reason is that, there may not be any market for second hand plant and equipment and they may have to be sold out only at a loss.

(d) The capital budgeting decisions require an assessment of future events which are uncertain. It is really a difficult task to estimate the probable future events, and the expected benefits and costs in uncertain conditions.

## 2.2 Evaluation Techniques: Payback, Accounting Rate of Return, Net Present Value, Internal Rate of Return, Profitability Index - Comparison of DCF Techniques

Capital budgeting decisions are extremely crucial for any organisation for the following reasons.

(a) The amount involved in these proposals is very huge and after investing such an amount, if the projects prove to be failure, it will result into tremendous amount of losses. Sometimes the entire organisation may be wiped off due to such failed projects.

(b) The capital budgeting decisions are normally not reversible and if at all they are reversed, there may be at a loss. For example, if a firm decides to invest in modernisation of machinery and due to some reason, this decision proves to be a failure, reversal of this decision can be done only at a loss.

In view of the above, before any capital budgeting decision is taken, careful evaluation of the same should be done and if they are likely to be viable, then only they should be accepted. For evaluation of capital budgeting proposals, the following techniques are used.

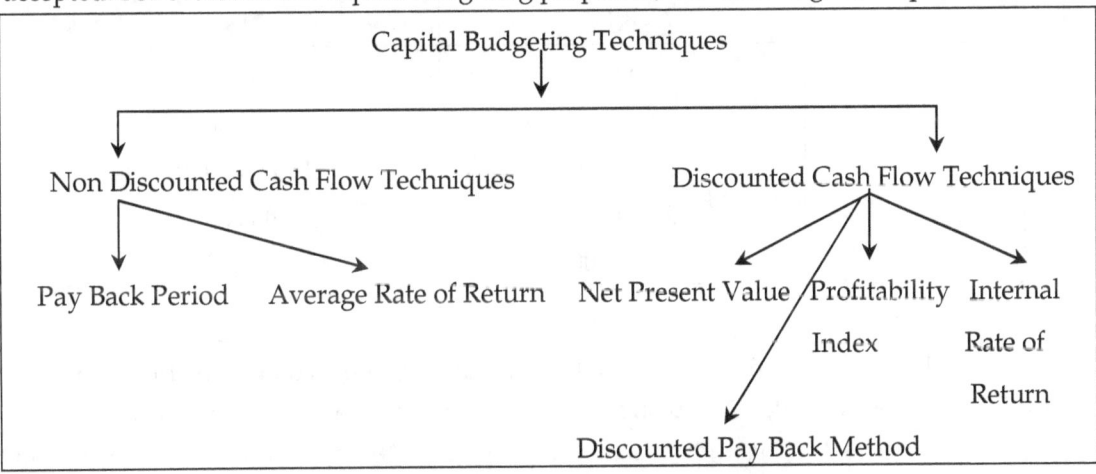

**Fig. 2.1: Capital Budgeting Techniques**

These techniques are discussed in detail in the following paragraphs.

## (A) Non Discounted Cash Flow Techniques

Evaluation of capital budgeting proposals is done on the basis of cash inflows and outflows rather than on the basis of accounting profits. Non discounted cash flow means the estimated cash flows during the entire life time of the project without taking into consideration their time value, i.e. the present value of the future cash inflows. The following techniques are included in this category.

## [I]  Pay Back Period:

The Pay Back Period is the number of years in which the initial investment made in a capital budgeting proposal is recovered back. Thus, for example, if the initial investment in a proposal is ₹ 20,00,000 and the projected cash inflows per year are ₹ 4,00,000 each, the pay back period will be $\dfrac{₹\,20,00,000}{₹\,4,00,000}$ = 5 years. This means that the initial investment made in the proposal will be recovered in a period of 5 years. The pay back period is calculated as given below.

- When the projected cash inflows from a capital budgeting proposal are equal, the pay back period is computed with the help of the following formula.

$$\text{Pay Back Period} = \frac{\text{Initial Investment}}{\text{Projected Annual Cash Inflows}}$$

- When the projected cash inflows from a capital budgeting are not uniform, the pay back period will be computed as given below:

Initial Investments: ₹ 50,00,000.

**Projected Cash Inflows:**

| Year | Amount [₹] | Cumulative Cash Inflows [₹] |
|:---:|:---:|:---:|
| 01 | 12,00,000 | 12,00,000 |
| 02 | 19,00,000 | 31,00,000 |
| 03 | 25,00,000 | 56,00,000 |
| 04 | 27,00,000 | 83,00,000 |
| 05 | 26,00,000 | 1,09,00,000 |
| Total | 1,09,00,000 | |

The cumulative cash inflows shown in the third column shows that in the first two years out of the initial investment, ₹ 31,00,000 are recovered while at the end of the third year, total ₹ 56,00,000 are recovered. This indicates that the Pay Back Period is more than two years but less than three years. The following formula will be used to calculate the exact Pay Back Period.

**Pay Back Period:**     $\dfrac{2 + \text{Unrecovered balance at the end of the second year}}{\text{Cash Inflows of the subsequent year}}$

=   2 + 19,00,000/56,00,000

=   2 + .33

=   2.33 years.

The Pay Back Period of 2.33 years shown above, indicates that the initial investment made in the project, will be recovered in that period. For any proposal, the lesser the pay back, the better it is. Hence, if the Pay Back Period technique is to be used for evaluation of capital budgeting proposals, the decision making will be on the basis of the following points.

(a) In case there are mutually exclusive proposals, i.e. either proposal X or proposal Y is to be accepted, the lesser the pay back period, the better it is. In other words, in such cases, the proposal with a lesser pay back period will be selected.

(b) In case, there is only one proposal, which is either to be accepted or rejected, the firm may decide some target pay back period and if the projected pay back period is less than that, then only the proposal will be selected. For example, if there is a proposal to accept or reject and the target pay back period is 5 years, while the projected pay back period is 4 years, the proposal may be accepted. On the other hand, if the projected pay back period is 6 years, it may be rejected.

## Merits of Pay Back Period Technique:

The Pay Back Period technique has the following merits.

1. It is a rough and ready method of computing the number of years in which the initial investments are recovered.

2. The Pay Back Period is easy to compute and understand, even a common man can understand the implications of this technique.

3. The number of years in which the initial investment is going to be recovered are known, which facilitates the planning of the investment.

## Limitations of Pay Back Period Techniques:

However, the Pay Back Period has the following limitations.

1. The main limitation of the pay back period is that the present value of money is not taken into consideration. The present value of money goes on declining with the passage of time and therefore projected cash inflows should be adjusted to this factor. However this is not done in the case of pay back period and hence the utility of this technique is reduced substantially. In order to remove this limitation, discounted pay back period is computed by discounting the cash inflows.

2. In this technique, the number of years in which the initial investment is recovered is given more importance as the emphasis is on the recovery of the initial investment. However the post pay back period profitability is ignored and hence there is a possibility of profitable projects being rejected only because the pay back period of these projects is more. The following illustration will make the point clear.

**Proposal X:**

Initial Investments: ₹ 50,00,000.

Projected Cash Inflows:

| Year | Amount (₹) | Cumulative Cash Inflows (₹) |
|------|-----------|------------------------------|
| 01 | 12,00,000 | 12,00,000 |
| 02 | 19,00,000 | 31,00,000 |
| 03 | 25,00,000 | 56,00,000 |
| 04 | 27,00,000 | 83,00,000 |
| 05 | 26,00,000 | 1,09,00,000 |
| **Total** | **1,09,00,000** | |

As shown in the above illustration, the Pay Back Period in this proposal is 2.33 years.

Now, consider the proposal Y, which also has the initial investment of ₹ 50,00,000 and the estimated life of 5 years. The projected cash inflows are as follows.

| Year | Amount (₹) | Cumulative Cash Inflows (₹) |
|------|-----------|------------------------------|
| 01 | 10,00,000 | 10,00,000 |
| 02 | 15,00,000 | 25,00,000 |
| 03 | 24,00,000 | 49,00,000 |
| 04 | 35,00,000 | 84,00,000 |
| 05 | 38,00,000 | 1,22,00,000 |
| **Total** | **1,22,00,000** | |

The Pay Back Period in the above case is as follows.

$$\text{Pay Back Period:} \quad = 3 + \frac{1,00,000}{84,00,000}$$

$$= 3.011 \text{ years}$$

Thus, it can be observed that the pay back period for proposal Y is more than that of X and therefore proposal X will be selected on the basis of pay back criteria. However, if the total cash inflows are taken into account, proposal Y is more profitable than X as the total of cash inflows is ₹ 1,22,00,000 while that of X is ₹ 1,09,00,000 but this fact will be ignored as more importance is given to the faster recovery of the initial investment.

## [II] Average Rate of Return/Accounting Rate of Return:

This is an age old technique used for evaluating capital expenditure proposals. It has been defined in many ways, which led to Peter Drucker to say that this is a 'rubber of infinite elasticity'. This rate of return indicates the percentage return projected on the investment made in the proposal. In this method, projected net profit after income tax is computed for the expected life of the proposal and its average is worked out. The percentage of this average net profit to the investments is computed which is the average rate of return or also called as accounting rate of return. The formula for computing this rate is as follows.

Average Rate of Return [Accounting Rate of Return] =

$$\frac{\text{Projected Average Incremental} \times \text{Net Profits after income tax}}{\text{Investments} \times 100}$$

Average Rate of Return is also computed by taking the average investments made in the proposal which is calculated as given below.

$$\text{Average Investments} = \frac{\text{Opening Investments} + \text{Closing Investments}}{2}$$

The illustration of Average Rate of Return is given below.

Initial Investments: ₹ 20,00,000, residual value: nil

Effective life: 5 years.

Projected Net Profits after depreciation and income tax:

| Year | Amount (₹) |
|------|-----------|
| 1 | 4,50,000 |
| 2 | 6,00,000 |
| 3 | 7,00,000 |
| 4 | 7,50,000 |
| 5 | 7,00,000 |
| **Total** | **32,00,000** |

The average profits will be:

$$\frac{₹\,32,00,000}{5} = ₹\,6,40,000$$

$$\text{The Average Rate of Return} = \frac{\text{Average Profits}}{\text{Average Investments}} \times 100$$

$$= \frac{₹\,6,40,000}{₹\,10,00,000} \times 100 = 64\%$$

* Average investment is computed by taking the total of the opening balance plus the closing balance and dividing the total by two, i.e. $\dfrac{₹\,20,00,000 + \text{Nil}}{2} = ₹\,10,00,000.$

**Decision-Making:** In case of a single proposal, the decision- making depends on the cost of funds required for that proposal. If the projected accounting rate of return is more than the cost of funds, the proposal may be accepted, otherwise it may not. In case there are two mutually exclusive proposals, the one with higher rate of return should be accepted.

**Merits of Accounting Rate of Return Technique:**

The main merits of this method are as follows.

1. This method is easy to understand and simple to compute. Hence it is easily understandable.

2. Feasibility of a proposal can be understood properly in the form of percentage of rate of return on the investment.

**Demerit/Limitation of Accounting Rate of Return Technique:**

However this method suffers from a major limitation.

1. The present value of money is not taken into consideration and hence not much useful for evaluation of proposals, which are of longer duration.

## (B) Discounted Cash Flow Techniques

**[I]  Net Present Value:**

The Net Present Value is the difference between the total present value of projected cash inflows arising from a proposal and the initial investment made in the proposal. For computing the Net Present Value, the following steps are taken.

(a) Cash in flows arising out of a capital budgeting proposal are projected for the entire life time of a proposal.

(b) A rate of discount at which the cash inflows are to be discounted should be fixed. The rate of discount depends on the cost of funds required for the proposal and the inflation rate in the economy.

(c) Present value of projected cash inflows is computed by applying the rate of discount selected.

(d) Net present value is computed by deducting the initial investment amount [cash outflow] from the total present value of the cash inflows. If the net present value is positive, the proposal may be accepted and if it is negative, it may be rejected. In case of mutually exclusive proposals, a proposal with higher net present value will be selected.

## Illustration:

X Ltd. is considering a proposal of investing ₹ 25,00,000 with an expected life of 5 years and no salvage value at the end of the life. The projected cash inflows are as follows.

1st Year: ₹ 5,00,000, 2nd year: ₹ 7,00,000, 3rd year: ₹ 9,50,000, 4th year: ₹ 10,00,000 and 5th year: ₹ 11,00,000.

The company uses 10% rate of discount. Calculate the Net Present Value of this proposal.

## Solution:

| Year | Amount (₹) | P.V. Factors @ 10% | Present Value of Cash Inflows (₹) |
|---|---|---|---|
| 1st | 5,00,000 | .909 | 4,54,500 |
| 2nd | 7,00,000 | .826 | 5,78,200 |
| 3rd | 9,50,000 | .751 | 7,13,450 |
| 4th | 10,00,000 | .683 | 6,83,000 |
| 5th | 11,00,000 | .621 | 6,83,100 |
| Total | 42,50,000 | | 31,12,250 |

Net Present Value = Total present value of cash inflows – Initial investments

₹ 31,12,250 – ₹ 25,00,000 = ₹ 6,12,250

As the net present value is positive, the proposal may be accepted.

## [II] Internal Rate of Return:

This is an alternative technique for use in making capital investment decisions that also takes into consideration the present value of money. The internal rate of return represents the true interest rate earned on an investment over the course of its useful life. This is the rate of discount at which the net present value is neither positive or negative. In other words, the rate of discount at which the net present value is nil, is the internal rate of return.

## Merits of Internal Rate of Return Technique:

The Internal Rate of Return has the following merits.

1. Time value of money is taken into consideration.

2. It considers all cash flows occurring over the entire life of the project to calculate the rate of return.

3. It is consistent with the shareholders' wealth maximisation objectives. Whenever a project's internal rate of return is greater than the opportunity cost of capital, the shareholders' wealth will be maximised.

The computation of internal rate of return involves trial and error process up to a certain stage and then exact internal rate of return is computed by applying a formula. Before applying the formula, the following steps are required to be taken.

(a) Initially, the cash inflows arising out of a particular proposal will be discounted at a particular rate, say 10%.

(b) If the net present value at 10% is positive, a higher rate of discount than 10% will be tried for arriving at negative net present value. In other words, a pair of rate, one with a positive net present value and another with a negative net present value will have to be found out by trial and error process.

(c) After establishing the pair of rate, the next step will be the application of the following formula to find out exact rate of return. The formula for the same is as follows.

$$\text{Internal Rate of Return} = \frac{\text{Lower Rate} + \text{Net Present Value at lower rate}}{\text{Difference between the present value}} \times \text{Difference in rates}$$

[Illustration is given in the solved examples]

**Decision Making:** If there is a single proposal, which is either to be accepted or rejected, the internal rate of return is compared with the cost of funds and if it is found that the internal rate of return is more than the cost of funds, the project may be accepted. On the other hand, if the internal rate of return is less than the cost of funds, the project may be rejected. In case of mutually exclusive proposals, the proposal with a higher internal rate of return may be accepted.

## [III] Profitability Index:

This is also termed as cost benefit ratio and is computed by dividing the total present value of cash inflows by the initial investment. The profitability index indicates the return available per rupee invested in a proposal and is useful when decision making is to be made from mutually exclusive proposals involving different amount of investments.

## [IV] Discounted Pay Back Period:

One of the serious limitation of the Pay Back Period as discussed above is that the present value of cash inflows is not taken into consideration. In other words, the cash flows are not discounted for the computation of the pay back period. In order to remove this limitation, for the computation of the pay back period, the present value of the cash flows are taken into consideration and then the pay back period is computed. This is called as 'Discounted Pay Back Period'. However the limitation that post pay back period cash flows are not taken into consideration still continues in spite of the discounting of the cash flows. The computation of discounted pay back period is shown in the illustrations given below.

**Comparison of Net Present Value and Internal Rate of Return:** The Net Present Value and Internal Rate of Return, both are the techniques of evaluation of capital expenditure proposals by using discounted cash flows. A question arises as to whether these techniques will give same results or whether they will reveal conflicting results in the evaluation of a capital expenditure proposal? For example, suppose a company is evaluating proposal X and proposal Y, which are mutually exclusive and their net present values and internal rate of return reveal the following things.

| Proposal | Initial Investments (₹) | Net Present Value (₹) | Internal Rate of Return [%] |
|---|---|---|---|
| X | 20,00,000 | 8,90,000 | 20% |
| Y | 20,00,000 | 9,50,000 | 22% |

In the above situation, it is clear that proposal Y is giving higher net present value and its internal rate of return is also greater than that of X, which means that on both the criteria, proposal Y is better. This is confirmed by both the techniques used for the evaluation. Thus it has been observed that in the case of conventional projects, [in which an initial cash outflow is followed by a series of cash inflows] that are independent of each other [i.e. where the selection of a particular project does not preclude the choice of the other], both Net Present Value and Internal Rate of Return will lead to same accept/reject decisions. However, there are also situations where the Internal Rate of Return method may lead to different decisions being made from those that would follow the adoption of the Net Present Value procedure.

The Net Present Value and Internal Rate of Return will give conflicting rankings to the capital expenditure proposals, which are mutually exclusive, under the following conditions.

- The cash flow pattern may differ. That is, the cash flows of one project may increase over time, while those of others may decrease or vice versa.
- The cash outlays, i.e. initial investment may differ for the projects.
- The projects may have different expected lives.

These factors are discussed below.

**(a) Timing of cash flows:** The most commonly found condition for the conflict between the NPV and IRR is the timing of cash flows. The following example will clarify the point.

Suppose, there are two projects, M and N with the following details.

| Project | Cash Outlays C0 | Cash Inflows C1 | Cash Inflows C2 | Cash Inflows C3 | Net Present Value @ 9% | Internal Rate of Return |
|---|---|---|---|---|---|---|
| M | − 1680 | 1400 | 700 | 140 | 301 | 23% |
| N | − 1680 | 140 | 840 | 1510 | 321 | 17% |

It can be seen that at 9% rate of discount, the NPV of project M is ₹ 301 which is less than the NPV of project N, but the IRR of project M is higher than that of N. A question arises as to why this happens? In such situation, which project should be accepted?

Let us see how the NPVs of both the projects behave with discount rates. This is shown in the following table.

| Discount Rate [%] | Project M | Project N |
|---|---|---|
| 0 | 560 | 810 |
| 5 | 409 | 520 |
| 10 | 276 | 276 |
| 15 | 159 | 70 |
| 20 | 54 | – 106 |
| 25 | – 40 | – 257 |
| 30 | – 125 | – 388 |

It can be seen from the above table that the net present value of project N falls sharply as the rate of discount increases. The reason is that its largest cash inflows are quite late in life, when the compounding effect of time is most significant. This is exactly opposite as compared to project M as this project has larger amounts of cash inflows in the early part of the life when compounding effect is not much. The internal rate of returns for both the projects are 23% and 17% respectively for M and N. The NPV profiles of two projects intersect at 10% rate of discount which is shown below. This is called as Fisher's Intersection.

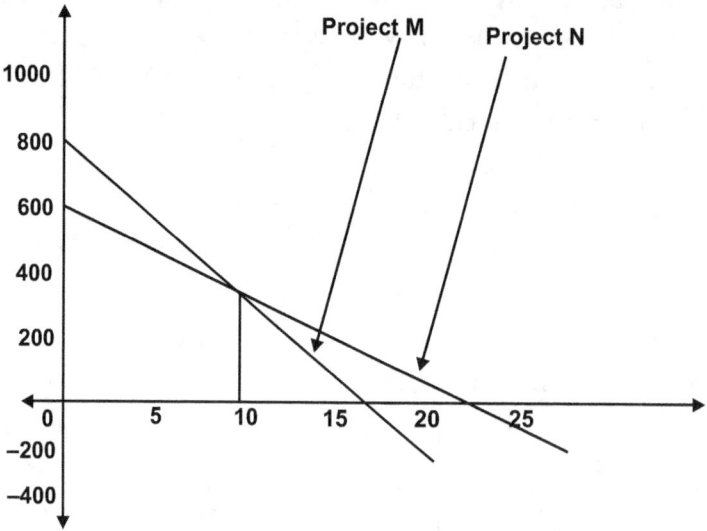

Fig. 2.2

Fisher's intersection occurs at the discount rate where the net present values of both the projects are the same, i.e. ₹ 276. The intersection rate can be determined with the help of the following method.

$$\frac{-1680 + 1400}{(1 + r^*)} + \frac{700}{(1 + r^*)^2} + 140\,(1 + r^*)^3 = -1680 + 140\,(1 + r^*) + 840\,(1 + r^*)^2 + 1510\,(1 + r^*)^3$$

Solving the above equation we get $r^* = 10\%$

It can be noticed from the above graph that at the rate of discount less than the intersection rate [10%], project N has the higher net present value but lower internal rate of return of 17%. On the other hand, at the discount rate higher than the intersection rate of 10%, project M has both, higher net present value as well as higher internal rate of return of 23%. Thus, if the required rate of return is greater than the intersection rate, both, net present value and internal rate of return will yield consistent results. That is, the project with higher internal rate of return will also have higher net present value. However, if the required rate of return is less than the intersection rate, the two methods will give contradictory results. That is, project with higher internal rate of return will have lower net present value and vice versa.

Another question that is to be answered is that in such a conflicting situation, which project should be chosen? Both projects generate positive net present value at 9% but project N is better as it is generating higher net present value. If the internal rate of return criteria is used, project M is generating higher internal rate of return. If project N is chosen, we will be richer by an additional value of ₹ 20. Should we have the satisfaction of earning a higher rate of return or should we like to be richer? The net present value is consistent with the objective of maximising wealth and hence when a choice is to be made between mutually exclusive projects, the project with higher net present value should be selected.

(b) Incremental Approach: It is argued that the internal rate of return method can still be used to choose between mutually exclusive projects, if we adopt it to calculate rate of return on the incremental cash flows. If we prefer project N to project M, there should be incremental benefits in doing so. To see this, let us calculate the incremental flows of project N over project M. The following results are obtained.

| Project | Initial Cash Outflows C0 | Cash Inflows C1 | Cash Inflows C2 | Cash Inflows C3 | Net Present Value @ 9% | Internal Rate of Return [%] |
|---------|--------------------------|-----------------|-----------------|-----------------|------------------------|------------------------------|
| [N – M] | 00 | -1260 | 140 | 1370 | 20 | 10 |

The internal rate of return is 10%. It is more than the opportunity cost of 9%. Therefore project N should be accepted. It is better than project M despite its lower internal rate of return because it offers all benefits that project M offers plus the opportunity of an incremental investment at 10%, a rate higher than the required rate of return of 9%. It may be noticed that the net present value of incremental flows is the difference of the net present value of project N over that of project M, this is so because of value adding principle.

The incremental approach is a satisfactory way of salvaging the internal rate of return rule. But the series of the incremental cash flows may result in negative and positive cash flows. [i.e. lending and borrowing type pattern] This would result in multiple internal rate of return and ultimately the net present value method will have to be used.

(c) **Scale of Investment:** Another condition under which the net present value and internal rate of return methods will give contradictory ranking to the projects, is when the cash outlays are of different sizes. Let us consider projects A and B involving following cash flows.

| Project | Cash Outflows [Initial] (₹) | Cash Inflows 1st year (₹) | Net Present Value at 10% | Internal Rate of Return [%] |
|---------|------------|------------|------------|------------|
| A | − 1000 | 1500 | 364 | 50% |
| B | − 1,00,000 | 1,20,000 | 9091 | 20 |

The net present value of project A is ₹ 364 at 10% rate of discount and the internal rate of return in 50% while in case of project B, the net present value is ₹ 9091 at 10% rate of discount and the internal rate of return is 20%. Thus these two projects are ranked separately under the two methods.

As discussed earlier, the net present value method gives unambiguous results. Since the net present value of project B is higher, it should be accepted. The same result can be obtained if we calculate the internal rate of return on incremental investment.

| Project | Cash Outflows [Initial] (₹) | Cash Inflows 1st year (₹) | Net Present Value at 10% | Internal Rate of Return [%] |
|---------|------------|------------|------------|------------|
| [A-B] | -99000 | 1,18,500 | 8727 | 19.7 |

The incremental investment of ₹ 99,000 [₹ 1,00,000 − ₹ 1,000] will generate cash inflows of ₹ 1,18,500 after a year. Thus the return on the incremental investment is 19.7%, which is in excess of 10% required rate of return. Thus project B is preferable to project A.

(d) **Project Life Span:** Difference in the life span of two mutually exclusive projects can also give rise to the conflict between the net present value method and internal rate of return method. The following is illustrated in the following illustration.

| Projects | [Cash Outflows] C0 | Cash Inflows C1 | C2 | C3 | C4 | C5 | Net Present Value @ 10% | Internal Rate of Return % |
|---|---|---|---|---|---|---|---|---|
| X | 10000 | 12000 | | | | | 909 | 20 |
| Y | 10000 | 0 | 0 | 0 | 0 | 20,120 | 2493 | 15 |

Both the projects require initial cash outlays of ₹ 10000 each. Project X generates cash flow of ₹ 12000 at the end of one year, while Project Y generated cash flow of ₹ 20,120 at the end of the fifth year. At 10% required rate of return, the net present value of the project X is ₹ 909 while that of Y is ₹ 2493. Internal rate of return in case of project X is 20% while that of Y is 15%. Thus the two methods rank the projects differently. The net present value can be used to choose between the projects since it is always consistent with the wealth maximising principle. Thus project Y should be preferred since it has higher net present value.

## 2.3 Project Selection Under Capital Rationing

### (A) Meaning

A firm may have several projects which may yield positive net present value. However there is a situation where some ceiling limit is to be put on the total capital expenditure that a firm wishes to incur. Financial constraints may force a firm to put restrictions on the total volume of capital expenditure that may be incurred in a particular period. Thus capital rationing is a situation where a firm cannot undertake all positive net present value projects it has identified because of shortage of capital. It is quite natural that in such a situation, even some viable proposals have to be rejected due to shortage of funds. A firm has to answer a question in this situation that how to allocate available funds to the acceptable proposals which require more funds than they are available? Various aspects of capital rationing are discussed in detail in the following paragraphs.

### (B) Factors Responsible for Capital Rationing

Capital rationing situation may arise in the following situations.

(a) **External Factors:** Capital rationing may arise due to external factors like imperfections of capital market or deficiencies in the market information which may affect the availability of capital. Sometimes the market is not able to mop up the necessary financial resources required by a firm. It may also happen that the Government may put some restrictions on the market which will limit the capital availability in the market. For example, to control inflation, the Government may increase the rate of interest which will affect the capital flow adversely in the market. Due to these restrictions, a firm may not be able to mop the amount of capital required by them for various projects.

**(b) Internal Factors:** Internal factors responsible for capital rationing are as follows:

(i) Apprehension of the Management regarding the issue of fresh equity share capital for the fear of loosing the control over the company.

(ii) Conservative policy of the Management regarding raising funds through debt may affect the financing of a particular proposal.

(iii) Reluctance to accept some viable proposals because of its inability to manage the firm in the scale of operation resulting from inclusion of all the viable projects.

## (C) Decision making in Capital Rationing Situations

Under capital rationing situations, the crucial decision is that how to distribute the scarce capital amongst the most profitable proposals. The Management has to decide not only the profitable investments opportunities but also decide that combination of the profitable projects which will give the highest net present value within the available funds amount.

As per the theoretical principles, proposals should be undertaken to the point where the return is just equal to the cost of financing these proposals. However, in capital rationing situations, it may so happen that a firm may have to sacrifice some of the profitable proposals due to paucity of funds. Hence as mentioned above, funds should be allocated amongst different proposals in such a manner that the net present values from all these proposals will be the highest.

The following illustrations will make the concept further clear.

**Illustration 1:** The following proposals are available for a firm. Their net present values and initial investments are given below.

| Project | Required Initial Investments (₹) | Net Present Value at appropriate cost of capital (₹) |
|---------|----------------------------------|-------------------------------------------------------|
| A | 1,00,000 | 20,000 |
| B | 3,00,000 | 35,000 |
| C | 50,000 | 16,000 |
| D | 2,00,000 | 25,000 |
| E | 1,00,000 | 30,000 |

Total funds available are ₹ 3,00,000. Determine the optimal combination of proposals assuming that the projects are divisible.

**Solution:** The various proposals will have to be ranked as shown below for arriving at the optimum combination.

| Project | Required Initial Investments (₹) | Net Present Value at the appropriate cost of capital (₹) | Profitability Index (3/2) | Rank |
|---|---|---|---|---|
| (1) | (2) | (3) | (4) | (5) |
| A | 1,00,000 | 20,000 | 0.2 | 3 |
| B | 3,00,000 | 35,000 | 0.117 | 5 |
| C | 50,000 | 16,000 | 0.32 | 1 |
| D | 2,00,000 | 25,000 | 0.125 | 4 |
| E | 1,00,000 | 30,000 | 0.3 | 2 |

From the above table, it is clear that the proposal C has the highest rank and then there are other proposals according to their profitability index. The profitability index is used for ranking the proposals.

The following table shows the allocation of the funds amongst different projects so as to maximise the return.

| Rank of Investment | Project | Required Initial Investment (₹) |
|---|---|---|
| 1 | C | 50,000 |
| 2 | E | 1,00,000 |
| 3 | A | 1,00,000 |
| 4 | 1/4th of D [1/4th of ₹ 200000] | 50,000 |
| Total | | 3,00,000 |

Thus it can be seen that the optimum combination of proposals in capital rationing situation is C, E, A and 1.4th of D. This combination will optimize the return.

### Illustration 2:

X Ltd, has six proposals in hand. Their cash flows are given below.

[₹ 000s]

| Year | A | B | C | D | E | F |
|------|------|------|-------|-------|-------|-------|
| 0 | (100) | (50) | ---- | (10) | (100) | ------- |
| 1 | (50) | (70) | (100) | (20) | (100) | -------- |
| 2 | (25) | 100 | (30) | 50 | 200 | (200) |
| 3 | 100 | 100 | 150 | (100) | 100 | 300 |
| 4 | 100 | ----- | 200 | 100 | 50 | 100 |
| 5 | 100 | ------- | ------- | 100 | -------- | 100 |

The required rate of return for the proposals is 10%. This rate is expected to remain constant over the next five years. Based on the 10% rate of discount, the net present values of the proposals are as follows.

| Project | Net Present Value [₹ 000s] |
|---------|----------------------------|
| A | 39.4 |
| B | 44.1 |
| C | 133.6 |
| D | 68.4 |
| E | 83.6 |
| F | 190.5 |

In order to implement the above proposals, the following investments are required.

| Year | ₹ |
|------|-----------|
| 0 | 2,60,000 |
| 1 | 3,40,000 |
| 2 | 2,55,000 |
| 3 | 1,00,000 |
| 4 | ------------ |
| 5 | ------------ |

## 2.4 Inflation and Capital Budgeting

Inflation can be simply defined as an increase in the average price of goods or services. The accepted measure of general inflation is the Retail Price Index which is based on the assumed expenditure patterns of an average family. General inflation is a factor in investment appraisal but of more concern is that may be termed specific inflation, i.e. the changes in price of the various factors which may increase the cash outflows, for example, wage rates, material costs, energy costs, transportation charges etc. In view of this every effort should be made to estimate the rate of inflation and its likely impact on the inflows and outflows. Every attempt should be made to estimate specific inflation for each element of the project in a detailed manner. The following factors are quite important in this respect.

(a) **Synchronised and Differential Inflation:** Inflation is differential when costs and revenues change at differing rates of inflation or where the various items of cost and revenues move at different rates. This is the normal situation but the concept of synchronised inflation, where costs and revenues are changing at the same rate may occur very rarely.

(b) **Money Cash Flows and Real Cash Flows:** Money cash flows are the actual amounts of money changing hands whereas real cash flows are the purchasing power equivalents of the actual cash flows. In a world of zero inflation there would be no need to distinguish between money and real cash flows as they would be identical. However this situation will take place very rarely and in the real life situations, a firm will have to encounter some degree of inflation. Where inflation does exist, then a difference arises between money cash flows and their real value and this difference is the basis of the treatment of inflation in project appraisal. The real discount factor can be calculated with the help of the following formula.

$$\text{Real discount factor} = \frac{1 + \text{Money discount factor}}{1 + \text{Inflation rate}} - 1$$

**Illustration:** A machine costs ₹ 10000 and is expected to yield the following net cash flows. [estimated at current prices]

| Year | 1 | 2 | 3 |
|------|------|------|------|
| ₹ | 5000 | 8000 | 6000 |

Expected rate of inflation is 5% p.a. and the cost of capital is 15.5%.

The impact of inflation on the cash flows is computed as given below.

₹

| Year | Current Prices | Actual Cash Flows |
|------|----------------|-------------------|
| 0 | (10000) | (10000) |
| 1 | $5,000 \times 1.05$ | 5,250 |
| 2 | $8,000 \times (1.05)^2$ | 8,820 |
| 3 | $6,000 \times (1.05)^3$ | 6,946 |

For each flow, we have added inflation @ 5% by multiplying by $(1.05)n$ where n is the number of years inflation. Having calculated the actual cash flows, we will not compute the net present value by discounting in the usual manner. This is shown below.

₹

| Year | Cash flows | Discount Factor @ 15.5% | Present Value |
|------|-----------|--------------------------|---------------|
| 0 | (10000) | 1 | (10000) |
| 1 | 5,250 | $1/1.155$ | 4,545 |
| 2 | 8,820 | $[1/1.155]^2$ | 6,612 |
| 3 | 6,946 | $[1/1.155]^3$ | 4,508 |
| Total | | | NPV = 5665 |

Since the net present value is positive, the proposal may be accepted.

## 2.5 Concept and Measurement of Cost of Capital - Specific Cost and Overall Cost of Capital

A company raises funds from various sources for financing long-term requirements. These sources principally consist of, (i) Equity capital, (ii) Reserves and surplus, (iii) Long term loans and (iv) Debentures.

Each of the above sources cost the company something. Cost of capital, therefore, can be defined as cost of raising funds through different sources. Alternatively, it can also be defined as the rate of return that a company must earn on its investments so that the expectations of the investors are satisfied. In other words, the minimum rate of return mentioned above will maintain the existing position which means that if the present situation is not improved, at least it will not deteriorate further. This rate of return is in turn calculated on the basis of the cost of raising funds from different sources for financing the investments of the company.

Before discussing further the components of cost of capital and its components, it will be appropriate to view the cost of capital with respect to risk associated with a particular investment opportunity because the expected rate of return is bound to change with risk.

There may be three situations viz.

(i)     Riskless rate of return may be offered from a particular proposed investment. This means that there is absolutely no risk involved from such investments. The rate of return expected in such cases is minimum which means cost of capital is also minimum.

(ii)    In some investments, there is a risk known as business risk. Such risk arises out of the need to market the product successfully. For such proposals, expected rate of return is naturally high and, therefore, cost of capital is also high.

(iii)   In addition to the business risk, there is a financial risk also in some proposals. This risk arises because of financing pattern of the project. If the major portion is financed through debt or preference capital, there will be an obligation on the part of the company to pay interest or preference dividend. This risk results into higher expected rate of return which implies higher cost of capital.

In view of the above discussion, it can be said that cost of capital can be stated as:

$$k = k_0 + k_1 + k_2 \text{ where,}$$
$$k = \text{Total cost of capital}$$
$$k_0 = \text{Riskless cost/rate of return}$$
$$k_1 = \text{Premium for business risk}$$
$$k_2 = \text{Premium for financial risk.}$$

## Uses of Cost of Capital

The cost of capital, which is a very useful concept, is used in the following decisions:

(i)     Capital budgeting decisions: Capital budgeting decisions may be either: (a) accept or reject a particular proposal or (b) selection of a particular proposal from various alternative proposals available. For taking any of the above decisions, the cash inflows from various proposals are discounted at a rate of discount. This rate of discount can be decided on the basis of cost of capital of that capital expenditure proposal.

(ii)    In planning of the capital structure also, cost of capital is a very relevant concept. According to traditional approach, cost of capital is very vital in determining the optimum capital structure of a company. In fact the optimum capital structure according to the traditional approach is such a combination of debt and equity that the aggregate cost of capital is minimum at that level.

## Types of Cost of Capital

Cost of capital can be divided into the following types:

(i)   **Specific Cost:** The specific cost of capital is the cost of specific source of capital i.e. equity capital, debt, retained earnings etc. It is measured as the rate of discount which equates the present value of the expected payments to that source of finance with the net funds received from that source of finance.

(ii)  **Weighted Average Cost of Capital:** This cost of capital, which is the aggregate cost of capital, is calculated on the basis of the weights assigned to each source of capital based on either book values or market values. The following illustration will clarify the concept. Suppose, a company is using debt and equity for financing various investment proposals. The specific cost and weighted average cost is shown in the following table:

| Source of capital | Book value [₹] | Weights on the basis of book value | Specific cost [%] | Weighted Average cost [%] [weights × specific cost] |
|---|---|---|---|---|
| Equity | 40,000 | .40 | .16 | .064 |
| Debt | 60,000 | .60 | .09 | .054 |
| | 1,00,000 | 1.00 | | .118 |

Therefore, the weighted average cost is 11.8%.

(iii) **Historical cost:** The cost of capital in relation to funds raised in the past is the historical cost of capital.

(iv)  **Future cost:** The cost of funds that will be raised in future is the future cost of capital.

## Calculation of Cost of Capital

(i)  **Cost of debt:** The cost of debt capital is measured as the rate of discount which equates the present value of post–tax interest and principal repayments with the net proceeds of the debt issue. In the calculation of cost of debt, the annual debt interest payment is multiplied by the factor $(1 - t)$, where $t$ = taxation rate. The reason is that the interest is a tax deductible expense.

The formula for calculation of cost of debt is as follows:

$$k_d = \frac{I(1-t) + \dfrac{F-P}{n}}{\dfrac{P+F}{2}}$$

where
$k_d$ = Cost of debt,
$I$ = Amount of interest,
$t$ = Taxation rate,
$F$ = Face value of debenture,
$P$ = Net amount realised,
$n$ = Number of years for maturity.

**Illustration:** A company sells 15 years, 14% debentures of the face value of ₹ 1,000 at ₹ 970. In addition an underwriting fee of 1.5% of the face value is incurred. Rate of taxation is 50%.

The cost of debentures is calculated as follows:

$$k_d = \frac{140\,(1 - .50) + \dfrac{1,000 - 955}{15}}{\dfrac{1,000 + 955}{2}} = 6.75\%$$

**(ii) Cost of Term Loan:** The term loans from financial institutions is also a very important source. These loans are generally repayable over a period of 8 to 11 years, equal annual or half yearly or quarterly instalments after an initial grace period of 1 to 3 years. There is no question of repayment at premium and there is hardly any issue expense. The cost of such loan can be calculated as follows:

$$k_d = \text{Interest}\,(1 - \text{tax rate})$$

**(iii) Cost of Preference Capital:** Preference capital carries a fixed rate of dividend. However, this dividend is not a tax deductible expense. The formula for calculation of cost of preference capital is as follows:

$$k_p = \frac{PD + \dfrac{(F - P)}{n}}{\dfrac{F + P}{2}}$$

where

$k_p$ = Cost of preference capital,

PD = Preference dividend,

F = Repayable value,

P = Net amount realised,

n = Maturity period.

For example,

XYZ Ltd. issues ₹ 100 face value preference shares carrying 14% dividend which are repayable at par after 10 years. The net amount realised per share is ₹ 92.

The $k_p$ is calculated below:

$$k_p = \frac{14 + \left(\dfrac{100 - 92}{10}\right)}{\dfrac{100 + 92}{2}} = 15.42\%$$

**(iv) Cost of Equity Capital:** There is a controversy regarding whether the equity capital has cost or not. However, it is now accepted that equity capital is not a cost-free source of financing. However, as compared to Pref. capital and debt where estimate rate of return required by the suppliers of funds can be estimated fairly and easily, for equity capital it is a bit difficult. The reason is that the benefits expected by them cannot be measured easily. In order to remove this difficulty, several approaches have been proposed. These approaches are explained below.

(a) **Dividend/Price Approach:** As per this approach, the market price per share is equal to the present value of the expected dividends discounted at the rate of return required by equity shareholders. In other words, from the given market price and expected dividends by equity shareholders, the rate of return required by equity shareholders can be calculated. The cost of equity capital in this case will be:

$$k_e = \frac{D}{P}$$

where     D  =  Dividend per share,

                P  =  Market price,

                $k_e$  =  Cost of equity capital.

(b) **Dividend / Price + Growth rate approach:** In the above approach, the expected dividend per share by equity shareholders is presumed to be constant. However, if the rate of dividend is expected to grow in future, the cost of equity capital will be,

$$k_e = \frac{D}{P} + g$$

where     g  =  growth rate.

**Illustration:** The market price per share of the equity capital of ABC Ltd. is ₹ 150. The expected dividend is ₹ 15 per share and expected growth rate is 7% p.a. The cost of equity capital will be

$$k_e = \frac{15}{150} + .07$$

$$= .10 + .07$$

$$= .17 \text{ or } 17\%$$

(c) **Earnings / Price approach:** As per this approach, earnings per share are more important than dividend per share. Therefore, cost of equity capital will be,

$$k_e = \frac{EPS}{P}$$

(d) **Realised yield approach:** According to this approach, the actual yield realised by equity shareholders in the past is taken as the cost of equity capital. In other words, it is the rate of discount which equates the cash outflow and the present value of cash inflows realised by investors.

(v) **Cost of retained earnings:** The cost of retained earnings is in the nature of opportunity cost for the investors. When the company prefers to retain the earnings rather than distribute it among the shareholders, the shareholders lose something in the form of return, which in turn is taken as the cost of retained earnings. The formula for calculation of this cost is as follows:

$$k_r = k_e \frac{1-t_p}{1-t_g}$$

where    $k_e$ = Cost of equity capital,

$t_p$ = Ordinary personal income-tax rate,

$t_g$ = Personal long-term capital gains.

## Practical Problems

**Problem 1:** ABC Ltd is considering investing in a project that is expected to cost ₹ 12,00,000 and has an effective life of 5 years. The projected cash inflows for this period are as follows.

| Year | Amount (₹) |
|------|------------|
| 1 | 3,00,000 |
| 2 | 3,00,000 |
| 3 | 4,50,000 |
| 4 | 4,50,000 |
| 5 | 7,50,000 |
| **Total** | **22,50,000** |

Calculate: [A] Pay Back Period [B] Net Present Value @ 10% rate of discount [C] Profitability Index. [D] Discounted Pay Back Period at 10% rate of discount.

**Solution: [A] Pay Back Period**

| Year | Amount (₹) | Cumulative Cash Inflows (₹) |
|------|------------|------------------------------|
| 1 | 3,00,000 | 3,00,000 |
| 2 | 3,00,000 | 6,00,000 |
| 3 | 4,50,000 | 10,50,000 |
| 4 | 4,50,000 | 15,00,000 |
| 5 | 7,50,000 | 22,50,000 |
| **Total** | **22,50,000** | **57,00,000** |

Thus from the above table, it is clear that out of the initial investment of ₹ 12,00,000, at the end of the third year ₹ 10,50,000 are recovered and at the end of the fourth year ₹ 15,00,000 are recovered. This means that the Pay Back Period is more than 3 years and less than 4 years. For calculating the exact pay back period, the following formula will be utilised.

$$\text{Pay Back Period} = 3 + \frac{1,50,000}{4,50,000} = 3.33 \text{ years.}$$

**Note:** ₹ 1,50,000 is the unrecovered balance of the initial investment at the end of the third year, while ₹ 4,50,000 is the cash inflow of the subsequent year, i.e. cash inflow of the fourth year.

**[B] Net Present Value @ 10%**

| Year | Amount (₹) | Present Value Factors @ 10% | Present Value of Cash Inflows |
|---|---|---|---|
| 1 | 3,00,000 | .909 | 2,72,700 |
| 2 | 3,00,000 | .826 | 2,47,800 |
| 3 | 4,50,000 | .751 | 3,37,950 |
| 4 | 4,50,000 | .683 | 3,07,350 |
| 5 | 7,50,000 | .621 | 4,65,750 |
| **Total** | **22,50,000** | | **16,31,550** |

Net Present Value = Total Present Value of Cash Inflows – Initial Investments

= ₹ 16,31,550 – ₹ 12,00,000 = ₹ 4,31,550

**[C] Profitability Index:** The formula for the Profitability Index is as follows.

$$\frac{\text{Total Present Value of Cash Inflows}}{\text{Initial Investments}}$$

$$= \frac{₹ 16,31,550}{₹ 12,00,000} = 1.359$$

**[D] Discounted Pay Back Period:** The following table, similar to the table prepared for computing the Net Present Value is prepared to compute the cumulative discounted cash inflows and then the Discounted Pay Back Period.

| Year | Amount (₹) | Present Value Factors @ 10% | Present Value of Cash Inflows | Cumulative Cash Inflows (₹) |
|---|---|---|---|---|
| 1 | 3,00,000 | .909 | 2,72,700 | 2,72,700 |
| 2 | 3,00,000 | .826 | 2,47,800 | 5,20,500 |
| 3 | 4,50,000 | .751 | 3,37,950 | 8,58,450 |
| 4 | 4,50,000 | .683 | 3,07,350 | 11,65,800 |
| 5 | 7,50,000 | .621 | 4,65,750 | 16,31,550 |
| **Total** | **22,50,000** | | **16,31,550** | **16,31,550** |

Thus it is clear from the above computation, that the Discounted Pay Back Period is more than 4 years but less than 5 years. The following formula will have to be used for computing the exact Discounted Pay Back Period

$$\text{Discounted Pay Back Period} = 4 + \frac{34,200 *}{4,65,750 **} = 4.073 \text{ years}$$

\* Un recovered balance at the end of the 4th year

\*\* Cash inflows of the subsequent year, i.e. 5 th year.

**Problem 2:** A firm whose cost of capital is 10% is considering two mutually exclusive proposals, X and Y, the details of which are as follows.

| Particulars | Proposal X (₹) | Proposal Y (₹) |
|---|---|---|
| Initial Investments | 15,00,000 | 15,00,000 |
| Projected Cash Inflows | | |
| 1st year | 1,00,000 | 6,50,000 |
| 2nd year | 2,50,000 | 6,00,000 |
| 3rd year | 3,50,000 | 6,00,000 |
| 4th year | 5,50,000 | 5,75,000 |
| 5th year | 7,50,000 | 5,25,000 |
| Total | 20,00,000 | 29,50,000 |

Calculate:

[A] Pay Back Period

[B] Net Present Value @ 10% rate of discount

[C] Profitability Index

[D] Internal Rate of Return.

**Solution: [A] Pay Back Period:**

| Particulars | Proposal X (₹) | Proposal Y (₹) | Cumulative Cash Inflows Proposal X | Cumulative Cash Inflows Proposal Y |
|---|---|---|---|---|
| Projected Cash Inflows | | | | |
| 1st year | 1,00,000 | 6,50,000 | 1,00,000 | 6,50,000 |
| 2nd year | 2,50,000 | 6,00,000 | 3,50,000 | 12,50,000 |
| 3rd year | 3,50,000 | 6,00,000 | 7,00,000 | 18,50,000 |
| 4th year | 5,50,000 | 5,75,000 | 12,50,000 | 24,25,000 |
| 5th year | 7,50,000 | 5,25,000 | 20,00,000 | 29,50,000 |
| Total | 20,00,000 | 29,50,000 | | |

Proposal X: From the cumulative cash inflows, it is clear that the pay back period is more than 4 years but less than 5 years. The exact period is calculated with the help of the following formula.

$$\text{Pay Back Period [Proposal X]} = 4 + \frac{2,50,000*}{7,50,000**} = 4.33 \text{ years}$$

$$\text{Pay Back Period [Proposal Y]} = 2 + \frac{2,50,000*}{6,00,000**} = 2.41 \text{ years}$$

\* Unrecovered balance at the end of the particular year, i.e. 4th year in case of Proposal X and 2nd year in case of Proposal Y.

\** Cash inflows of the subsequent year.

### [B] Net Present Value

#### (a) Proposal X:

| Particulars | Projected Cash Inflows (₹) | Present Value Factors @ 10% | Present Value of Cash Inflows (₹) |
|---|---|---|---|
| Projected Cash Inflows | | | |
| 1st year | 1,00,000 | .909 | 90,900 |
| 2nd year | 2,50,000 | .826 | 2,06,500 |
| 3rd year | 3,50,000 | .751 | 2,62,850 |
| 4th year | 5,50,000 | .683 | 3,75,650 |
| 5th year | 7,50,000 | .621 | 4,65,750 |
| Total | 20,00,000 | | 14,01,650 |

Net Present Value = Total Present Value of Cash Inflows – Initial Investment

= ₹ 14,01,650 – ₹ 15,00,000

= (–) ₹ 98,350

#### (b) Proposal Y:

| Particulars | Proposal Y (₹) | Present Value Factors @ 10% | Present Value of Cash Inflows (₹) |
|---|---|---|---|
| Projected Cash Inflows | | | |
| 1st year | 6,50,000 | .909 | 5,90,850 |
| 2nd year | 6,00,000 | .826 | 4,95,600 |
| 3rd year | 6,00,000 | .751 | 4,50,600 |
| 4th year | 5,75,000 | .683 | 3,92,725 |
| 5th year | 5,25,000 | .621 | 3,26,025 |
| Total | 29,50,000 | | 22,55,800 |

Net Present Value = Total Present Value of Cash Inflows – Initial Investment

= ₹ 22,55,800 – ₹ 15,00,000 = ₹ 7,55,800

### [C] Profitability Index:

$$\text{Proposal X} = \frac{\text{Total present value of cash inflows}}{\text{Initial investments}}$$

$$= \frac{₹\,14,01,650}{₹\,15,00,000} = 0.934$$

$$\text{Proposal Y} = \frac{₹\,22,55,800}{₹\,15,00,000} = 1.503$$

**[D] Internal Rate of Return:** Internal rate of return is trial and error process up to a certain stage, before the application of the formula. In case of Proposal X, the net present value at 10% rate of discount is coming negative and hence we will have to find out another rate at which the net present value will come positive. The calculation is done as shown below. For having positive net present value, a lower rate than 10% will have to be tried and hence the net present value is computed at 5% rate of discount.

**Proposal X:**

| Particulars | Proposal Y (₹) | Present Value Factors @ 10% | Present Value of Cash Inflows (₹) |
|---|---|---|---|
| Projected Cash Inflows | | | |
| 1st year | 1,00,000 | .952 | 95,200 |
| 2nd year | 2,50,000 | .907 | 2,26,750 |
| 3rd year | 3,50,000 | .864 | 3,02,400 |
| 4th year | 5,50,000 | .823 | 4,52,650 |
| 5th year | 7,50,000 | .784 | 5,88,000 |
| **Total** | **20,00,000** | | **16,65,000** |

If the net present value at 5% rate of discount is worked out it will be ₹ 16,65,000 – ₹ 15,00,000 = ₹ 1,65,000. Now we have two rates, one is 5% at which the net present value is positive and the other one is 10% at which the net present value is negative. This means that the Internal Rate of Return is between 5% and 10%. For computing exact Internal Rate of Return, the following formula will have to be used.

$$\text{Internal Rate of Return} = \frac{\text{Lower Rate + Net Present Value at lower rate}}{\text{Difference between the present values} \times \text{Difference in rates}}$$

$$= 5\% + \frac{₹\,1,65,000}{₹\,16,65,000 - ₹\,14,01,650} \times 5\%$$

$$= 8.1\%$$

**Proposal Y:** For proposal Y, the net present value at 10% rate of discount is coming positive and hence we will have to try a rate which is higher than 10% to get a negative net present value. The calculations are shown below.

Proposal Y:

| Particulars | Proposal Y (₹) | Present Value Factors @ 35% | Present Value of Cash Inflows (₹) |
|---|---|---|---|
| Projected Cash Inflows | | | |
| 1st year | 6,50,000 | .740 | 4,81,000 |
| 2nd year | 6,00,000 | .548 | 3,28,800 |
| 3rd year | 6,00,000 | .406 | 2,43,600 |
| 4th year | 5,75,000 | .301 | 1,73,075 |
| 5th year | 5,25,000 | .223 | 1,17,075 |
| **Total** | **29,50,000** | | **13,43,550** |

The total present value of cash inflows is ₹ 13,43,550, which is less than the initial investment of ₹ 15,00,000 and hence the net present value at 35% is negative. Now, we have two rates, one is 10% at which the net present value is positive and the second is 35% at which the net present value is negative. This means that the internal rate of return is between 10% and 35%. For computing the exact internal rate of return, the following formula will have to be used.

**Internal Rate of Return:**

$$\frac{\text{Lower Rate + Net Present Value at lower rate}}{\text{Difference between the present values} \times \text{Difference in rates}}$$

$$= 10\% + \frac{₹\,7,55,800}{₹\,22,55,800 - ₹\,13,43,550} \times 25\%$$

$$= 30.71\%$$

**Problem 3:** Z Ltd. is examining two mutually exclusive proposals for new capital investment. The data on the proposals are as follows:

| Particulars | Proposal A (₹) | Proposal B (₹) |
|---|---|---|
| Initial cash outflow | 27,00,000 | 30,00,000 |
| Salvage value | Nil | Nil |
| Expected life | 6 years | 6 years |
| Depreciation | Straight line method | Straight line method |

| Earnings before depreciation and income-tax year | (₹) | (₹) |
|---|---|---|
| 1 | 6,50,000 | 9,75,000 |
| 2 | 7,25,000 | 10,00,000 |
| 3 | 8,75,000 | 11,00,000 |
| 4 | 9,50,000 | 10,25,000 |
| 5 | 9,00,000 | 9,50,000 |
| 6 | 8,00,000 | 8,50,000 |
| Total | 49,00,000 | 59,00,000 |

The corporate income-tax rate is 30% Calculate the following:

(i) Pay-back period

(ii) Net present value at 15%

(iii) Average rate of return.

Rank the proposals under each of the technique.

**Solution:** For calculation of the (i) and (ii) above, it will be necessary to calculate cash inflows from the given figures of earnings before depreciation and tax.

**Proposal A:**

| | I | II | III | IV | V | VI | VII |
|---|---|---|---|---|---|---|---|
| Year | EBDT | Depreciation | EBT | Income tax at 30% | EAT | Depreciation | Cash inflows |
| | (₹) | (₹) | (₹) | (₹) | (₹) | (₹) | (₹) |
| 1 | 6,50,000 | 4,50,000 | 2,00,000 | 60,000 | 1,40,000 | 4,50,000 | 5,90,000 |
| 2 | 7,25,000 | 4,50,000 | 2,75,000 | 82,500 | 1,92,500 | 4,50,000 | 6,42,500 |
| 3 | 8,75,000 | 4,50,000 | 4,25,000 | 1,27,500 | 2,97,500 | 4,50,000 | 7,47,500 |
| 4 | 9,50,000 | 4,50,000 | 5,00,000 | 1,50,000 | 3,50,000 | 4,50,000 | 8,00,000 |
| 5 | 9,00,000 | 4,50,000 | 4,50,000 | 1,35,000 | 3,15,000 | 4,50,000 | 7,65,000 |
| 6 | 8,00,000 | 4,50,000 | 3,50,000 | 1,05,000 | 2,45,000 | 4,50,000 | 6,95,000 |
| Total | 49,00,000 | | | | 15,40,000 | | 42,40,000 |

Calculation of (i) Pay-back, (ii) NPV and (iii) ARR:

| Year | Cash inflows (₹) | P.V. Factors @ 15% | P.V. of cash inflows |
|---|---|---|---|
| 1 | 5,90,000 | .869 | 5,12,710 |
| 2 | 6,42,500 | .756 | 4,85,730 |
| 3 | 7,47,500 | .657 | 4,91,108 |
| 4 | 8,00,000 | .571 | 4,56,800 |
| 5 | 7,65,000 | .497 | 3,80,205 |
| 6 | 6,95,000 | .432 | 3,00,240 |
| Total | 42,40,000 | Total | 26,26,793 |

(i)         Pay-back period $= 3 + \dfrac{7,20,000}{8,00,000} = 3.9$ years

(ii)                        NPV = Present values of cash inflows – Initial cash outflows

= 26,26,793 – 27,00,000 = ₹ (–) 73,207

(iii) Average rate of return: This is calculated as follows:

$$ARR = \frac{\text{Average income}}{\text{Average investment}} \times 100$$

$$= \frac{₹\,2,56,667}{13,50,000} \times 100 = 19.01\%$$

**Note:** Average income is total of Earnings After Tax, [Column 'V' in the table I] divided by number of years i.e. 6 years [₹ 15,40,000 ÷ 6 = ₹ 2,56,667].

Average investment is Initial Investment + Salvage value divided by 2

i.e.        $\dfrac{₹\,27,00,000 + \text{Nil}}{2} = ₹\,13,50,000.$

**Proposal B:**

| | I | II | III | IV | V | VI | VII |
|---|---|---|---|---|---|---|---|
| Year | EBDT | Depreciation | EBT | Income tax at 30% | EAT | Depreciation | Cash inflows |
| | (₹) | (₹) | (₹) | (₹) | (₹) | (₹) | (₹) |
| 1 | 9,75,000 | 5,00,000 | 4,75,000 | 1,42,500 | 3,32,500 | 5,00,000 | 8,32,500 |
| 2 | 10,00,000 | 5,00,000 | 5,00,000 | 1,50,000 | 3,50,000 | 5,00,000 | 8,50,000 |
| 3 | 11,00,000 | 5,00,000 | 6,00,000 | 1,80,000 | 4,20,000 | 5,00,000 | 9,20,000 |
| 4 | 10,25,000 | 5,00,000 | 5,25,000 | 1,57,500 | 3,67,500 | 5,00,000 | 8,67,500 |
| 5 | 9,50,000 | 5,00,000 | 4,50,000 | 1,35,000 | 3,15,000 | 5,00,000 | 8,15,000 |
| 6 | 8,50,000 | 5,00,000 | 3,50,000 | 1,05,000 | 2,45,000 | 5,00,000 | 7,45,000 |
| | 59,00,000 | | | | 20,30,000 | | 50,30,000 |

Calculation of (i) Pay-back, (ii) NPV, (iii) ARR.

| Year | Cash inflows (₹) | P.V. Factors @ 15% | P.V. of cash inflows |
|------|------------------|--------------------|----------------------|
| 1 | 8,32,500 | .869 | 7,23,443 |
| 2 | 8,50,000 | .756 | 6,42,600 |
| 3 | 9,20,000 | .657 | 6,04,440 |
| 4 | 8,67,500 | .571 | 4,95,343 |
| 5 | 8,15,000 | .497 | 4,05,055 |
| 6 | 7,45,000 | .432 | 3,21,840 |
| **Total** | **50,30,000** | | **31,92,721** |

(i)          Pay-period  =  3 + 3,97,500/8,67,500 = 3.46 years

\* = Un recovered balance at the end of the 3rd year

+ = Cash inflow of the subsequent year, i.e. of the 4th year.

(ii)          NPV  =  ₹ 31,92,721 – ₹ 30,00,000  =  (–) ₹ 1,92,721

(iii)          ARR  =  3,38,333/15,00,000 X 100 = 22.56%

**Summary:**

| Particulars | Proposal A (₹) | Proposal B (₹) |
|-------------|----------------|----------------|
| (i) Pay-back period | 3.9 years | 3.46 years |
| (ii) NPV | (-) ₹ 73,207 | (-) ₹ 1,92,721 |
| (iii) ARR | 19.01% | 22.56% |

From the above mentioned summary, Proposal B is better than Proposal A in all respects except the net present value. Its pay-back period is lesser than A while ARR is more than A. In case of NPV, both the proposals are showing a negative NPV, but Proposal A is having lesser negative NPV than B

**Problem 4:** Y Ltd. is considering to purchase a machine in order to produce a new product. It is expected that the new product will generate an annual profit of ₹ 15,00,000 per year for first 5 years. The material cost required for this production is expected to be ₹ 4,50,000 p.a., labour of ₹ 5,50,000 and other expenditure ₹ 1,50,000 p.a. The cost of the machine is ₹ 5,00,000 with expected scrap value nil, with a life of 5 years. The company uses a straight line method of depreciation. The income–tax rate is 30% and the cost of capital 12%. The machine will also require an investment of working capital of ₹ 75,000 which will be recovered at the end of the 5th year.

Advise the company about purchase of the machine by using net present value method.

**Solution:**

The total cash outflow from the machine is as follows:

| | |
|---|---|
| Cost | ₹ 5,00,000 |
| (+ Working capital | ₹ 75,000 |
| **Total** | **₹ 5,75,000** |

The cash inflows are calculated as follows:

Statement showing cash inflows:

| Particulars | | Amount (₹) |
|---|---|---|
| | ₹ | |
| Sales | | 15,00,000 |
| **Less:** Expenses | | |
|    (i)   Material | 4,50,000 | |
|    (ii)  Labour | 5,50,000 | |
|    (iii) Other expenses | 1,50,000 | 11,50,000 |
| **Profit before depreciation:** | | **3,50,000** |
| **Less:** Depreciation | | |
|     [₹ 5,00,000 ÷ 5] | | 1,00,000 |
| **Profit before tax** | | **2,50,000** |
| **Less:** Income–tax @ 30% | | 75,000 |
| **Profit after tax** | | **1,75,000** |
| **Add:** Depreciation | | 1,00,000 |
|     **Cash inflows** | | **2,75,000** |

**Present value of cash flows:**

| | | |
|---|---|---|
| 1 – 5 year @ 12% p.v. factors Rs 2,75,000 × 3.605 | = | 9,91,375 |
| [Cumulative p.v. factors] | | |
| **Add:** Working capital recovery | | |
| ₹ 75,000 × .567 | | 42,557 |
| | | 9,48,818 |
| **Less:** Cash outflow | | 5,75,000 |
| Net present value | | **3,73,818** |

**Conclusion:** Since the NPV is positive, the machine should be purchased.

**Problem 5:** An existing machine has been in operation for the last 2 years with remaining useful life of 10 years. The management of the company is considering to replace it with an improved model which will result in greater productivity. The existing machine can be sold at a price of ₹ 1,00,000. The relevant particulars are as follows:

| Particulars | Existing machine | New machine |
|---|---|---|
| Purchase price | ₹ 2,40,000 | ₹ 4,00,000 |
| Estimated life | 12 years | 10 years |
| Salvage value | Nil | Nil |
| Annual operating hours | 2,000 | 2,000 |
| Selling price per unit | ₹ 10 | ₹ 10 |
| Output per hour | 15 units | 30 units |
| Material cost per unit | ₹ 2 | ₹ 2 |
| Labour cost per hour | 20 | 40 |
| Consumable stores p.a. | 2,000 | 5,000 |
| Repairs & maintenance p.a. | 9,000 | 6,000 |
| Working capital | 25,000 | 40,000 |

The company follows the straight line method of depreciation and is subject to 50% tax. Whether the present machine should be replaced ? The cost of capital is 15%.

**Solution:**

I. **Cash outflows:**

|  |  | ₹ |
|---|---|---|
| Purchase price |  | 4,00,000 |
| **Add:** Additional working capital |  | 15,000 |
|  |  | 4,15,000 |
| **Less:** Sale price of old machine: | 1,00,000 |  |
| Tax savings due to loss on sale |  |  |
| [Book value ₹ 2,00,000 – |  |  |
| ₹ 1,00,000 sale price = |  |  |
| ₹ 1,00,000 loss] | 50,000 | 1,50,000 |
| Net cash outflows |  | 2,65,000 |

II. **Cash inflows:**

| Particulars | Existing machine | New machine | Difference |
|---|---|---|---|
| 1 | 2 | 3 | 4 |
| A. Sales–units | 30,000 | 60,000 | 30,000 |
| B. Sales value | ₹ 3,00,000 | ₹ 6,00,000 | ₹ 3,00,000 |
| C. Expenses: |  |  |  |
| (i) Material | 60,000 | 1,20,000 | 60,000 |
| (ii) Labour | 40,000 | 80,000 | 40,000 |
| (iii) Consumable stores | 2,000 | 5,000 | 3,000 |
| (iv) Repairs & Main. | 9,000 | 6,000 | (3,000) |
| (v) Depreciation | 20,000 | 40,000 | 20,000 |
| Total – [C] | 1,31,000 | 2,51,000 | 1,20,000 |

| D. Earnings before tax [B – C] | 1,69,000 | 3,49,000 | 1,80,000 |
|---|---|---|---|
| E. Earnings after tax [Tax 50%] | 84,500 | 1,74,500 | 90,000 |
| F. Cash inflow [E + Depreciation] | 1,04,500 | 2,14,500 | 1,10,000 |

**Net Present Value:**

| Year | Cash inflows (₹) | P.V. Factors at 15% | P.V. of cash inflows |
|---|---|---|---|
| 1 – 10 | 1,10,000 | 5.019 | 5,52,090 |
| | 15,000* | .247 | 3,705 |
| | *Working capital Recovery | | |
| | | Cash inflow | 5,55,795 |
| | | (–) Cash outflow | 2,65,000 |
| | | NetPresent Value | 2,90,795 |

The NPV is positive and, therefore, the machine can be replaced.

**Problem 6:** A manufacturing company is considering to purchase a machine for improving its productivity. Two choices in the form of Machine C and Machine D are available. The details of the two machines are as follows:

| Particulars | Machine C | Machine D |
|---|---|---|
| Purchase price (₹) | 6,00,000 | 6,00,000 |
| Expected life | 10 yrs. | 10 yrs. |
| Additional fixed costs | | |
| [Excluding depreciation] | 30,000 | 32,000 |
| Additional capacity | 2,00,000 Hrs. | 2,10,000 Hrs. |
| Salvage value | Nil | Nil |
| Installation cost | 1,00,000 | 1,25,000 |

The company at present is producing three products viz. X, Y and Z. The additional demand of the product that can be met with the new machine and the contribution per unit is as follows:

| Particulars | X | Y | Z |
|---|---|---|---|
| (₹) | (₹) | (₹) | (₹) |
| Contribution per unit | 40 | 52 | 46 |
| Additional demand [units] | 2,000 | 2,500 | 4,000 |
| No. of machine hrs. per unit | 25 | 30 | 23 |

The income–tax rate is 30%. The required rate of return is 10%. Advise the company about proper choice.

**Solution:**

In order to take the decision about X or Y, net present value of both the machines will have to be calculated. For calculation of cash inflows, sales mix will have to be calculated. Since three products are being produced and number of available machine hours is limited for both the machines, priority will have to be decided among the three products on the basis of contribution per machine hour. This is done in the following manner.

**Machine C:**

I.  **Statement showing priority of the products:**

| Particulars | X | Y | Z |
|---|---|---|---|
| Contribution per unit [₹] | 40 | 52 | 46 |
| Machine hrs. per unit | 25 | 30 | 23 |
| Contribution per machine hour | 1.6 | 1.73 | 2 |
| Priority | III | II | I |

II.  **Statement showing no. of units of each product:**

| | Units | Hrs. per unit | Total Hrs. |
|---|---|---|---|
| Product Z [Highest possible units to be produced] | 4,000 | 23 | 92,000 |
| Product Y | 2,500 | 30 | 75,000 |
| Product X | 1320 | 25 | Balance Hrs. 33,000 |

III. **Statement showing cash inflows:**

| Particulars | ₹ |
|---|---|
| Contribution: | |
| Z  4,000 units × ₹ 46   = | 1,84,000 |
| Y  2,500 units × ₹ 52   = | 1,30,000 |
| X  1,320  units × ₹ 40  = | 52,800 |
| | 3,66,800 |
| | |
| **Less:** (i)  Fixed costs                    30,000 | |
| (ii)  Depreciation                70,000 | (–) 1,00,000 |
| [7,00,000 ÷ 10] | |
| Profit before tax | 2,66,800 |
| **Less:** Income–tax 30% | (–)   80,040 |
| Profit after tax | 1,86,760 |
| **Add:** Depreciation | (+)  70,000 |
| Cash inflows | 2,56,760 |
| Present value of cash inflows at 10% | |
| From year 1 to year 10 | |
| ₹ 2,56,760 × 6.145    = | 15,77,790 |
| **Less:** Initial cash outflow | (–) 7,00,000 |
| Net Present value | 8,77,790 |

## Machine D:

Like Machine C, firstly the product mix will have to be decided on the basis of priority decided earlier.

### I. Statement showing no. of units of each product:

|  | Units | Hrs. per unit | Total hours |
|---|---|---|---|
| Z | 4,000 | 23 | 92,000 |
| Y | 2,500 | 30 | 75,000 |
| X | 1,720 | 25 | Bal. 43,000 |
|  |  |  | **2,10,000** |

### II. Statement showing cash inflows:

| Particulars | ₹ |
|---|---|
| Contribution: | |
| Z  4,000 units × ₹ 46    = | 1,84,000 |
| Y  2,500 units × ₹ 52    = | 1,30,000 |
| X  1,720  units × ₹ 40   = | 68,800 |
| Total contribution | **3,82,000** |
| **Less:** (i)  Fixed costs                32,000 | |
| (ii)  Depreciation          72,500 | (−) 1,04,500 |
| Profit before tax | 2,78,300 |
| **Less:** Income–tax 30% | (−) 83,490 |
| Profit after tax | **1,94,810** |
| **Add:** Depreciation | (+) 72,500 |
| Cash inflows | **2,67,310** |
| Present value of cash inflows | |
| 1 year – 10 years – 2,67,310 × 6.145 | 16,42,620 |
| **Less:** Initial cash outflows | (−) 7,25,000 |
| Net present value | **9,17,620** |

**Conclusion:** NPV of machine D is greater than NPV of Machine C and, therefore, Machine D can be selected.

## Questions for Discussion

1. What is Capital Budgeting? State its importance.
2. Explain the process of Capital Budgeting.
3. Explain: Inflation and Capital Budgeting.
4. Describe the various Evaluation Techniques.
5. Describe Calculation of Cost of Capital.
6. Explain: Project Selection under Capital Budgeting.
7. Write short notes on:

    (a) Net Present Value

    (b) Internal Rate of Return

    (c) Cost of Capital

    (d) Capital Investment Decisions.

■■■

**CHAPTER 3**

# Financing and Dividend Decision

*Contents ...*

## 3.1 Financial and Operating Leverage

Leverage is a very general term which represents influence or power. In financial analysis it can be explained as the influence of one financial variable over the other related financial variable. Leverages are classified into three categories:

(a) Operating leverage,

(b) Financial leverage,

(c) Combined leverage.

These concepts are explained in the following paragraphs:

**(a) Operating leverage:** The operating leverage measures the change in the EBIT (Earnings Before Interests and Tax] as a result of change in sales. This leverage arises because of the presence of fixed cost in the cost structure. If fixed cost is nil in the total cost structure, the operating leverage will be nil and the EBIT will change in the same proportion of change in sales. The EBIT will change by a higher percentage than the percentage change in sales, if fixed costs are present in the cost structure. A higher operating leverage indicates that the proportion of fixed costs is higher. It also indicates that EBIT will increase at a higher rate than the rate of increase in sales. But at the same time it cannot be overlooked that if the sales decrease, the EBIT will decrease at a higher rate. Therefore, it can be said that operating leverage is a double edged weapon.

Operating leverage is calculated with the help of the following formula:

$$\text{Operating leverage} = \frac{\text{Contribution}}{\text{EBIT}}$$

**Illustration:**

Calculate operating leverage from the following information:

(i) Sales – 20000 units @ ₹ 8 per unit

(ii) Variable cost – ₹ 2 per unit.

(iii) Fixed costs – ₹ 30,000.

**Solution:**

|  | ₹ |
|---|---|
| Sales 20,000 units @ ₹ 8 per unit | 1,60,000 |
| **Less:** Variable cost @ ₹ 2 per unit | 40,000 |
| Contribution | 1,20,000 |
| **Less:** Fixed costs | 30,000 |
| EBIT | 90,000 |

$$\text{Operating leverage} = \frac{\text{Contribution}}{\text{EBIT}}$$

$$= \frac{1,20,000}{90,000}$$

$$= 1.33$$

**Interpretation:** Operating leverage in the above illustration is 1.33 which means that if sales increases by 1%, the EBIT will increase by 1.33% and if it [sales] decreases by 1%, EBIT will decrease by 1.33%. This can be proved as follows.

Suppose sales increases by 1%

| Sales = ₹ 1,60,000 + 1% | = | 1,61,600 |
|---|---|---|
| **Less:** Variable costs ₹ 40,000 + 1% | = | 40,400 |
| Contribution |  | 1,21,200 |
| **Less:** Fixed costs |  | 30,000 |
| EBIT |  | 91,200 |

The EBIT has increased by 1.33% due to change in sales by 1%.

**(b) Financial leverage:** Financial leverage measures the percentage change in EBT (Earnings Before Tax) as a result of changes in EBIT. Financial leverage will be higher if the difference between EBIT and EBT is higher. This difference will be higher if amount of interest is higher because the difference between EBIT and EBT is the amount of interest. Therefore, it indicates that if proportion of debt in capital structure is high, the amount of interest and also the financial leverage will be high.

**Formula for calculation:**

$$\boxed{\text{Financial leverage} = \frac{\text{EBIT}}{\text{EBT}}}$$

**Illustration:**

Calculate financial leverage from the following:

| | ₹ | |
|---|---|---|
| Interest | 5,000 | |
| Sales | 50,000 | |
| Sales | 1000 | units |
| Variable costs | 25,000 | |
| Fixed costs | 15,000 | |

**Solution:**

| | ₹ |
|---|---|
| Sales | 50,000 |
| **Less:** Variable costs | 25,000 |
| Contribution | 25,000 |
| **Less:** Fixed costs | 15,000 |
| EBIT | 10,000 |
| **Less:** Interest | 5,000 |
| EBT | 5,000 |

$$\text{Financial leverage} = \frac{\text{EBIT}}{\text{EBT}}$$

$$= \frac{10,000}{5,000} = 2$$

**Interpretation:** Financial leverage in the above example is 2, which indicates that if EBIT increases by 1%, EBT will increase by 2%.

The degree of financial leverage [DFL] can be calculated as follows:

$$\text{DFL} = \frac{\Delta\text{EPS}/\text{EPS}}{\Delta\text{EBIT}/\text{EBIT}}$$

The degree of financial leverage explains changes in EPS in response to variations in EBIT. The financial risk refers to variability of EPS caused due to employment of debt capital. The degree of financial leverage as mentioned above helps to identify the financial risk.

**(c) Combined leverage:** It expresses the relationship between contribution and the taxable income. It helps in finding out the resulting percentage change in taxable income on account of percentage changes in sales.

$$\boxed{\text{Combined leverage} = \text{Operating leverage} \times \text{Financial leverage}}$$

**Illustration:**

A company has sales of ₹ 2 lakhs. The variable costs are 40% of sales while fixed costs are ₹ 40,000. The amount of interest on long-term loan is ₹ 10,000. Calculate combined leverage.

**Solution:**

In order to calculate the combined leverage, fixed operating leverage and then financial leverage will have to be calculated.

|  |  | ₹ |  |
|---|---|---|---|
| Sales |  | 2,00,000 |  |
| **Less:** Variable costs |  | 80,000 | [40% of sales] |
| Contribution |  | 1,20,000 |  |
| **Less:** Fixed costs |  | 40,000 |  |
| EBIT |  | 80,000 |  |
| **Less:** Interest |  | 10,000 |  |
| EBT |  | 70,000 |  |

(i) $\quad$ Operating leverage $= \dfrac{\text{Contribution}}{\text{EBIT}}$

$\qquad\qquad\qquad\qquad = \dfrac{1,20,000}{80,000} = 1.5$

(ii) $\quad$ Financial leverage $= \dfrac{\text{EBIT}}{\text{EBT}}$

$\qquad\qquad\qquad\qquad = \dfrac{80,000}{70,000} = 1.142$

(iii) $\quad$ Combined leverage $=$ Operating leverage $\times$ financial leverage

$\qquad\qquad\qquad\qquad = 1.5 \times 1.142 = 1.713$

The conclusion that can be drawn from the above discussion is that if operating leverage as well as financial leverage is on the higher side, fresh capital should be raised preferably through equity shares rather than debt. Generally, it is said that low leverage should be accompanied by the other higher leverage. If operating leverage is on the lower side, financial leverage can be kept on the higher side by employing more debt in the capital structure.

## 3.2 Capital Structure

*"Capital Structure is the make up of a firm's capitalisation i.e. it represents the mix of different sources of long term funds in the total capitalisation of the company."* **- C.W. Gerstenberg**

Capital Structure represents only long term funds, i.e., long term debts; shareholder's equity etc. and excludes all short term loans and advances. The selection of appropriate capital structure is a very crucial decision and depends on a number of factors such as the nature of a company's business; the risks involved, the requirements of the Government, regularity of earnings, condition of the money market and the terms relevant in the industry and the attitude of the investor etc. Theoretically, Capital structure of the company can be of the following four patterns:

(a) Capital structure with equity shares only.

(b) Capital structure with both equity and preference shares.

(c) Capital structure with equity shares and debentures.

(d) Capital structure with equity shares, preferences shares and debentures.

## 3.3 Cost of Capital and Valuation

A company raises funds from various sources for financing long-term requirements. These sources principally consist of: (a) Equity capital, (b) Reserves and surplus, (c) Long term loans and (d) Debentures.

Each of the above sources cost the company something. Cost of capital, therefore, can be defined as cost of raising funds through different sources. Alternatively, it can also be defined as the rate of return that a company must earn on its investments so that the expectations of the investors are satisfied. In other words, the minimum rate of return mentioned above will maintain the existing position which means that if the present situation is not improved, at least it will not deteriorate further. This rate of return is in turn calculated on the basis of the cost of raising funds from different sources for financing the investments of the company.

Before discussing further the components of cost of capital and its components, it will be appropriate to view the cost of capital with respect to risk associated with a particular investment opportunity because the expected rate of return is bound to change with risk.

There may be three situations viz.

(a) Riskless rate of return may be offered from a particular proposed investment. This means that there is absolutely no risk involved from such investments. The rate of return expected in such cases is minimum which means cost of capital is also minimum.

(b) In some investments, there is a risk known as business risk. Such risk arises out of the need to market the product successfully. For such proposals, expected rate of return is naturally high and, therefore, cost of capital is also high.

(c) In addition to the business risk, there is a financial risk also in some proposals. This risk arises because of financing pattern of the project. If the major portion is financed through debt or preference capital, there will be an obligation on the part of the company to pay interest or preference dividend. This risk results into higher expected rate of return which implies higher cost of capital.

In view of the above discussion, it can be said that cost of capital can be stated as:

$$k = k_0 + k_1 + k_2 \text{ where,}$$
$$k = \text{Total cost of capital}$$
$$k_0 = \text{Riskless cost/rate of return}$$
$$k_1 = \text{Premium for business risk}$$
$$k_2 = \text{Premium for financial risk.}$$

## Uses of Cost of Capital

The cost of capital, which is a very useful concept, is used in the following decisions:

(a)  Capital budgeting decisions: Capital budgeting decisions may be either: (a) accept or reject a particular proposal or (b) selection of a particular proposal from various alternative proposals available. For taking any of the above decisions, the cash inflows from various proposals are discounted at a rate of discount. This rate of discount can be decided on the basis of cost of capital of that capital expenditure proposal.

(b)  In planning of the capital structure also, cost of capital is a very relevant concept. According to traditional approach, cost of capital is very vital in determining the optimum capital structure of a company. In fact the optimum capital structure according to the traditional approach is such a combination of debt and equity that the aggregate cost of capital is minimum at that level.

## Types of Cost of Capital

Cost of capital can be divided into the following types:

(a)  **Specific Cost:** The specific cost of capital is the cost of specific source of capital i.e. equity capital, debt, retained earnings etc. It is measured as the rate of discount which equates the present value of the expected payments to that source of finance with the net funds received from that source of finance.

(b)  **Weighted Average Cost of Capital:** This cost of capital, which is the aggregate cost of capital, is calculated on the basis of the weights assigned to each source of capital based on either book values or market values. The following illustration will clarify the concept. Suppose, a company is using debt and equity for financing various investment proposals. The specific cost and weighted average cost is shown in the following table:

| Source of capital | Book value [₹] | Weights on the basis of book value | Specific cost [%] | Weighted Average cost [%] [weights × specific cost] |
|---|---|---|---|---|
| Equity | 40,000 | .40 | .16 | .064 |
| Debt | 60,000 | .60 | .09 | .054 |
|  | 1,00,000 | 1.00 |  | .118 |

Therefore, the weighted average cost is .118%.

(c) **Historical cost:** The cost of capital in relation to funds raised in the past is the historical cost of capital.

(d) **Future cost:** The cost of funds that will be raised in future is the future cost of capital.

## Calculation of Cost of Capital

(i) **Cost of debt:** The cost of debt capital is measured as the rate of discount which equates the present value of post–tax interest and principal repayments with the net proceeds of the debt issue. In the calculation of cost of debt, the annual debt interest payment is multiplied by the factor $(1 - t)$, where $t$ = taxation rate. The reason is that the interest is a tax deductible expense.

The formula for calculation of cost of debt is as follows:

$$k_d = \frac{I(1-t) + \dfrac{F-P}{n}}{\dfrac{P+F}{2}}$$

where    $k_d$ = Cost of debt,

       $I$ = Amount of interest,

       $t$ = Taxation rate,

       $F$ = Face value of debenture,

       $P$ = Net amount realised,

       $n$ = Number of years for maturity.

## Illustration:

A company sells 15 years, 14% debentures of the face value of ₹ 1,000 at ₹ 970. In addition an underwriting fee of 1.5% of the face value is incurred. Rate of taxation is 50%.

The cost of debentures is calculated as follows:

$$k_d = \frac{140(1 - .50) + \dfrac{1,000 - 955}{15}}{\dfrac{1,000 + 955}{2}} = 6.75\%$$

(ii) **Cost of Term Loan:** The term loans from financial institutions is also a very important source. These loans are generally repayable over a period of 8 to 11 years, equal annual or half yearly or quarterly installments after an initial grace period of 1 to 3 years. There is no question of repayment at premium and there is hardly any issue expense. The cost of such loan can be calculated as follows:

$$k_d = \text{Interest} (1 - \text{tax rate})$$

**(iii) Cost of Preference Capital:** Preference capital carries a fixed rate of dividend. However, this dividend is not a tax deductible expense. The formula for calculation of cost of preference capital is as follows:

$$k_p = \frac{PD + \dfrac{(F-P)}{n}}{\dfrac{F+P}{2}}$$

where

$k_p$ = Cost of preference capital,

PD = Preference dividend,

F = Repayable value,

P = Net amount realised,

n = Maturity period.

For example,

XYZ Ltd. issues ₹ 100 face value preference shares carrying 14% dividend which are repayable at par after 10 years. The net amount realised per share is ₹ 92.

The $k_p$ is calculated below:

$$k_p = \frac{14 + \left(\dfrac{100-92}{10}\right)}{\dfrac{100+92}{2}} = 15.42\%$$

**(iv) Cost of Equity Capital:** There is a controversy regarding whether the equity capital has cost or not. However, it is now accepted that equity capital is not a cost-free source of financing. However, as compared to Pref. capital and debt where estimate rate of return required by the suppliers of funds can be estimated fairly and easily, for equity capital it is a bit difficult. The reason is that the benefits expected by them cannot be measured easily. In order to remove this difficulty, several approaches have been proposed. These approaches are explained below.

(a) **Dividend/Price Approach:** As per this approach, the market price per share is equal to the present value of the expected dividends discounted at the rate of return required by equity shareholders. In other words, from the given market price and expected dividends by equity shareholders, the rate of return required by equity shareholders can be calculated. The cost of equity capital in this case will be:

$$k_e = \frac{D}{P}$$

where

D = Dividend per share,

P = Market price,

$k_e$ = Cost of equity capital.

**(b) Dividend / Price + Growth rate approach:** In the above approach, the expected dividend per share by equity shareholders is presumed to be constant. However, if the rate of dividend is expected to grow in future, the cost of equity capital will be,

$$k_e = \frac{D}{P} + g$$

where      g  =  growth rate.

**Illustration:** The market price per share of the equity capital of ABC Ltd. is ₹ 150. The expected dividend is ₹ 15 per share and expected growth rate is 7% p.a. The cost of equity capital will be

$$k_e = \frac{15}{150} + .07$$

$$= .10 + .07$$

$$= .17 \text{ or } 17\%$$

**(c) Earnings / Price approach:** As per this approach, earnings per share are more important than dividend per share. Therefore, cost of equity capital will be,

$$k_e = \frac{EPS}{P}$$

**(d) Realised yield approach:** According to this approach, the actual yield realised by equity shareholders in the past is taken as the cost of equity capital. In other words, it is the rate of discount which equates the cash outflow and the present value of cash inflows realised by investors.

**(v) Cost of retained earnings:** The cost of retained earnings is in the nature of opportunity cost for the investors. When the company prefers to retain the earnings rather than distribute it among the shareholders, the shareholders lose something in the form of return, which in turn is taken as the cost of retained earnings. The formula for calculation of this cost is as follows:

$$k_r = k_e \frac{1-t_p}{1-t_g}$$

where      $k_e$  =  Cost of equity capital,

$t_p$  =  Ordinary personal income-tax rate,

$t_g$  =  Personal long-term capital gains.

# 3.4 Designing Capital Structure

## (A) Theories of Capital Structure

The following are the theories of capital structures.

(a) Net Income approach.

(b) Net Operating Income approach.

(c) Traditional position.

(d) Modigliani – Miller approach (MM').

(a) **Net Income Approach:** This approach says that a relationship definitely exists between cost of capital and capital structure. The approach further says that cost of debt $[k_d]$ is less than cost of equity $[ke]$. Therefore, the aggregate cost of capital $[k_a]$ will start decreasing when a firm increases the percentage of debt in its capital structure. Therefore, the valuation of a firm will increase because the aggregate cost of capital is falling down. [The valuation of a firm has inverse relationship with cost of capital].

In mathematical terms, the approach can be described as follows:

$$k_a = k_d \left[ \frac{B}{B+S} \right] + K_e \left[ \frac{S}{B+S} \right]$$

where        $k_a$ = Aggregate cost of capital

$B$ = Borrowings

$S$ = Share capital

$k_e$ = Cost of equity capital

$k_d$ = Cost of debt

The approach can also be presented in the form of a graph as follows:

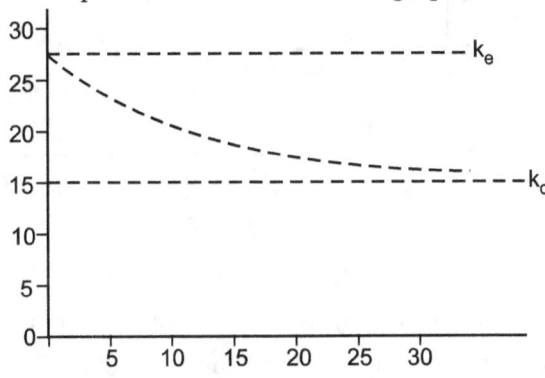

Fig. 3.1: Net Income Approach

Though it may be admitted that cost of debt $[k_d]$ is less than cost of equity, the cost of debt may not remain the same at all levels of debts. In case of a company which is already loaded with debt, the cost of debt may be higher than a company, predominantly employing equity capital. Similarly, with the introduction of more debt, the hidden costs also increase. This hidden cost is not taken into consideration in this approach.

Therefore, this approach quite rightly says, that cost of capital and capital structure are connected with each other, the assumptions are not that correct making the approach as a one sided.

(b) **Net Operating Income Approach:** According to this approach, cost of capital and capital structure are not connected with each other. This means that the pattern of financing has no effect on overall cost of capital. The reason behind this is summarized in the following paragraph.

The approach says that in case a firm increases the proportion of debt in the capital structure, the initial reaction is that, aggregate cost of capital decreases because the cost of debt is less than cost of equity. However, this decrease is compensated by an increase in the cost of equity capital. The cost of equity capital increases because equity shareholders expect more from a risky firm. The firm becomes more risky due to increase in the proportion of debt in the capital structure. Therefore, the aggregate cost of capital remains at the same level as it was before the introduction of debt.

The graphical presentation of this approach can be shown below:

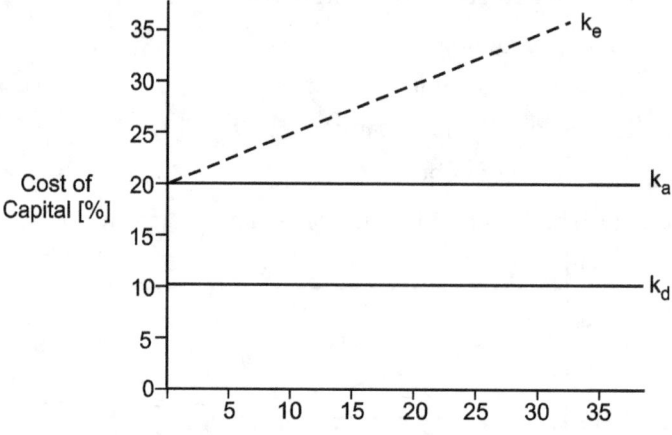

**Fig. 3.2: % of debt in capital structure**

The approach is mainly advocated by **David Durand** who argued that marked value of the firm depends upon its net operating income and not on the pattern of financing. The change in the leverage changes only the distribution of income. Therefore, the value of the firm remains unchanged, irrespective of the pattern of financing.

**(c) Traditional Approach:** This approach resembles a certain extent of the Net Income approach. The similarity is that this approach also says that the aggregate cost of capital reduces with the introduction of more debt in the capital structure. However, this fall in the aggregate cost of capital is not unchecked. A stage comes when the aggregate cost of capital does not fall even after introduction of more debt in the capital structure. It remains constant for some time and after introduction of more debt, the aggregate cost again starts rising. The combination of debt and equity at which the aggregate cost of capital is minimum can be called as *optimum capital structure*. The graphical presentation of this approach can be shown below:

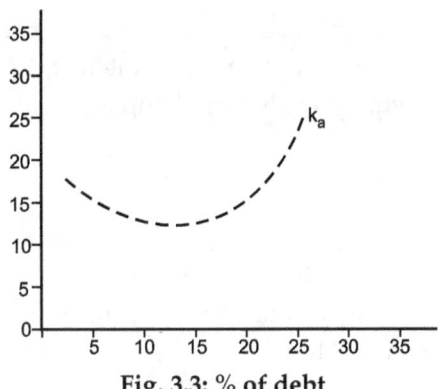

**Fig. 3.3: % of debt**

(d) **Modigliani – Miller Approach (MM'):** The basic aspect of MM' approach is that the total market value of a firm is equal to its expected operating income divided by the discount rate appropriate to its risk class. The market value, therefore, is not connected with the capital structure. According to MM' approach, a process called as arbitrage process proves their argument. The arbitrage process is explained below:

**Table 3.1: The Arbitrage Process**

|  | X Ltd.<br>(₹) | Y Ltd.<br>(₹) |
|---|---|---|
| Total capital employed | 20,00,000 | 20,00,000 |
| Equity capital | 20,00,000 | 12,00,000 |
| Debt | nil | 8,00,000 |
| Net operating income | 2,00,000 | 2,00,000 |
| Interest on loan | nil | 40,000 [5%] |
| Market value of debt | nil | 8,00,000 |
| Earnings for equity shareholders | 2,00,000 | 1,60,000 |
| Equity capitalisation rate | 10% | 12% |
| Market value of equity | 20,00,000 | 13,33,333 |
| Total market value of the firm | 20,00,000 | 21,33,333 |

According to the table the value of levered firm Y Ltd. is more than that of levered firm X Ltd. As per the MM' approach, this solution cannot last for long because equity shareholders will sell their equity investments to Y Ltd., and invest in the equity of X. This will be done by substituting corporate leverage by personal leverage. The arbitrage process is explained below.

Suppose a person holds 1% of total equity of Company Y. He will sell this holding for ₹ 13,333.33. He will borrow ₹ 8,000 at 5% rate of interest. With ₹ 13,333.33 + ₹ 8,000 = ₹ 21,333 he will purchase the equity capital in Company X. It will result in the following income.                                                                       ₹

| | |
|---|---|
| Income on Investment in X Ltd. | 2,132 |
| (–) Interest 5% on ₹ 8,000 | 400 |
| **Net income** | **1,732** |

The net income of ₹ 1,732 is higher than a net income of ₹ 1600 that is foregone by the shareholder when he sold shares in Y Ltd.

₹ 1600 being 1% of available profits.

**Note:** The person is holding 1% of total equity of Company Y. As he is selling that equity, he will borrow ₹ 8,000 which is 1% of the borrowings of Y Ltd. This is known as substitution of personal borrowings to corporate borrowings. As funds available with him are ₹ 21,333 [₹ 13,333.33 + ₹ 8,000] and they are approximately 1.066% of capital employed of company X, he will purchase 1.066% of the equity capital of company X. Therefore, he will be entitled for 1.066% of the earnings available for equity shareholders of company X. The amount comes to ₹ 2,132 and after deducting ₹ 400 as interest on borrowings; his net income comes to ₹ 1,732. To conclude, it can be said that by maintaining the same proportion of investments in X Ltd., the person can improve his net income from that company. This process is called as the Arbitrage process.

**Criticism of MM' Approach:** This approach is based on the assumption that the capital markets are perfect. However, in the real world perfections do not exist and, therefore, the capital structure of a firm may affect its valuation.

Another assumption of this approach is that there is an absence of corporate income-tax. This assumption is also unrealistic in the modern context. However, this assumption was removed later.

**Conclusion:** Due to corporate taxation, it can be said that the cost of capital is definitely the financial leverage. Due to increase in financial leverage the cost of capital is certainly reduced. However, due to costs like bankruptcy costs and agency costs which increase due to financial leverage, the cost of capital increases. Therefore, it can be concluded that between cost of capital and capital structure, a relationship definitely exists.

## (B) Factors to be Considered While Planning Capital Structure

### (a) Analysis of Debt Capacity:

Before planning the capital structure it will be highly beneficial to analyse the debt servicing capacity of a firm. The reason for this is that a firm should borrow only that much where it can serve even in adverse conditions. Employment of debt capital results into two types of obligations on a firm: (a) repayment of the principal amount and (b) interest on loan.

One of the tools used for the assessment of debt capacity of a firm is to calculate some key ratios, which are as follows:

(i) **Interest coverage ratios:** This ratio indicates the coverage of income before interest and tax to annual interest payments. In other words, this ratio indicates as to how many times the income is before interest and taxes as compared to the interest. This ratio is calculated with the help of the following formula.

$$\text{Interest coverage ratio} = \frac{\text{Earnings before interest and tax}}{\text{Annual interest on debt}}$$

The following illustration will clarify the point.

Suppose the EBIT for X Ltd. is ₹ 10,00,000 and the amount of interest is ₹ 2,00,000. The interest coverage ratio will be:

$$\frac{₹\,10,00,000}{₹\,2,00,000} = 5 \text{ times}$$

The indication given by the above ratio is that the EBIT is 5 times as compared to the interest.

The main drawback of this ratio is that it takes into consideration only the interest component and not the repayment of principal. Secondly, it takes into account the earnings before interest and tax and not the cash flows. Actually analysis of cash flows is more relevant than the earnings. Another aspect of the ratio is that there is no standard or ideal ratio against which the ratio of a particular firm can be compared.

In order to have a better idea about the debt servicing capacity of a firm, the following ratio is used.

(ii) **Cash flow coverage ratio:** This ratio takes into account both, the interest payment and the principal payments. The formula is as follows:

$$\text{Cash flow coverage ratio} = \frac{\text{EBIT} + \text{Depreciation} + \text{Non Cash Expenses}}{\text{Interest on debt} + \dfrac{\text{Loan repayment instalment}}{[1 - \text{tax rate}]}}$$

**Illustration:**

The EBIT of XYZ Ltd. is ₹ 25,00,000. Depreciation provided is ₹ 5,00,000. Interest on debt ₹ 2,00,000 and other non-cash expenses are ₹ 3,00,000. The annual installment of loan repayment is ₹ 8,00,000. The cash flow coverage ratio will be as follows:

$$\frac{25,00,000 + 5,00,000 + 3,00,000}{2,00,000 + \dfrac{8,00,000}{(1 - .50^*)}} = 1.83$$

* Income – tax rate.

This ratio indicates the coverage of cash flows for the interest as well as for principal repayments and, therefore, is definitely a better measure to assess the debt servicing capacity of a firm.

After analysing the above ratios, it can be concluded that if the ratios consistently show a declining trend, it will be dangerous to raise fresh debt. However, it must be mentioned that a cash flow analysis is also required before coming to any decision. Cash flow analysis is explained in the following point.

### (b) Cash flow Analysis:

Many times it is seen that a high debt-equity ratio may not necessarily indicate a bad situation because the debt servicing capacity of the firm is quite satisfactory. On the other hand, a low debt ratio may be quite burdensome on a firm as the debt servicing capacity of the firm is quite inadequate. The debt servicing capacity of a firm, indicated by the ratios mentioned above, depends upon the cash flow position of a firm.

It is essential to predict the cash inflows under different situations. The different situations mean optimistic, pessimistic and most likely situations. That level of debt should be maintained, which the firm will be able to service even under pessimistic conditions.

### (c) Control:

In designing capital structure of a company, the desire of management to retain control over the company should also be taken into consideration. The promoters of the company can retain their control on the company as long as their holding in the company is more than 50%. To retain the control over the company, it is suggested that there should be issue of debt as the holders of debt do not have any voting rights in the company. Similarly, issue of Preference shares will also not dilute the control of existing management. While raising the debt, care should be taken that it is not disproportionately high, otherwise there will be problems in repayment. The suppliers of debt may also put a lot of restrictions on the companies to protect their interests. A very excessive amount of debt may create liquidity problems which can result in the company being caught in a debt trap. This may invite sickness which means a total loss of control.

Therefore, the conclusion here is that to retain control it is advisable to go in for debt and preference capital but with proper caution so that the company does not turn into a debt loaded company.

### (d) Flexibility:

Flexibility refers to the ability of a firm to raise capital from any source it wishes to tap. Flexibility ensures maneuverability to the finance manager. Flexibility can be ensured by keeping some of the debt raising capacity in reserve so that the firm can raise debt whenever need arises. Flexibility can also be ensured by early repayment of debt and preference capital if discretion is available to the company. This will result in replacing a cheaper source of finance with an expensive source of finance. However, flexibility, has its own drawbacks especially for a growth firm. In order to keep reserve capacity of debt, a firm may issue equity shares at a time when the market is not favourable. This will not be beneficial to the company in the sense that the selling price of equity shares may be lesser than the intrinsic value based on expected growth. To conclude, it can be said that the financial plan of the company should ensure such flexibility that the capital structure can be changed as per the operating strategy of the company.

**(e) Timings of the Issue:**

The situation in the capital market is also one of the important considerations in capital structure planning. The conditions in the capital markets may not be always favourable for tapping a particular source. If there is a general decline in the share prices [including its own share prices] in the stock markets and if the trend is expected to continue in the future, it will be advisable to raise debt from the market at present. In future, when the market is expected to improve, equity shares can be issued. If the situation in the capital market is quite encouraging i.e. shares trading at higher prices, it will be prudent to raise funds by equity shares rather than debt. A word of caution can be added here and that is, even if the situation is favourable for a particular type of issue, reserve capacity for that source should always be kept. For example, if the situation is favourable for debt issue, a company should not exhaust its borrowing powers totally. Similarly, the company should always take advantage of the present situation and not wait for improving the situation in future.

**(f) Growth rate:**

Companies which are growing at a faster rate prefer more debt rather than equity. The reason for this is that due to the high financial requirements of the company, issue of shares may prove to be inadequate. Similarly, cost of equity tends to be more than the cost of debt and this is also one of the reasons for preference to debt. However, companies with growth opportunities may find debt financing more costly if there is absence of proper collateral security being offered.

**(g) Stability of Earnings:**

Capital structure planning also depends on the stability of earnings of a company. The debt servicing capacity of a firm depends to a great extent on the cash flows of the firm and the cash flows in turn [operating cash inflows], depend on the stability of its earnings. If the earnings are expected to remain fairly stable in the future, a firm can afford to rely more on the debt than equity. The reason is that its debt servicing capacity is fairly high in such cases. On the other hand, if the earnings are expected to fluctuate violently in the future, conservative ways of financing like equity shares should be tapped.

**(h) Attitude of the Lenders:**

Sometimes, the attitude of the lenders may not be positive in sanctioning debts. In such cases, it is always better to rely on shares. In some cases, especially institutional lenders, may put more and more restrictions on the borrowers. This also may lead firms to rely more on shares than on debt.

**(i) Taxation Structure in the Country:**

If the rate of taxes in the country are high, debt is cheaper than equity, as the interest on debt is a tax deductible item for calculation of taxable income. But as mentioned earlier, there should not be an overdose of debt only because it is cheaper. The debt servicing capacity of the firm should always be kept in mind while raising the debt.

**(j) Asset Structure:**

The asset structure of a company will also affect the capital structure decisions. Companies holding a large proportion of tangible fixed assets will be able to raise higher amount through debt. This is due to the fact that these assets will be useful for giving security to the lenders. On the other hand, companies having large amount of assets in the form of intangible assets will not be able to raise higher amount of debt due to the fact that they will not be able to offer such security to the lenders in the form of fixed assets. Hence the composition of asset structure plays an important role in planning the capital structure.

**(k) Sustainability:**

The financing policy of a company should be sustainable and feasible in the long run. This means that a company should use a sustainable model which will help the company to survive and grow in the long run. In other words, when a financing model is chosen, there should not be only short term view but a long term view should be taken with an objective that the company should exist for a long period of time. The sustainable model assumes that a company uses the internal financing and debt with a target debt equity ratio for raising finance and there is no use of shares in raising the money. This model indicates the target growth rate that the company should target. However, the model also indicates that if a different growth rate is targeted than indicated by the sustainable growth model, it will have to alter the financial policies in the form of the change in the debt-equity ratio or the payout ratio or both. Thus the financing model depends on the company. In other words, the capital structure decisions will differ for a company which targets a sustainable growth rate as compared to a company which is adopting a different rate than indicated by the sustainable growth mode.

**Conclusion:** Planning of capital structure is a very crucial decision for a finance manager. Efforts should be made to achieve an optimum capital structure. But, optimum capital structure is very difficult to achieve in practice and, therefore, atleast capital structure should be designed after considering the above mentioned points.

## 3.5 Dividend Policy - Aspects of Dividend Policy - Practical Consideration - Forms of Dividend Policy

### (A) Meaning of Dividend

The dictionary meaning of **"Dividend"** is sum payable as interest on loan or as profit of a company to the creditors of an insolvents estate or an individuals share of it.

In commercial usage, however, dividend is the share of company's profits distributed among the members.

**Features:**

The important features of dividend are as follows:

(a) Dividend is a portion of profits paid to the shareholders.

(b) Dividend is payable only out of profits of the company.

(c) Dividend is recommended by the Board and sanctioned by the shareholders in Annual General Meeting.

(d) Payment of dividend is an appropriation of profits and it involves application of assets of the company for distribution among the shareholders.

(e) Dividend is not paid on calls received in advance.

(f) The rate of dividend may vary from year to year, except preference shares, where the rate is fixed.

### (B) Dividend Policy

Dividend is the portion of earnings which is distributed among the shareholders. In other words, dividend policy determines the division of earnings between payment to shareholders and retained earnings. Formulation of proper dividend policy is one of the major financial decision to be taken by the financial managers.

**Meaning and Significance of Dividend Policy:**

Dividend policy is closely related to retained earnings. Retained earnings are one of the most important sources of internal funds for meeting the financial needs of the company for its growth and development. The dividend distribution to equity shareholder involve the outflow of cash. Both growth of the company and dividend distribution to shareholders are desirable, But these two goals are in conflict. A higher dividend rate means less retained earnings, which may consequently result in slower growth and lower market rate per share. In view of this, determining the dividend policy is one of the important functions of finance manager and he must very carefully divide the allocation of earnings between dividends and retained earnings.

Dividend policy may have a critical influence on the value of the firm. If the value of the firm is a function of its dividend payment ratio, the dividend policy will affect directly the firm's cost of capital.

A company which wants to pay dividends and also needs funds to finance its investment opportunities will have to depend on external source of finance such as issuing debentures and equity shares. Dividend policy of the firm thus affects both long-term financing and the wealth of share holders.

If strict dividend policy was formulated to retain large share of earnings, sufficiently large resources would be available to the company for its growth and modernisation purposes. This will give rise to business earnings. In view of improved earnings position and financial health of the enterprise, the value of share will increase and a capital gain will result. Thus, shareholders earn capital gain in lieu of dividend income, the former in the long-run while the latter in the short-run; the reverse holds true if liberal dividend policy is followed to pay out higher dividends to shareholders. As a result of this, the stockholder's dividend earnings will increase but the possibility of earning capital gains is reduced. Investors desirous of immediate income will value shares with high dividend greatly. The stock market may, therefore, respond to this development and the value of shares may surge.

## (C) Aspects of Dividend Policy - Practical Considerations

The first question that has to be answered by a finance manager is how much payout ratio should be adopted? This decision is extremely tricky because it involves a conflict of interests between shareholders and the management. The shareholders will always expect a higher payout because they are interested in getting maximum return on their investments. On the other hand the management looks upon the divisible profits as a means for financing the requirements of the company. Instead of depending upon external sources to raise the finance, it will be always advisable to utilise the retained earnings which is the company's own source. Therefore, a dividend payout ratio will have to be decided after a careful consideration of the following factors:

(a) **Shareholders' Expectations:** It is mentioned in the above paragraph that shareholders are always interested in high dividends. However, in case the majority of the shareholders are from a higher income bracket, they may prefer lower rates of dividends. On the other hand, if a shareholder is a retired person with a small income, he will expect a higher amount of dividend. Though, it can be admitted that expectations of all the shareholders cannot be taken into considerations, at least a payout ratio which satisfies the expectations of majority of shareholders should be followed. Since, shareholders are the owners of the company, their wishes must be taken into account.

(b) **Liquidity:** As per the provisions of the Companies Act, 1956, dividends are to be paid in cash. Therefore, before deciding of a payout ratio, liquidity position of the company should be examined carefully. In case of a growing firm, liquidity may not be very high because of their substantial investments and other commitments. These firms may not be in a position to pay a high dividend even though they wish to do so. On the other hand, a mature firm may have greater liquidity as the investment opportunities have declined. Availability of cash and sound financial position is also an important factor in dividend decisions. A dividend represents a cash outflow, the greater the funds and the liquidity of the firm, the better the ability to pay dividend. The liquidity of a firm depends very much on the investment and financial decisions of the firm which in turn determines the rate of expansion and the manner of financing. If cash position is weak, stock dividend will be distributed and if cash position is good, company can distribute the cash dividend.

(c) **Projections of Funds:** Another vital factor to be taken into account is the need of funds in the future. A forecast for the funds required in the future can be prepared and accordingly a payout ratio can be fixed. Firms which have substantial opportunities for investments require more funds than those firms whose opportunities are comparatively less. The firms having more investment opportunities can keep a low payout ratio and plough back the profits. If the firms do not see much of the requirements of funds in future, a high payout ratio can be adopted.

(d) **Capital Structure:** Capital structure of a company is the combination of various sources like equity capital, preference capital and long-term loans. If the capital structure of a company is highly geared i.e. consisting of a higher proportion of preference capital and term loans, there will be a heavy commitment on the part of the company to pay preference dividend and interest on the loan. This will force the firm to reduce the payout ratio as much of the earnings will be distributed for such commitments. On the other hand, if in the capital structure, equity capital is higher than the other two sources, dividend commitments are not high and, therefore, a high payout ratio can be maintained.

(e) **Control:** If finance is raised from external sources, there is a danger that the existing management will lose the control. The exception to this is the rights issue. If funds are raised from internal financing like the retained earnings, there is no risk of losing control. In such cases, the payout ratio is kept low.

(f) **Access to Capital Market:** If a firm has easy accessibility to the capital market, a high payout ratio can be adopted inspite of a lower liquidity. Easy accessibility to capital market ensures greater flexibility to the firm in paying dividends as well as in meeting the obligations of the firm. Thus, greater the ability of the firm to raise funds in the capital markets, the greater will be its ability to pay dividends even if it has lower liquidity.

**(g) Restrictions by Lenders:** The lenders may put some restrictions on the company. A firm may have to agree with the lender to restrict the payment of dividend payments. These restrictions may be in different forms. For example, a restriction can be, not to pay dividends unless some amount of the earnings is transferred to the sinking fund. In such cases, the payout ratio will have to be kept low.

**(h) Legal Restrictions:** In deciding on the dividend, the directors take the legal requirements too into consideration. In order to protect the interests of creditors and outsiders, the Companies Act 1956 prescribes certain guidelines in respect of the distribution and payment of dividend. Moreover, a company is required to provide for depreciation on its fixed and tangible assets before declaring dividend on the shares. It proposes that Dividend should not be distributed out of capital, in any case. Likewise, contractual obligation should also be fulfilled, for example, payment of dividend on preference shares in priority over ordinary dividend. The legal provisions will have to be kept in mind before fixing a dividend policy. As per Companies Act, 1956, dividends shall be paid only out of profits and for this current profits as well as past profits can be used. The profits mentioned above should be profits after providing depreciation. In special cases, if it is in public interest, the Central Government may permit a company to declare dividends without providing for depreciation. The dividends are to be paid in cash but a company is allowed to capitalise its profits and issue bonus shares. The bonus issues should be effected according to the guidelines issued by SEBI.

These legal restrictions will have to be taken into consideration before the dividend policy is fixed.

**(i) Inflation:** Inflation actually can act as a constraint on paying dividends. Depreciation is provided on the original cost of an asset and, therefore, it may not be an adequate source for replacement of the asset. Therefore, some part of the earnings should be retained in order to maintain the capital intact.

**(ii) Stability of Dividends:** Inspite of any dividend payout ratio fixed by a firm, the fact remains that the stability in dividend payments is considered as one of the desirable features in the dividend policy. This policy is desirable from the point of view of the shareholders also as they can plan their incomes accordingly. The question that arises is, what is stability? Whether it is stable payout ratio or stable dividend per share?

To answer this question, we will have to examine the different forms of stability. These forms are discussed in detail in the following paragraphs.

**(a) Stable Payout Ratio:** According to this policy, a fixed payout ratio is decided and it is followed consistently year after year. For example, a firm may decide that payout ratio should be 40%. If the divisible profits are ₹ 7,00,000, the total dividend payment will be

₹ 2,80,000. If the profit figure changes to ₹ 6,00,000, the dividend payment will be 40% of ₹ 6,00,000 i.e. ₹ 2,40,000. The stable payout ratio can be illustrated with the help of the following diagram.

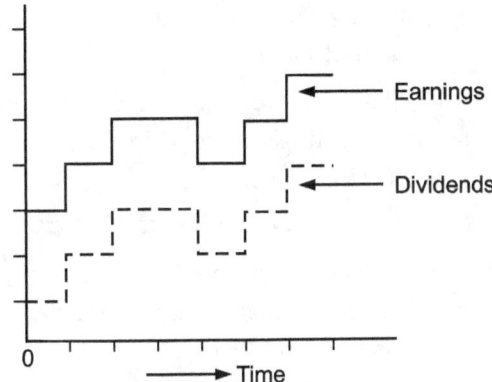

**Fig. 3.4: Stable Payout Ratio**

The feature of this policy is that if profits fluctuate, dividend per share also fluctuates. The stability of dividend per share, therefore, cannot be maintained. If amount of profits is nil, no dividends are paid to the shareholders. However, there is an inbuilt flexibility in this policy which ensures that if profits are high, dividends will also be high and if profits are low, dividends are also very low.

**(b) Stable Dividend per Share:** In this policy, a stable dividend per share is paid irrespective of profits. For example, a company may decide that 20% dividend per share is to be paid. If the share is of ₹ 100 each, the amount of dividend per share is ₹ 20. If profits in a particular year are very high, the same dividend per share is maintained and the remaining amount can be ploughed back to profits. When profits decline, the past accumulated profits can be utilised to maintain the same dividend per share. This policy can be explained with the help of the following diagram.

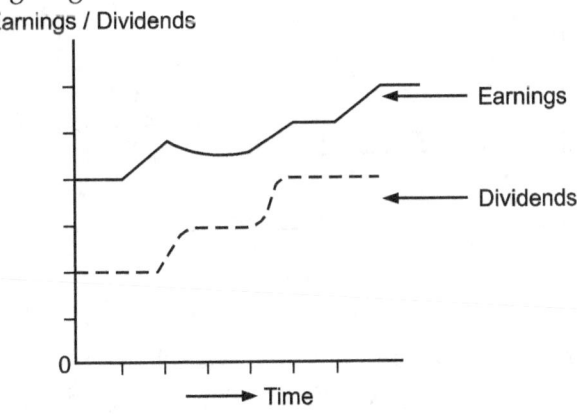

**Fig. 3.5: Stable Dividend Per Share**

In the above diagram, the dividend line is shown as going up periodically. The indication given is that extra dividend per share can be paid if profits increase permanently. This means that if profits increase temporarily, it may not be distributed as dividends. But if profits increase permanently, they should be distributed as extra dividend because otherwise there will be a stagnation in dividends.

To conclude, it can be said that stability of dividends is desirable from the investor's side because it eliminates uncertainty regarding dividend income. Similarly, it creates a faith in their minds about the return on their investments.

## (D) Forms of Divided Policy

The dividend decision in a firm is taken in the light of the firm's operating and financial conditions. Following are the different types of dividend policies and the firm has to choose one of the policy which suits its existing conditions.

**(a) Stable Dividend Policy:**

When a firm constantly pays a fixed amount of dividends and maintains it for all times to come regardless of fluctuations in the level of its earnings, it is said to have pursued a relatively stable dividend policy. In such a policy, stockholders are assured of a fixed dividend per share. During periods of prosperity the firm withholds all extraordinary income of the business to use them to maintain dividend amount during lean years. Stability of dividend policy does not mean stagnation in dividend payout ratio. In fact, slow but steady change is the prime feature of a stable dividend policy. The behavioural relationship between earnings and dividends is exhibited in Fig. 3.6.

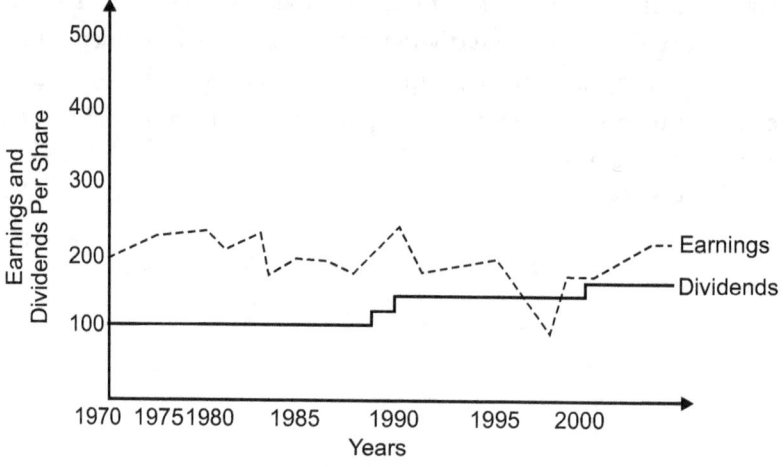

Fig. 3.6: Behavioural Relationship between Earnings and Dividends

It may be noted from the above figure that when the company's earnings tend to rise regularly and management feels satisfied that increased earnings are sustainable, permanent dividend per share is increased. Likewise, dividend will not be allowed to decline in correspondence with a fall in business earnings until it is felt that the firm will not be able to recover from the setback. It is also observed that, while earnings fluctuate, from year to year, dividend will rise only after yearly rise in earnings takes a 'long-run tendency'.

**(b) Policy of no Immediate Dividend:**

Generally this policy of no immediate dividend is persued in the following circumstances:

(i)    When the firm is a new and rapidly growing and it needs tidy amount of funds to finance its expansion programmes.

(ii)   When the firm's access to capital market is difficult or when availability of fund is costlier.

(iii)  Where shareholders have agreed to accept higher return in future or they have strong preference for long-term capital gains as opposed to short-term dividend income.

Very often, the management may decide to declare no dividend despite large earnings of the company.

**(c) Policy of Regular and Extra Dividends:**

Companies following regular dividend policy payout dividends constantly to stockholders at constant rate and do not change the payout ratio unless it is believed that changes in earnings are permanent. When profits of the company swell, the management may decide to distribute a part of the increased earnings as extra dividends instead of enhancing the regular dividend payout ratio. Extra dividends are declared only in the year in which earnings exceed annual dividend requirement by some given amount.

**(d) Policy to pay Irregular Dividends:**

Firm following this policy does not pay out fixed amount of dividend per share. Instead, dividend per share is varied in correspondence with change in level of earnings.

Generally, this policy is adopted by firms with unstable earnings. Under this policy, a large part of profits may be ploughed back in the year in which the firm has host of highly profitable investment opportunities. In the subsequent year, when the firm will have no or limited investment opportunities to seize the management may distribute larger share of earnings which would otherwise have remained unutilised.

**(e) Policy of Regular Stock Dividend:**

The company adopting this policy pays dividends in stock instead of in cash. Stock dividend is also designated 'bonus shares' which is very frequently used to capitalise reinvested earnings of the company. Issue of bonus shares does not effect the liquidity position of the company. It increases indeed the shareholding of residual owners but not their equity in the company.

## 3.6 Forms of Dividend

Generally, the alternative forms of dividend are: Scrip dividend, Cash dividend, Property dividend, Bond dividend, Stock dividend.

But in India only cash dividend and stock dividend are declared and paid.

**(a) Scrip Dividend:** When earnings of the company justify dividend, but the company's cash position is temporarily weak and does not permit cash dividend, it may declare dividend in the form of scrips. In this method of dividend, the share holders are issued transferable promissory notes which may or may not be interest bearing. Scrip dividends are justified only when the company has really earned profit and has only to wait for the conversion of other current assets into cash in the course of operations.

**(b) Cash Dividend:** Cash dividend is the dividend which is distributed to the shareholders in cash out of the earnings of the business.

**(c) Property Dividend:** This involves a payment with assets other than cash. This form of dividend may be followed wherever there are assets that are no longer necessary in the operation of the business.

**(d) Bond Dividend:** Sometimes, the dividends are paid in bonds or notes that have a long enough term to fall beyond the current liability group. Effect of both scrip dividends and bond dividends is the same except that the payment is postponed in the bond dividends.

**(e) Stock Dividend:** Stock dividend is the dividend which is paid to the shareholders in kind. When stock dividends are paid, a portion of the surplus is transferred to the capital account and shareholders are issued additional share certificates. Such shares are known as bonus shares and this process is known as capitalisation of profit.

### 3.6.1 Theories of Dividend

An important question that is to be answered is that whether there is any connection between the dividends declared and the market price of shares of a particular company. There are contradictory theories on this aspect.

The theories of dividend can be broadly classified into: (i) Relevance and (ii) Irrelevance. The Relevance theories advocate that dividend decisions definitely affect market prices while Irrelevance theories say that between dividend and market price there is no connection at all. These theories are explained below:

**(i) Relevance theories:** Under these theories, the following theories or models are quite significant.

**(A) Walter's Model:** Prof. J. E. Walter advocates that between dividends and market prices of share, there is a definite connection. In order to explain this connection, Walter says that business firms can be classified into three categories on the basis of rate of return on investments [r] and cost of capital [k]. He further says that for a growth firm, the rate of return is more than the cost of capital i.e. r > k. If rate of return is less than k, the firm is called as declining firm. In case rate of return = cost of capital, the firms are called as indifferent firms. If r > k i.e. for a growth firm, the optimum dividend policy will be 100% retention or zero percent payout. The market price of the shares will go on increasing when dividend payout ratio starts decreasing.

On the other hand, market price will start reducing when payout ratio starts increasing. In the case of a declining firm the situation is exactly reverse. The optimum dividend policy for such firms will be 100% payout and nothing should be retained. It means that market price will start increasing when the dividend payout starts increasing. In case of indifferent firms when r = k, high or low dividend payout ratio will not make any difference. The reasons for these types of changes in the market prices of shares are that in case of a growth firm, there are a number of profitable opportunities outside and hence instead of declaring dividend, if the amount of profit is retained, the market price of shares will rise. In case of declining firms, exactly opposite things take place. As the opportunities outside are not available, instead of retaining profits, it is better to distribute the profits as dividends. In case of indifferent firms, whether dividends are declared or whether there is retention of profits, it will not make any difference. The model can be summarised as below:

r > k  Growth firm       – 100% retained will be optimum policy

r < k  Declining firm    – 100% payout will be optimum

r = k  Indifferent firm  – 100% payout or zero percent will not make any
difference.

Walter's model can be expressed in a mathematical formula as given below:

$$P = \frac{D + \left[\dfrac{r}{ke}\right](E-D)}{ke}$$

P = Market price per share

D = Dividend per share

r = Rate of return

E = Earnings per share

ke = Cost of capital (Equity)

**The assumptions on which Walter's model is based are as follows:**

(a) Retained earnings are the only sources of financing new investments.

(b) The rate of return i.e. 'r' as well as 'ke' are always constant.

(c) The life of the firm is indefinite.

**Illustrations:**

Calculate the market price of share of a company if rate of return is 15% and cost of capital is 12%. The dividend payout is 40% while earnings per share is ₹ 30.

What should be the optimum dividend policy of the company as per Walter's model?

**Solution:**

As per Walter's model,

$$P = \frac{D + \left[\dfrac{r}{ke}\right](E - D)}{ke}$$

$$= \frac{12 + \left[\dfrac{.15}{.12}\right](30 - 12)}{.12} = ₹\ 287.5 = \text{Market price}$$

As per Walter's model, the firm is a growth firm because r > ke. Therefore, the optimum dividend policy should be 100% retention. Market price will be the highest, if retention ratio is 100% or payout ratio is zero percent. This is shown below:

$$P = \frac{0 + \left[\dfrac{.15}{.12}\right](30 - 0)}{.12} = ₹\ 312.5$$

**Note:** Dividend per share – 40% of ₹ 30 = ₹ 12.

The Walter's model has got a very limited application in real life situations due to the various assumptions. However, its usefulness cannot be denied in the sense that it shows the effect of dividends policy under varying profitabilities.

**(B) Gordon's model:** Gordon has also advocated a model which is similar to Walter's model. Gordon also agrees that market prices of shares are connected with the dividends declared by the firm. Like Walter's, Gordon also classifies firms into three categories. There are growth firms for whom rate of return [r] is greater than discount rate [k], for declining firms r < k while for indifferent firms r = k. The optimum dividend policies for these firms are as follows:

r  >  k   Growth firm      –   100% retained is optimum

r  <  k   Declining firm   –   100% payout is optimum

r  =  k   Indifferent firm –   No change in price of shares inspite of dividend payout

The formula for calculation of market price, as suggested by Gordon is as follows:

$$P = \frac{E(1 - b)}{k - br}$$

where              P  =  Market price

                     b  =  Retention ratio

            (1 - b)  =  Dividend payout ratio

$$K = \text{Rate of discount}$$
$$br = \text{Growth rate of earnings and dividends}$$
$$r = \text{Rate of return}$$
$$E = \text{Earnings per share}$$

**Illustration of Gordon's Model:**

| Growth firm | Indifferent/ Normal firm | Declining firm |
|---|---|---|
| $r > k$ | $r = k$ | $r < k$ |
| $r = 30\%$ | $r = 30\%$ | $r = 20\%$ |
| $k = 20\%$ | $k = 30\%$ | $k = 30\%$ |
| $E = ₹\,10$ | $E = ₹\,10$ | $E = ₹\,10$ |
| $b = 40\%$ | $b = 40\%$ | $b = 40\%$ |
| $P = \dfrac{10(1-.40)}{.20-(.40\times.30)}$ | $P = \dfrac{10(1-.40)}{.30-(.40\times.30)}$ | $P = \dfrac{10(1-.40)}{.30-(.40\times.20)}$ |
| $= \dfrac{6}{.20-.12}$ | $= \dfrac{6}{.18}$ | $= \dfrac{6}{.22}$ |
| $= \dfrac{6}{.08}$ | $= ₹\,33.33$ | $= ₹\,27.27$ |
| $= ₹\,75$ | $b = 60\%$ | $b = 60\%$ |
| $b = 60\%$ | $P = \dfrac{10(1-.60)}{.30-(.60\times.30)}$ | $P = \dfrac{10(1-.60)}{.30-(.60\times.20)}$ |
| $P = \dfrac{10(1-.60)}{.20-(.60\times.30)}$ | $= \dfrac{4}{.12}$ | $= \dfrac{4}{.18}$ |
| $= \dfrac{4}{.02} = ₹\,200$ | $= ₹\,33.33$ | $= ₹\,22.22$ |

**Gordon's model is based on the following assumptions:**

(a) Retained earnings represent the only source of financing for the firm.

(b) The rate of return and the cost of capital of the firm is constant.

(c) The growth rate of the firm is the product of its retention ratio and its rate of return.

(d) The firm has an indefinite life.

(e) Tax does not exist.

**Revised model of Gordon's earlier model:** Since Risk and Uncertainty factors have to be considered, Gordon has revised his earlier model. He says that discount rates in the future should be increased because risk and uncertainty increases with time. Gordon's revised equation is,

$$P_0 = \frac{D_0}{(1+k_1)} + \frac{D_1}{(1+k_2)} + \ldots\ldots \frac{D_t}{(1+k_t)}$$

In this case is $k_1 < k_2$ and so on.

Gordon argues that dividend policy in such a case matters even when the rate of return on investment (r) is equal to the average of all ks.

**(C) Traditional position:** This theory advocated by **Graham** and **Dodd**, says that shareholders always prefer dividends to retained earnings. Therefore, market prices will tend to increase if dividend payout is on the higher side. According to this approach, "Given two companies in the same general position and with the same earning power, the one paying the larger dividend will always sell at a higher price."

**(D) Radical Approach: Michael J. Brennan** and other advocates of low payout position argue that a policy of low dividend payout ratio promotes the welfare of the shareholders. The reason for this is that, for taxation purposes capital gains are taxed more favourably [long-term capital gains] than the income from dividends. The investors, therefore, will prefer those shares which provide more capital appreciation and less dividend income. This is possible when the dividend payout ratio is on the lower side. If the shareholders of a company are from a higher income bracket, this model may be applicable. However, in the absence of any evidence, it is difficult to generalise this conclusion.

**(ii) Irrelevance theory:** Under this approach, the thought is that the market price of shares and the value of a firm is not at all dependent on the percentage of dividends declared. Modigliani and Miller are the strong advocates of this thought. Their arguments are as follows:

**Modigliani - Miller Model:** According to this model, the value of a firm is solely dependent on the earning capacity of the firm. How a firm is distributing its earnings is not the deciding factor in the valuation. The MM argument says that a firm may retain its earnings or it may distribute them. If the earnings are retained, it will lead to capital appreciation. On the other hand, if dividends are distributed, the shareholders will enjoy dividend income which is equal to the amount by which his capital would have appreciated if the company would have retained its earnings. The shareholders, therefore, do not make any differentiation between present dividend and retained earnings.

The MM' model is based on certain assumptions. These assumptions are as follows:

(a) There are perfect capital markets and investors are rational.

(b) Information is freely available and there are numerous transactions.

(c) An investor cannot influence prices.

(d) Floatation costs are nil.

(e) There are no taxes.

(f) The firm has a fixed investment policy.

(g) Risk of uncertainty does not exist.

Modigliani and Miller have has also given a mathematical proof for their argument. This is explained with the help of the following illustration.

**Illustration:**

A company has a P/E (Price/Earnings) ratio of 10. The amount of share capital is ₹ 50,00,000 divided into shares of ₹ 100 each. The company expects declaration of dividend of ₹ 8 per share. On the assumption that the company pays dividend, its net income is ₹ 5,00,000 and it makes new investments of ₹ 10,00,000 during the period, prove under MM' assumption that the value of the firm remains unchanged when (a) dividends are paid and (b) dividends are not paid.

**Solution:**

(i)  (a)  **Price $P_1$ when dividend is not declared.**

$$P_0 = \frac{D_1 + P_1}{1 + ke}$$

$$100 = \frac{P_1}{(1 + .10)}$$

$$= ₹\ 110 = P_1$$

(b)  **When dividends are declared**

$$P_0 = \frac{D_1 + P_1}{1 + ke}$$

$$= 100 = \frac{8 + P_1}{1.10}$$

$$P_1 = ₹\ 102$$

$P_0$ = Prevailing market price

ke = Cost of capital

$D_1$ = Dividend to be received at the end of period one.

$P_1$ = Market price of a share at the end of period one.

(ii) (a)  **Amount required for new financing I – [y – n $D_1$] that is,**

$$= ₹\ 10,00,000 - [₹\ 5,00,000 - ₹\ 4,00,000]$$

$$= ₹\ 9,00,000$$

I = Amount of investment

y = Earnings

$nD_1$ = Amount of dividend [₹ 8 × 50,000 shares]

(b)  **New shares to be issued**

$$An = \frac{₹\ 9,00,000}{₹\ 102 \left[ \begin{array}{c} \text{Market price when} \\ \text{dividends are declared} \end{array} \right]}$$

$$= 8823.52 \text{ or } 8824$$

### (iii) Value of the firm when dividends are declared

$$V = \frac{1}{(1 + ke)} \left[ nD_1 + (n + An)\, P_1 - I + y - nD_1 \right]$$

$$= \frac{1}{(1 + .10)} \left[ \begin{array}{l} 4,00,000 + \left(50,000 + \dfrac{9,00,000}{102}\right) 102 \\ -10,00,000 + 5,00,000 - 4,00,000 \end{array} \right]$$

or

$$\frac{4,00,000 + \left[ \begin{array}{l} \dfrac{50,000 + 9,00,000}{102} \times 102 \\ -10,00,000 + 5,00,000 - 4,00,000 \end{array} \right]}{1.10}$$

or

$$\frac{55,00,000}{1.10}$$

$$= ₹\ 50,00,000$$

### (iv) Value of the firm if dividends are not declared:

$$V = \frac{1}{(1 + ke)} \left[ (N + An)\, p_1 - I + y \right]$$

$$= \frac{1}{1.10} \left[ \begin{array}{l} \left(50,000 + \dfrac{5,00,000}{110}\right) \\ \times 110 - 10,00,000 + 5,00,000 \end{array} \right]$$

$$= \frac{60,00,000 - 10,00,000 + 5,00,000}{1.10}$$

$$= ₹\ 50,00,000$$

In the above formula, the explanations of the various terms are as follows:

$V$ = Value of the firm

$Ke$ = Cost of capital

$$\left[ \text{P/E ratio is 10. Therefore, cost of capital is } \frac{1}{10} = .10 \right]$$

$N$ = Number of existing equity shares

$An$ = New shares

$nD_1$ = Total dividends

$P_1$ = Price of shares after dividend is declared or when no dividend is declared

$I$ = Amount of investment

$Y$ = Earnings

## 3.7 Share Splits

Share split is also known as a 'stock split'. Share split/Stock split increases the number of shares in a public company.

Stock split is done to infuse liquidity and to make shares affordable to various investors who could not buy the shares of that company before due to high prices.

When a company declares stock split, the number of shares of that company increases, but the market capital remain the same. As the number of shares increase, price per share goes down. Stock split is an issue of new shares in a company to existing shareholders in proportion to their current holdings.

## Practical Problems

### Capital Structure

**Problem 1:**

A limited company is considering different methods to finance its investment proposal. It is estimated that initially ₹ 40,00,000 will be needed. Two alternative methods are available for raising the funds:

(i) To raise ₹ 20,00,000 by sale of equity shares of ₹ 100 each and balance at 18% term loan.

(ii) To raise the entire amount by sale of equity shares of ₹ 100 each.

The existing capital structure of the company consists of:

(i) 50,000 equity shares of ₹ 100 each and

(ii) 17% term loan of ₹ 20,00,000.

The expected EBIT (Earnings before interest and tax) is ₹ 15,00,000. Advise the company on the basis of EPS (Earnings per share) in each alternative.

**Solution:**

Statement showing earnings per share under different alternatives.

| Particulars | Alternative I [₹ 20,00,000 Equity ₹ 20,00,000 Debt at 18%] ₹ | II [All equity] ₹ |
|---|---|---|
| A. EBIT (Earnings before interest and tax) | 15,00,000 | 15,00,000 |
| B. Interest on loan | | |
|    (i) Existing | 3,40,000 | 3,40,000 |
|    (ii) Fresh | 3,60,000 | – |
|    Total – [B] | **7,00,000** | **3,40,000** |
| C. Earnings before tax [A – B] | 8,00,000 | 11,60,000 |
| D. Income tax at 50% | 4,00,000 | 5,80,000 |
| E. Earnings after tax [C – D] | 4,00,000 | 5,80,000 |
| F. Number of equity shares [Existing + New] | 70,000 | 90,000 |
| G. Earnings per share [E ÷ F] | 5.71 | 6.44 |

**Conclusion:** Since EPS is higher in case of alternative II involving sale of equity shares, it is advisable to use that source.

## Problem 2:

A new project under consideration by your company requires a capital investment of ₹ 150 lakhs. The required funds can be raised either through the sale of equity shares or borrowed from a financial institution. Interest on term loan is 15% and tax rate is 50%. If the debt–equity ratio of 2: 1 is to be maintained calculate the indifference point of the project.

## Solution:

Capital investment of ₹ 150 lakhs is to be made. If a debt-equity ratio of 2: 1 is to be maintained, equity will be $1/3^{rd}$ i.e. ₹ 50 lakhs and debt will be $2/3^{rd}$ i.e. ₹ 100 lakhs. The indifference point is calculated as follows:

$$\frac{x[1-t]}{N_1} = \frac{[x-I][1-t]}{N_2}$$

where,
$$x = \text{EBIT at indifference level}$$
$$t = \text{Income tax rate}$$
$$I = \text{Interest}$$
$$N_1 = \text{No. of equity shares in alternative I}$$
$$N_2 = \text{No. of equity shares in alternative II}$$

Therefore,
$$\frac{x[1-.30]}{1,50,00,000} = \frac{[x-5,00,000][1-.30]}{50,00,000}$$

$$x = ₹7,50,000$$

**Note:** In the illustration, the value of equity shares on per share basis is not given and therefore, in $N_1$ and $N_2$ the total values of equity shares is taken instead of the number of shares.

## Problem 3:

XYZ Ltd. has currently an ordinary share capital of ₹ 250 lakhs consisting of equity shares of ₹ 100 each. The company is planning to raise another ₹ 200 lakhs for financing a major expansion program. The following four options are available.

(i)      Entirely through ordinary shares.

(ii)     ₹ 100 lakhs through ordinary shares and the balance by 15% term loan.

(iii)    ₹ 50 lakh through ordinary shares, ₹ 150 lakhs through long-term borrowing at 15% rate of interest.

(iv)    ₹ 100 lakhs through ordinary shares, and ₹ 100 lakhs through preference shares with 14% dividend.

Expected EBIT of the company is ₹ 80 lakhs. Calculate EPS under each alternative and advise the company about the most beneficial alternative.

Income-tax rate can be taken as 50%.

**Solution:**

EPS under different alternatives:

| Particulars | Alternative I [Ordinary shares] | II [100 lakhs Ord. Shs 100 lakhs balance term loan] | III [50 lakhs Ord. Shs. 150 lakhs term loan] | IV [100 lakhs Ord. Shs. 100 lakhs Pref.] |
|---|---|---|---|---|
| | [₹] | [₹] | [₹] | [₹] |
| A. EBIT | 80,00,000 | 80,00,000 | 80,00,000 | 80,00,000 |
| B. Interest | – | 15,00,000 | 22,50,000 | – |
| C. Earnings before tax [A – B] | 80,00,000 | 65,00,000 | 57,50,000 | 80,00,000 |
| D. Income-tax at 50% | 40,00,000 | 32,50,000 | 28,75,000 | 40,00,000 |
| E. EAT [C – D] | 40,00,000 | 32,50,000 | 28,75,000 | 40,00,000 |
| **Less:** Pref. Dividend | – | – | – | 14,00,000 |
| Earnings of equity | 40,00,000 | 32,50,000 | 28,75,000 | 26,00,000 |
| F. No. of equity shares | 4,50,000 | 3,50,000 | 3,00,000 | 3,50,000 |
| G. EPS [E ÷ F] | 8.88 | 9.28 | 9.58 | 7.42 |

**Conclusion:** As per the above statement, earnings per share under Alternative III involving equity issue of ₹ 50 lakhs and term loan of ₹ 150 lakhs, is the highest. Therefore, it is advisable to follow that alternative:

_____

*Pref. dividend

**Problem 4:**

A company gives you the following figures:

| Particulars | Amount (₹) |
|---|---|
| Profit before interest and tax | 24,00,000 |
| **Less** Interest on debentures @12.5% | 2,00,000 |
| Interest on long term loans @ 16% | 2,00,000 |
| Total Interest | **4,00,000** |
| Profit before tax | 20,00,000 |
| **Less** Income-tax at 50% | **10,00,000** |
| Profit after tax | 10,00,000 |
| Number of equity shares [₹ 10 each] | 4,00,000 |
| Earnings per share | 2.50 |
| Current market price | 20.00 |
| Price earnings ratio | 8 |

The company has undistributed reserves and profits of ₹ 81,50,000. The company needs to raise ₹ 36,00,000 for repayment of debentures and modernisation of plants. Two alternative sources are available for raising this money.

(i) Raising the entire amount through term loans @18% interest.

(ii) Raising partially by sale of ₹ 1,00,000 equity shares at an expected price of ₹ 18 per share and the balance through term loan @16% interest.

The company expects that the rate of return i.e. before tax and interest on funds employed will improve by 4% because of modernisation and if debt–equity ratio [debt/debt plus shareholders funds] exceeds 25% the P/E ratio will go down to 6.

Advise the company about the proper course of action.

**Solution:**

### Statement showing evaluation of alternative financing plans

| Particulars | | Plan I [Term loan @16%] | Plan II [Equity ₹ 18,00,000 16% Debt ₹ 18,00,000] |
|---|---|---|---|
| | | ₹ | ₹ |
| I. | Earnings before interest and tax [Working note no 1] | 34,00,000 | 34,00,000 |
| II. | Interest | | |
| | (a) Existing | 2,00,000 | 2,00,000 |
| | (b) Fresh | 5,76,000 | 2,88,000 |
| | Total – (II) | **7,76,000** | **4,88,000** |
| III. | Earnings before tax (I – II) | 26,24,000 | 29,12,000 |
| IV. | Income-tax @50% | 13,12,000 | 14,56,000 |
| V. | Earnings after tax (III – IV) | 13,12,000 | 14,56,000 |
| VI. | No. of equity shares | 4,00,000 | 5,00,000 |
| VII. | Earnings per share [V ÷ VI] | ₹ 3.28 | ₹ 2.91 |
| VIII. | Price earnings ratio | 6 times | 8 times |
| IX. | Market price per share [VII × VIII] | ₹ 19.68 | ₹ 23.28 |

Plan No. II, involving combination of equity and term loan, is better than Plan I as it maximises market price of equity shares.

**Working Notes:**

1. EBIT percentage on capital employed is expected to increase by 4% after modernisation. The capital employed is calculated as follows:

| Particulars | Capital employed before modernisation ₹ | Capital employed after modernisation ₹ |
|---|---|---|
| Equity Capital | 40,00,000 | 40,00,000 |
| Reserves and Surplus | 81,50,000 | 81,50,000 |
| 12.5% Debentures | 16,00,000 | Repaid |
| 16% Term loan | 12,50,000 | 12,50,000 |
| Additional funds |  | 36,00,000 |
| **Total** | **1,50,00,000** | **1,70,00,000** |

EBIT at present is ₹ 24,00,000 which is 16% on capital employed, i.e. ₹ 1,50,00,000. After modernisation it will be 20% on ₹ 1,70,00,000 i.e. ₹ 34,00,000.

2. Debt to equity ratio after raising debt of ₹ 36,00,000 will be as follows:

$$\frac{36,00,000 + 12,50,000}{36,00,000 + 12,50,000 + 40,00,000 + 81,50,000} \times 100 = 28.52\%$$

Since it is more than 25%, as per information given in the example, the P/E ratio is reduced to 6 from the present 8 times.

**Problem 5:**

A company wants to have an optimum mix of debt and equity. The cost of debt and cost of equity at a different debt equity ratio is as follows:

| Debt equity ratio | Cost of debt % [Post-tax] | Cost of equity [%] |
|---|---|---|
| – | – | 12.5 |
| 10: 90 | .05 | 13.0 |
| 20: 80 | .05 | 13.6 |
| 30: 70 | .06 | 14.3 |
| 40: 60 | .07 | 16.0 |
| 50: 50 | .08 | 18.0 |
| 60: 40 | .10 | 20.0 |

What is the optimum capital structure of the company?

**Solution:**

Calculation of combined cost of capital.

| Debt–equity ratio | Cost of debt post–tax [%] | Cost of equity [%] | Combined cost [%] |
|---|---|---|---|
| – | – | 12.5 | 12.5 |
| 10: 90 | .05 | 13.0 | $.10 \times .05 + .90 \times .13 = 12.2$ |
| 20: 80 | .05 | 13.6 | $.20 \times .05 + .80 \times .136 = 11.88$ |
| 30: 70 | .06 | 14.3 | $.30 \times .06 + .70 \times 14.3 = 10.028$ |
| 40: 60 | .07 | 16 | $.40 \times .07 + .60 \times 16 = 9.628$ |
| 50: 50 | .08 | 18 | $.50 \times .08 + .50 \times .18 = 13$ |
| 60: 40 | .10 | 20 | $.60 \times .10 + .40 \times .20 = 14$ |

From the above table at a combination of 30: 70 debt (–) equity the aggregate cost of capital is minimum and, therefore, it is an optimum capital structure.

**Problem 6:**

A company needs ₹ 5,00,000 for modernisation. The following three plans are available. (i) Issue of 50,000 equity shares of ₹ 10 per share. (ii) Issue of Rs 25,000 equity shares of ₹ 10 per share and 2,500 debenture of ₹ 100 each at 14% rate of interest. (iii) Issue of 25,000 equity shares and the balance through 10% preference shares.

If the company's earnings before interest and tax are ₹ 10,000, ₹ 20,000, ₹ 40,000, ₹ 60,000 and ₹ 1,00,000, what will be the earnings per share under each of the three financial plans? Assume an income–tax rate of 50%.

**Solution:** Statement showing EPS

**Financial Plan I**

|  | ₹ | ₹ | ₹ | ₹ | ₹ |
|---|---|---|---|---|---|
| EBIT | 10,000 | 20,000 | 40,000 | 60,000 | 1,00,000 |
| **Less:** Interest | nil | nil | nil | nil | nil |
| Earnings before tax | 10,000 | 20,000 | 40,000 | 60,000 | 1,00,000 |
| **Less:** Income–tax at 50% | 5,000 | 10,000 | 20,000 | 30,000 | 50,000 |
| Earnings after tax | 5,000 | 10,000 | 20,000 | 30,000 | 50,000 |
| No. of Eq. shares EPS | 50,000 | 50,000 | 50,000 | 50,000 | 50,000 |
| [EAT ÷ No. of Shares] | .10 | .20 | .40 | .60 | 1.00 |

**Financial Plan II**

| | ₹ | ₹ | ₹ | ₹ | ₹ |
|---|---|---|---|---|---|
| EBIT | 10,000 | 20,000 | 40,000 | 60,000 | 1,00,000 |
| Less: Interest | 35,000 | 35,000 | 35,000 | 35,000 | 35,000 |
| Earnings before tax | (25,000) | (15,000) | 5,000 | 25,000 | 65,000 |
| Less: Income–tax at 50% | (12,500) | (7,500) | 2,500 | 12,500 | 32,500 |
| Earnings after tax | (12,500) | (7,500) | 2,500 | 12,500 | 32,500 |
| No. of Eq. shares | 25,000 | 25,000 | 25,000 | 25,000 | 25,000 |
| EPS | (.50) | (.30) | .10 | .50 | 1.3 |

**Financial Plan III**

| | ₹ | ₹ | ₹ | ₹ | ₹ |
|---|---|---|---|---|---|
| EBIT | 10,000 | 20,000 | 40,000 | 60,000 | 1,00,000 |
| Less: Interest | nil | nil | nil | nil | nil |
| Earnings before tax | 10,000 | 20,000 | 40,000 | 60,000 | 1,00,000 |
| Less: Income–tax at 50% | 5,000 | 10,000 | 20,000 | 30,000 | 50,000 |
| Earnings after tax | 5,000 | 10,000 | 20,000 | 30,000 | 50,000 |
| Less: Pref. dividend | 25,000 | 25,000 | 25,000 | 25,000 | 25,000 |
| Earnings for Equity Shareholders | (20,000) | (15,000) | (5,000) | 5,000 | 25,000 |
| No. of Equity shares | 25,000 | 25,000 | 25,000 | 25,000 | 25,000 |
| EPS | (.80) | (.60) | (.20) | .20 | 1 |

**Conclusion:** The selection of a financial plan depends upon the EBIT. If sales are increasing, EPS under the second plan will be the highest. If sales are either remaining stagnant or reducing, equity shares will be the best alternative.

**Problem 7:**

AB Ltd. needs ₹ 10,00,000 for expansion. The expansion is expected to yield an annual EBIT of ₹ 1,60,000. While choosing a financial plan, AB Ltd. Has an objective of maximizing earnings per share. It is considering the possibility of issuing equity shares and raising debt of ₹ 1,00,000 or ₹ 4,00,000 or ₹ 6,00,000. The market price per share currently is ₹ 50 and is expected to drop upto ₹ 40, if funds are borrowed in excess of ₹ 5,00,000. Funds can be borrowed at the rates indicated below:

(a)   Upto ₹ 1,00,000 @ 8%,

(b)   Over ₹ 1,00,000 upto ₹ 5,00,000 @12%

(c)   Over ₹ 5,00,000 @ 18%

Assuming a tax rate of 50%, calculate EPS under the three financing plans.

## Solution:

Statement showing calculation of EPS

| Particulars | Alternatives | | |
|---|---|---|---|
| | I [Debt ₹ 1,00,000] | II [Debt ₹ 4,00,000] | III [Debt ₹ 6,00,000] |
| EBIT | 1,60,000 | 1,60,000 | 1,60,000 |
| **Less:** Interest | 8,000 | 44,000 | 74,000 |
| Earnings before tax | 1,52,000 | 1,16,000 | 86,000 |
| **Less:** Income tax 50% | 76,000 | 58,000 | 43,000 |
| Earnings after tax | 76,000 | 58,000 | 43,000 |
| No. of shares | 36,000 | 24,000 | 20,000 |
| EPS [EAT ÷ No. of shares] | 2.11 | 2.42 | 2.15 |

EPS is highest in alternative II so Alternative II should be selected.

## Working notes:

The interest is calculated as follows:

| Alternative II: | 8% on ₹ 1,00,000 | = | 8,000 |
|---|---|---|---|
| | 12% on ₹ 3,00,000 | = | 36,000 |
| | Total | | **44,000** |
| Alternative III: | 8% on ₹ 1,00,000 | = | 8,000 |
| | 12% on ₹ 4,00,000 | = | 48,000 |
| | 18% on ₹ 1,00,000 | = | 18,000 |
| | Total | | **74,000** |

## Leverages

## Problem 1:

From the following figures, calculate operating, financial and combined leverages of Aditya Ltd. and Amar Ltd.

| Particulars | Aditya Ltd. | Amar Ltd. |
|---|---|---|
| Selling price per unit | ₹ 75 | ₹ 75 |
| Profit volume ratio | 40% | 60% |
| Fixed costs | ₹ 40,00,000 | ₹ 60,00,000 |
| Capital structure: | | |
| Equity capital | ₹ 20,00,000 | ₹ 35,00,000 |
| Term loan | ₹ 15,00,000 at 18% | ₹ 10,00,000 at 17% |
| Production capacity | 2,00,000 units p.a. | 3,50,000 units p.a. |
| Capacity utilisation | 90% | 80% |

**Solution:**

Profitability Statement of Aditya Ltd. & Amar Ltd.

| Particulars | Aditya Ltd. | Amar Ltd. |
|---|---|---|
| Production units | 1,80,000 | 2,80,000 |
| Selling price per unit | 75 | 75 |
| Sales value (Production × Price p/u] | 1,35,00,000 | 2,10,00,000 |
| Contribution: | | |
| 40% of sales | 54,00,000 | |
| 60% of sales | | 1,26,00,000 |
| **Less:** Fixed cost | 40,00,000 | 60,00,000 |
| EBIT | 14,00,000 | 66,00,000 |
| **Less:** Interest | 2,70,000 | 1,70,000 |
| **EBT** | **11,30,000** | **64,30,000** |

$$\text{Operating leverage} = \frac{\text{Contribution}}{\text{EBIT}}$$

$$\text{Aditya Ltd.} ₹ \quad \frac{54,00,000}{14,00,000} = 3.86$$

$$\text{Amar Ltd.} ₹ \quad \frac{1,26,00,000}{66,00,000} = 1.91$$

$$\text{Financial leverage} = \frac{\text{EBIT}}{\text{EBT}}$$

$$\text{Aditya Ltd.} \quad \frac{14,00,000}{11,30,000} = 1.24$$

$$\text{Amar Ltd.} \quad \frac{66,00,000}{64,30,000} = 1.03$$

Combined leverage: Operating × Financial leverage

$$\text{Aditya Ltd.} = 3.86 \times 1.24 = 4.7864$$
$$\text{Amar Ltd.} = 1.91 \times 1.03 = 1.9673$$

**Conclusion:** From the above calculations, it is clear that leverages for Aditya Ltd. are greater than that of Amar Ltd. Therefore, risk is higher for Aditya Ltd. than Amar Ltd. comparatively.

**Problem 2:**

From the following particulars, calculate the operating, financial and combined leverages.

**Balance Sheet of Zenith Ltd. as on 31st March, 2016**

| Liabilities | ₹ | Assets | ₹ |
|---|---|---|---|
| Equity share capital [₹ 10 each] | 12,00,000 | Fixed Assets [Net] | 21,00,000 |
| 15% Debentures | 8,00,000 | Current Assets | 19,00,000 |
| General Reserve | 7,00,000 | | |
| Current liabilities | 13,00,000 | | |
| **Total** | **40,00,000** | **Total** | **40,00,000** |

**Additional Information:**

1.  The earnings before interest and tax (EBIT) is 20% on sales for the year ended 31st March 2016.

2.  The profit volume ratio is 40%.

3.  The total asset turnover [Sales/Total asset] for the year is 2.

**Solution:**

The total asset turnover is 2 and therefore Sales are ₹ 40,00,000 × 2 = ₹ 80,00,000. P/v ratio is 40%.

Therefore, contribution    =    ₹ 32,00,000 [40% of sales]

EBIT = 20% on sales    =    ₹ 16,00,000

(i)   Operating leverage    $= \dfrac{\text{Contribution}}{\text{EBIT}}$

$$= \dfrac{32,00,000}{16,00,000} = 2$$

(ii)   Financial leverage    $= \dfrac{\text{EBIT}}{\text{EBT}} = \dfrac{16,00,000}{14,80,000} = 1.08$

[EBT = ₹ 16,00,000 – ₹ 1,20,000]

Interest on Debentures

(iii) Combined leverage    =   Operating leverage × Financial leverage

                           =   2 × 1.08

                           =   2.16

**Comment:** All the leverages for the company are quite low and, therefore, operating, financial and combined risks are quite low.

**Problem 3:**

From the following particulars, prepare income statements of Sure Ltd., Slow Ltd., and Fast Ltd., for the year ended 31st March 2016.

| Particulars | Sure Ltd. | Slow Ltd. | Fast Ltd. |
|---|---|---|---|
| Operating leverage | 5 | 6 | 4 |
| Financial leverage | 4 | 5 | 3 |
| Interest [₹] | 3,000 | 4,000 | 2,000 |
| p/v ratio | 40% | 25% | 50% |
| Income–tax rate | 50% | 50% | 50% |

**Solution:**

Income statements

| Particulars | Sure Ltd. | Slow Ltd. | Fast Ltd. |
|---|---|---|---|
| A. Sales | 50,000 | 1,20,000 | 24,000 |
| B. Variable cost | 30,000 | 90,000 | 12,000 |
| C. Contribution [A – B] | 20,000 | 30,000 | 12,000 |
| D. Fixed cost | 16,000 | 25,000 | 9,000 |
| E. EBIT [C – D] | 4,000 | 5,000 | 3,000 |
| F. Interest cost | 3,000 | 4,000 | 2,000 |
| G. EBT [E – F] | 1,000 | 1,000 | 1,000 |
| H. Income-tax 50% | 500 | 500 | 500 |
| I. EAT [G – H] | 500 | 500 | 500 |

**Working notes:**

$$\text{Operating leverage} = \frac{\text{Contribution}}{\text{EBIT}}$$

$$\text{Contribution} - \text{Fixed cost} = \text{EBIT}$$

$$\text{Financial leverage} = \frac{\text{EBIT}}{\text{EBT}}$$

$$\text{EBIT} - \text{Interest} = \text{EBT}$$

For Sure Ltd., Financial leverage is 4 which means EBIT is 4 times of EBT. In other words if EBIT is 4, EBT is 1 which means interest = 3 [4 – 1 = 3].

| Now, if interest | = 3 = ₹ 3,000 |
|---|---|
| | 4 = ₹ 4,000 = EBIT |
| Similarly, for Slow Ltd. | = 4 = ₹ 4,000 |
| | 5 = ₹ 5,000 = EBIT |
| Fast Ltd. | 2 = 2,000 |
| | 3 = ₹ 3,000 = EBIT |

From operating leverage and EBIT, contribution for all the companies can be calculated.

$$\text{Contribution} = \text{Operating leverage} \times \text{EBIT}$$

| Sure Ltd. | 5 × 4,000 = ₹ 20,000 |
|---|---|
| Slow Ltd. | 6 × 5,000 = ₹ 30,000 |
| Fast Ltd. | 4 × 3,000 = ₹ 12,000 |

Sales for all the companies can be calculated from p/v ratio and contribution.

Sure Ltd.: P/v ratio 40% contribution ₹ 20,000.

$$\text{Sales} = ₹ 50,000$$

Slow Ltd.                     P/v ratio  =  60%
                              Contribution  =  ₹ 30,000
                                     Sales  =  ₹ 1,20,000
Fast Ltd.                     P/v ratio  =  50%
                              Contribution  =  ₹ 12,000
                                     Sales  =  ₹ 24,000

Fixed cost is the difference between contribution and EBIT.

**Note**: EBIT = Earnings before interest and tax

                              EBT  =  Earnings before tax
                              EAT  =  Earnings after tax

## Problem 4:

Calculate the operating leverage, financial leverage and combined leverage from the following details:

        Selling price per unit   =  ₹ 150
        Variable cost per unit   =  ₹ 100
        Fixed costs              =  ₹ 6,00,000
        Production & sales       =  20,000 units

The capital structure of the company under alternate financing plan is as follows:

| Particulars | Plan I ₹ | Plan II ₹ |
|---|---|---|
| Equity Capital | 20,00,000 | 10,00,000 |
| 16% Debentures | 10,00,000 | 20,00,000 |
| **Total** | **30,00,000** | **30,00,000** |

## Solution:

Calculation of leverages:

| Particulars | Plan I ₹ | Plan II ₹ |
|---|---|---|
| A.  Sales units | 20,000 | 20,000 |
| B.  Sales value [₹ 150 per unit] | 30,00,000 | 30,00,000 |
| C.  Variable cost [per unit ₹ 100] | 20,00,000 | 20,00,000 |
| D.  Contribution [B – C] | 10,00,000 | 10,00,000 |
| E.  Fixed costs | 6,00,000 | 6,00,000 |
| F.  EBIT [D – E] | 4,00,000 | 4,00,000 |
| G.  Interest | 1,60,000 | 3,20,000 |
| H.  EBT [F – G] | 2,40,000 | 80,000 |

1.                    Operating leverage $= \dfrac{\text{Contribution}}{\text{EBIT}}$

$$= \dfrac{10,00,000}{4,00,000}$$

$$= 2.5$$

Since fixed cost is the same for both, Plan I and Plan II, operating leverage is same for both the plans.

2 .                   Financial leverage $= \dfrac{\text{EBIT}}{\text{EBT}}$

Plan I $= \dfrac{4,00,000}{2,40,000} = 1.67$

Plan II $= \dfrac{4,00,000}{80,000} = 5$

3.            Combined leverage $=$ Operating leverage $\times$ Financial leverage

Plan I                    $2.5 \times 1.67 = 4.175$

Plan II                   $2.5 \times 5 = 12.5$

**Conclusion:** In Plan II, since major amount is raised by debentures, the plan is more risky. It is clearly shown by the higher financial leverage accompanied by high combined leverage.

**Problem 5:**

The income statement of a company is as follows:

| Particulars | Amount [₹] |
|---|---|
| Sales | 20,00,000 |
| Variable costs [70%] | 14,00,000 |
| Contribution | 6,00,000 |
| Fixed costs | 5,00,000 |
| Earnings before interest & tax | 1,00,000 |

The capital structure of the company is as follows:

|  | ₹ |
|---|---|
| Equity Capital [₹ 10 each] | 2,50,000 |
| 14% Debt | 1,50,000 |
| **Total** | **4,00,000** |

**Calculate:**

1. The earnings per share.
2. The percentage change in EPS as a result of 25% increase in sales.
3. Financial leverage. [Income–tax rate is 30%]

**Solution:**

1.   Statement of EPS at existing level of sales

| Particulars | Amount [₹] |
|---|---|
| Earnings before interest and tax | 1,00,000 |
| **Less:** Interest and debt | 21,000 |
| Earnings before tax | 79,000 |
| No. of equity shares | 25,000 |
| Earnings per share | 3.16 |

2.   Statement showing changes in EPS

| Particulars | + 25% in sales [₹] | – 25% in sales [₹] |
|---|---|---|
| Sales | 25,00,000 | 15,00,000 |
| **Less:** Variable costs [70%] | 17,50,000 | 10,50,000 |
| Contribution | 7,50,000 | 4,50,000 |
| **Less:** Fixed costs | 5,00,000 | (5,00,000) |
| EBIT | 2,50,000 | (50,000) |
| **Less:** Income–tax | 1,25,000 | (25,000) |
| EBT | 1,25,000 | (25,000) |
| No. of Equity Shares | 25,000 | 25,000 |
| EPS | 5 | (1) |
| Change in EPS | + 58.22 | – |

3.   $$\text{Financial leverage} = \frac{\text{EBIT}}{\text{EBT}}$$

$$\text{At present} = \frac{1,00,000}{79,000} = 1.27$$

$$\text{Increase of 25\%} = \frac{2,50,000}{2,29,000} = 1.09$$

## Cost of Capital

**Problem 1:**

Annual net profit earned by a company amounted to ₹ 50,000. It is expected that retained earnings can be invested by the shareholders in a similar type of company @10%. If the same are distributed among the shareholders, the shareholders also have to incur by way of brokerage and commission @3% of the net dividends. Rate of tax is 40%. Calculate the cost of retained earnings.

**Solution:**

The calculation of cost of retained earnings can be done with the help of the following formula:

$$k_r = k_e \, (1-t) \, (1-b)$$

where            $k_r$ = cost of retained earnings

                   $k_e$ = cost of equity capital

                     $t$ = taxation rate

                     $b$ = brokerage and / or commission.

Therefore,       $k_r$ = .10 $(1-.40)\,(1-.03)$

                    = 5.82%

---

**Problem 2:**

A company issues 10% debentures for ₹ 2,00,000. Rate of income tax is 40%. Calculate the cost of debt if the debentures are issued:

(i)     at par,

(ii)    at a discount of 10%, and

(iii)   at a premium of 10%.

**Solution:**

The cost of debt is always post-tax cost.

The formula for calculating the same is as follows:

$$k_d = \frac{I}{P} \, [1-t]$$

where,            $k_d$ = Cost of debt,

                    $I$ = Annual interest payment,

                    $P$ = Net proceeds

                    $t$ = Taxation rate.

(i)     Debt issued at par

$$k_d = \frac{20,000}{2,00,000} \, [1-.40] = 6\%$$

(ii)    Debt issued at discount of 10%

$$k_d = \frac{20,000}{1,80,000} \, [1-.40] = 6.6\%$$

(iii)   Debt issued at a premium of 10%

$$k_d = \frac{20,000}{2,20,000} \, [1-.40] = 5.45$$

**Note:** Since the period of repayment is not mentioned, it is not taken into consideration.

**Problem 3:**

X Ltd. has the following capital structure

|  |  |
|---|---:|
|  | ₹ |
| Equity share capital [20,000 shares] | 4,00,000 |
| 6% Preference shares | 1,00,000 |
| 8% Debentures | 3,00,000 |
|  | 8,00,000 |

The market price of equity share is ₹ 20. It is expected that the company will pay a current dividend of ₹ 2 per share which will grow @ 7% forever. Rate of tax is 40%. Calculate the weighted average cost of capital.

**Solution:**

Before we calculate weighted average cost of capital, specific cost of capital will have to be calculated.

(i)   Cost of Equity Capital $k_e = \dfrac{D}{P} + g$

where,

$$\begin{aligned}
D &= \text{Dividend per share} \\
P &= \text{Market price} \\
g &= \text{Growth rate} \\
&= \frac{2}{20} + .07 = 0.17
\end{aligned}$$

(ii)  Cost of Debentures $= k_d = (1-t)\,R$

$$\begin{aligned}
&= (1-.40)\,.08 \\
&= .048 \text{ or } 4.8\%
\end{aligned}$$

(iii) Cost of Pref. Capital $= k_p = \dfrac{PD + \left[\dfrac{P-NP}{n}\right]}{\dfrac{P+NP}{2}}$

where

$$\begin{aligned}
PD &= \text{Preference dividend} \\
P &= \text{Face value} \\
NP &= \text{Net proceeds} \\
n &= \text{Number of years}
\end{aligned}$$

$\therefore \qquad k_p = \dfrac{6 + \left[\dfrac{100-100}{10}\right]}{\dfrac{100+100}{2}} = 0.06$

**Note:** It is assumed in the absence of information that the face value and net proceeds from the preference share are ₹ 100 each and their redemption period is 10 years.

**Weighted Average Cost of Capital:**

| Sources | Amount | Capital structure proportion [weights] | Specific cost | Weighted average cost |
|---|---|---|---|---|
| Equity Capital | 4,00,000 | .50 | .17 | 0.085 |
| Preference Capital | 1,00,000 | .125 | .048 | 0.006 |
| 8% Debentures | 3,00,000 | .375 | .060 | 0.0225 |
| **Total** | **8,00,000** | **1.000** | | **0.1135 or 11.35** |

Weighted average cost = 11.35%

## Problem 4:

M/s. ABC & Co. has the following capital structure as on 31st March 2015.

| Particulars | Amount (₹) |
|---|---|
| 12% Debentures | 3,00,000 |
| 9% Preference shares | 2,00,000 |
| Equity – 5,000 shares of ₹ 100 each | |
| | 5,00,000 |
| **Total** | **10,00,000** |

The equity shares of the company are quoted at ₹ 102 and expected dividend is ₹ 9 per share for 2014-15. A growth rate of 7% was registered in the past which is expected to be maintained. On the assumption that the applicable income-tax rate for the company is 40%, calculate the weighted average cost of capital.

## Solution:

The calculation of specific cost of capital will have to be done before calculating the weighted average cost of capital.

(i)    Cost of Equity Capital:

$$k_e = \frac{D}{P} + g = \frac{9}{102} + .07 = .1582$$

(ii)    Cost of Preference Capital

$$k_p = \frac{PD + \left[\dfrac{P - NP}{n}\right]}{\dfrac{P + NP}{2}} = \frac{9 + \left[\dfrac{100 - 100}{10}\right]}{\dfrac{100 + 100}{2}} = \frac{9}{\dfrac{200}{2}} = .09$$

**Note:** It is assumed that face value and net proceeds of preference shares are ₹ 100 each and the redemption period is 10 years.

(iii)    Cost of Debentures:

$$k_d = [1 - t]\,R$$
$$= [1 - .40]\,.\,12 = .072$$

Calculation of weighted average cost of capital:

| Source | Amount (₹) | Capital structure proportion [weight] | Specific cost | Weighted average cost |
|---|---|---|---|---|
| Equity Capital | 5,00,000 | .50 | .1582 | .0791 |
| Pref. Capital | 2,00,000 | .20 | .09 | .018 |
| 12% Debentures | 3,00,000 | .30 | .072 | .0216 |
| | 10,00,000 | | | .1187 |

Weighted average cost of capital = 11.87%

**Problem 5:**

From the following data, calculate the value of each firm as per the Modigliani Miller approach.

| Particulars | Firm A (₹) | Firm B (₹) | Firm C (₹) |
|---|---|---|---|
| Earnings before interest and tax | 13,00,000 | 13,00,000 | 13,00,000 |
| Number of shares | 3,00,000 | 3,00,000 | 3,00,000 |
| 12% Debentures | – | 9,00,000 | 10,00,000 |

Every firm expects 12% return on investments.

**Solution:**

According to Modigliani Miller approach, the market value of the firm is calculated by the following formula,

$$V_m = \frac{EBIT}{k_O}$$

where,

$EBIT$ = Earnings before interest and tax,

$k_O$ = Overall cost of capital,

$V_m$ = Total market value of the firm.

$$V_m = \frac{13,00,000}{.12} = ₹\ 108.33\ lakhs$$

Since EBIT and overall cost of capital for each of the firm is the same, value of every firm will be the same. Number of shares and debentures are not relevant.

Overall cost of capital is equal to expected rate of return on investment.

**Problem 6:**

Assuming that a company pays income-tax @ 40%, calculate the after-tax cost of capital in the following cases:

(a)   A 8.5% preference share sold at par redeemable after 5 years.

(b)   A perpetual bond with 8% rate of interest.

(c)   A ten years 8% ₹ 1,000 debenture sold at ₹ 950 less 4% underwriting commission.

(d) A preference share sold at ₹ 100 with 9% dividend and redemption price of ₹ 110 and redemption period of 7 years.

(e) An ordinary share selling at a market price of ₹ 120 and current dividend of ₹ 9 per share which is expected to grow at 8%.

**Solution:**

(a)
$$k_p = \dfrac{PD + \left[\dfrac{P - NP}{n}\right]}{\dfrac{P + NP}{2}} = \dfrac{8.5 + \left[\dfrac{100 - 100}{5}\right]}{\dfrac{100 + 100}{2}} = 8.5\%$$

**Note:** The par value and net proceeds are presumed to be ₹ 100 each.

(b)      $k_d = [1 - t]R = [1 - .40].08 = .048$ or 4.8%

(c)
$$k_d = \dfrac{I + \left[\dfrac{P - NP}{2}\right]}{\dfrac{P + NP}{2}}$$

$$= \dfrac{80 + \left[\dfrac{1000 - 910}{2}\right]}{\dfrac{1000 + 910}{2}} = 13.09\%$$

This 13.08% is the pre-tax cost of debentures. The post-tax cost is calculated as follows:

$$k_d = [1 - .40].13.08 = 7.84\%$$

$$k_d = \dfrac{PD + \left[\dfrac{P - NP}{n}\right]}{\dfrac{P + NP}{2}}$$

$$= \dfrac{9 + \left[\dfrac{110 - 100}{7}\right]}{\dfrac{110 + 100}{2}} = \dfrac{10.43}{105} = .0993 \text{ or } 9.93\%$$

**Note:**      P = Redemption value, if redemption value is different from face value.

(e)      $k_e = \dfrac{D}{P} + g = \dfrac{9}{120} + .08 = .155$ or 15.5%

---

**Problem 7:**

A company has the following long-term capital outstanding as on 31st March 2015.

(a) 10% Debentures with a face value of ₹ 5,00,000, [₹ 1000 each] redemption period of 10 years.

(b) Preference shares with a face value of ₹ 4,00,000 annual dividend 12%, redemption period 10 years.

(c) 60,000 equity shares of ₹ 10 each, the market price is ₹ 50 per share and growth rate of 12% realised. Dividend per share ₹ 7.

Calculate weighted average cost of capital. Assume income tax rate as 40%.

## Solution:

Calculation of specific cost of capital:

(i)    Cost of Debentures    $k_d$ = $\dfrac{I + \left[\dfrac{P - NP}{n}\right]}{\dfrac{P + NP}{2}}$

$$= \dfrac{100 + \left[\dfrac{1000 - 1000}{10}\right]}{\dfrac{1000 + 1000}{2}} = \dfrac{100}{1000} = 10\%$$

Post-tax cost of debt  = $[1 - .40]\ .10 = 6\%$

(ii)   Cost of Preference Capital

$$k_p = \dfrac{PD + \left[\dfrac{P - NP}{n}\right]}{\dfrac{P + NP}{2}} = \dfrac{12 + \left[\dfrac{100 - 100}{10}\right]}{\dfrac{100 + 100}{2}} = 12\%$$

(iii)  Cost of Equity Capital

$$k_e = \dfrac{D}{P} + g = \dfrac{7}{50} + .12 = 26\%$$

Calculation of weighted average cost of capital:

| Sources of capital | Amount (₹) | Proportion in capital structure | Specific cost | Weighted average cost |
|---|---|---|---|---|
| Equity Capital | 6,00,000 | .40 | .26 | .104 |
| Preference Capital | 4,00,000 | .2667 | .12 | .032 |
| Debentures | 5,00,000 | .3333 | .06 | .0199 |
| | **15,00,000** | | | **.1559** |

Weighted average cost of capital = 15.59%

## Problem 8:

A company has the following specific cost of capital with the indicated book value and market value weights.

| Type of capital | Cost | Book value weight | Market value market |
|---|---|---|---|
| Equity | 18% | .40 | .58 |
| Preference shares | 15% | .30 | .17 |
| Long term debt | 7% | .30 | .25 |

(i)  Calculate the weighted average cost of capital.

(ii) Calculate the weighted average cost of capital, using marginal weights if the company intends to raise the needed funds using 50% long-term debt, 35% preference shares and 15% retained earnings.

## Solution:

### Weighted average cost according to book value weight

| Sources of capital | Weight [%] | Specific cost [%] | Weighted average cost [%] |
|---|---|---|---|
| Equity | .40 | .18 | .072 |
| Preference shares | .30 | .15 | .045 |
| Long term debt | .30 | .07 | .021 |
| | | | **.138** |

Weighted average cost = 13.8%

### Weighted average cost as per market value weight

| Sources of capital | Weight [%] | Specific cost [%] | Weighted average cost |
|---|---|---|---|
| Equity | .58 | .18 | .1044 |
| Preference shares | .17 | .15 | .0255 |
| Long term debt | .25 | .07 | .0175 |
| | | | **.1474** |

Weighted average cost = 14.74%

### Calculation of revised cost of capital

| Sources of capital | Weight [%] | Specific cost [%] | Weighted average cost |
|---|---|---|---|
| Long-term debt | .50 | .07 | .035 |
| Preference shares | .35 | .15 | .0525 |
| Retained earnings | .15 | .18 | .0270 |
| | | | **.1145** |

Weighted average cost = 11.45%

## Questions for Discussion

1. Define Leverage. What is operational leverage?
2. What is Cost of Capital?
3. Explain: Calculation of Cost of Capital.
4. Explain the various Theories of Capital Structure.
5. Explain the various Factors to be considered while Planning Capital Structure.
6. Describe the practical considerations in Dividend Policy.
7. Write short notes:
   (a) Dividend policy.
   (b) Forms of policy.
   (c) Forms of Dividend.
8. Explain:
   (a) Theories of Dividend.
   (b) Share Splits.

■■■

# CHAPTER 4

# Working Capital Management

## Contents ...

## 4.1 Principles of Working Capital: Concept, Needs and Determinants

### (A) Concept of Working Capital

The concept of working capital can be broadly divided into two categories: (a) Gross working capital (b) Net working capital

**(a) Gross working capital:** This concept implies the total of all current assets of a business firm. A current asset is that asset which can be converted into cash or into other current assets within an accounting year or an operating cycle.

Current assets include cash and bank balances, debtors, bills receivables, inventories, prepaid expenses and short-term investments.

**(b) Net working capital:** This concept of working capital is the difference between current assets and current liabilities. While current assets have been defined above, current liabilities can be explained as those liabilities which are expected to mature for payment within an accounting year and will be paid either out of existing current assets or by creating other current liabilities.

Current Liabilities include creditors, bills payable, outstanding expenses, bank overdraft and other short-term loans.

Net working capital can be positive or negative. If current assets exceed current liabilities, the difference is positive net working capital and when current liabilities exceed current assets, the difference is negative working capital.

Working capital is required to run the day to day activities of the business and hence it not only involves managing of current assets but also involves raising the amount of working capital required, through various sources including short-term and long-term sources.

Working capital can also be divided into categories:

(i) fixed working capital

(ii) fluctuating working capital.

Every business requires some minimum amount of working capital inspite of the level of operations, throughout the year. This amount represents the fixed amount of working capital.

In many business firms, the levels of operations fluctuate from time to time depending upon the demand pattern. In case, the demand picks up in a particular season, the need for working capital also increases and during low demand periods, the need for working capital also comes down. This aspect of working capital can be shown in a better way with the help of the following diagram.

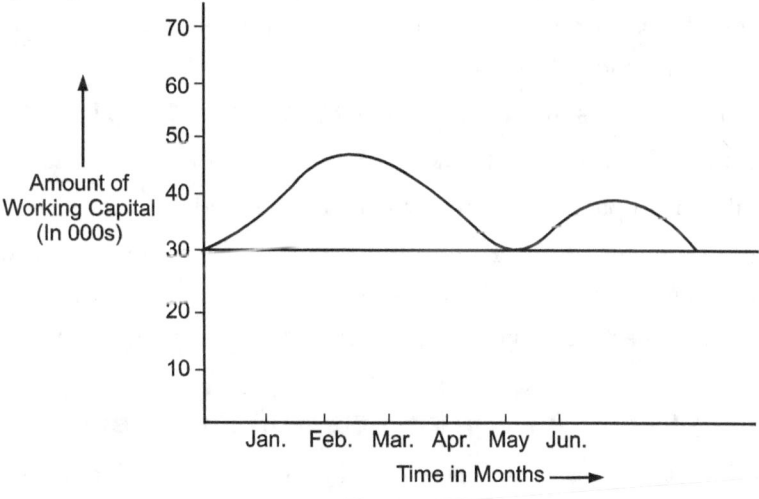

Fig. 4.1

The fixed amount of working capital also go on increasing as the time passes because of the growth of the firm. This can be shown in the following diagram.

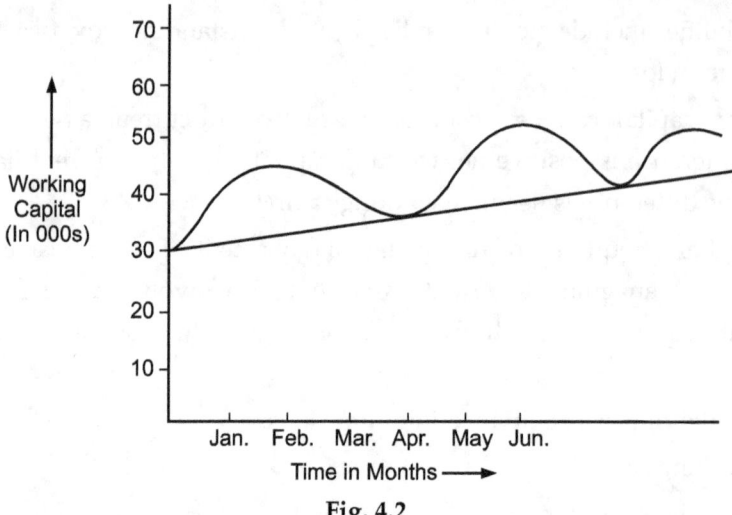

Fig. 4.2

## (B) Nature of Working Capital Management

Working Capital means current assets such as cash, accounts receivable and inventory and so on, minus the current liabilities. The management of current assets is as important as or rather more important than the management of fixed assets. This is because the fate of most of the business very largely depends upon the manner in which their working capital is managed.

The study of working capital management is incomplete unless we have an overall look on the management of current liabilities. Determining the appropriate level of current asset, current liabilities and of working capital involves fundamental decisions regarding firm's liquidity and the composition of firm's debts.

**There are two fold objectives of the Management of Working Capital:**

(a) Maintenance of working capital at appropriate level and,

(b) Availability of ample funds as and when they are needed.

In the accomplishment of these two objectives the management has to consider the composition of current assets pool. The working capital position sets the various policies in the business with respect to general operation, purchasing, financing, expansion and dividend etc.

## (C) Scope for Working Capital Management

(a) There is a positive correlation between the sale of the product of the firm and the current assets. An increase in the sale of the product requires a corresponding increase in current assets. It is therefore indispensable to manage the current assets properly and efficiently.

(b) More than half of the total capital of the firm is generally invested in current assets. It means less than half of the capital is blocked in fixed assets. We pay due attention to the management fixed assets through the capital budgeting process. Management of working capital too, therefore, attracts the attention of the management.

(c) In emergency (non-availability of funds etc.) fixed assets can be acquired on lease but there is no alternative for current assets. Investment in current assets, i.e., inventory or receivables can in no way be avoided without sustaining loss.

(d) Working capital needs are more often financed through outside sources so it is necessary to utilise them in the best possible way.

(e) The management of working capital is more important for small units because they scarcely rely on long term capital market and have an easy access to short term financial sources i.e. trade credit, short term bank loan etc.

(f) In the modern system approach to management, the operations of the firm are viewed as a total that is an integrated system. In this sense it is not possible to study one segment of the firm individually or leave it out completely. Hence an overall look on the management of working capital is necessary.

## (D) Need of Working Capital

(a)   To enable a company to meet its obligations.

(b)   To ensure the solvency of a company.

(c)   To ensure the credit standing of a company.

(d)   To facilitate obtaining credit from banks without difficulty.

## (E) Types of Working Capital

Various types of working capital are as discussed below:

(a) **Gross Working Capital:** Gross working capital is equal to total current assets only. It indicates the quantum of working capital available to meet current liabilities.

(b) **New Working Capital:** Net working capital is the excess of current assets over current liabilities. It is a qualitative concept.

(c) **Permanent Working Capital:** It is the minimum aggregate of cash, inventory and debtors maintained to carry on business operations smoothly at any time during an accounting period.

(d) **Temporary Working Capital:** It is also called as 'circulating working capital'. It is influenced by seasonal fluctuations of businesses concerned.

(e) **Special Working Capital:** This is the amount of working capital to meet unforeseen eventualities that may arise during the course of operations.

(f) **Regular Working Capital:** This is the amount of working capital required for the continuous operations of an enterprise.

## (F) Determinants of Working Capital

The working capital needs of a firm are affected by numerous factors. The important factors are as follows:

(a) **Nature of business:** In some business organisations, the sales are mostly on cash basis and the operating cycle is also very short. In these concerns, the working capital requirement is comparatively less. Mostly service giving companies come in this category. In some of the manufacturing concerns, usually the operating cycle is very long and a firm has to give credit to customers for improving sales. In such cases, the working capital requirement is more.

(b) **Production policy:** Working capital requirements also fluctuate according to the production policy. Some products have a seasonal demand but in order to eliminate the fluctuations in working capital, the manufacturer plans the production in a steady flow throughout the year. This policy will even out the fluctuations in working capital.

(c) **Market conditions:** Due to competition in the market, the demands for working capital fluctuate. In a competitive environment, a business firm has to give liberal credit to customers. Similarly, it will have to maintain a large inventory of finished goods to service the customers promptly. In this situation, larger amount of working capital will be required.

On the other hand, when a firm is in seller's market, it can manage with a smaller amount of working capital because sales can be made on cash basis and there will be no need to maintain large inventory of finished goods because customers can be serviced with delay.

(d) **Seasonal fluctuations:** A firm which is producing products with seasonal demands requires more working capital during peak seasons while the demand for working capital will go down during slack seasons. During the season, all activities such as production, purchase and sales are at their peak and hence the working capital need increases.

For example, a sugar factory has the crushing season from October to April and during this period all activities are in full swing. The need for working capital is high during this period. On the other hand, after the crushing season ends, level of different activities is reduced and hence the working capital requirements also come down.

(e) **Growth and expansion activities:** The working capital needs of the firm increase as it grows in terms of sales or fixed assets. A growing firm may need to invest funds in fixed assets in order to sustain its growth of production and sales. This will in turn increase investments in current assets which will result in increase in working capital needs.

(f) **Operating efficiency:** For any business organisation, resources available are always scarce and it is of paramount importance that they should be used with utmost care. Thus a firm's operations can be called as efficient if the scarce resources are used extremely effectively so that the productivity is highest and the cost is minimum. Due to the operational efficiency, the working capital is used efficiently and the need for it is reduced. On the other hand, the need for working capital will go on increasing if the operating efficiency cannot be achieved.

(g) **Credit policy:** The working capital requirements of a firm depend to a great extent on the credit policy followed by a firm for its debtors. A liberal credit policy followed by a firm will result in huge funds blocked in debtors which will enhance the need for working capital. The situation will be further deteriorated if the collection procedure is also slack. If a liberal credit policy is followed without inquiring into the credit worthiness of customers, there can be a problem of recovery in future which will further push up the working capital requirements.

The need for working capital is also affected by the credit policy followed by the firm's creditors. If the creditors are ready to supply materials and goods on liberal credit, working capital requirements are substantially reduced. On the other hand, if purchases are mainly for cash, working capital needs go up. While planning the working capital, due attention should be given towards the credit policies followed by the firm and its creditors.

(h) **Sales growth:** As the sales grow, the working capital needs also go up. Actually it is very difficult to establish an exact proportion of increase in current assets, as a result of increase in sales. Advance planning of working capital becomes essential because current assets will have to be employed even before growth in sales takes place.

Once sales start increasing, they must be sustained. For this a firm will have to expand its production facilities which will require more investments in fixed assets. This will in turn result in more requirements of current assets which will increase working capital needs.

(i) **Dividend policy:** A firm pays dividend out of profits earned by it. As per the provisions of the Companies Act 1956, if dividend is to be paid, it must be paid in cash and not in kind. This means that if a firm follows a liberal dividend policy, it will have to make provision for sufficient liquidity and it will result in increasing the need of the working capital. On the other hand, if the dividend policy is kept on conservative basis, the requirements of working capital will be lower.

## (G) Operating Cycle

The net working capital is the difference between current assets and current liabilities. A firm acquires current assets to convert them into cash so that the current liabilities can be satisfied. On the other hand, fixed assets such as land and building, plant and machinery etc.

are acquired with a long-term objective. The amount of capital invested in fixed assets is recovered after a long period of time. On the other hand, amount blocked in current assets is expected to recover as early as possible. The concept of operating cycle is based on this aspect.

The concept of operating cycle implies the time period that is required from the time cash is put in the business along with other inputs to the time it is recovered from the amount of sales made by the firm.

A firm puts cash as an input and the inputs like raw materials are purchased with the help of cash. The raw material is converted into finished product and for this additional cash may be required. The finished product is converted into sale and if the sale is made for cash, the operating cycle is complete as cash is recovered back. On the other hand, if sales are on credit, sales are converted into debtors and debtors are converted into cash.

The length of the operating cycle depends upon several factors. These factors are as follows:

**(a) Length of the manufacturing process:** If the manufacturing process is quite lengthy, the operating cycle will be prolonged. On the other hand, if the manufacturing process is of shorter duration, the length of the operating cycle will also be of a shorter duration.

For example, in case of hotels and restaurants, the manufacturing process is relatively short which reduces the duration of operating cycle. In case of heavy engineering industries, since the manufacturing process itself is very lengthy, the operating cycle also becomes very long.

**(b) Holding period of inventories:** On an average for how long the firm holds inventory is also one of the factors affecting operating cycle. If the firm holds inventory of raw material for a longer duration due to safety precautions, operating cycle is prolonged. Firms following hand to mouth policies regarding inventories of raw materials will have a shorter operating cycle.

Similarly, in case of work-in-process, if the time duration is long before being converted into finished product, operating cycle will be of a longer period. In case of finished goods inventory also, the same principle exists. If finished goods are quickly converted into sales, operating cycle will be shorter. But if finished goods inventory is not converted into sale quickly and liberal credit is extended to the customers, operating cycle becomes lengthy.

## (H) Working Capital Policy

The basic objective of working capital management is that there should be an optimum investment in working capital. There should not be either excessive working capital or shortage of working capital. In order to decide the optimum investment in working capital, there is a need to consider different policies of working capital. The different policies are discussed below:

**(a) Ratio of current assets to sales:** The current assets change as a result of changes in the sales. A firm has to decide about the proportion of current assets to be maintained in relation to sales. There can be aggressive, moderate or conservative current assets policies.

If an aggressive current assets policy is followed, a firm will maintain a very low level of current assets in relation to sales. On the other hand, a conservative policy implies carrying of a very high level of current assets in relation to sales. A moderate policy is a via media between the two extreme policies mentioned above and results into a moderate proportion of current assets to sales. The result of a conservative current asset policy is that the risk is reduced. The surplus current assets will ensure that the firm is able to cope up with fluctuation in sales as well as production. Besides this, the higher liquidity in this method will help in eliminating the risk of technical insolvency. However, profitability will have to be sacrificed in this method.

An aggressive current policy implies that there is a minimum investment in current assets in relation to sales. This means that the firm is taking greater risk. This method definitely ensures higher profitability but at the same time, it exposes the firm to greater risk of technical insolvency as well as lack of capacity to cope up unanticipated changes in market, changes in the market place and operating conditions. A moderate current asset policy tries to balance risk and profitability by keeping moderate level of current assets in relation to sales.

The various policies discussed above are shown in the following figure.

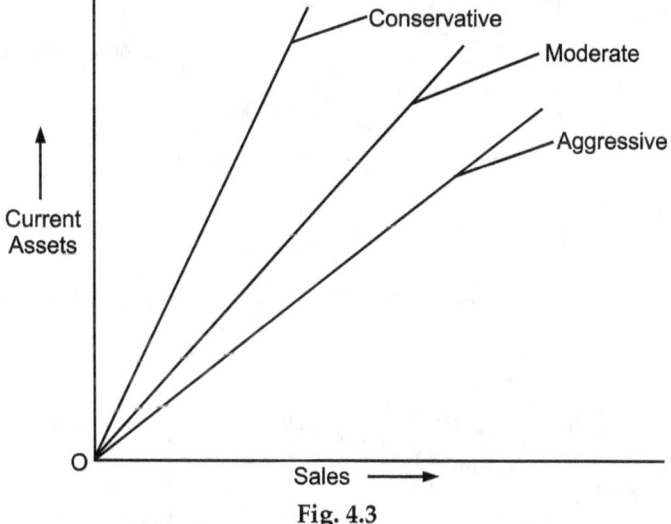

**Fig. 4.3**

**(b) Financing of current assets: Short term vs Long-term financing.** Another important question which a finance manager has to answer is that how to finance the current assets? What should be the mix of short term and long-term financing? There are two broad policy options i.e. (i) Conservative current asset financing policy and (ii) An aggressive current asset financing policy.

In conservative current asset financing policy, a firm relies more on long-term financing such as shares, debentures, preference shares, long-term debt and retained earnings. In this method, as the emphasis is on long-term financing, the firm has less risk of facing problems of shortage of funds.

An aggressive policy is said to be followed by a firm, when it relies heavily on short-term bank financing and other short term sources. Even some part of fixed assets is financed by short-term funds. The policy exposes the firm to a higher degree of risk but reduces the average cost of financing. Conservative current assets financing policy reduces the risk but has a higher cost of financing.

In addition to the above mentioned ways of financing, there is one more way which is called as hedging approach. In this approach long-term sources are used for financing fixed assets and permanent current assets while short-term funds are used for financing temporary or variable current assets. However, exact matching is not possible because of the uncertainty about the expected lives of the assets. The different approaches explained above are shown in the following figures.

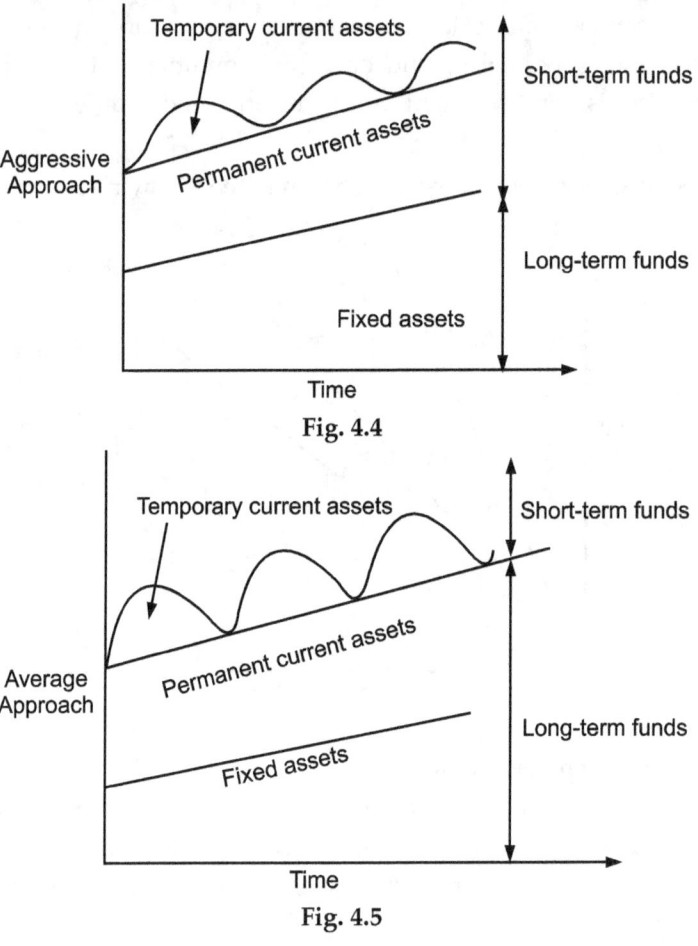

Fig. 4.4

Fig. 4.5

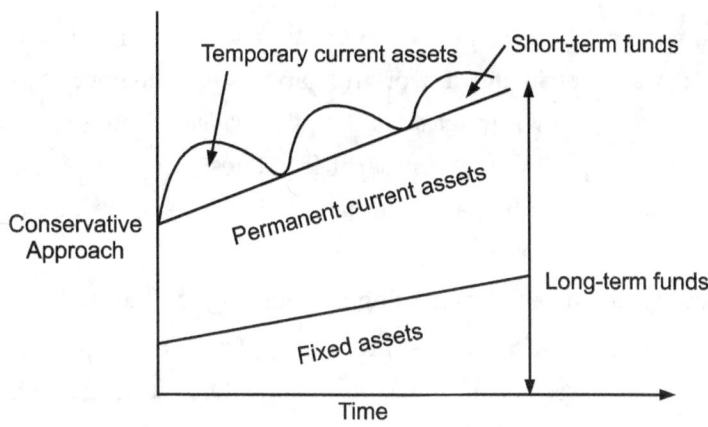

Fig. 4.6: Hedging Approach

(c) **Ratio of current assets to fixed assets:** A firm needs fixed assets and current assets to support a particular level of output. When level of output is increased, the level of current assets is increased but not in the proportion of the increase in output. A ratio of current assets to fixed assets indicates the level of current assets. This ratio is calculated by dividing current assets by fixed assets. Assuming a constant level of fixed assets, higher current assets to fixed assets ratio indicates a conservative current assets policy while a lower ratio indicates an aggressive current assets policy. This is illustrated with the help of the following figure.

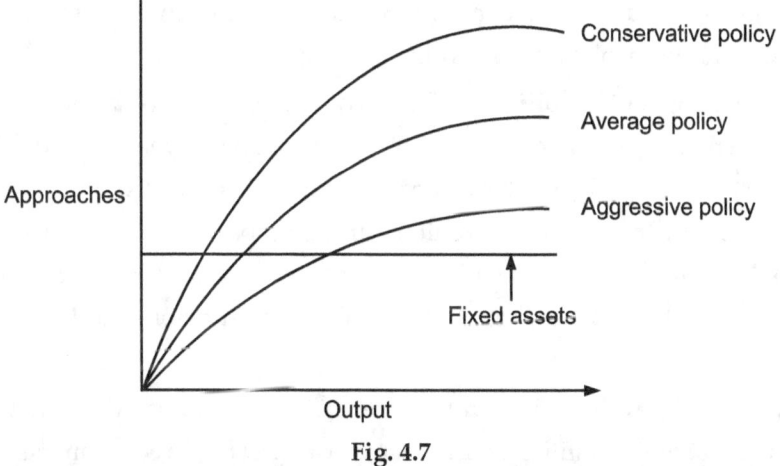

Fig. 4.7

## 4.2 Issues and Estimation of Working Capital

The excessive current assets result into higher amount of working capital which ensures safety but at the cost of profitability. On the other hand, if investment in current assets is reduced, it will lower the amount of working capital but there will be a greater risk accompanied by higher profitability.

A firm has to ensure a balance between the two and for doing this it is of paramount importance to prepare an estimate of working capital. A statement showing estimate of working capital is also known as *working capital budget*. The greatest advantage of preparation of working capital budget is that it facilitates planning of the level of holding current assets. Similarly, it also helps to compare the projected working capital and actual working capital.

The following steps are taken in predicting the working capital needs:

(a) **Estimating current assets:** In the prediction of working capital, it is essential to predict the current assets. Current assets include the following assets.

   (i)   Stock of raw materials, work-in-process and finished goods.

   (ii)  Sundry debtors.

   (iii) Any advance payment of expenses.

   (iv)  Cash and bank balances.

   For predicting the level of inventories, it is necessary to calculate the expected holding period of each type of inventory or stock. In case of debtors, on an average how much credit will be allowed to the debtors should be estimated. For advance payments it is necessary to estimate the amount that will have to be paid as advance. As far as cash and bank balance is concerned, how much amount the firm wants to hold as cash and bank balance should be estimated.

(b) **Estimating current liabilities:** The second step in estimating working capital requirement is to estimate the current liabilities. The current liabilities include trade creditors, bills payable, bank overdraft, expenses due but not paid and other short-term liabilities. In estimating creditors and bills payable, how much credit will be allowed by the creditors, should be estimated carefully. In case of other current liabilities, what will be expected, delay in the payment of such liabilities should be estimated.

(c) **Contingency margins:** The difference between estimated current assets and estimated current liabilities will be net working capital requirements. To be on the safer side of contingency margin of 10% to 15% may be added in the net figure calculated as per the above explanation.

In addition to the above mentioned points, any proposed additions in fixed assets should also be taken into consideration if it is going to affect the working capital position. Similarly, how far changes in sales are going to affect the level of current assets should also be taken into consideration.

The format of working capital budget is given below.

### Working Capital Budget

| Particulars | Amount [₹] | Amount [₹] |
|---|---|---|
| **[A] Current Assets:** | | |
| (i) Stock-in-trade | | |
| (a) Raw materials | | |
| (b) Work-in-process | | |
| (c) Finished goods | | |
| (ii) Debtors | | |
| (iii) Prepaid expenses | | |
| (iv) Cash and bank balance | | |
| Total [A] | | |
| **[B] Current Liabilities:** | | |
| (i) Creditors | | |
| (ii) Delay in payment of expenses | | |
| Total [B] | | |
| **[C] Net Working Capital:** | | |
| [A – B] | | |
| **[D] Add:** Contingency margin if any | | |
| **[E] Total working capital requirement** | | |

## 4.3 Accounts Receivable Management

## (A) Introduction

Any business organisation, which is in manufacturing sector or in a service sector uses two types of capitals – fixed and circulating or working capital. Fixed capital is the amount of capital, which is invested in fixed assets. Fixed assets are those assets, which are not acquired for resale. In other words, the fixed assets are used in the business for enhancing the earning capacity. Plant and machinery, land and building, furniture, vehicles are some of the examples of fixed assets. Working capital is the amount of capital, which is required for running the day-to-day business. This capital is also called as circulating capital and it is defined as excess of current assets over current liabilities.

There are two concepts of working capital – gross and net. *Gross working capital is the total amount invested in the current assets of the firm while net working capital is the difference between the current assets and current liabilities.* Current assets are those assets, which are acquired or created in the business with an intention of converting them into cash or other current assets. Inventories, Debtors, Bills Receivables, Short- term investments, expenses prepaid and cash and bank balance are examples of current assets. Current liabilities are the liabilities, which are expected to mature within a period of one year from the date of creation and are expected to be paid either out of existing current assets or by creating a new current liability. Trade creditors, bank overdraft, cash credits, expenses outstanding and bills payable are the examples of current liabilities. The difference between the current assets and current liabilities is known as net working capital as mentioned above.

If we analyse the components of current assets, it will be observed that a substantial part of current assets is in the form of 'Trade Debtors'. In case of several Indian companies, it has been noticed that the 'Trade Debtors', after inventories are the major components of current assets. Though this proportion may vary from industry to industry and also on firm- to- firm basis, it is a fact that nearly 25% of the current assets are in the form of Trade Debtors. This amount is blocked in the Trade Debtors and if proper control is not exercised the firm may face shortage of working capital and it may result in the firm being caught in the debt trap. The management of Trade Debtors, which is also called as 'Credit Management' thus becomes of paramount importance for any management. The basic principle of managing the Trade Debtors is the tradeoff between liquidity and profitability or in other words it is striking balance between too liberal credit and too conservative credit. The basic principles of a sound 'Credit Management' are discussed in detail in this chapter in the subsequent paragraphs.

## (B) Trade Credit – Background

Let us trace the origin of 'Trade Debtors' and find out the cause behind the creation of this current asset. If we try to peep into the transactions of sale of any business organisation, whether in manufacturing sector or in service sector, we will realise that sales are basically of two types. The first one is cash sale where the transaction is settled then and there only. In other words, goods or services are sold and the cash is recovered on spot. Thus neither there is any risk in such transactions nor there is any need for creation of records as the transaction is over then and there only. However, all the sales cannot be on cash as customers are bound to expect some credit facilities from the firm. If the firm is in the seller's market, it can dictate terms with its customers and can insist on cash sales only. However in the present day era of cut-throat competition, a firm has to offer credit facilities to the customers and thus the credit offered by the firm creates Trade Debtors. Thus the Trade Debtors are created due to the credit offered by the firm to its customers. Trade Debtors are also called as Sundry Debtors or Book Debts. Accounts Receivables is yet another term used to describe the debtors. However Accounts Receivables include both, debtors on open account as well as debtors who have accepted bill of exchange drawn by the firm. A bill of exchange is a negotiable instrument drawn by the firm and accepted by the debtor. It contains an unconditional order given by the creditor [the firm] to the debtor to pay a certain sum of money on a certain date to a certain person or to his order. Thus a debtor who has accepted a bill of exchange is considered to be safer than the debtor on open account. It should be noted that wherever the word 'Trade Debtors' or 'Sundry Debtors' or 'Book Debts' has been used, it means both, debtors on open account and also debtors who have accepted the bill of exchange. It is also to be noted that the amount of Trade Credit will go on increasing if a firm follows liberal credit policy and on the other hand if a conservative credit policy is followed, the Trade Credit amount will be naturally on the lower side. However if a very liberal credit policy is followed, a firm will have to take the risk of bad debts as well as excessive investments in the debtors though the amount of sales may show an upward trend. On the other hand, a conservative credit policy may improve the liquidity position but there is a risk of losing some of the market share to the competitors. Hence there is a need of a well- defined credit policy, which will ensure a tradeoff between a very conservative policy and a liberal policy.

## (C) Causes Behind Granting Credit

As mentioned in the above paragraph, debtors are the result of trade credit granted by the firm. A question may be asked, why the firms grant credit at all? What benefits they are expecting out of the trade credit in spite of the risks associated with the same? It will be interesting to see the causes behind granting trade credit by various firms. These causes are discussed in the following paragraphs.

(a) Credit is granted to the customers to face the growing competition successfully. The market world over is becoming highly competitive and offering credit to customers can be additional selling point for a firm. Hence to obtain a sustainable competitive advantage, firms grant trade credit.

(b) It has been observed that in several business segments, buyers as well as the dealers prefer granting of credit, as they themselves have to extend credit to their customers. In other words they will not be able to operate without credit being extended to them and hence firms have to grant credit to such buyers. Credits are also offered to build up long- term relationship with dealers.

(c) When a new product is introduced, it requires some push in the beginning to establish its self. In such cases, credits are offered as a marketing policy to customers to attract them.

(d) Industry practices also play an important role in the decisions regarding granting of credit. If it is a regular practice in an industry to grant credit to customers, a firm has to follow that policy otherwise there is a danger of loosing customers.

(e) A firm uses credit policy as a leverage for growth. A judicious credit policy will definitely help a firm to magnify its sales and this can lead to enhanced market share. Thus credit policy can be used as a tool for improving the growth.

# (D) Objectives of Credit Policy

There are benefits and drawbacks of liberal credit and conservative credit as well. Allowing extremely liberal credit or following a very conservative credit policy are the two extremes of any credit policy and hence the objective of the credit policy of any firm will be to have a tradeoff between too liberal and too conservative credit policy. Accounts Receivables [debtors] of a firm depend on two things, first the volume of credit sales and second the collection period or the credit period allowed to the debtors. Thus for example, if the daily credit sales of a firm are ₹ 15 lakhs and the average collection period is 30 days, the amount of investment in debtors will be ₹ 15 lakhs × 30 days = ₹ 450 lakhs. In other words, daily credit sales will be blocked for 30 days and hence the investments in debtors will be so high. In the light of this, it is necessary to have a well- defined credit policy and follow the same so that balancing between liberal credit and conservative credit will be possible. Credit policy of a firm involves decisions regarding the following.

(a) **Credit Standards:** These standards represent the basic criteria for the extension of credit to customers. The standards involve decisions regarding granting credit to the customers. The quantitative basis of establishing credit standards are factors such as credit rating, credit references, average payment periods and certain financial ratios such as current ratio, liquidity ratio and debt equity ratio.

(b) **Credit Analysis:** Apart from credit standards, a firm should also conduct credit analysis. Credit analysis involves developing procedures for evaluation applications for credit. In other words, when customers apply for credit, there should be some mechanism for evaluation of these applications. Credit analysis precisely means this thing. The basis of this evaluation is obtaining information about credit standing of customers through various available sources and processing the same for evaluation of credit.

(c) **Credit Terms:** A firm has to take decision about the credit terms that are allowed to the customers. Credit terms include the credit period, quantum of cash discount to be allowed as well as the period of cash discount. The cash inflows will depend to a large extent on credit terms and hence these aspects should be evaluated carefully before a final decision is taken.

(d) **Collection Policies:** These policies involve laying down procedures to collect account receivables after the credit period is over. The collection of receivables should be made promptly and for this, there should be proper collection policy.

The points mentioned above are discussed in the following paragraphs in detail.

(a) **Credit Standards:** Credit standards are the criteria, which a firm follows in selecting customers for the purpose of credit extension. An important question that is to be answered is, what standards of credit the firm should follow? Whether credit should be granted to anyone and everyone or whether we should be extremely choosy in granting credit? Actually there are two extreme policies regarding granting of credit, the first one is to grant credit to anyone who demands the same and the second one is not to grant credit to any one irrespective of their credit standing. Between these extreme policies, lies the middle path, which really decides the credit standards that are to be followed. Therefore it becomes of paramount importance that a firm should fix credit standards so that decision making will be easier.

In order to determine the credit standards, careful analysis of alternate standards should be made. It should be remembered that if the credit standards were extremely liberal, there would be an impressive growth in sales. However due to the liberal standards, there will be huge losses due to bad debts as several customers may commit default in payment. The cost of collection as well as the cost of holding the investment in Accounts Receivables will also go up. On the other hand, if credit standards are extremely strict, there will be loss of sales but there will be substantial reduction in the bad debts. The collection costs and also the cost of holding the investments in Accounts Receivables will also be less. Therefore the cost/benefit analysis of alternate credit standards should be conducted to find out incremental sales and incremental cost of relaxing standards. If this analysis is favourable to the firm, i.e. if the incremental sales are more than the incremental costs, relaxation will be beneficial to the firm otherwise not. Thus, the choice of optimum credit standards involves a tradeoff between incremental return and incremental costs.

(b) **Credit Analysis:** Besides establishing credit standards, it is necessary for a firm to develop procedures for evaluating the credit applications. Thus the second aspect of credit policies of a firm is 'credit analysis and investigation'. For taking decisions regarding the grant of credit the first step is to obtain the credit information about the customers and secondly analysing the information. Decisions regarding the grant of credit are taken after carefully analysing information gathered from various sources. These steps are explained below.

(I) **Gathering Credit Information:** Information about customers can be gathered from various sources. Sources of collecting information are mainly of two types.

(i) **Internal Sources:** Information about customers is collected by asking them to fill up various forms and documents. Thus information about their financial transactions can be collected. Customers may also be asked to furnish trade references, which can be cross-verified for obtaining credible information. In addition to these sources, a firm can also verify past records of customers with them, i.e. their past transactions with the firm can be verified to obtain this crucial information.

(ii) **External Sources:** In addition to the internal sources, a firm can use external sources for collecting information. External sources include financial statements of the customer's firm. Financial statements include Profit and Loss A/c and Balance sheet. These statements contain useful information and aspects like financial viability, liquidity, profitability, and solvency can be analysed. Though these aspect may not guarantee the future payments and also do not indicate the regularity of past payments, they can be useful in understanding the financial position of a firm. Another useful external source for collecting information is 'Bank References'. Information about the customer's financial position can be collected from the firm's bankers. Alternatively information about customer's financial position may be collected from the customer's bank. In addition, information can also be collected from specialist 'Credit Bureau Reports' from organisations specializing in supplying credit information.

(II) **Analysis of Credit Information:** After collecting information from various sources, the next step is to analyse the information. This is necessary to determine credit worthiness of the applicant. For analysing the information, the following methods can be used.

**Quantitative Methods:**

Under this method, use of quantitative methods is made for credit analysis. The following methods are used in this category.

- Ad hoc approach/ Numerical Credit Scoring: A firm may develop its own ad hoc approach of numerical credit scoring to determine the credit worthiness of the customers. Attributes assigned by the firm may be assigned weights depending on their importance and be combined to create an overall score or index. For example, a firm may list down desired attributes such as character, integrity, past record, profitability, and so on and weights may be assigned to each of this attribute. A total of these weights may be taken to decide the total score of the customer's firm and then a decision may be taken.

The following table shows the use of this procedure for assigning a rating index.

| Factor | Factor Weight | Rating 5 | Rating 4 | Rating 3 | Rating 2 | Rating 1 | Factor Score |
|--------|---------------|----------|----------|----------|----------|----------|--------------|
| Past Payment | 0.30 | | _/ | | | | 1.20 |
| Net Profit margin | 0.20 | | _/ | | | | 0.80 |

*contd. ...*

| | | | | | | | |
|---|---|---|---|---|---|---|---|
| Current ratio | 0.20 | | | _/ | | | 0.60 |
| Debt-equity ratio | 0.10 | | _/ | | | | 0.40 |
| Return on equity | 0.20 | _/ | | | | | 1.00 |
| Rating Index | | | | | | | 4.00 |

- **Simple Discriminant Analysis:** This is more objective method of analyzing customers. In this method a single discriminant factor is decided on the basis of which credit granting decision is taken. For example, empirical analysis may show that the ratio of earnings before depreciation, interest and taxes [EBDIT] to sales is a significant factor in discriminating between good and bad customers. The next step is to determine the cutoff point, which will distinguish between the good customers and bad customers. For this the good customers [paying] and bad customers [non paying] customers are arranged by the magnitude of EBDIT to Sales ratio. The next step will be selection of a cutoff point to divide the array into two parts with a minimum number of misclassification. The cutoff point is selected by visual inspection. The firm can consider granting credit to those customers who have the EBDIT to Sales ratio above the cutoff point.

- **Multiple–discriminant Analysis:** Credit worthiness of a customer depends on many factors that may interact with each other. This technique of multiple-discriminant analysis combines many factors according to the importance [weight] to be given to each factor and determines a composite score to differentiate good customers from bad customers. Altman, an expert financial analyst from USA, has developed and used a multiple discriminant analysis to predict bankruptcy of firms. His model is as given below.

$$Z = 0.012 \ [NWC/TA] + 0.014 \ [RE/TA] + 0.033 \ [EBIT/S] + 0.006 \ [MV/D] + 0.010[S/TA], \text{ where,}$$

$NWC$ = Net working capital

$TA$ = Total assets

$RE$ = Retained earnings

$EBIT$ = Earnings before interest and tax

$S$ = Sales

$MV$ = Market value of equity

$D$ = Book value of debt

On the basis of statistical analysis, Altman's model established a cut-off score of Z of 2.675, which means that firms with a score above 2.675 are financially strong while those below this score have a very high likelihood of becoming bankrupt.

**Example:** You are considering extending credit to firms X and Y, which have the following financial rations. What are their Z scores if you use Altman's model?

| Firms | NWC/TA | RE/TA | EBIT/S | MV/D | S/TA |
|-------|--------|-------|--------|------|------|
| Firm X | 20% | 10% | 7.5% | 360% | 2.8 |
| Firm Y | 16% | 12% | 6.5% | 210% | 2.5 |

Z score for firm X and Y is computed as under,

Firm X = Z = $0.012 \times 20 + 0.014 \times 10 + 0.033 \times 7.5 + 0.006 \times 360 + 0.010 \times 2.8 = 2.8155$

Firm Y = Z = $0.012 \times 16 + 0.014 \times 12 + 0.033 \times 6.5 + 0.006 \times 210 + 0.010 \times 2.5 = 1.8595$

As mentioned above, the cut off score of Z is 2.675; firm X is above the cut off score and hence credit may be extended to them. Firm Y has a score less than the cut off score and hence credit may not be extended to them.

The quantitative models mentioned above no doubt give objective results. However it should be remembered that these models are based on past data and hence can be misleading. Therefore a firm will have to use their judgment also in addition to the models described above.

Risk Classification Scheme: On the basis of information and analysis in the credit management process, customers may be classified into various risk categories. A simple risk classification scheme is shown in the following figure.

| Risk Class | Description |
|------------|-------------|
| 1 | Customers with no risk of default |
| 2 | Customers with negligible risk of default [default rate of less than 2%] |
| 3 | Customers with little risk of default [default rate between 2% and 5%] |
| 4 | Customers with some risk of default [default rate between 5 and 10%] |
| 5 | Customers with significant risk of default [default rate in excess of 10%] |

The risk classification scheme described above is one of the many risk classification schemes that may be used. Each firm would have to develop a risk classification scheme as per its need and requirements.

**Qualitative Methods:**

The quantitative methods described above should be supported by qualitative methods. These methods will include mainly subjective judgment and will mainly cover aspects relating to the quality of management. Hence quantitative methods should be supported by the qualitative methods also. The assessment of prospective customers can be done on the basis of the 'five C's of credit'

- **Character:** Willingness of the customer to honor his obligations
- **Capacity:** Ability of customer to meet credit obligations
- **Capital:** Financial reserves of the customer
- **Collateral:** Security offered by the customer
- **Conditions:** The general economic conditions that affect the customer.

## (E) Credit Terms

The stipulations under which a firm sells on credit to customers are called as 'Credit Terms'. These stipulations include I] Credit Period and II] Cash Discount. These are discussed in the following paragraphs.

**Credit Period:**

The length of time allowed to customers for payment for their purchases is known as credit period. It is generally stated in terms of a net date. For example, if the firm's credit terms are 'net 35', it is expected that the customers will repay the credit obligations not later than 35 days. Normally the factors influencing the credit period are industry practices, severity of competition and also the cash flow position of the firm. However a firm may allow higher credit period in order to push up the sales while it may tighten the credit period if customers are defaulting too frequently and bad debts loses are mounting up. If the credit period is increased, sales will increase, however the operating profits will go up only when the cost of extending the credit period is less than the incremental profits. If sales increase, increase in the investment in accounts receivables will also increase, which will result in increased cost of investment in accounts receivables. Thus extending credit period will be beneficial only when the incremental sales will be more than the increased cost. The following example will clarify the point.

**Illustration:** XYZ Ltd. is considering increase its credit period from net 35 to net 50. The firm's expected sales to increase from ₹ 120 lakhs to ₹ 180 lakhs and average collection period to increase from 35 days to 50 days. The bad debts loss ratio and collection costs ratio are expected to remain at 5% and 6% respectively. The variable costs of the firm are 85% of the sales, corporate tax rate is 35% and the required post tax return is 20%. What are the implications of this decision?

The implications of these decisions are shown below.

**Statement Showing Impact of Relaxation of Credit Policy**

| Particulars | Amount ₹ In Lakhs |
|---|---|
| 1.  Incremental Sales | 60.00 |
| 2.  Incremental Contribution 15% of sales | 09.00 |
| 3.  Incremental bad debts and collection costs | 06.60 |
| 4.  Incremental operating profit [2-3] | 02.40 |
| 5.  Incremental after tax operating profit [3-4] | 4.20 |
| 6.  Incremental investment in receivables * | 13.20 |
| 7.  Cost of investment in receivables | 2.64 |
| 8.  Net increase in operating profit | 4.20 – 2.64 = 1.56 |

The proposed relaxation in credit period is not advisable as it will result in reduction in operating profits.

* Incremental Investment In Receivables:

**Existing investments:** $35/365 \times$ ₹ 120 lakhs = ₹ 11.51 lakhs

Investments after increase in credit period: $50/365 \times$ ₹ 180 lakhs = ₹ 24.66 lakhs

Incremental investments = ₹ 13.15 lakhs

## Cash Discount:

A cash discount is reduction in the payment offered to customer in order to encourage prompt payment i.e. before the expiry of credit period allowed to customers. For example, if a firm sales on credit of ₹ 5 lakhs to customer 'A' on a credit of 30 days, it may offer a 2% cash discount if the payment is made within 15 days. Thus the customer may get motivated to make the payment before the due date in order to get a discount of 2%. A cash discount may be expressed as 2/15 net 30, which means that the customer can avail of the discount if he makes payment within 15 days and if he does not opt for the same, he can make the payment within 30 days.

Cash discount can be used effectively to increase not only the sales but also to expedite the payment. However before taking decision to allow cash discount, a firm will have to carefully think about the comparative costs and benefits of allowing cash discounts. The following illustration will clarify the point.

## Illustration:

Rachana Ltd. currently makes all sales on credit and offers no cash discount. It is considering a 2% cash discount for payment within 10 days. The firm's current average collection period is 60 days. Sales at present are 200000 units, selling price ₹ 30 per unit, variable cost per unit ₹ 20 per unit and average cost per unit is ₹ 25 at the current sales volume.

It is expected that the change in credit terms will result in increase in sales to 225000 units and the average collection period will fall to 45 days. However due to increased sales, increased working capital required will be ₹ 100000 [it does not take into account the effect on debtors] Assuming that 50% of the total sales will be on cash discount and 20% is the required return on investment, should the proposed discount be offered?

**Solution:** Statement Showing Effect Of Extending Cash Discount To Customers

| Particulars | Amount ₹ |
|---|---|
| Increased sales revenue [25,000 × ₹ 30] | 7,50,000 |
| **Less:** Variable cost [25,000 × ₹ 20] | 5,00,000 |
| Incremental contribution | 2,50,000 |
| **Add:** Saving in cost due to decrease in investment in debtors * | 29,167 |
| **Less:** Cost of additional working capital required ** | (20,000) |
| **Less:** Cost involved in cash discount *** | (67,500) |
| Profit | 1,91,667 |

It is advisable that the firm should extend cash discount to its customers as it will result into an incremental profit of ₹ 1,91,667.

* Savings in cost due to decrease in investment in debtors

Present investment in debtors [without cash discount]

$$= ₹ 2, 00, 000 × ₹ 25/ 6 \#$$

$$= ₹ 8, 33, 333$$

# 360 days/60 days average collection period = 6

**Cost of additional working capital = ₹ 1, 00, 000 × .20 = ₹ 20, 000

*** Cost involved in cash discount = 0.02 × 2, 25, 000 units × ₹ 30 × 0.5 = ₹ 67, 500

**Note:** In the above computation regarding the cash discount, it is given that 50% of sales will avail the cash discount and hence the same has been taken into computation.

**Collection Policies:** Collection policies refer to the procedures followed for collecting accounts receivables when they become due after the expiry of credit period. There is a need of a well-defined collection policy because all the customers do not pay the firm's dues in time. Hence the main object of the collection policy is to accelerate the collections. If a firm analyzes the accounts receivables, it will be observed that some customers are slow payers and these customers need follow up. This follow up is ensured through the collection policy. The regular collection ensures regular cash flows, keeps collection costs and bad debts within limits and maintains overall collection efficiency. Debtors are also kept alert and they tend to pay their dues promptly. The collection program of the firm, which is aimed at timely collections of receivables, may consist of the following.

- Monitoring the state of receivables.
- Despatch of letters to customers whose due date is approaching.
- Telegraphic and telephonic advice to customers around the due date
- Threat of legal action to overdue accounts
- Legal action against overdue accounts.

The following aspects should be kept in mind while fixing the collection policy.

(i)   There should be proper procedure laid down for collection. This procedure should be well defined and should be followed rigorously to ensure regular collections.

(ii)  The responsibility for collection and follow-up should be fixed explicitly. Depending upon the requirements, either a separate credit department may be established or this responsibility should be assigned to sales or accounts department. It is necessary to have a close co-ordination among various departments, especially sales and accounts. Accounts department maintains the credit record and information while past information and current transactions are recorded by the sales department.

(iii) Though collection procedures should be established firmly, individual cases should be dealt with on their merits. There is a possibility that some customers might be in temporary difficulty and may not be able to pay due to their tight monetary position. This may be due to reversionary conditions or other factors, which are beyond the control of the customer. Special consideration is required in such cases.

For accelerating collections, the firm should chalk out a policy of offering cash discount to customers. Cash discount is a cost to the firm for ensuring faster recovery of cash. Some customers fail to pay within the specified discount period, yet they may make payment after deducting discount. Such cases must be identified promptly and necessary action should be initiated against them to recover full amount.

**Illustration:**

A firm is contemplating stricter collection policies. The following details are available.

1.   At present, the firm is selling 36,000 units on credit at a price of ₹ 32 each, the variable cost per unit is ₹ 25 per unit while the average cost per unit is ₹ 29, average collection period is 58 days, and collection expenses amount to ₹ 10,000. Bad debts are 3%

2.   If the collection procedures are tightened, additional collection charges amounting to ₹ 20,000 would be required, bad debts will be 1%, the collection period will be 40 days, sales volume is likely to decline by 500 units.

Assuming a 20% rate of return on investments, what will be your recommendations? Should the firm implement the decision?

**Solution:**

(i)  Bad debts expenses:    Present plan: 3% of ₹ 11,52,000 = ₹ 34,560

Proposed plan: 1% of ₹ 11,36,000 = ₹ 11,360

Saving in bad debts expenses = ₹ 23,200

(ii)  Average collection period/average investment in receivables.

Present plan = 36,000 × ₹ 29/360/58 = ₹ 1,68,200

Proposed plan = [36,000 × ₹ 29] – [500 × ₹ 25] /360/40 = ₹ 1,14,611

Savings in average investments = ₹ 1,68,200 – ₹ 1,14,611 = ₹ 53,589

Assuming a 20% return, the firm will be able to earn ₹ 10718 on this saving.

(iii) Sales volume: since the sales volume will decline by 500 units, there would be a loss of ₹ 3,500 [500 × ₹ 7].

(iv) Additional collection charges ₹ 20,000.

(v)  Thus the total benefits from a tightening of the collection policy will be ₹ 33,918 [₹ 23,200 + ₹ 10,718 ] and the total cost will be ₹ 23,500 [₹ 3,500 + ₹ 20,000]. Therefore there would be a net gain of ₹ 10,418 [₹ 33,918 – ₹ 23,500]. It is advisable therefore for the firm to implement the proposed strategy.

## (F) Control Techniques

A firm has to constantly monitor and control its receivables to ensure the success of the collection efforts. Methods used for controlling and monitoring the receivables are:

(a)  Average Collection Period and

(b)  Aging Schedule and

(c)  Collection Experience Matrix.

These methods are discussed below in detail.

**(a)  Average Collection Period:** Average collection period is the average number of days required for collection of the amount of receivables. In other words, it indicates the number of days of credit granted to the customers. For computing the average collection period, debtors turnover is computed and from the debtors turnover, average collection period can be computed. The debtors turnover is computed as follows.

Debtors Turnover Ratio = Credit Sales/Average Accounts Receivables.

**Note:** Average Accounts Receivables means opening balance of accounts receivables plus closing balance accounts receivables divided by 2.

**Example:** Credit Sales of a firm are ₹ 25,00,000 for a particular period. The Accounts Receivables at the beginning of the period were ₹ 6, 00, 000 and at the close of the period were ₹ 7, 00, 000. The debtors' turnover will be,

Debtors' turnover  =  Credit Sales / Average Accounts Receivables

=  ₹ 25, 00, 000/ ₹ 6, 50, 000 * = 3.84 times or 4 times

* Average Accounts Receivables is computed as ₹ 6,00,000 + ₹ 7,00,000/2 = ₹ 6,50,000

Now the turnover of debtors' is 4 times, which indicates that the debtors are paying the money 4 times in a year. It means that the average collection period is 12/4 = 3 months.

The average collection period thus computed is compared with the firm's stated credit period to judge the efficiency of the collection efforts. For example, if the credit period of the firm is 60 days, then a collection period of 4 months, i.e. 120 days is not at all satisfactory.

It should be remembered that an extended credit period delays cash inflows, thus affecting the liquidity position of the company. Besides this, the chances of bad debts losses also increase. Thus the average collection period is a fairly good indicator of the quality of receivables as it indicates the speed of recovery.

However one of the limitations of this method is that it provides an average picture of collection experience and is based on aggregate data. Secondly it is susceptible to sales variations and the period over which sales and receivables have been aggregated.

**(b) Aging Schedule:** The aging schedule classifies outstanding accounts receivables at a given point of time into different age brackets. In other words, it breaks down receivables according to length of time for which they have been outstanding. An illustrative aging schedule is given below.

| Age Group [In days] | % of Receivables |
|---|---|
| 0-30 | 35 |
| 31-60 | 40 |
| 61-90 | 20 |
| Above 90 | 5 |

The above aging schedule indicates that 40% of the receivables are outstanding for 31-60 days while 5% of the receivables are outstanding for more than 90 days. Thus the aging schedule helps to identify the slow-paying customers and is extremely useful for understanding the pattern of payment of the receivables. For better control, it is necessary to compare the actual aging schedule with some standard one to determine whether the accounts receivables are within control or not.

**(c) Collection Matrix:** The average collection period and the aging schedule have traditionally been very popular measures for monitoring receivables. However they suffer from a limitation in that they are influenced by the sales pattern as well as by the payment behavior of the customers. If sales are increasing, the average collection period and the aging schedule will differ from what they would be if sales would have been constant. This holds even when the payment behavior of the customers remains unchanged. The reasons is quite simple, a greater portion of sales is billed currently. Similarly, decreasing sales leads to same results. The reason here is that a smaller portion is billed currently. Therefore in order to study the changes in the payment behavior of customers it is necessary to look at the pattern of collections associated with sales. This is illustrated in the following table.

## Collection Matrix

| % of Receivables collected during the | January Sales | February Sales | March Sales | April Sales | May Sales | June Sales |
|---|---|---|---|---|---|---|
| Month of sales | 13 | 14 | 15 | 12 | 10 | 9 |
| First following month | 42 | 35 | 40 | 40 | 36 | 35 |
| Second following month | 33 | 40 | 21 | 24 | 26 | 26 |
| Third following month | 12 | 11 | 24 | 19 | 24 | 25 |
| Forth following month | ----- | ------ | ------ | 5 | 4 | 5 |

The above matrix shows that credit sales during the month of January are collected as follows.

13% in January, 42% in February [the first following month], 33% in March [the second following month], and 12% in April [the third following month]

From the collection pattern, one can judge whether the collection is improving, stable or deteriorating. A secondary benefit of such an analysis is that it provides a historical record of collection percentages that can be useful in projecting monthly receipts for each budgeting period. Thus Collection Matrix is an extremely useful method of monitoring and controlling receivables.

# 4.4 Factoring

A firm has to strike a balance between too liberal credit and too strict credit policy. In case of a very liberal credit policy, the amount of sales will increase considerably but at the same time the cost of holding the investments and the amount of bad debts will increase substantially. If the credit policy is too strict and the firm is very much selective in granting credit, some amount of sales is bound to be lost. The ideal credit policy should be such that the difference between the benefits and costs is maximum. One thing which can be understood from the discussion is that granting of credit to the customers cannot be avoided. For surviving in the competitive environment, some credit facility to the customers is a must and it means that certain amount is locked in debtors or accounts receivable. A firm has to wait for some time before the amount is recovered. If there is some agency which can be given some relief to the firm by providing money immediately by purchasing the book debts, it will be most welcome for the firm. The factoring services concept was born out of this need only.

## (A) Nature of Factoring

As described above, granting credit to customers results into blocking of funds in accounts receivable. A factor purchases a book debt from the firm and makes instant payment to the firm. Later on the amount is recovered from the debtors by the factor. In the modern days, the factors also provide administrative support in credit collection and also other financial services. The procedure to be followed between the factoring company and the client depends upon the agreement between the two. Before purchasing the book debts, the factor may like to evaluate the credit worthiness of the customer and if he is satisfied, the book-debts will be purchased and cash payment will be made instantly. Information will have to be given to the customer that the payment is to be made directly to the factor. Purchasing the book debts of the client are the basic services provided by the factoring company. However, in addition to these services, a factoring company may provide services regarding credit administration to the clients. Under this a factor may offer full consultancy services to the clients regarding granting credit to the customers. Full details of the customer's accounts are maintained with factoring company and it facilitates the collection from customer. As stated earlier, advance even upto 80%, 90% against the book debts may be paid to the client and the risk of bad debts may also be assumed by the factoring company depending upon the agreement.

**(B) Types of Factoring**

The following are the types of factoring services available to the clients:

(a) **Full service non-recourse:** In this type of factoring, the factor assumes 100% of the risk involved in the collection of debtors. In other words, if some amount becomes bad, the factor bears this loss and the client gets the entire amount of book debts. Usually, 80 – 90% amount of the debtors is paid in advance to the clients and the balance on recovery. Since the customer gets full amount from the factor, this method is widely welcomed by the clients.

(b) **Full service recourse factoring:** Under this method, the risk of bad debts is not assumed by the factor. The client has to bear the loss on account of bad debts if any. Naturally, if 100% amount is advanced to the client and subsequently if there are bad debts, some amount will have to be refunded. This type of factoring is comparatively less risky from factoring company's point of view.

(c) **Bulk/Agency factoring:** This type of factoring is used as a method of financing book-debts. Under this method, the credit administration is maintained by the client himself and only advance is given either with or without recourse. Clients having efficient credit administration prefer this type of factoring.

(d) **Non-notification factoring:** Under this system the factoring company does not maintain the accounts of the customers. Similarly, the customers are not informed about assignment of their accounts to the factor. The factor collects the money through the client company with or without recourse. In other words, the factor performs all his functions without informing the client that he owns the book-debts.

## 4.5 Inventory Management

### (A) Introduction

One of the important constituents of current assets is the 'inventory'. In several business organisations, inventories account for nearly 50-60% if the total current assets of an organisation. The more the inventory, the more is the amount of funds locked in it and thus results in increase in the amount of the cost of the funds so locked up. Hence there is a need for effective management of the inventory so that the twin objectives of inventory management, i.e. minimizing the amount of investment in inventory and at the same time making sure that the production flow is not affected will be served. The various aspects of inventory management in the light of these objectives are discussed in detail in the following paragraphs.

### (B) Inventory – What is Included?

Inventories include the following:

(a) **Raw materials:** This is the material which is used for conversion into the finished product. For example, oil seeds will be raw material for the edible oil industry, cotton will be the raw material for the textile industry. Organisations purchase material after considering the production requirements and unused raw material at the end of a particular period, say at the end of an accounting year is the inventory of raw materials.

(b) **Work-in-progress:** At the end of an accounting year, there are some materials on hand which are neither fully raw, neither fully finished. Thus these material are in semi-finished stage and are called as work-in-progress.

(c) **Finished goods:** These are the finished goods remaining unsold at the end of a particular accounting period. The finished goods inventory ensures that the demand from the consumers is easily met and hence certain stock is required. However a large inventory of finished goods may indicate either sluggish demand or lack of demand.

(d) **Stores and spares:** Inventory also includes the stores and spares which are required for the running of machines. For example, stock of coolants, lubricating oil, spare parts of machinery etc are required to ensure that, they can be used in the repairs of the machinery.

### (C) Techniques of Inventory Control

The main objectives of inventory management are:

(a) To ensure that the investment in inventory is not too high. Thus overstocking of materials and other inventories should be avoided at any cost. This objective can be achieved by systematically reducing the level of inventory by careful planning of various activities. For example, the raw material inventory can be reduced by planning of the production and purchasing as per the exact production planning. The overstocking of material results in locking of funds and the business organisation may face shortage of working capital. For meeting the working capital needs, the firm may have to borrow and thus the interest cost will rise. There is a danger that the firm will be caught in the debt trap and it will be difficult to come out.

(b) Another objective of inventory management is ensure that the supply of raw material to the production departments is smooth and uninterrupted. As for the finished goods, the stock should be sufficient to meet the demand of the customers.

For achieving the above conflicting objectives, a number of techniques are available. These techniques are as follows.

## (D) Economic Order Quantity

One important question that is to be answered by the Purchase Manager is how much to purchase at any one time? In other words, how much quantity is to be ordered at any one point of time? Whether there are any costs associated with the ordering quantity apart from the purchase price? It will be noticed that there are costs attached to the ordering quantity. These costs are of two types, the first is the ordering cost and the other one is the carrying cost. We will discuss about these costs. Ordering cost is the cost of placing an order. In other words, it can be said that when an order is placed, the company has to incur certain costs at the time of order. These costs include costs like handling and transportation costs, stationery costs, costs incurred for inviting quotations and tenders etc. The more is the frequency of order, the more are these costs.

On the other hand, there are certain costs that are called as carrying costs. The cost of carrying the inventory is the real out of pocket cost associated with having inventory on hand, such as warehouse charges, insurance, lighting, losses due to handling, spoilage, breakage etc, and another important component of carrying cost is the amount of interest lost due to the investment in the inventory. Carrying costs will go on increasing if the quantity of material in inventory goes on increasing.

Both, the carrying costs and the ordering costs are variable costs, however their behavior is exactly opposite of each other. It orders are more frequent, ordering costs will go on increasing but as the material ordered will be in less quantity, the carrying costs will decrease. On the other hand, if number of orders are reduced, the quantity per order will increase and the carrying cost will increase. The ordering cost will come down due to reduction of number of orders.

In this situation, the most desirable quantity to be ordered is that quantity at which both, the ordering costs and carrying costs will be minimum. This quantity is called as 'Economic Order Quantity'. This quantity can be calculated with the help of the following formula.

Economic Order Quantity $= \sqrt{2CO/I}$

Where,                          C = Annual consumption,

O = Ordering cost

I = Carrying cost

The Economic Order Quantity is an important concept as it guides the Purchase Manager regarding the quantity to be purchased of a particular material. However this concept is based on some assumptions. These assumptions are as follows.

- The concerned material will be available all the time without any difficulty.
- The price of the material will remain constant.
- Ordering cost and carrying costs are variable.
- Impact of quantity discounts on the prices is negligible.

## (E) Fixation of Level

Another important aspect of material procurement is not to purchase too much or too little. Similarly the timing of the purchase is also important. Fixation of levels of materials is done precisely with these objectives in mind. The following levels of materials are fixed for achieving objectives like avoiding overstocking, ensuring that the material is ordered at right time and also avoiding shortage of materials.

(a) **Maximum Level:** This is the highest level of material beyond which the inventory of material is not allowed to rise. Obviously this level is fixed with the objective of avoiding overstocking. This level is fixed after taking into consideration the consumption of material and the re-order period. Mathematically the level is fixed as under.

**Maximum Level =Re-order Level + Re-order Quantity –**

**[Minimum Consumption × Minimum Re-order period]**

(b) **Minimum Level:** This level is fixed with the objective of avoiding shortage of material. If production is held up due to shortage of material, there will be huge loss to the company. In order to avoid this, the minimum level is fixed. Care is taken that the stock do not fall below this level. The minimum level is fixed in the following manner.

**Minimum Level = Ordering Level –**

**[Average rate of consumption × Re-order period]**

(c) **Re-order Level:** This level is fixed for deciding the time of placing an order. If the stock of materials reaches this level, fresh order is placed so that by the time the material is procured, the level of material may fall up to minimum level but not below that. This level is fixed in the following manner.

**Re-order Level  =  Maximum Usage per Period × Maximum Re-order Period**

**(d) Average Level** = This level is the average of the maximum and minimum level and computed in the following manner.

**Average Level  =  Maximum Level + Minimum Level / 2**

**(e) Danger Level** = Generally the danger level of stock is indicated below the safety or minimum stock level. Sometimes, depending on the practices of the firm and circumstances prevailing, the danger level is determined between the re-order level and minimum level.

## (F) Perpetual Inventory System

Perpetual Inventory system means continuous stock taking. Chartered Institute of Management Accountants (CIMA) defines perpetual inventory system as *'the recording as they occur of receipts, issues and the resulting balances of individual items of stock in either quantity or quantity and value'*. Under this system, a continuous record of receipt and issue of materials is maintained by the stores department and the information about the stock of materials is always available. Entries in the Bin Card and the Stores Ledger are made after every receipt and issue and the balance is reconciled on regular basis with the physical stock. The main advantage of this system is that it avoids disruptions in the production caused by periodic stock taking. Similarly it helps in having a detailed and more reliable check on the stocks. The stock records are more reliable and stock discrepancies are investigated and appropriate action is taken immediately.

## (G) ABC System

In this technique, the items of inventory are classified according to the value of usage. Materials are classified as A, B and C according to their value.

Items in class 'A' constitute the most important class of inventories so far as the proportion in the total value of inventory is concerned. The 'A' items constitute roughly about 5-10% of the total items while its value may be about 80% of the total value of the inventory.

Items in class 'B' constitute intermediate position. These items may be about 20-25% of the total items while the usage value may be about 15% of the total value.

Items in class 'C' are the most negligible in value, about 65-75% of the total quantity but the value may be about 5% of the total usage value of the inventory.

The numbers given above are just indicative, actual numbers may vary from situation to situation. The principle to be followed is that the high value items should be controlled more carefully while items having small value though large in numbers can be controlled periodically.

## (H) Just In Time Inventory

This is the latest trend in inventory management. This principle envisages that there should not be any intermediate stage like storekeeping. Material purchased from supplier should directly go the assembly line, i.e. to the production department. There should not be any need of storing the material. The storing cost can be saved to a great extent by using this technique. However the practicality of this technique in Indian conditions should be verified before practicing the same. The benefits of Just In Time system are as follows,

(a) Right quantities are purchased or produced at right time.

(b) Cost effective production or operation of correct services is possible.

(c) Inventory carrying costs are eliminated totally.

(d) The stores function is eliminated and hence there is a considerable saving in the stores cost.

(e) Losses due to breakage, wastage, pilferage etc are avoided.

## (I) VED Analysis

This analysis divides items into three categories in the descending   order of their criticality as follows.

(a) 'V' stands for vital items and their stock analysis requires more attention. The reason is that if these items are not available, the resulting stock outs will cause heavy losses due to stoppage of production. Thus these items are required to be stored adequately to ensure smooth operation of the plant.

(b) 'E' means essential items. Such items are considered essential for efficient running but without these items, the system will not fail. Care must be taken to see that they are always in stock.

(c) 'D' stands for desirable items, which do not affect production immediately but availability of these items will lead to more efficiency and less fatigue.

(d) Thus VED analysis can be very useful to capital intensive process industries. As it analyses items based on their importance and it can be used for those special raw materials which are difficult to procure.

## (J) FSND Analysis

Age of the inventory indicates the duration of inventory in the organisation. It shows the moving position of inventory during the year. This analysis divides the items of inventory into four categories in the descending order of their usage rate as follows.

(a) 'F' stands for fast moving items and stocks of such items are consumed in a short span of time. Stock of fast moving items must be observed constantly and replenishment orders be placed in time to avoid stock out position.

(b) 'S' indicates slow moving items, existing stock of which would last for two years or so. These items must be reviewed carefully before eliminating them.

(c) 'N' means normal moving items and such items are exhausted over a period of time, i.e. say one year. The order levels and quantities for such items should be on the basis of a new estimate of future demand to minimise the risks of a surplus stock.

(d) 'D' stands for dead stork which means that there will not be any further demand for the same. It is necessary to identify these items and if there cannot be any alternative use for the same, should be eliminated.

## (K) Inventory Turnover Ratio

There are several items in the store which are slow moving which means that they are issued to the production after a long time gap. Some items are such that they are never issued to the production as they have become obsolete or outdated and need to be disposed off. For identifying these items, it is necessary to compute the inventory turnover ratio. Inventory turnover ratio enables the management to avoid the capital being locked in such items. This ratio indicates the efficiency or inefficiency with which inventories are maintained. Inventory turnover ratio is calculated in the following manner.

| **Inventory Turnover Ratio:** Cost of material consumed/Cost of average stock held during the year |
| --- |

The cost of average stock here is taken as the average of opening stock and closing stock. The inventory turnover ratio can also be calculated in days as below.

**Days during the period / Inventory turnover ratio**

Detection of Slow Moving and Non Moving or Obsolete Materials: It is essential for any business unit to detect slow moving and non moving or obsolete materials. Obsolete materials become useless or obsolete due to change in the product, process, design or method of production. Obsolete materials are different from slow moving materials and non- moving materials. Slow moving materials move at a slow rate. In the case of slow moving materials as well as non moving materials, capital remains blocked unnecessarily and also cost of storing continue to be incurred of these materials are kept in the store in excess of the requirements. Management should make proper investigations into slow moving and obsolete materials and try to minimise the capital investments in the same. It is necessary to have an efficient Management Information System which will enable to generate regular reports to examine the situations relating to these stocks so that the non moving and obsolete stocks can be disposed off in time.

**Conclusion**: Thus it can be seen that there are various tools and techniques that can be used to achieve the objectives of inventory management. By effectively controlling the level of inventory, a business organisation can manage the working capital effectively

## 4.6 Cash Management

Cash is the most liquid asset in any business. It is a very crucial asset in the day-to–day operations of a business firm. Cash is the basic input required to run the business continuously and at the same time it is also the ultimate output expected to be realised by selling the service or product manufactured by the firm. A firm has to strike a balance between maintaining a very high cash balance and a very small amount of cash balance. If excessive cash balance is maintained, the excess cash will remain idle affecting the profitability of the business adversely. On the other hand, if too small amount of cash balance is maintained, it will lead to shortage of cash resulting into disruption of manufacturing operations of a business firm. Therefore, the major aspect of cash management is to keep a proper cash balance.

The term cash with reference to cash management is used in two senses. In a narrow sense, it is used broadly to cover cash [currency] and generally accepted equivalent of cash such as cheques, bank drafts and demand deposits in banks. The broader view of cash also includes 'near–cash assets' such as marketable securities and time deposits in banks. The main characteristic of these assets is that they can be readily sold and converted into cash. They also provide a short-term investment outlet for excess cash and are also useful for meeting planned outflow of funds.

Cash management thus is concerned with, the managing of,

(a) Cash flows into and out of the firm.

(b) Cash flows within the firm.

(c) Cash balances held by the firm at a point of time by financing deficit or investing surplus cash.

The management of cash assumes more importance because of the difficulties experienced in predicting cash flows, especially inflows. During some periods cash flows will be extremely erratic. It is also possible that at times cash outflows will exceed cash inflows while during some periods cash inflows will be quite higher than cash outflows. Due to these factors, considerable time of the management is to be devoted to cash management even though cash constitutes a small portion of the total current assets of the firm. This section, therefore, is divided into sections which are as follows:

**(A) Objectives of holding cash:**

A business firm needs cash for the following three objectives or motives.

(a) **Transactions motive:** There are several transactions like purchases, sales, payment of expenses, wages and salary payments etc., taking place in the day-to-day business operations. For these transactions a firm needs cash. However, if there is perfect synchronisation between cash inflows and cash outflows, there would not be any need for maintaining cash. But in practise, this synchronisation is hardly possible. Therefore whenever cash payments exceed cash receipts, cash balance is to be maintained for meeting the payments. A firm may invest surplus cash in marketable securities, so that necessary cash can be available by disposing off these securities whenever required.

**(b) Precautionary motive:** A business firm may face an emergency situation in future. In order to meet this situation in future, some cash may be held. The cash balance held will work as a cushion or buffer to face the unexpected emergency. If cashflows of the future can be predicted with reasonable accuracy, less cash balance will have to be maintained. Similarly, if the firm can borrow from outside the cash required, large amount of cash need not be maintained. The cash maintained for such purpose can be invested in high liquid and low risk marketable securities.

**(c) Speculative motive:** If cash is held to take advantage of profit-making opportunities arising out of changes in the value of securities, the cash holding is called speculative holding of cash. The firm may also speculate on materials prices. If it is expected that material prices will fall in the future, the firm may purchase materials in the future by postponing the purchases at present.

## (B) Cash Planning and Forecasting:

**(a) Cash planning:** It is quite possible that a business may suffer from shortage of cash inspite of satisfactory profits. On the other hand there may be surplus cash available remaining idle and thus affecting profitability adversely. These situations arise due to either poor planning of cash or no planning at all. Therefore, proper cash planning becomes absolutely necessary for any business. Cash planning is nothing but estimating future cash flows with reasonable accuracy. This helps in avoiding cash shortages as well as reduce the excessive cash balance by investing surplus cash. Cash planning can be done for short term, medium term or long term depending on the requirements of the firm. A cash planning can be for as short period as one week. A monthly cash planning, however, is more commonly followed.

**(b) Forecasting of cash:** Cash budgeting or cash forecasting is the principal tool of cash planning as well as of cash management. A cash budget is a statement showing expected cash inflows and outflows for a specific future period. A cash budget can be prepared for a period of one year which is broken down to a budget for each month. The cash budget can also be prepared on weekly or even on daily basis. Generally, cash budgets upto one year is a short-term forecasting while if it exceeds one year, it is a long-term forecasting.

## Short-term Forecasting:

The short-term cash forecasting, as explained above is in the form of cash budgets. Cash budgets are extremely helpful in (a) estimating cash require-ments, (b) planning of short–term financing, (c) planning capital expenditure, (d) planning of purchasing materials and (e) developing credit policies.

The mostly used methods of short-term forecasting or cash budgeting are as follows. (a) The Receipts and Payments method and (b) The adjusted net income method.

**(a) The Receipts and Payments Method:** In this method the receipts and payments are anticipated for a specific future period and the difference between the two is the expected cash balance at the end of that period. Both types of receipts i.e. revenue and capital are estimated while both types of payments i.e. revenue and capital are estimated. The basis of estimation of each item depends upon the nature of that item. e.g. Cash sales are dependent on estimated sales and its division between cash and credit sales while the payment for purchases depends on estimated purchases and its division between cash and credit purchases. The following illustration will clarify the method of preparation of this budget.

**Illustration 1:**

Summarised below are the income and expenditure forecasts for the months of March to August 2015.

| Month | Sales (₹) | Purchases (₹) | Wages (₹) | Overheads (₹) |
|-------|-----------|---------------|-----------|---------------|
| March | 60,000 | 36,000 | 9,000 | 10,000 |
| April | 62,000 | 38,000 | 8,000 | 9,500 |
| May | 64,000 | 33,000 | 10,000 | 11,500 |
| June | 58,000 | 35,000 | 8,500 | 9,000 |
| July | 56,000 | 39,000 | 9,500 | 9,500 |
| August | 60,000 | 34,000 | 8,000 | 8,500 |

You are requested to prepare the cash budget for three months starting on May 1st, 2015 in view of the following information.

1. Cash balance as on 1st May, 2015: ₹ 8,000.

2. Sales and purchases are all on credit.

3. Plant costing ₹ 16,000 is due for delivery in July, 2015, payable 10% of delivery and the balance after 3 months.

4. Advance tax instalments of ₹ 8,000 each are payable in March and June.

5. The period of credit allowed by suppliers is 2 months and allowed to customers is 1 month.

6. Lag in payment of all expenses is one month.

**Solution:**                                   **Cash Budget ......**

**Period: May – July 2015**

| Particulars | May (₹) | June (₹) | July (₹) |
|---|---|---|---|
| [A] Opening cash balance | 8,000 | 16,500 | 13,000 |
| [B] Expected cash receipts | | | |
|    (i) Credit sales | 62,000 | 64,000 | 58,000 |
| [C] Total cash available [A + B] | 70,000 | 80,500 | 71,000 |
| [D] Expected cash payments: | | | |
|    (i) Wages | 8,000 | 10,000 | 8,500 |
|    (ii) Overheads | 9,500 | 11,500 | 9,000 |
|    (iii) Purchases | 36,000 | 38,000 | 33,000 |
|    (iv) Purchase of plant | – | – | 1,600 |
|    (v) Advance tax | – | 8,000 | – |
| [E] Total payments | 53,500 | 67,500 | 52,100 |
| [F] Closing balance [C – E] | 16,500 | 13,000 | 18,900 |

**(b) Adjusted Net Income Method:** In this method, there are three sections: sources of cash, uses of cash and the adjusted cash balance. In the preparation of this statement, items like dividends, depreciation, net profit etc. can be easily understood from financial statements. Major difficulties may be faced in estimating working capital requirements and changes. Ratio's relating to sales and receivables can be used conveniently to predict these changes. The major benefit of this method is that it keeps a control over working capital and anticipating financial requirements.

**Long-term Cash Forecasting:**

The long-term forecasts of cash may be for a period of 2 yrs, 3 yrs or even for five years. These forecasts are prepared to give an idea about the financial requirements of the firm in the distant future. A firm requires finance for new product development as well as introduction of new product, purchase of new plant and machinery and other such needs arising in the future. The long-term cash forecasting helps the firm to make necessary provision of cash for these requirements.

Long-term cash forecasts may not be in as much details as short-term cash forecasting. But it definitely helps in improving corporate planning as well as evaluation of capital expenditure proposals.

**(C) Monitoring collections and disbursements:**

To enhance the efficiency of cash management, collections and disbursements must be properly monitored. The following factors are of considerable importance in this respect.

(a) **Efficient and prompt collections:** The collections from customers should be as prompt as possible. For this purpose the bills for goods sold should be sent as promptly as possible. Similarly cash collections can be accelerated by reducing the gap between the time and customer pays the bill and the cheque is collected and funds become available for the use of the firm. In addition to quick handling of cheques a firm receiving remittances by cheques from different parts of the country can decentralise its collections and reduce the delay in the conversion of cheques into cash. The customers may be asked to send their remittances to the regional or local offices rather than to the head office. The regional office of the bank may be asked to transfer the excess cash balance after keeping minimum cash balance in the regional office, to the head office. Periodic checking of these transactions will be helpful in ensuring smooth functioning of this system.

(b) **Control of payables:** As far as payables are concerned, it should be ensured that the payments should be done only when they are due. The payables and their disbursements can be centralised. Delaying disbursements results in maximum availability of cash. However, care should be taken that the credit worthiness of the firm is not adversely affected by such delayed disbursements.

**Playing the float:** The technique of playing the float can be very usefully applied. When the firm's actual bank balance is greater than the balance shown by the firm's books, the difference is called as 'payment float.' The difference between the total amount of cheques drawn on a bank account and the balance shown on bank's books is caused by transit and processing delays. If the financial manager can accurately estimate when the cheques issued will be deposited and collected, he can invest the 'float' during the float period to earn a return.

**(D) Maintaining optimum cash balance:**

In the above paragraphs, cash forecasting as well as controlling of cashflows are discussed. Another important aspect of cash management is to maintain an optimum cash balance which will be neither excessive nor in short. The question that arises is how to arrive at this balance? Which factors should be considered in determining the optimum cash balance?

To answer these questions, two models of optimum cash balance are discussed in the following paragraphs:

(a) **Baumol Model:** The model proposed by William J. Baumol is similar to the economic order quantity concept in inventory management. Baumol suggests that two types of costs are associated with the cash balance. The first type of cost is the transaction cost which is incurred when marketable securities are converted in cash. The second type of cost is the holding cost which is nothing but income foregone due to holding of cash balance. Both these costs are variable in nature but if one cost is reduced, the other type of cost will increase and vice versa. For example: if large cash balance is maintained, the transaction costs will be reduced while holding costs will increase and on the other hand if minimum cash balance is maintained, holding costs will be reduced while transaction costs will shoot up. The optimum size of cash balance will be reached when the total cost is minimised.

The optimum size of the cash balance can be found out either by preparing tables or the following formula can also be used for that purpose.

$$C = \sqrt{\frac{2bT}{I}}$$

where

| | | |
|---|---|---|
| C | = | optimum cash balance, |
| b | = | requirement of cash |
| T | = | Transaction costs |
| I | = | Interest |

**(b) Miller–Orr Model:** As per this model there are upper control limits and lower control limits. The cash balance at any point of time is not allowed to go above the upper control limit while it is not allowed to fall below the  lower control limit. In between these two levels, there is a 'returning point'. Upward changes in cash balances are allowed till the cash balance reaches the upper control limit as shown in the following figure. As this level is reached, the cash balance is reduced to the 'returning point' by investing in marketable securities. On the other hand, the downward changes are permitted till the cash balance is reached the lower control limit and once it touches that, enough marketable securities are disposed off to restore the cash balance to return point.

The following figure will explain this point.

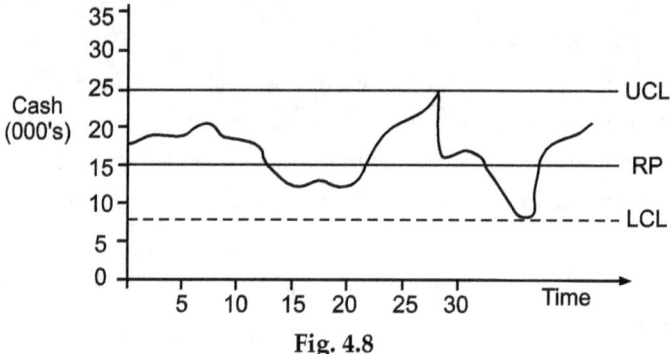

Fig. 4.8

**(E) Cash Budget**

   A Cash Budget is an estimate of the receipts and payments for each month or other period forming part of the whole budget period. It is essential to allow for the time-lag between certain transactions and the receipt or payment of the relative cash. The necessity and consequently, the objective of cash budget is to ensure that sufficient cash is available for both the revenue and capital expenditure to indicate when additional finance is required and how much and to show any expected surplus funds which may be invested profitably outside the business.

**Important Functions of Cash Budget:**

- To ensure that sufficient cash is available when required.
- To reveal any expected shortage of cash whether long-term or short-term.
- To reveal any expected surplus of cash, whether long term or short-term.
- To preserve the liquidity.
- To reveal the seasonal requirements such as payment of 'Income-Tax'.
- To assist in sound-investment policy.
- To indicate the availability of cash discounts.
- To indicate the availability of funds for replacement of assets, additions to assets, expansion schemes, new schemes, modification of existing plant etc.

**(F) Performa (Cash Budget)**

|  | | Jan. | Feb. | Mar. | April | May | June | July | Aug. | Sept. | Oct. | Nov. | Dec. |
|---|---|---|---|---|---|---|---|---|---|---|---|---|---|
|  | | (₹) | (₹) | (₹) | (₹) | (₹) | (₹) | (₹) | (₹) | (₹) | (₹) | (₹) | (₹) |
| (A) | Op. Cash Bal.: | | | | | | | | | | | | |
| (B) | Cash Receipts | | | | | | | | | | | | |
| | (i)   Cash Sales | | | | | | | | | | | | |
| | (ii)  Collection from Debtors | | | | | | | | | | | | |
| | (iii) Sale of Fixed Assets | | | | | | | | | | | | |
| | (iv)  Collection from B/R | | | | | | | | | | | | |
| | (v)   Loan from Banks | | | | | | | | | | | | |
| | (vi)  Interest on Investments | | | | | | | | | | | | |
| | (vii) Issue of Shares | | | | | | | | | | | | |
| | (viii) Issue of Debentures | | | | | | | | | | | | |
| | [Receipts (A) + (B)] | | | | | | | | | | | | |
| (C) | Cash Payments: | | | | | | | | | | | | |
| | (i)   Cash Purchases | | | | | | | | | | | | |
| | (ii)  Payment of Suppliers | | | | | | | | | | | | |
| | (iii) B/P Payment | | | | | | | | | | | | |
| | (iv)  Payment of Exps. & Taxes | | | | | | | | | | | | |
| | (v)   Payment of Dividend | | | | | | | | | | | | |
| | (vi)  Interest on Loans | | | | | | | | | | | | |
| | (vii) Purchase of Fixed Assets | | | | | | | | | | | | |
| | (viii) Payment of Loans | | | | | | | | | | | | |
| | Total Payments (C) | | | | | | | | | | | | |
| | Closing Cash Bal. [(A) + (B) – (C)] | | | | | | | | | | | | |

## 4.7 Working Capital Finance: Trade Credit, Bank Finance

The important aspect of working capital management is to finance the working capital needs. There are different approaches for financing working capital needs of a business firm. Exclusive long-term sources of funds can be used for financing working capital or exclusively short-term sources can also be used for financing the working capital. A compromise approach in the sense that short-term sources of funds to be used for financing fluctuating amount of working capital and long-term sources of funds should be utilised for financing permanent or core amount of working capital can also be used. Normally funds available for a period of less than one year or for one year are called as short-term sources. In India, borrowings from bank and trade credit are the two short-term sources which are very popular in financing the working capital.

## (A) Trade Credit

The trade credit implies the credit allowed by the supplier to the purchasing firm. Trade credits do not actually mean raising of money from outside but is only the postponement of the payment to the creditors. Trade credit is quite a useful mode of financing working capital needs and many firms rely on such credit. However, any supplier would investigate the credit worthiness of its customers before granting such credit.

Credit granted by the supplier can be on open account which implies that goods are sold on credit without any formal instrument and the customer is expected to make the payment according to the credit period. In some cases, the creditor [supplier] prepares an instrument known as bill of exchange which is accepted by the purchaser [firm]. From the purchaser's angle it is a bills payable. The amount of the bills payable is to be paid after the expiry of the period of credit.

The biggest advantage of trade credit to the purchaser is that it is available easily or almost instantly. Of course, the credit worthiness of the purchaser is verified. Similarly, if the relations between the supplier and the purchaser are informal, the trade credit can be highly flexible. It can be adjusted to suit the individual needs.

## (B) Bank Financing

Another commonly used source for financing working capital needs is the bank finance. Normally a bank assesses the requirements of customers for working capital needs. This assessment is done on the basis of the sales level as well as production plans of the firm. How much amount of current assets should be maintained is also assessed by the bank.

After deducting the margin money from the total requirements, the balance amount is financed by the bank. There may be separate financing limits for peak periods and non-peak periods. The bank borrowing may be in the following forms:

(a) **Bank Overdraft:** This is most common method of bank financing. A customer is allowed to withdraw more amount than the balance at his credit in the account.

For example, if bank balance to the credit of a customer is ₹ 20,000 he may be allowed to withdraw ₹ 30,000 thus indicating that there is a bank overdraft of ₹ 10,000. How much amount is allowed to be withdrawn as overdraft depends upon the limit sanctioned by the bank. The limits are decided after a careful scrutiny of the bank account transactions of the customer. Interest is charged only on the amount which is withdrawn as overdraft.

Like trade credit, bank overdraft arrangements can also offer wide flexibility, once relations between the bank and the customer are developed.

**(b) Cash Credit:** Like overdraft, in this method also, a bank sanctions a particular limit up to which a borrower can borrow. It is not necessary for a borrower to withdraw the entire amount of borrowing immediately. He can withdraw the amount as per his requirements. Interest is charged only on the amount withdrawn and not on the entire amount sanctioned. A bank may demand security in the form of a current asset.

Similar to overdraft, cash credit also offers wide flexibility and, therefore, is very popular method of financing.

**(c) Bills Discounting:** A bill of exchange which is drawn by a creditor on his debtor is a negotiable instrument. It contains an unconditional order to pay a certain sum of money after a certain period of time to the creditor. But the creditor has to wait till the maturity date before he receives the payment. His money remains blocked till the period is over. In order to remove this difficulty, the creditor can discount the bill with his bank. The bank deducts certain amount as discount from the amount of the bill and the remaining amount is paid to the creditor. However, before giving this facility to the drawer or the creditor, the credit rating of the drawer is checked by the bank.

**(d) Letter of Credit:** In international trade as a security, the sellers insist on the buyers to get letter of credit. When the letter of credit is issued by the buyer's bank, the bank undertakes to pay in case the buyer fails to pay the price of the purchases made. A bank opens a letter of credit in the name of the buyer and payment is made by the bank in case the buyer fails to make the payment. Thus the risk is passed on to the bank from the buyer.

Cash credits or overdrafts are direct ways of financing the working capital requirements while letter of credit is an indirect way of financing and bank's liability arises only if the purchaser fails to make the payment.

**(e) Working Capital Loans:** In addition to the above mentioned methods, sometimes temporary working capital loans may also be sanctioned by the bank.

For all the financing modes discussed above, a bank will usually demand some kind of security. The security may be in the form of hypothecation, pledge, mortgage or lien.

In addition to the sources of raising finance for working capital needs, one more source in the form of accrued expenses or outstanding expenses is available. Like trade credit, this source also does not actually generate funds but it only postpones the payment of certain expenses. The greater the postponement, the greater is the amount available for financing. Legal aspects should be taken into consideration before using this source.

**(C) Regulations of Bank Finance:**

As described above, bank credit is a very popular source of financing working capital needs. This is due to various reasons like easy availability, higher degree of flexibility etc.

But it has been observed that in the past there has been a misuse of bank finance by the borrowers. Loans taken for working capital purposes were diverted to finance long term requirements. Similarly, the management of funds by many companies was unprofessional and unscientific. As a result, many companies became sick and a large amount of bank money was blocked in the sick units. All these reasons made it necessary to have some regulations on the bank financing and accordingly, various study groups were appointed by the Reserve Bank of India to have guidelines for providing bank finance.

The norms of working capital finance followed by banks were based on Tandon Committee Report (Mid 70's). The Chore Committee further made recommendations to follow certain norms and procedure for providing working capital finance. The important norms and guidelines suggested by these committees are summarised in the following paragraphs.

**(I) Tandon Committee:** The Reserve Bank of India appointed a study group headed by Mr. P. L. Tandon who was the then Chairman of Punjab National Bank. The group suggested some guidelines regarding the bank borrowing for working capital purpose. The Tandon Committee suggested that the borrower should be allowed to hold a reasonable level of current assets. Particularly in the case of inventories, the Tandon committee suggested that the level of inventory should be as per the requirement only and in any case excessive investments in the inventories should be avoided. The banker should finance only those receivables which are in tune with the practices of the borrower's company and industry. In order to avoid excessive investments in inventories, there is a need for having some uniform norms. The Tandon Committee in its final report has suggested norms for 15 industries. Industries like heavy engineering and sugar were omitted.

The Tandon Committee has also suggested norms for determining borrowing limits. As per the norms, the banker is required to finance only a part of working capital gap and the remaining amount should be financed through long-term sources. The following three methods are suggested by the committee:

(a) In the first method, 25% of the working capital gap will be contributed by the borrower and 75% will be financed by bank borrowings. This method will give a minimum of current ratio of 1:1.

(b) In the second method, 25% of the total current assets will be contributed by the borrower and the remaining will be financed by bank. This method will give a current ratio of 1.3: 1.

(c) In the third method, borrower will contribute 100% of core assets and 25% of the balance of current assets. The remaining of the working capital gap can be financed by the borrowings.

The committee recommended that the first method should be used mainly as stop gap and the borrowers ultimately should move to the third method. The borrowers who are already in the second stage should not be allowed to enter into first stage. They should be encouraged to enter into the third stage. The committee has also suggested a change in the style of bank lending. The total credit limit should be divided into fixed part and fluctuating part. The fixed part shall be treated as a demand loan and will be minimum borrowing level. The fluctuating part will be taken care of by a demand cash credit. The interest rate on the loan component should be lower than cash credit system.

The committee also recommended that there should be regular supply of information from the borrower to the lender. Projected financial statements, funds flow statements and budgets should be supplied on regular basis. Actual figures supplied quarter wise give idea about the performance of the borrower's business. There is a responsibility on the part of the bank that the stipulated credit limit is not exceeded and also to see that the bank borrowings are used for the purpose of which it is taken.

**(II) Chore Committee Recommendations:** A working group under the chairmanship of Mr. K. B. Chore was formed in April 1979 by the Reserve Bank of India. The main terms of reference for this group were to review the cash-credit system and suggest modifications and if required, suggest alternate credit system. The important recommendations made by this committee are as follows:

(a)    As far as possible, the borrower, should try to reduce the dependence on bank credit. Therefore, the second method suggested by Tandon committee is recommended. If necessary, the borrower should be granted a working capital term loan which should be repaid in semi-annual installments of 5 years with a higher rate of interest than the cash credit.

(b)    For every borrower, limits should be fixed according to 'peak level' and 'normal non-peak level'. This limit is to be fixed for all the borrowers borrowing in excess of ₹ 10 lakhs and will be according to peak and non-peak periods. It will be the duty of the borrower to indicate his needs well in advance. If actual borrowing exceeds this limit by more than 10%, appropriate action will be taken against the borrower.   Ad-hoc or temporary credit limits should be discouraged by the banks.

(c)    All borrowers [except sick units] with working capital requirements of ₹ 10 lakhs and above to be placed under second method of lending recommended by Tandon Committee.

(d)    The banks should continue the existing system of three types of lending viz., cash credits, loans and bills. However, cash credit system should be gradually replaced by loans and bills. The division of cash credit account into fixed and fluctuating components as per suggestions of Tandon committee should be discontinued.

Advances against book-debts should be converted to bills wherever possible and at least 50% of the cash credit limit utilised for financing of raw material inventory should be changed to bills system.

(e) The requirement of submitting information on quarterly basis should be continued and should be made more strict. However the format should be simpler.

**(III) Nayak Committee Recommendations:** The Nayak Committee's recommendations were accepted by the Reserve Bank of India, keeping in view the contribution of small scale industry in providing employment, promoting exports and in its support in the overall industrial production. This committee headed by Mr. P. R. Nayak made the following important recommendations.

(a) There should be priority given to village industries, tiny sector and small scale sector in the same order while giving credit to the small scale sector.

(b) For the requirements of credit of village industries, tiny sector units and other small scale units upto aggregate fund based working capital limits up to ₹ 50 lakhs from the banking sector, the norms for inventory and receivables as also the methods of lending as per Tandon Committee will not apply. On the contrary, for such units, the working capital limit will be computed at 20% of their projected annual turnover for new as well as existing units. Margin money requirements for these units which will have to be brought by these units will be 5% of their annual turnover. This means that 25% of their output value should be computed as working capital requirements out of which 20% should be provided by banking sector and remaining 5% will be the margin money which is the contribution of the borrower.

(c) The SSI unit, who has availed of the bank credit should prepare budget every year in case of the working capital requirement on the basis of 'bottom ups'.

(d) The banks should follow a 'single window system' for working capital loans as well as term loans. This system will help bank to provide term loans and working capital loans to small scale sector whose project investments are upto ₹ 20 lakhs and working capital requirements are up to ₹ 10 lakhs.

(e) A grievance cell should be established by banks so that in case of difficulties the small scale units can approach it.

(f) In order to have speedy disposal of the loan applications from the small scale sector, the banks should process and dispose of the applications from the small scale sector at the earliest and hence, the time limit laid down is that the applications up to ₹ 25000 should be disposed off within 15 days while in other cases it should be disposed off within a period of 8 to 9 weeks. Similarly in order to expedite the processing of the loan applications, the banks are advised to adopt a committee approach, in which decisions are taken by the competent authority after discussion with the concerned Branch Manager.

(g) There should be a system of appealing in the sense that in case of rejection by an authority, there should be a higher authority to whom the applicant can approach.

(h) There should not be a pre-condition of deposit mobilisation.

(i) The bank officers should have right approach, attitude and skills to handle the small scale sector.

**(IV) Vaz Committee Recommendations:** The Vaz Committee recommended that the recommendations of Nayak Committee should be extended to all the business organisations and these recommendations are accepted. The borrower will have to provide margin money of 5% of the projected turnover, from the long term sources and 20% will be provided by the bank. In arriving this 25%, four working capital cycles have been assumed by the Committee.

## 4.8 Commercial Paper

### (A) Meaning of Commercial Paper

An emerging source of financing working capital requirements of corporate enterprise is **commercial paper**. Commercial paper is a short term money market instrument, consisting of unsecured promissory notes with a fixed maturity, usually between seven days and three months, issued in bearer form and on a discount basis. Thus, commercial paper is a certificate evidencing an unsecured corporate debt of short maturity. It represents a promise by the borrowing company to repay loan at a specified date. In law, the commercial paper comes closest to a promissory note.

### (B) Advantages and Disadvantages of a Commercial Paper

**Advantages:**

(i) A commercial paper is sold on an unsecured basis and does not contain any restrictive conditions;

(ii) As it is a freely transferable instrument, it has high liquidity;

(iii) It provides more funds compared to other sources. Generally, the cost of Commercial Paper to the issuing firm is lower than the cost of commercial bank loans;

(iv) A commercial paper provides a continuous source of funds. This is because their maturity can be tailored to suit the requirements of the issuing firm. Further, maturing commercial paper can be repaid by selling new commercial paper;

(v) Companies can park their excess funds in commercial paper thereby earning some good return on the same.

**Disadvantages:**

(i) Only financially sound and highly rated firms can raise money through commercial papers. New and moderately rated firms are not in a position to raise funds by this method.

(ii) The size of money that can be raised through commercial paper is limited to the excess liquidity available with the suppliers of funds at a particular time.

(iii) Commercial paper is an impersonal method of financing. As such if a firm is not in a position to redeem its paper due to financial difficulties, extending the maturity of a commercial paper is not possible.

## Practical Problems

## Working Capital Management

**Problem 1:**

The Board of directors of XYZ Engineering Co. Pvt. Ltd. requests you to prepare a statement showing the working capital requirements for a level of activity of 1,56,000 units of production. The following information is available for your consideration.

| Per unit | (₹) |
|---|---|
| [A] Raw materials | 90 |
| Direct labour | 40 |
| Overheads | 75 |
| **Total cost** | **205** |
| Profit | 60 |
| **Selling price per unit** | **265** |

[B] (i)  Raw materials are in stock on an average one month.

(ii)  Materials are in process 50% complete on an average two weeks.

(iii)  Finished goods are in stock on an average one month.

(iv)  Credit allowed by suppliers one month.

(v)  Time lag in payment from debtors two months.

(vi)  Lag in payment of wages $1^{1}/_{2}$ weeks.

(vii)  Lag in payment of overheads one month. 20% of the output is sold against cash. Cash in hand and bank expected ₹ 60,000.

Assume that production is carried on evenly throughout the year, wages and overheads accrue similarly and a time period of 4 weeks is equivalent to a month.

## Solution:

**XYZ Engineering Co. Pvt. Ltd.**
**Statement Showing Working Capital Requirements**
**Particulars**

| | | |
|---|---|---|
| **[A] Current Assets** | | **Amount (₹)** |

(i) Stock of raw materials for one month

$$\left[\frac{1,56,000 \times ₹\,90 \times 1}{12}\right] \qquad\qquad 11,70,000$$

(ii) Work in process for 2 weeks

(a) Materials

$$\frac{1,56,000 \times ₹\,90 \times 2}{48} \quad = \quad 5,85,000$$

(b) Wages

$$\frac{1,56,000 \times ₹\,40 \times 2}{48} \quad = \quad 2,60,000$$

(c) Overheads

$$\frac{1,56,000 \times ₹\,75 \times 2}{48} \quad = \quad \underline{4,87,500}$$

$$\qquad\qquad\qquad\qquad\qquad 13,32,500 \qquad 6,66,250 \text{ [50\% complete]}$$

(iii) Finished goods stock for one month

$$\frac{1,56,000 \times ₹\,205\,[\text{Total cost}] \times 1}{12} \qquad\qquad 26,65,000$$

(iv) Debtors for 2 months [At cost]

$$\frac{1,24,800 \times ₹\,205 \times 2}{12} \qquad\qquad 42,64,000$$

(v) Cash in hand and at bank $\qquad\qquad\qquad\qquad\quad \underline{60,000}$

| | | |
|---|---|---|
| **Total – A** | | **88,25,250** |
| **[B] Current liabilities** | | **Amount (₹)** |

(i) Creditors (1 month)

$$\frac{1,56,000 \times ₹\,90 \times 1}{12} \qquad\qquad 11,70,000$$

(ii) Time lag in payment of wages

$$\frac{1,56,000 \times ₹\,40 \times 1.5}{48} \qquad\qquad 1,95,000$$

(iii) Time lag in payment of overheads

$$\frac{1,56,000 \times ₹\,75 \times 1}{12} \qquad\qquad 9,75,000$$

| | | |
|---|---|---|
| **Total – B** | | **23,40,000** |
| **[C] Net Working Capital [A – B]** | | **64,85,250** |

**Problem 2:**

ABC cements Ltd. sells its products on a gross profit of 20% on sales. The following information is extracted from its annual accounts for the current year ended on 31st March 2016.

|  | ₹ |
|---|---|
| Sales at 3 months credit | 40,00,000 |
| Raw materials | 12,00,000 |
| Wages paid-average time lag 15 days | 9,60,000 |
| Manufacturing expenses paid–one month in arrears | 12,00,000 |
| Administrative expenses paid-one month in arrears | 4,80,000 |
| Sales promotion expenses payable half year in advance | 2,00,000 |

The company enjoys one month's credit from the suppliers of raw materials and maintains a 2 months stock of raw materials and one and half month's stock of finished goods. The cash balance is maintained at ₹ 1,00,000 as a precautionary measure. Assuming a 10% margin, find out the working capital requirements of the company.

**Solution:**

**ABC Cements Ltd.**

**Statement showing the calculation of working capital requirements**

| Particulars | Amount (₹) |
|---|---|
| **[A]  Current Assets** | |
| (i)   Inventory: | |
| (a)  Raw materials (₹ 12,00,000 × 2/12] | 2,00,000 |
| (b)  *Finished goods $\left[\dfrac{₹ 32,00,000 \times 1.5}{12}\right]$ | 4,00,000 |
| (ii)  *Debtors $\left[\dfrac{₹ 36,80,000 \times 3}{12}\right]$ | 9,20,000 |
| (iii)  Prepaid sales expenses $\left[\dfrac{₹ 2,00,000 \times 6}{12}\right]$ | 1,00,000 |
| (iv)  Cash balance | 1,00,000 |
| Total – A | 17,20,000 |
| **[B]  Current liabilities** | |
| (i)   Creditors for goods $\left[\dfrac{₹ 12,00,000 \times 1}{12}\right]$ | 1,00,000 |
| (ii)  Wages $\left[\dfrac{₹ 9,60,000 \times 1}{2 \times 12}\right]$ | 40,000 |
| (iii)  Manufacturing expenses $\left[\dfrac{₹ 12,00,000 \times 1}{12}\right]$ | 1,00,000 |
| (iv)  Administrative expenses $\left[\dfrac{₹ 4,80,000 \times 1}{12}\right]$ | 40,000 |
| Total – B | 2,80,000 |

**[C]  Net working capital [A – B]**                                    14,40,000
     **Add:** 10% margin for contingencies                          1,44,000
     Total working capital requirement                           **15,84,000**

*Finished goods are calculated on the basis of cost of production which is sales – gross profit [20% of sales].

|                                              |         ₹ |
| :------------------------------------------- | --------: |
| Cost of production therefore in sales        | 40,00,000 |
| **Less:** Gross profit                       |  8,00,000 |
| **Cost of production**                       | 32,00,000 |

$$^{*}\text{Debtors} = ₹\,32,00,000 + ₹\,4,80,000 = ₹\,36,80,000$$

$$\text{Cost of goods sold} + \text{Administrative expenses}$$

## Problem 3:

A newly formed company has to prepare an estimate of working capital requirements for the coming year. The information about the projected Profit & Loss A/c. of the company is as under:

| Particulars                                      |          | Amount (₹) |
| :----------------------------------------------- | -------: | ---------: |
| Sales:                                           |          |  21,00,000 |
| **Less:** Cost of goods sold                     |          |  15,30,000 |
| **Gross profit**                                 |          |   5,70,000 |
| **Less:** Administrative expenses                | 1,40,000 |            |
| Selling expenses                                 | 1,30,000 |   2,70,000 |
| Profit before tax                                |          |   3,00,000 |
| Provision for tax                                |          |   1,00,000 |
| Cost of goods sold has been derived as follows:  |          |   6,70,000 |
| Materials used                                   |          |   8,40,000 |
| **Add:** Wages and other manufacturing expenses  |          |   6,25,000 |
| **Add:** Depreciation                            |          |   2,35,000 |
|                                                  |          |  17,00,000 |
| **Less:** Stock of finished stock                |          |            |
| [10% produced not yet sold]                      |          |   1,70,000 |
|                                                  |          |  15,30,000 |

The figures above relate only to the goods that have been finished and not to those in process, goods equal to 15% of the year's production [in terms of physical units] are in process, requiring on an average full materials but only 40% of other expenses. The company believes in keeping two months consumption of material in stock.

All expenses are paid in one month in arrears; suppliers of materials extend $1^1/_2$ months credit. Sales are 20% cash and the rest at two months credit, 70% of the income-tax has to be paid in advance in quarterly installments. Cash balance desired is ₹ 40,000.

**Solution:**

**Statement showing working capital requirements**

| Particulars | Amount (₹) |
|---|---|
| **[A] Current Assets** | |
| (I)   Inventory: | |
|    (a) Raw materials $\left[\dfrac{₹\,8,40,000 \times 2}{12}\right]$ | 1,40,000 |
|    (b) Work in progress: | |
|    (i)   Raw materials $\left[\dfrac{₹\,8,40,000 \times 15}{100}\right]$ | 1,26,000 |
|    (ii)  Wages and other manufacturing expenses $\left[\dfrac{₹\,6,25,000\ \times 40 \times 15}{100 \times 100}\right]$ | 37,500 |
|    (c) Stock of finished goods: [₹ 1,70,000 – 23,500 Dep] | 1,46,500 |
| (II)  Debtors – 2 months credit [See working note No. 1] | 2,11,800 |
| (III) Cash | 40,000 |
| **Total –A** | **7,01,800** |
| **[B] Current liabilities** | |
| (I)   Lag in payment of expenses (1 month) | |

| | | |
|---|---|---|
| (i)   Wages and manufacturing expenses | 6,25,000 | |
| (ii)  Administrative expenses | 1,40,000 | |
| (iii) Selling expenses | 1,30,000 | |
| | 8,95,000 | |
| $\left(\dfrac{8,95,000}{12}\right)$ | 74,583 | |
| (II)  Creditors – $1^1/_2$ months credit | | |
| $\left(\dfrac{8,40,000 \times 3}{24}\right)$ | 1,05,000 | |
| **Total – B** | | **1,79,583** |
| **[C]  Net working capital [A – B]** | | 5,22,217 |
| **Add:** 10% contingency margin | | 52,221 |
| Total working capital requirements | | **5,74,438** |

**Working Note:**

1. Calculation of Debtors                                                    ₹

   Cost of goods sold:                                                  15,30,000

   **Less:** Depreciation                                                 2,11,500

                                                                        13,18,500

   **Add:** Administrative exp.                                           1,40,000

   Selling exp.                                                           1,30,000

   Total                                                                 15,88,500

   Credit Sales: 80% of ₹ 15,88,500              =                       12,70,800

   Debtors = $12,70,800 \times \dfrac{2}{12}$       =                       2,11,800

2. Since depreciation is a non-cash expense, it is excluded from the cost of goods sold for determining work-in-process, finished goods and debtors.

## Problem 4:

The management of Gemini Ltd. has called for a statement showing the working capital needed to finance a level of activity of 3,00,000 units of output for the year. The cost structure for the company's product for the above mentioned activity level is detailed below:

| Cost per unit | (₹) |
|---|---|
| Raw materials | 20 |
| Direct labour | 5 |
| Overheads | 15 |
| **Total cost** | 40 |
| Profit | 10 |
| **Selling price** | 50 |

Past trend indicates that raw materials are held in stock, on an average for two months.

Work in progress [50% complete] will approximate to half a monthly production.

Finished goods remain in warehouse on an average for a month.

Suppliers for materials extend a month's credit.

For debtors two months credit is usually allowed. A minimum cash balance of ₹ 25,000 is expected to be maintained.

The production pattern is assumed to be uniform throughout the year.

**Solution:**

**Statement showing working capital requirements**

| Particulars | Amount (₹) |
|---|---|
| [A]  **Current Assets** | |
| (i)   **Inventory:** | |
| (a)   **Raw materials:** | |
| $\left[3,00,000 \text{ units} \times ₹\, 20 \times \dfrac{2}{12}\right]$ | 10,00,000 |

**(b) Work-in-progress:**

| | | |
|---|---|---|
| * Raw materials | | |
| [12,500 units × ₹ 10] | 1,25,000 | |
| * Direct labour | | |
| [12,500 units × ₹ 2.5] | 31,250 | |
| * Overheads | | |
| [12,500 units × ₹ 7.5] | 93,750 | 2,50,000 |

      * 50% complete

**(c) Finished goods for one month:**

| | |
|---|---|
| 25,000 units × ₹ 40 | 10,00,000 |
| (ii) Debtors: 3,00,000 units × ₹ 40 × $\dfrac{2}{12}$ | 20,00,000 |
| (iii) Minimum cash balance | 25,000 |
| **Total [A]** | **42,75,000** |

**[B] Current liabilities**

Creditors for one month:

$$3,00,000 \text{ units} \times 20 \times \dfrac{1}{12} \qquad\qquad 5,00,000$$

**[C] Net working capital [A – B]**            **37,75,000**

**Problem 5:**

Finix Ltd. has investigated the profitability of its assets and the cost of its funds.

The results indicate,

| | | |
|---|---|---|
| (i) | Current assets earn | 10% |
| (ii) | Fixed assets return | 15% |
| (iii) | Current liabilities cost | 4% |
| (iv) | Average cost of long-term funds | 12% |

The current balance-sheet is as follows:

| Liabilities | ₹ | Assets | ₹ |
|---|---|---|---|
| Current liabilities | 20,000 | Current assets | 40,000 |
| Long-term funds | 1,40,000 | Fixed assets | 1,20,000 |
| **Total** | **1,60,000** | **Total** | **1,60,000** |

(i) What is the net profitability?

(ii) The company plans to reduce its working capital by ₹ 10,000 by either (a) reducing current assets by ₹ 10,000 by shifting them to fixed assets or (b) by shifting ₹ 10,000 from long-term liabilities to current liabilities.

Advise the company about proper course of action.

**Solution:**

**(i)  Net profitability**                                                                              ₹

    (a)  Earnings on current assets 10% on ₹ 40,000        =        4,000
    (b)  Earnings on fixed assets 15% on ₹ 1,20,000        =       18,000
                    **Total**                                                       **22,000**
    (c)  Cost of current liabilities 4% on ₹ 20,000        =          800
    (d)  Cost of long-term funds 12% on ₹ 1,40,000         =       16,800
                    **Total**                                                       **17,600**
    (e)  Profitability = [Earnings – Cost]                                4,400

**(ii)  (a)  Shifting ₹ 10,000 from current assets to fixed assets**

    (b)  Earnings on current assets 10% on ₹ 30,000                      3,000
    (c)  Earnings on fixed assets 15% on ₹ 1,30,000                     19,500
                    **Total**                                                       **22,500**
        **Less:** Cost as calculated above                           (–) 17,600
    **Profitability**                                                      4,900

**(iii)  Shifting ₹ 10,000 to current liabilities from long-term funds.**

    (a)  Cost of current liabilities 4% on ₹ 30,000                      1,200
    (b)  Cost of long-term funds 12% on ₹ 1,30,000                      15,600
                                                                       **16,800**
            Profitability = ₹ 22,000 – ₹ 16,800        =                **5,200**

**Conclusion:** Shifting ₹ 10,000 to current liabilities from long-term funds are more profitable.

**Problem 6:**

A client of yours Swift Ltd. is about to commence a new business and finance has been provided in respect of fixed assets. They ask your advice about the working capital requirements of the company. The following information is available for your information:

| Particulars | Average credit period | Estimate for first year (₹) |
|---|---|---|
| Purchase of materials | 6 weeks | 26,00,000 |
| Wages | 11/2 weeks | 19,50,000 |
| **Overheads:** | | |
| Rent | 6 months | 1,00,000 |
| Directors & Manager's salaries | 1 month | 3,60,000 |
| Office salaries | 2 weeks | 4,55,000 |
| Traveller's commission | 3 months | 2,00,000 |
| Other overheads | 2 months | 6,00,000 |
| Cash sales | – | 1,40,000 |
| Credit sales | 7 weeks | 65,00,000 |
| Average amount of stock & WIP | – | 3,00,000 |
| Average amount of undrawn profits | – | 3,10,000 |

Sales were made at an even rate throughout the year.

Calculate the working capital requirements for the company.

**Solution:**

### Swift Ltd. statement showing working capital requirements

| Particulars | | Amount (₹) |
|---|---|---|
| **[A]** | **Current Assets** | |
| (i) | Average amount of stocks and W.I.P. | 3,00,000 |
| (ii) | Debtors for 7 weeks $\left[\dfrac{₹\,65,00,000 \times 7}{52}\right]$ | 8,75,000 |
| | | 11,75,000 |

**[B] Current Liabilities**

(i) Lag in payment of expenses:

(a) Wages $-\left(1^1/_2 \text{ weeks}\right) \quad = \dfrac{19,50,000 \times 1.5}{52} = 56{,}250$

(b) Rent ₹ $1,00,000 \times \dfrac{6}{12} \quad = 50{,}000$

(6 months)

(c) Directors & Manager's salaries (1 month)

$\qquad ₹\,3,60,000 \times \dfrac{1}{12} = 30{,}000$

(d) Office salaries (2 weeks)

$\qquad \dfrac{₹\,4,55,000 \times 2}{52} = 17{,}500$

(e) Traveler's commission (3 months)

$\qquad ₹\,2,00,000 \times \dfrac{3}{12} = 50{,}000$

(f) Other overheads (2 months)

$\qquad ₹\,6,00,000 \times \dfrac{2}{12} = 1{,}00{,}000$ ............ 3,03,750

(ii) Creditors – 6 weeks credit

$\qquad \dfrac{₹\,26,00,000}{52} \times 6$ ............ 3,00,000

| | | |
|---|---|---|
| | **Total B** | 6,03,750 |
| **(C)** | **Net Working Capital [A – B]** | 5,71,250 |

**Note:** In the above problems, debtors are calculated by taking the cost of sales. They can also be calculated by taking selling price.

## Management of Cash

**Problem 1:**

ABC company wishes to arrange for overdraft facilities with its bankers during the period April to June 2015. You are required to prepare a Cash–budget for the above period, indicating the extent of bank overdraft required, if any for each month.

| Month | Sales (₹) | Purchases (₹) | Wages (₹) | Overheads (₹) |
|---|---|---|---|---|
| February | 4,00,000 | 2,80,000 | 60,000 | 75,000 |
| March | 6,50,000 | 4,00,000 | 80,000 | 1,80,000 |
| April | 8,00,000 | 6,80,000 | 95,000 | 1,95,000 |
| May | 10,00,000 | 8,50,000 | 1,10,000 | 2,00,000 |
| June | 13,00,000 | 12,00,000 | 1,15,000 | 2,40,000 |

**Additional information:**

1. Expected cash balance as on 1st April, 2015 is ₹ 45,000.
2. Credit allowed to Debtors is 1 month and by creditors 2 months.
3. Wages and overheads are paid in the first week of the subsequent month.
4. All Sales and Purchases are on credit.

**Solution:**

ABC Comp. Cash Budget period 1st April to 30th June, 2015

| Particulars | April (₹) | May (₹) | June (₹) |
|---|---|---|---|
| A. Opening balance | 45,000 | 1,55,000 | 2,65,000 |
| B. Expected cash receipts | 6,50,000 | 8,00,000 | 10,00,000 |
| C. Total cash available [A + B] | 6,95,000 | 9,55,000 | 12,65,000 |
| D. Expected cash payments | | | |
|    (i) Purchases | 2,80,000 | 4,00,000 | 6,80,000 |
|    (ii) Wages | 80,000 | 95,000 | 1,10,000 |
|    (iii) Overhead | 1,80,000 | 1,95,000 | 2,00,000 |
|    Total – D | 5,40,000 | 6,90,000 | 9,90,000 |
| E. Closing balance [C – D] | 1,55,000 | 2,65,000 | 2,75,000 |

**Conclusion:** From the above budget it is clear that overdraft facilities are not required in these three months. However, if any major expense arises, it may be required.

**Problem 2:**

From the following particulars, prepare a Cash budget from January to March, 2015.

| Month | Sales | Purchases | Overheads | | |
|---|---|---|---|---|---|
| | | | Administrative | Production | Selling |
| | ₹ | ₹ | ₹ | ₹ | ₹ |
| Oct. 2014 | 11,00,000 | 6,50,000 | 95,000 | 1,00,000 | 65,000 |
| Nov. 2014 | 12,00,000 | 7,00,000 | 1,25,000 | 1,30,000 | 90,000 |
| Dec. 2014 | 14,50,000 | 9,00,000 | 1,25,000 | 1,60,000 | 1,15,000 |
| Jan. 2015 | 16,00,000 | 11,00,000 | 1,75,000 | 1,70,000 | 1,45,000 |
| Feb. 2015 | 19,00,000 | 13,00,000 | 2,00,000 | 1,95,000 | 1,60,000 |
| March 2015 | 19,00,000 | 14,00,000 | 2,10,000 | 2,00,000 | 1,70,000 |

**Additional information:**

1.  Expected cash balance as on 1st January, 2015 is ₹ 80,000.

2.  Out of the total sales 50% are Cash Sales. Credit allowed to debtors is one month.

3.  All the purchases are on credit. The suppliers allow 2 months credit.

4.  Capital expenditure proposed to be incurred on acquisition on Machinery in March, 2015 is ₹ 4,00,000.

5.  Income–tax payable in March, 2015 is ₹ 90,000.

6.  Interest receivable on Investment ₹ 35,000 in January, 2015.

7.  Lag in the payment of overhead expenses is one month.

**Solution:**

**ABC Company**

**Cash Budget (from 1.1.2015 to 31.3.2015)**

| Particulars | January (₹) | February (₹) | March (₹) |
|---|---|---|---|
| A.  Cash balance: opening | 80,000 | 5,40,000 | 9,00,000 |
| B.  Expected receipts: | | | |
|    (i)  Cash Sales [50%] | 8,00,000 | 9,50,000 | 9,50,000 |
|    (ii)  From Debtors | 7,25,000 | 8,00,000 | 9,50,000 |
|    (iii)  Interest on Investments | 35,000 | – | – |
| C.  Total Cash available    [A + B] | **16,40,000** | **22,90,000** | **28,00,000** |
| | | | |
| D.  Expected payments | | | |
|    (i)  Purchases | 7,00,000 | 9,00,000 | 11,00,000 |
|    (ii)  Administrative overheads | 1,25,000 | 1,75,000 | 2,00,000 |
|    (iii)  Production  overheads | 1,60,000 | 1,70,000 | 1,95,000 |
|    (iv)  Selling overheads | 1,15,000 | 1,45,000 | 1,60,000 |
|    (v)  Capital Exp. on Machinery purchases | – | – | 4,00,000 |
|    (vi)  Income–tax payable | – | – | 90,000 |
|    Total [D] | 11,00,000 | 13,90,000 | 21,45,000 |
| E.  Closing Bal. [C – D] | 5,40,000 | 9,00,000 | 7,45,000 |

**Problem 3:**

From the following information prepare a Cash budget for 6 months from January to June, 2015.

₹

A. Sales forecasts:

| | | |
|---|---|---|
| | January' 2015 | 6,00,000 |
| | February | 8,00,000 |
| | March | 8,00,000 |
| | April | 12,00,000 |
| | May | 10,00,000 |
| | June | 8,00,000 |

B. Actual sales:

| | | |
|---|---|---|
| | November 2014 | 14,00,000 |
| | December 2014 | 12,00,000 |

C. Gross profit margin is 20% on sales.

D. Wages and Salaries are ₹ 80,000 per month for first 3 months and thereafter expected to increase by ₹ 15,000 per month. They are to be paid in the same month in which they become due.

E. The company had expected that stock of goods as on 1st January, 2015, is ₹ 1,10,000. Thereafter the inventory level is to be kept at an uniform level of ₹ 1,15,000 per month.

F. Interest on ₹ 20,00,000 @ 14% on Debentures is due by March end and June end.

G. 40% of total sales are on Cash basis. Out of the remaining, 60% are recovered in the month following the sales and balance in subsequent month.

H. Creditors are paid in the same month.

I. Balance of Cash on 1st January 2015: ₹ 60,000.

### Cash Budget (Period January – June 2015)

| Particulars | Jan. [₹] | Feb. [₹] | March [₹] | April [₹] | May [₹] | June [₹] |
|---|---|---|---|---|---|---|
| A. Opening balance | 60,000 | 5,83,000 | 7,67,000 | 8,09,000 | 8,09,000 | 10,33,000 |
| B. Expected Cash receipts | | | | | | |
| (i) Cash Sales | 2,40,000 | 3,20,000 | 3,20,000 | 4,80,000 | 4,00,000 | 3,20,000 |
| (ii) Collections from Debtors [Working note no. 1] | 7,68,000 | 5,04,000 | 4,32,000 | 4,80,000 | 6,24,000 | 6,48,000 |
| C. Total cash available [A + B] | 10,68,000 | 14,07,000 | 15,19,000 | 17,69,000 | 18,33,000 | 20,01,000 |
| D. Expected payments | | | | | | |
| (i) Purchases[Working note No. 2] | 4,05,000 | 5,60,000 | 5,60,000 | 8,65,000 | 7,05,000 | 5,45,000 |
| (ii) Wages & salaries | 80,000 | 80,000 | 80,000 | 95,000 | 95,000 | 95,000 |
| (iii) Interest on Debenture | – | – | 70,000 | – | – | 70,000 |
| Total [D] | 4,85,000 | 6,40,000 | 7,10,000 | 9,60,000 | 8,00,000 | 7,10,000 |
| E. Closing Balance [C – D] | 5,83,000 | 7,67,000 | 8,09,000 | 8,09,000 | 10,33,000 | 12,91,000 |

**Working notes: 1**

1.   **Collections from Debtors**

|  | | ₹ |
|---|---|---|
| **January 2015** | | |
| Cash Sales @40% of total sales | | 2,40,000 |
| Therefore, credit sales | | 3,60,000 |

**Cash received:**

| | | |
|---|---|---|
| 60% of credit sales of Dec. 2014 | | 4,32,000 |
| 40% of credit sales of Nov. 2014 | | <u>3,36,000</u> |
| | | **7,68,000** |

| | **February 2015** | |
|---|---|---|
| (i) | 60% of credit sales in Jan. 2015 | 2,16,000 |
| (ii) | 40% of credit sales of Dec. 2014 | <u>2,88,000</u> |
| | | **5,04,000** |

| | **March 2015** | |
|---|---|---|
| (i) | 60% of credit sales of Feb.' 2015 | 2,88,000 |
| (ii) | 40% of credit sales of Jan.' 2015 | <u>1,44,000</u> |
| | | **4,32,000** |

| | **April 2015** | |
|---|---|---|
| (i) | 60% of credit sales of March 2015 | 2,88,000 |
| (ii) | 40% of credit sales of Feb.' 2015 | <u>1,92,000</u> |
| | | **4,80,000** |

| | **May 2015** | |
|---|---|---|
| (i) | 60% of credit sales of April 2015 | 4,32,000 |
| (ii) | 40% of credit sales of March 2015 | <u>1,92,000</u> |
| | | **6,24,000** |

| | **June 2015** | |
|---|---|---|
| (i) | 60% of credit sales of May 2015 | 3,60,000 |
| (ii) | 40% of credit sales of April 2015 | <u>2,88,000</u> |
| | | **6,48,000** |

**Working Note No 2:** Purchases are not given in the example. Therefore, from Gross Profit Margin and Cost of goods sold, purchases are found out as follows:

| Particulars | | Jan. | Feb. | March | April | May | June |
|---|---|---|---|---|---|---|---|
| | | [₹] | [₹] | [₹] | [₹] | [₹] | [₹] |
| Sales | | 6,00,000 | 8,00,000 | 8,00,000 | 12,00,000 | 10,00,000 | 8,00,000 |
| Cost of goods sold | | | | | | | |
| [80% of sales] | | 4,80,000 | 6,40,000 | 6,40,000 | 9,60,000 | 8,00,000 | 6,40,000 |
| **Add:** Closing stock | | 1,15,000 | 1,15,000 | 1,15,000 | 1,15,000 | 1,15,000 | 1,15,000 |
| | Total | 5,95,000 | 7,55,000 | 7,55,000 | 10,75,000 | 9,15,000 | 7,55,000 |
| **Less:** | | | | | | | |
| Opening stock | | 1,10,000 | 1,15,000 | 1,15,000 | 1,15,000 | 1,15,000 | 1,15,000 |
| Wages | | 80,000 | 80,000 | 80,000 | 95,000 | 95,000 | 95,000 |
| **Purchases** | | **4,05,000** | **5,60,000** | **5,60,000** | **8,65,000** | **7,05,000** | **5,45,000** |

**Observations:** From the above calculations, it is seen that balance of cash is very high right from January 2015. The company is advised to invest at least a part of it, so that cash will not be idle.

## Problem 4:

From the following information and the additional information, prepare a cash budget for 6 months from January 2015.

| Month | Purchases | Salaries & Wages | Prod. overheads | Office & selling overheads | Sales |
|---|---|---|---|---|---|
| | ₹ | ₹ | ₹ | ₹ | ₹ |
| January | 50,000 | 20,000 | 12,000 | 11,000 | 1,44,000 |
| February | 62,000 | 24,200 | 12,600 | 13,400 | 1,94,000 |
| March | 51,000 | 21,200 | 12,000 | 15,000 | 1,72,000 |
| April | 61,200 | 50,000 | 13,000 | 17,800 | 1,77,200 |
| May | 74,000 | 44,000 | 16,000 | 22,000 | 2,05,000 |
| June | 77,600 | 46,000 | 16,400 | 23,000 | 2,17,400 |

1. 50% of total sales are cash sales. Remaining are recovered in the subsequent month.

2. Suppliers allow one month's credit.

3. Dividend of ₹ 35,000 is to be paid in June.

4. Overheads are paid in the same month in which they become due.

5. Income tax payable in March ₹ 40,000.

6. Cash balance as on 1st January 2015 ₹ 80,000.

Solution:

### Cash Budget for January–June, 2015

| Particulars | Jan. [₹] | Feb. [₹] | March [₹] | April [₹] | May [₹] | June [₹] |
|---|---|---|---|---|---|---|
| A. Opening balance | 80,000 | 1,09,000 | 1,77,800 | 2,10,600 | 2,53,400 | 3,01,300 |
| B. Expected cash receipts: | | | | | | |
| (i) Cash Sales | 72,000 | 97,000 | 86,000 | 88,600 | 1,02,500 | 1,08,700 |
| (ii) From Debtors | – | 72,000 | 97,000 | 86,000 | 88,600 | 1,02,500 |
| C. Total cash available [A + B] | 1,52,000 | 2,78,000 | 3,60,800 | 3,85,200 | 4,44,500 | 5,12,500 |
| D. Expected cash payments: | – | 50,000 | 62,000 | 51,000 | 61,200 | 74,000 |
| (i) Purchases | 20,000 | 24,200 | 21,200 | 50,000 | 44,000 | 46,000 |
| (ii) Salaries & Wages | 12,000 | 12,600 | 12,000 | 13,000 | 16,000 | 16,400 |
| (iii) Prod. overheads | | | | | | |
| (iv) Office & Selling | 11,000 | 13,400 | 15,000 | 17,800 | 22,000 | 23,000 |
| (v) Income–tax | – | – | 40,000 | – | – | – |
| Total –D | 43,000 | 1,00,200 | 1,50,200 | 1,31,800 | 1,43,200 | 1,59,400 |
| E. Closing Cash balance [C – D] | 1,09,000 | 1,77,800 | 2,10,600 | 2,53,400 | 3,01,300 | 3,53,100 |

## Inventory Management

**Problem 1:**

From the following figures relating to two components X and Y, compute Re-order Level, Minimum Level, Maximum Level and Average Stock Level.

| Particulars | Component X | Component Y |
|---|---|---|
| Maximum consumption per week | 75 units | 75 units |
| Average consumption per week | 50 units | 50 units |
| Minimum consumption per week | 25 units | 25 units |
| Reorder period | 4 to 6 weeks | 2 to 4 weeks |
| Reorder quantity | 400 units | 600 units |

Solution:

The computation of various levels is shown below.

[A] Reorder Level = Maximum Consumption × Maximum Reorder Period

Component X = 75 units × 6 weeks  = 450 units

Component Y = 75 units × 4 weeks  = 300 units.

[B] Minimum Level = Reorder Level – Average Consumption × Average Reorder Period

Component X = 450 units – [50 units × 5 weeks] = 200 units

Component Y = 300 units – [50 units × 3 weeks] = 150 units

[C] Maximum Level = Reorder Level + Reorder Quantity –

[Minimum Consumption X Minimum Reorder Period]

Component X = 450 units + 400 units - [25 units X 4 weeks] = 750 units

Component Y = 300 units + 600 units – [25 units X 2 weeks] = 850 units

[D] Average Level = ½ [Maximum Level + Minimum Level]

Component X = ½ [750 units + 200 units] = 475 units

Component Y = ½ [150 units + 850 units] = 500 units

**Problem 2:**

A manufacturer purchases 800 units of a certain component p.a. @ ₹ 30 per unit from outside supplier. The annual usage is 800 units, order placing and receiving cost is ₹ 100 per order and cost of holding one unit of the component for one year is ₹ 4. Calculate the Economic Order Quantity by tabular method. Also calculate the number of orders to be placed per year.

**Solution:**

The following table is prepared to compute the Economic Order Quantity.

| Annual Consumption | Number of orders p.a. | Units per order | Average inventory Units | Carrying cost @ ₹ 4 per unit on average inventory (₹) | Order placing and receiving cost @ ₹ 100 per order (₹) | Total annual costs (₹) |
|---|---|---|---|---|---|---|
| 800 | 1 | 800 | 400 | 1600 | 100 | 1700 |
|  | 2 | 400 | 200 | 800 | 200 | 1000 |
|  | 3 | 267 | 133 | 532 | 300 | 832 |
|  | 4 | 200 | 100 | 400 | 400 | 800 * |
|  | 5 | 160 | 80 | 320 | 500 | 820 |
|  | 6 | 133 | 67 | 268 | 600 | 868 |

* The total annual cost of ₹ 800 is the lowest when number of orders placed are 4 in a year. This means that the quantity per order of 200 [4 orders per year] is the Economic Order Quantity.

## Questions for Discussion

1. What is working capital? Explain the factors affecting working capital.
2. Explain: Financing of Working Capital Requirements.
3. Explain: Estimating of Working Capital Requirements.
4. State the nature and need for Working Capital Management.
5. What is Factoring? Explain its nature and types.
6. Explain the concept of Operating Cycle.
7. Write short notes:
   (a) Working capital budget.
   (b) Commercial Paper.
   (c) Working capital policy.
8. Explain:
   (a) Accounts Receivables Management.
   (b) Techniques of Inventory Control.
   (c) Economic Order Quantity.
   (d) Aspects of Cash Management.

■■■

# CHAPTER 5

# Long Term Sources of Finance

*Contents ...*

## 5.1 Indian Capital and Stock Market - New Issues Market

### (A) Meaning of Capital Market

Capital Market is one of the significant components of every financial market and should be studied carefully. The capital market is basically a market for financial assets which have a long or indefinite maturity. Unlike money market instruments, the capital market instruments become mature for the period more than one year. It is an institutional arrangement to borrow and lend money for a longer period of time. It consists of financial institutions like IDBI, ICICI, UTI, LIC, etc. which play the role of lenders in the capital market. Business units and corporate are the borrowers in the capital market.

Capital market involves various instruments which can be used for financial transactions. Capital market provides long term debt and equity finance for the government and the corporate sector. Capital market can be classified into primary and secondary markets. The primary market is a market for new shares, whereas the existing securities are traded in the secondary market. Capital market institutions provide rupee loans, foreign exchange loans, consultancy services and underwriting.

### (B) Importance of Capital Market

Capital market is also very important like the money market and it plays a significant role in the national economy. A developed, dynamic and vibrant capital market can immensely contribute to speedy economic growth and development.

Mentioned below are the important functions and role of the capital market.

(a) **Mobilisation of Savings:** Capital market is an important source for mobilising idle savings from the economy. It mobilises funds from people for further investments in the productive channels of an economy. In that sense it activates the ideal monetary resources and puts them in proper investments.

(b) **Capital Formation:** Capital market helps in capital formation. Capital formation is net addition to the existing stock of capital in the economy. Through mobilisation of ideal resources, it generates savings. The mobilised savings are made available to various segments such as agriculture, industry, etc. This helps in increasing capital formation.

(c) **Provision of Investment Avenue:** Capital market raises resources for longer duration thereby providing an investment avenue for people who wish to invest resources for a long period of time. It also provides suitable interest rate returns to investors. Instruments such as bonds, equities, units of mutual funds, insurance policies, etc. definitely provide diverse investment avenues for the public.

(d) **Speed up Economic Growth and Development:** Capital markets make funds available for a long period of time and the financial requirements of businesses are met. It in turn helps in research and development and increasing production and productivity in economy, by generation of employment and development of infrastructure. Capital markets enhance production and productivity in the national economy.

(e) **Proper Regulation of Funds:** Capital markets not only help in fund mobilisation, but also in proper allocation of these resources. Capital market can have regulation over the resources so that it can direct funds in a qualitative manner.

(f) **Service Provision:** As a significant financial set up, capital markets provide various types of services. It includes long term and medium term loans to industry, underwriting services, consultancy services, export finance, etc. These services facilitate the manufacturing sector in a large spectrum.

(g) **Continuous Availability of Funds:** Capital market is a place where the investment opportunity is continuously available for long term investment. This is a liquid market as it makes funds available on a continuous basis. Both buyers and sellers can easily buy and sell securities as they are continuously available. Basically capital market transactions are related to the stock exchanges. Thus marketability in the capital market becomes easy.

## (C) Stock Market

Stock market or share market is a corporation or organisation which provides facilities for stock brokers and traders, to trade company stocks and other securities.

The securities traded on a stock market include: shares issued by companies, unit trusts and other mutual investment products and bonds.

## (D) New Issue Market

New Issue Market is also called as a 'Primary Market'. New Issue Market is one part of the capital market that deals with issuing of new securities.

Companies or public sector institutions can obtain funds through the sale of new stock or bond issues through new issue market.

The main function of new issue market is to facilitate the transfer of resources from savers to users.

The facilities of the New Issue Market are also utilised for selling existing concerns to the public as going concerns through conversions of existing proprietary enterprises or private companies into public companies. The new issues may take the form of equity shares, preference shares or debentures.

The firms raising fund may be new companies or existing companies planning expansion. The new companies need not always be entirely new enterprises. They may be private firms already in business, but 'going public' to expand their capital bases. 'Going public' means becoming public limited companies to be entitled to raise funds from the general public in the open market.

**Features of New Issue Market**

    (a)  It is related with new issues.

    (b)  It has no particular place.

## 5.2 Long-term Finance: Shares, Debentures and Term Loans, Lease, Hire Purchase, Venture Capital Financing, Private Equity

### (A) Shares

These shares are known as equity shares. As per Companies Act 1956, an equity share is that share which is not a preference share. A preference share is a share the holder of which has a priority for receiving dividend over equity shareholder and also priority regarding repayment of capital when a company goes into liquidation. Of course, the question of repayment of capital will arise only after the satisfaction of all third party liabilities. The above facts make it clear that equity shareholders do not have any priority regarding dividends or capital repayment.

**Features of Shares:**

The following are some of the features of equity or ordinary shares:

(a) Equity shareholders have a right to attend the annual general meeting of their company and they have a right to vote on all the matters. The most important proposals on which voting rights are to be exercised are election of directors, dividends, alteration of various clauses in the Memorandum of Association etc. As per the provisions of the Companies Act 1956, equity shareholders can appoint a proxy also. The proxy can attend the annual general meeting if the original shareholder is not able to attend the same and he can also vote in the meeting.

(b) Equity shareholders are entitled to a dividend on their shareholding. However, they do not have any priority over the preference shareholders as regards the dividend. Similarly, dividend on equity shares is never fixed. It is also not compulsory on the part of the board of directors to declare equity dividend every year. The board of directors only recommend dividends and it must be sanctioned in the annual general meeting. The shareholders can propose to reduce the rate of the dividend proposed by the directors but they cannot make a suggestion to increase it.

(c) Equity shareholders enjoy a pre-emptive right to maintain his proportionate share of ownership in the company. As per Company Law, equity shareholders have the right to purchase new shares in the same proportion as their current ownership. A shareholder may or may not exercise this right.

(d) Equity shareholders have a limited liability which is limited to the amount of their investments in shares. This principle of limited liability is actually the unique feature of a limited company. Once a shareholder has paid the entire price of his shareholding, he need not contribute anything more, even when his company is facing liquidation. But he has a residual share in the assets of his company. This means that at the time of liquidation of a company, after the satisfaction of all the third party liabilities, if some assets remain, the equity shareholders have a claim over them.

(e) If the company goes into liquidation, the claims of the lenders of the company are satisfied first, then the claims of preference shareholders are satisfied. If any amount is available after the satisfaction of these claims, then the equity shareholders claims are satisfied.

(f) As per the Companies Act 1956, a company can buy back the equity shares after satisfying the relevant provisions of the Companies Act.

**Benefits:**

The Benefits of Issuing Equity Shares are as follows:

(a) There is no question of redemption of the amount raised by equity shares. In other words, it is a permanent source of capital. Repayment will have to be done only when a company is being wound up and that too after the satisfaction of all third party liabilities. However, a company can buy back the equity shares subject to certain provisions of the Companies Act 1956.

(b) Another important advantage to the company is that there is no compulsion to pay dividends on equity shares. Payment of dividend is at the discretion of the directors and there is also no compulsion regarding the rate of dividend. If profits decrease sharply, the dividend can be skipped also.

(c) Equity shares serve as a base for a company and based on this, borrowings can be done. The borrowing capacity can be increased by issuing additional equity shares.

**Limitations:**

However, the equity capital suffers from the following limitations:

(a) Even though there is a controversy about the cost of equity capital, it is admitted that equity capital is not a cost free source of financing. Cost of equity capital is more than cost of borrowings and the main reason is that the dividend payment is not tax deductible.

(b) If investors' point of view is considered, there is considerable risk in the investment in the equity shares. This is due to the reason that there is no guarantee of dividend on equity shares. A company may or may not pay dividend to the equity shareholders. The dividend depends entirely on the profit available for distribution of dividend. However, rate of dividend can increase if sufficient profits are available. Thus there is no guarantee of a fixed return on the equity shares. Another factor is that in case of companies, whose shares are listed on the stock exchange, the market prices may fluctuate depending on the performance of the company and other factors like the economic condition of the country. Market price may fall if the performance of the company is not good and in such case the investors may suffer from heavy loss. On the other hand market prices may appreciate, again depending on the performance of the company and in that case equity shareholders may benefit. Thus there is considerable risk in investing in the equity shares.

(c) New equity issue results in dilution of earnings per share as well as there is a dilution of ownership pattern. Even though the Company Act, 1956 makes a provision to offer equity shares on rights basis to existing equity shareholders, it is not compulsory for them to purchase the shares.

## (B) Debentures

A company can also raise funds by sale of debentures. A debenture is an acknowledgement of a debt taken by the company. A debenture holder becomes a creditor of the company while shareholders, whether equity or preference are the owners of the company. A company has to repay the amount of debentures after the maturity period is over. Equity capital is an owned source of finance while debenture is a borrowed source of providing finance. The following are the important features of debentures:

(a) The rate of interest on debentures is fixed as per the terms of contract between the company and the debenture holders. The interest is payable on the par value (face value) even though the debenture may be issued at premium or discount. While calculating taxable profits of a company, the interest on debentures is an allowable deduction. However, the interest is taxable in the hands of debenture holders.

(b) A debenture may be either secured or unsecured. In case of secured debentures, some kind of security is offered to the debenture holders. Usually, the immovable property of the company is offered as security. If there is a default committed by the company in the payment of interest and principle amount, the debenture holders can obtain a decree to sell the property given as security and pay the amount to debenture holders. A debenture may be unsecured which gives them the status of an unsecured creditor.

(c) Debentures have a fixed maturity period. This means that, after the maturity period is over, the amount of debentures becomes payable.

(d) There may be a provision in the contract with debenture holders about retirement of debentures before the maturity period. In order to facilitate such a retirement, a company may establish a sinking fund. A sinking fund is created by setting aside certain amount of profit every year. The sinking fund is either managed by the company itself or by the trustees of a debenture trust deed.

(e) A buy-back provision may also be included in the debenture contract. Buy-back provisions enable the company to redeem debentures at a specified price before the maturity date.

(f) Debenture holders have a claim on the profits of the company ahead of equity shareholders. Similarly, they have a claim on the assets of the company ahead of other unsecured creditors if they [debentures] are secured.

Debentures may be non-convertible or fully convertible or partly convertible. In case of fully convertible debentures, they are fully converted into equity shares at a predetermined price. In such cases, an option is given to the debenture holders either to accept cash or equity shares. In case of partly convertible debentures, only a part of the debentures is converted into shares. Non-convertible debentures are, of course, not convertible at all.

The important advantage of issuing debentures is that they are less costly than issue of shares. The main reason behind this is that the interest payable on debentures is deductible from the profits for arriving at taxable profits. Another plus point of debentures is that there is no question of diluting of ownership as debenture holders are not the owners of the company like shareholders. On the contrary, if the funds raised through debentures are used efficiently, the earnings per equity share can be improved. This is known as *trading on equity*. During inflationary period, the real value of money goes on reducing but the amount of interest and the principal repayment remains same. Therefore, it can be said that the company stands to gain thorough issue of debentures during inflationary periods.

One thing which must be kept in mind is that debentures mean borrowings. Every rupee of borrowing brings additional repayment obligations. If the company is doing well, repayment will not be a problem but during adverse conditions there may be problems in repayment. If it is not possible to repay the principal amount and interest, it may result into liquidation of the company. It will be necessary for a company to plan for the cash out-flows arising on account of redemption of debentures well in advance. As the cash out-flows arising out of the redemption are quite substantial, it may create problems if proper planning is not made.

## (C) Term Loans

In addition to the debentures, a company can raise borrowings through term loans also. A term loan is a loan which has a maturity period of more than one year. Normally, such term loans are used in India for financing long-term requirements like capital expenditure proposals or diversification proposals etc. The following are the important features of term loans:

(a) As the name suggests, the term loans have a longer maturity period which varies from case to case and also from various lending institutions. However the maturity period varies from 6 to 10 years, though loans for a longer maturity period than 10 years are also given sometimes. In some cases, initial grace period of about 2 years may also be given in order to help the borrower to carry on the business in an efficient manner.

(b) Term loans are secured by a security given by the borrower. A floating charge may be created on the fixed assets of the company or alternatively, a fixed charge on specific assets may be created.

(c) The lender of the term loans is interested in the repayment of his money and therefore, to safeguard his interests, a number of restrictions may be put on the borrower. These are known as restrictive convenants. For example, there may be restriction on payment of dividend till the loan is repaid. The borrower has to provide full financial information to the lender through periodic financial statements. These convenants may be related to assets, liabilities, cash-flows or any other matter.

(d) Term loans may also be convertible into equity capital. Usually, the financial institutions provide this option.

**Repayment of loan:** The repayment of term loan is according to the repayment schedule showing the interest component and principal component repaid in each installment. The normal practice in India to amortise loan is to arrange repayment of principal amount in equal installments either annually or semi-annually and pay interest on the outstanding amount of loan. In this way, amount of interest paid in each installment will go on declining every year. Repayment of loan in such a manner helps a company to avoid a huge repayment of loan at the end of the maturity period.

# (D) Lease

## Meaning:

A lease is basically a contract between the owner of the asset who is known as *lessor* and the user of the asset who is known as *lessee*. According to this contract, the lessor grants to the lessee the right to use the asset for either a specific period or perpetually for a consideration called as lease rental. In other words, the lease agreement results in the transfer of possession of the asset in favour of the lessee without the transfer of ownership of that asset. The lease rental which is a consideration receivable by the lessor may be paid by the lessee at the beginning or at the end of a month, quarter, half year or year. Although generally fixed, the amount and timing of payment of lease rent can be tailored to the lessee's profits or cash-flows. In some types of lease agreements, more rentals are charged in the initial years and less in the later years of contract. These types of lease agreements are called as 'Up-fronted leases.' In 'Back-ended leases' during the initial years lower rentals are charged and the amount of rent goes on increasing in the later years. At the end of the lease agreement periods, the asset reverts to the lessor who is the legal owner of the asset.

Leasing of land, building etc. is existing in India from ancient times, but leasing of capital equipment is quite a recent development. Gradually, leasing as a source of long-term financing is gaining popularity in India.

## Types of Lease Agreements

Lease agreements can be divided into two categories.

**[a] Operating lease:** These agreements are short-term cancellable lease agreements. The features of these lease agreements can be summarised as follows:

(i)   The lease period is usually short and is shorter than the useful life of the asset.

(ii)  A single lease agreement may not fully amortise the original cost of the asset.

(iii) These agreements are cancellable at a short notice.

(iv) Due to short duration and the lessee's option to cancel the lease, the risk of obsolescence remains with the lessor. It is quite natural, therefore, due to shorter lease period and/or higher risk of obsolescence, the lease rentals will be higher.

(v) Computers, vehicles, furniture are examples of assets leased under this type.

**[b] Financial lease:** These contracts are long-term and non-cancellable. Since financial lease is for long term, the cost of assets can be fully amortised over the term of the lease. Therefore, they may also be called as Capital leases or full payout leases. Some of the features of financial lease are as follows:

(i) The contract is for long–term and is not cancellable.

(ii) The lessee is responsible for expenses like maintenance, taxes and other charges like insurance.

(iii) A financial lease agreement may provide for renewal of contract or purchase of the asset by the lessee after the contract expires. However in India, the option of purchasing the leased asset by the lessee is not incorporated in the lease agreement, because if such an option is incorporated, the lease may become a hire-purchase agreement.

Sometimes in a lease agreement, a firm which had purchased an asset may sell it to another firm and, afterwards, may acquire the same asset on lease. This arrangement is called as 'sale and lease back' arrangement.

For example: A Ltd. sells an asset to another company B Ltd. and immediately takes the same asset on lease from B Ltd. The benefit for A Ltd. is that it receives the amount of sale in lumpsum which improves its [A Ltd.'s] liquidity position.

Under one more type of lease agreement, the lessor borrows some portion of the purchase price of an asset or even the entire amount of purchase from a lender like a financial institution and then leases the asset to a lessee. The interest payments are met from the lease rentals received and as the owner of the asset, the lessor can claim substantial tax benefits.

**Benefits From Lease Financing**

A question that is bound to arise is that, what benefits can be derived from the lease agreement for a lessee company as against the option of purchasing the asset even by borrowing? The position from lessee's point of view can be summarised as per the following paragraphs.

(a) **Convenience and Flexibility:** In case of an operating lease, the contract can be terminated at will by the lessee and therefore, greater flexibility is ensured. Even long-term financial lease may offer this flexibility to the user, subject to the terms of contract. The flexibility ensures that the risk of obsolescence can be shifted to the lessor. However, this risk of obsolescence is usually offset to the lessor by charging high rent from the lessee.

The lease rent as described earlier are fixed periodic payments made by the lessee. However, the payments can be adjusted in such a way that they are suitable for the lessee's cashflows. The lease rentals may be adjusted to suit seasonal fluctuations in the cashflows of the lessee company. Similarly lease rentals may also be adjusted to enable the lessee to derive maximum tax advantage.

(b) **Expeditious Implementation:** In India, borrowing from banks and financial institutions involve long and complicated procedure. It may take three to six months and sometimes even a longer time. If compared to such a lengthy procedure, lease financing can be done much faster. Therefore, leasing facilitates are a very expeditious implementation of a project.

(c) **Maintenance:** In operating lease, the maintenance is to be borne by the lessee while in financial lease, the lessor is supposed to bear these charges. However, in both these types the lessee gets the advantage of specialized services offered by the lessor.

(d) **Control:** When term loans are raised, usually there is a clause in the agreement that provides for conversion of loan into equity and also for the appointment of a nominee director. In case of the conversion clause, the company fears about the potential danger of dilution of equity and in case of the nominee director there may be apprehensions about his [nominee director] nuisance value. In case of lease agreements, however, no such threat or danger exists and therefore, the companies prefer lease for borrowing.

(e) **Restrictive Clauses:** Apart from the facts mentioned in number (c) above, the loan agreement may provide for some restrictions on the borrowing company. These restrictions may be related to dividend payments, working capital position, additional financing, provision of bank guarantee etc. The lender organisation puts these restrictions with a view to ensure the repayment of their loan.

In contrast to the above, the lease agreements do not provide for more restrictions. However, restrictions may be put on the number of hours of use of an asset per week or per month. This type of restrictions are necessary for the protection of the asset.

(f) **Tax Benefits:** If an asset is purchased, the purchaser can claim the deduction of depreciation as he is the owner of the asset. However, if the company is already suffering from losses or making very low profits, full tax benefits cannot be availed of. But if an asset is taken on lease, the lease rentals can be claimed as full deduction for tax purposes.

From the point of view of the lessor, it can be said that the lessor gets the advantage of tax benefits due to depreciation on the asset which is purchased. However, the lease rent receivable by him is not exempted from tax. Similarly, he is not entitled for a concession in the Central Sales Tax.

**Procedural Aspects of Lease Agreement**

It should be remembered that lease agreement is a contract between the lessor and lessee. This agreement contains the following:

(i)   Description of the lessor, lessee and the asset.

(ii)  The amount of the lease rent, alongwith other conditions of payment like time, mode etc.

(iii) The terms and conditions regarding the payment of repairs and maintenance of the asset and the lessee's responsibility of the payment of such charges.

(iv) Restrictions if any put by the lessor on the use of the leased asset by the lessee.

(v)  Provisions regarding renewal, cancellation of lease or regarding return of equipment on expiry of lease period.

(vi) Variations in lease rentals in specific conditions like variation in bank rates, depreciation etc.

After selection of an asset, the lessee and lessor prepare an agreement as explained above and sign it. The lessee insures the equipment and endorses the insurance policy in favour of the lessor.

## (E) Hire Purchase

Hire purchase system is an agreement under which goods are sent on hire and under which hirer has an option to purchase them in installment, which is treated as hire charges until the payment of the last installment when ownership of goods is transferred from the seller to the purchaser.

**Features of Hire Purchase:**

(a) Agreement is made for supply of goods.

(b) Each installment is treated as a hire charge and not as a price.

(c) The purchaser agrees to pay for goods in the agreed installments.

(d) Possession of goods is transferred to the purchaser on signing of the agreement.

(e) The hire purchaser must keep the goods in good condition.

(f) On the payment of the last installment hire purchase becomes absolute purchase.

(g) The excess of total payment over the cash price is taken as interest.

# (F) Venture Capital Financing

**Meaning of Venture Capital**

Venture capital is provided to entrepreneurs who want to start a high-tech untried project having risk and at the same time high potential of profits. It is also meant for those who do not have long history of running businesses. Entrepreneurs who have new ideas of promising business but don't have funds, or cannot borrow due to the risk involved in the project, or due to hesitation of banks to finance such ideas, may approach venture capital institutions for finance. Venture capitalist, if find the proposed business to be worthy, may provide equity i.e. invest in the proposal. They take part in the management of the business, provide guidance to the promoters and exit after 5 to 7 years by way of 'Initial Public Issue' (IPO). Thus they realise their investment and make capital gain if the company succeeds in the venture.

**Definitions of Venture Capital**

(a) **According to Investopedia:** *"Money provided by investors to startup firms and small businesses with perceived long-term growth potential. This is a very important source of funding for start ups that do not have access to capital markets. It typically entails high risk for the investor, but it has the potential for above-average returns"*

(b) **According to Oxford Dictionary of Business and Management:** *"Capital invested in a project in which there is a substantial element of risk, especially money invested in a new venture or an expanding business. Risk capital is normally invested in the equity of the company in the hope of high returns, it is not a loan."*

(c) **According to Webster's New World Finance and Investment Dictionary:** *"Money that is given to entrepreneurs to invest in a start-up business or to develop a product. Venture capital is very risky investment and those investing money may lose their entire investment. However, if the business or the product becomes successful, the return can be huge. Venture capital is raised by venture capital firms who solicit investment from institutional investors, such as banks, private equity units, pension funds, or other investment management firms, as well as from wealthy individuals. Venture capital investments are made at different stages, with some venture capitalists focussing only on seed or initial investments, others on middle stages firms and others on later stage companies that have a viable product that is producing revenue."*

(d) **The 1995 Finance Bill, defines Venture Capital as:** *"Long-term equity investment in novel technology, based projects with display potential for significant growth and financial returns".*

New business ideas or untried ideas are very risky. The ideas may turn out to be a success and generate huge profits or may fail in which case the capitalist would lose everything invested. Firm of investors or wealthy individuals may be interested in taking the risk of providing funds for such business ideas in the form of equity and may exit after few years when their capital appreciates.

**Characteristic Features of Venture Capital:**

(a) Capital investment may be in the form of either equity or debt or both as a derivative instrument.

(b) It is made in hi-tech projects involving high risk and strong potential of high profitability.

(c) Venture capitalist finance the projects and wait for 5 to 7 years to reap the benefits of capital appreciation.

(d) Venture capital funds is not repaid rather is realised through exit route.

(e) The exit route may be any of the following:

    (i)   Public issue of shares,

    (ii)  Sale of share to entrepreneurs,

    (iii) Sale of company to another company,

    (iv) Finding new investor, or

    (v)  Liquidation.

(f) Venture capital organisation may be wholly owned subsidiaries of financial institutions, or owned by Government, or may be a group of individual venture capitalists.

(g) The financing of high-tech projects in the form of venture capital is done in various stages.

(h) Venture capitalists become member of the board in order to closely watch the performance of the business unit. The claim over management is decided on the basis of proportion of investment.

## (G) Private Equity

Private equity is equity capital that is not quoted on a public exchange.

Private equity is the money invested in firms which have not "gone public" and therefore are not listed on any stock exchange.

Private equity is highly illiquid as sellers of private stocks (called private securities) must first locate willing buyers.

Investors in private equity are generally compensated when:

(a) the firm goes public,

(b) it is sold or merges with another firm, or

(c) it is recapitalised.

Private equity refers to a type of investment aimed at gaining significant, or even complete control of a company in the hopes of earning a high return.

Private equity firms have been acquiring companies left right, paying sometimes very high premiums over these companies market values.

## Questions for Discussion

1. What do you mean by share? State its features.

2. Define Debentures. State the features of Debentures.

3. Define Lease. State the Types of Lease Agreements.

4. Explain the benefits from Lease Financing.

5. What is Venture Capital Financing?

6. Write short notes:

   (a) Indian Capital Market.

   (b) New Issues Market.

   (c) Advantages of Shares.

   (d) Term Loans.

   (e) Hire Purchase.

   (f) Private Equity.

■■■

www.ingramcontent.com/pod-product-compliance
Lightning Source LLC
Chambersburg PA
CBHW080903020726
47502CB00008B/2334